GADARA

The Story of the Gadarene Demoniac

Fiction

Based on a True Story

Kaleb Blackmar

BookLocker

Published by BookLocker.com, Inc., St. Petersburg, Florida.

Printed on acid-free paper.

This is a work of religious fiction. Except for those that appear in the bible, any similarity to real persons, living or dead, is coincidental and not intended by the author.

BookLocker.com, Inc.
2019

First Edition

Dedicated to Jesus of Nazareth

The Christ

The Son of the Living God

Who delivered me from a lifetime of darkness

And to the lost

Who Jesus came to seek and save

Through repentance

Also, to Alan and Deborah Midkiff

Whose help, encouragement and love

made this book possible

Preface

The idea of this story came to me years ago. The concept of a man who was hopelessly lost and rejected by the world, then delivered by Jesus himself and set upon a mission. The story of the Gadarene demoniac is well known in the Gospel account. Jesus cast a multitude of demons from a man into a vast herd of swine. They, in turn, ran into the Sea of Galilee and drowned. The local people came and found the former demoniac with Jesus, and in his right mind. The people then feared Jesus and told him to depart. The man wanted to go with him, but Jesus told him to stay and tell everyone what God had done for him. Unfortunately, the story of the man and his ministry that followed is lost to history.

I began researching everything I could find about the history around the story. Then I looked to some of the well-known biblical stories, as well as numerous accounts of Jesus and his disciples healing the sick and casting out demons. My main character was healed and ministered to by Jesus himself, as well as having residual knowledge from the demons. The result was a man of great faith who knew Jesus as the Son of God, and very grateful. I have endeavored to create characters: average people from different walks of life, as well as the formerly possessed; all impacted by a mighty and loving God. I've attempted to establish a first century world that people could relate to from the ruins of these locations and cities. The story is intended to be entertaining and yet encouraging; with action, adventure, romance and emotion with a touch of humor. Many scriptures are included; my goal was to take the actual accounts and build the story around it. All words from Jesus are his actual words from the KJV and referenced. The story interacts with the Bible but in no way re-interprets it. The Apocrypha, such as the book of Enoch, is also referenced or paraphrased. These texts were widely accepted in the first century; Peter and Jude both referred to them in their writings. The story offers a different point of view: Pagan Greeks confronted with the word of God by one of their own; a strong, fearless, loveable, devoted, scarred former demoniac with a mission.

There is the biblical account of the demoniac, but other than that it is only known to us through vague oral tradition, archaeological traces of locations, and the eventual results of his ministry. Christianity exploded in the region of the Decapolis (modern day northern Jordan and southern Syria) following the casting out of the demons. An important church headed by a bishop was established in Gadara about a century later. By 325 CE, the Church of Gadara sent a bishop to the important council of Nicaea. First century Gadara was a Greco-Roman city heavily involved in the pagan worship of Zeus and other gods of the Greek pantheon, which required sacrifices. Born in Gadara, the Greek poet Meleager referred to Gadara as the Syrian Athens, because of its numerous Pagan Temples. The Roman historian Josephus referred to it as a Greek city as well, and there was a heavy Roman presence. The Romans conquered the City of Gadara in 63 BC and spread their influence; their ruins can be found today in the ancient cities of Gadara, Gerasa (currently known as Jerash), Philadelphia (currently known as Aman), and Raqmu (currently known as Petra): the city of the Nabataeans. The Roman Army would travel with a Pagan Priest that would offer sacrifices on behalf of the soldiers; often swine. A standard for the Roman Tenth Legion depicted the wild boar. This gives authenticity to the two thousand plus herd of swine, for not only was pork a meat staple for the Romans and Greeks, but the demand for sacrifices would have been huge.

Jesus was told to depart following the casting out of the demons, likely for fear that he would curse the city as he did with Capernaum, Chorazin, and Bethsaida. It has been suggested that Jesus expressed authority over the Greek and Roman gods by destroying their sacrifices similar to the way God's authority was expressed through Moses and Aaron to the Egyptian gods (Exodus chapter 8 and on). This would explain why he allowed the demons to enter the swine. It would also explain the fear exhibited by the Gadarenes.

I believe it to be a fair assumption that the former demoniac did evangelize Gadara, as well as much of the Decapolis region. It would make perfect sense for Jesus to appoint a man from the region; a man with a powerful testimony, an evil demon-possessed man who had been restored, as evidence in the flesh of the power and authority of God. I believe that it is the nature of God to take that which the forces of darkness meant for destruction and turn it around for good. He would not have to be a trained evangelist but would simply present himself and say exactly what Jesus told him to say, that God had mercy and compassion upon him. He was able to change the minds and hearts of many people, as they would have been firmly entrenched in their long-held beliefs and traditions. Jesus returned months later to the eastern shores of the Sea of Galilee and was well received in the Decapolis. He performed a miracle healing a man who was deaf and mute, then feeding thousands with bread and fish (Mark 7:31-8:9). To accomplish what the former demoniac did, this was a man who had been touched by the Master's hand.

There is an archaeological site in the area near the Sea of Galilee known as the Kursi Memorial. It consists of the remains of an early fourth-century Byzantine chapel built by Queen Helena to preserve the site. It was abandoned in 749 CE due to a massive earthquake that destroyed it on January 18 of that year. The site was accidentally discovered in 1970 and identified after being forgotten for many centuries. It is believed by some to be the site where Jesus cast out the demons. This site is a memorial to the miracle, but I believe it to be misinterpreted from antiquity. There is a second site known to this day as *The Hill of the Swine* near the ancient harbor of Gadara. I believe it is likely the true site, which is where I set my story. The ability to land a boat, as well as the grassy slopes fit the biblical account. I strongly encourage the reader to look at the references, particularly the articles by Bill

Heinrich and Dr. Steven Anderson, for greater insight as they were a great resource and encouragement to the writing of this book.

This is also a work based on life experience, for I'm aware of the struggle. I walked in darkness for most of my life. Several years ago, I came to the end of myself after a lot of grief and came to the Lord Jesus in a very real way through deep repentance. This story was born in that time. My testimony is simply this: The Lord Jesus has delivered me from a lifetime of darkness. I pray for peace and healing upon anyone who I have hurt over the years in the name of Jesus. I'm currently living for God, as I have ever since. I have peace in my life that I never thought possible. I have a wife who has stood beside me and shares in this. We reach out to our community and try to be a blessing to others. I try to share the good news as much as possible. The struggle is very real. One of the subjects I've researched is stories of real demonic activity. I've searched for answers not only for myself, but for greater insight in preparation of writing this book. Together with my own experiences I came away with a unique understanding of a great many things. I present to you, the reader, my humble attempt to wrap my mind around a man inhabited by literally thousands of evil spirits, as well as a mighty God able to restore him. God loves every single one of us. Deep inside the worst of us I believe there is a soul yearning for the long-awaited touch of the Master's hand. There is no place in this world so deep, or dark, that Jesus cannot reach in and pull out that which was lost. The world needs more prayer.

Let us take a journey together, if you desire. Be sure to bring an outer garment, for the eastern Galilee can get a bit chilly at night, even in the summertime....

The Author

Table of Contents

Introduction:

A Collection of Forgotten Curiosities

It was a typical day at the museum. There was a cluttered basement office where much of the unseen work and research took place. Professor Adams had been going through archives of ancient Greek records and manifests, as he was assisting with trying to identify a well-preserved deep shipwreck recently found in the Black Sea. It was thought to be a Greek merchant ship from the first century. Very little decomposition had affected the wreck in the oxygen-free water. He stared at his computer screen, as he reviewed a virtual tour around the wreck while searching for clues. "This definition is amazing," he said to himself under his breath as he zoomed in on what appeared to be amphora laid out beside the wreck on the sea floor. Many were broken; however, a few were intact with the clay seal being visible on one. He opened a window to enlarge the image, then zoomed in on the seal. He could see an inscription, then enhanced the image the best he could. The professor couldn't read the entire inscription, but determined it had elements of Greek, Hebrew, and Latin. The elder researcher had always dreamed of that big discovery. This wasn't history changing in his opinion, but it was exciting. He squinted trying to read the Greek portion of the inscription while speaking under his breath, "H...house...can't quite make it out...A...Alethea, what a beautiful name." It was quiet in the basement room, as the professor stared at the image. He was quite pre-occupied with his work until the door opened: it was the curator.

"Good afternoon, Doctor Adams," the younger man said with a friendly greeting. He glimpsed at the image on the professor's large computer monitor and approached with an expression of curiosity. "It appears you found something interesting," he observed.

1

The professor replied, "Yes, this amphora has an inscription on the seal in Greek, Hebrew and Latin. I believe it to be wine, and the contents could still be present in some form. I'm going to make a recommendation for the next crew visiting the wreck to attempt a recovery. I'm not able to read the inscription clearly; too much distortion and silt. What I could read of the Greek portion was house, something, and then the name Alethea."

The curator commented, "What a beautiful name."

The professor just looked up at him with a smile.

"I have a new project I would like you to begin immediately. I apologize for interrupting your research, but there is a pressing matter that demands your expertise. We're going to open the new Roman exhibit soon, as you know. There are some artifacts that I would like to show you," the curator said as he gestured for him to follow.

The two men walked down the hall as the curator explained that the artifacts had been discovered a long time ago and forgotten. He stopped and opened the door to a large room filled with endless cabinets full of drawers. The men navigated through the maze of hidden treasures, then the curator stopped, smiled, and touched a long thin drawer. Both men put on clean gloves, then he opened the drawer.

"Ahh, early first century," the professor commented as he looked upon a well-preserved Roman short sword that was laid next to the scabbard. It was in relic condition but amazingly intact compared to most. He carefully picked it up with both hands and held it. He then let go very carefully with one hand and held it by the handle. He could feel the weight and the balance. The professor then carefully placed it back into the drawer. "I thank you, that was exciting, but what does this have to do with me? My expertise is ancient text," he said.

The curator said, "That is why I've called upon you, doctor. The artifacts were discovered in an obscure cave in the Jordanian desert in 1928. There is little known of the actual discovery; we have the location of the cave, but nothing else. There were a lot of cutbacks during the depression, so they were packed away and forgotten until just recently. The cache was found with a sealed jar containing scrolls: Greek scrolls. My hope is that you can find a connection or something that identifies the sword and other things. There were some mundane objects found such as a degraded leather pouch with an iron fire ring and flint, as well as many textile items. There's more," he said and then opened another drawer next to it and removed a wooden box. He opened it to reveal a Roman gold coin affixed to a gold chain. The curator continued, "This was found there as well. I think the project could be very interesting to you, for no one has ever translated or even read the scrolls. It appears someone started to once, as a note was found with them. All we know is the predominant author was apparently a man named 'Argus the Elder,' a resident of the ancient City of Gadara in what is now northern Jordan near the Syrian border. The cache is believed to have been made in the late first century: a period of Roman persecution of the early Christians."

The professor asked, "Are the scrolls well preserved?"

The curator responded, "Yes, considering they're two thousand years old they're remarkably well preserved. Some breaks and missing fragments; we've already prepared one of them for you. The conservators are preparing the remainder as well; I'll send someone to assist you." He looked at the professor. "I assume you do want to take on the assignment?" The curator asked and looked hopeful, as if he had been turned down by others.

The professor looked at the curator with a smile and replied, "Alright, I'll get on it right away. Don't get your hopes up too high, for an obscure cave in the middle of the desert probably won't be another Qumran. The last unknown scroll I translated was letters to a grandmother and a shopping list. I agree, however, that the value of an artifact being mentioned in ancient text makes it priceless."

The curator said, "A display case has already been established for the items, but we have no explanation as to how they ended up where they were. My hope is that you can provide a story to go with them."

"I can't wait to get started!" was the eager response from the professor. He had made a small discovery, but most of his current research was reviewing endless manifests and records. An unknown two-thousand-year-old document was, of course, more exciting. The curator smiled and patted his back, then led the professor to one of the clean rooms, where the ancient scroll had been carefully stretched out on a well-lit table. The curator spoke with him for a few moments, then left the room and closed the door behind him.

The professor once again indulged in his daydream of that big discovery, as he often did whenever he started a new project. He looked around the room, for he had a strange sensation that he wasn't alone. There were two small storage rooms in back with the doors slightly ajar. He called out, but there was only silence. The feeling was so strong that the professor even peeked into the rooms, but there was no one there. He slowly strolled back around the huge white table and gave the ancient scroll an overview. The elder man then looked around once more, smiled, shrugged his shoulders, and looked over the very nice task chair that had been provided for him. The professor sat down, then got comfortable and pulled out his magnifying glass as well as his notebook. The scroll had the professor's attention, then a figure slowly appeared right behind him. It was a tall figure with a powerful presence and was cloaked in a long garment covering his body and head, except the lower portion of his face. The stranger smiled as he raised a hand in a gesture of blessing. The professor felt a peculiar notion that someone was in the room once again and slowly looked over his shoulder. The figure vanished. He turned back around, then shook his head slightly and chuckled. As the professor read the faded text an incredible story began to emerge....

Prologue

Long ago there lived a man who dwelled in what was called The Decapolis Region. No man could tame him, and no one could approach him, for he was the embodiment of pure evil. Thousands of wicked spirits inhabited the man; spirits from a time before the great flood cleansed the earth. What remained lied buried beneath the absolute oppression of the fallen ones. His name was Jason. His own identity was denied him. The spirits within referred to themselves as Legion, for they were many.

Legion dwelled in places of death. Their sole purpose was to inflict pain, misery, and fear among those who inhabit the earth. Legion was the antithesis of God's creation; something that should not be. Deep within, however, there remained a man who desperately clung to hope. Hope that it would all come to an end. Years upon years the unholy cycle continued. One day, there came a man from the Galilee. His name was Jesus. He was the Son of God. Jesus defeated the evil that had destroyed Jason and set him free.

Jesus was rejected from the cities of the Decapolis out of fear. Jason longed to go with Jesus, and to become one of his disciples. Jesus forbade him and sent him to be among those who had rejected him. Jesus ministered to Jason, and equipped him, then sent him forth into the cities to share what God had done for him. This much is well known, as recorded within the pages of the Gospel of Peace. What became of the man, however, has been lost in the mists of time.

Until now....

GADARA

The Story of the Gadarene Demoniac

Fiction

Based on a True Story

The Decapolis, near the
Sea of Galilee

A.D. 28

Chapter One

The Herdsmen

The afternoon was giving way to evening on the southeast coast of the Sea of Galilee. The bright sun of the day was slowly changing to amber and crimson shades of color playing upon the rocky bluffs, steep grassy slopes, and trees of the landscape. There was a gentle breeze blowing from the west, as it stirred the grass and the trees slightly and brought with it a coolness, as well as the odors from the freshwater sea. The day had been quite warm but was cooling off quickly. A stretch of beach that was part of the harbor of Gadara gave way to an abrupt rise of the landscape from the sea. Atop the slope was a more level area; with rocky outcrops, intermittent oak trees, various bushes, and grass. A vast herd of more than two thousand swine were foraging there and were watched over by many herdsmen. For them, the air was dominated by the pungent odor of the swine. Two had stopped for a moment to adjust their clothing and put on their long, warm outer garments. The herdsmen had shed them in the heat of the day but were preparing for the coming chill and dampness of the night. The men were Greek and lived near the City of Gadara. They were about to bring their huge herd to market in a few days to supply the temple sacrifices, meat for the city, and for the enormous Roman Tenth Legion Camp near Gadara.

One was a young herdsman, Dimitri, lacking in experience but learning the trade from his elder mentor and friend, Aegeus. The elder herdsman was the leader; responsible for the other herdsmen, as well as the herd itself. Dimitri had known Aegeus all of his life, for he had been a friend of his father before he died. Aegeus had become a friend of the family, while helping Dimitri and his younger brother find their way in life. The young man had decided to follow the vocation of the elder herdsman. Dimitri was to learn the finer details of dealing in the marketplace, as well as hiring and managing men, plus herding and protecting the animals. The old man was also full of stories about encounters with predators and thieves which the young man found exciting. Dimitri sat down on a rock and laid his staff upon the ground, then uncovered his head to push his dark hair out of his face. He watched as the elder herdsman walked closer to the edge of the precipice. Aegeus surveyed the horizon and the sea to get an idea of what kind of weather to expect.

"Very curious," he said as he observed a group of rather dark, ominous clouds swirling in the distance over the sea, which was backlit by the orange glow of the setting sun. The sky was otherwise clear, except for high, thin wisps of clouds now colored in shades of yellow, crimson, and magenta. The old herdsman stood for some time watching the anomaly while leaning on his staff. Dimitri sat and watched the old man; the light of the sunset reflecting off his weathered face, his gray hair and beard, and his soft, worn clothing. He had become like a father to him.

"Do you think we should seek shelter among the rocks?" the young herdsman asked as he turned to his left, then pointed out one of the larger rock formations. The elder man turned and looked at several dark openings in the rock Dimitri had gestured to. Some were natural features; others were rock-cut tombs, which as he pondered the matter brought a grimace to his face.

"There's a wild beast that lives in those tombs," Aegeus said as he gripped his staff tightly. He closed his eyes for a moment while processing memories. "I once had an encounter with it," he added.

His countenance became somewhat nervous as he continued to scan the openings in the rock. "Not a normal beast," the elder man said as he turned back to observe the distant weather. It was becoming even more striking: the vibrant colors of the sky and the distant storm were now highlighted by occasional traces of lightning within the dark clouds.

It was obvious that the old man was a bit shaken by the issue of the mysterious beast. Changing the subject, he said, "There's plenty of good forage here for the swine; lots of acorns, grass, and low spots with mud too. I don't think we'll be needing shelter. That storm doesn't seem to be moving this way; in fact, it doesn't seem to be moving at all." He continued to look out over the sea.

"Does one ever get used to the smell?" Dimitri jokingly asked as he tried to relieve the tension a bit.

"No, you just learn to live with it," Aegeus said while chuckling. He then said, "We should walk the perimeter."

The men went about drawing the herd together, as they persuaded them firmly with their herding staffs which sent little puffs of dust into the air as they moved. The other forty or so herdsmen were also preparing for the coming darkness. Aegeus wanted to make sure the widely dispersed herdsmen were strategically placed to properly contain the herd overnight. The two were satisfied by their effort, then returned to the same spot which seemed to be a good place to camp. A slightly raised area of erosion deposit that would keep them up away from the animals, and there was plenty of room for the men and a fire. The young herdsman couldn't stop thinking about the beast his friend had brought up.

"What kind of beast is this you speak of?" the young man asked as he naturally wanted to hear a good story. "I've heard people tell of a wild *man* that no one can tame or capture, but I thought it was just a story," he said.

"There are things in this world that are better to be left alone," said the old man as he paused, then returned to looking out over the sea. He continued, "It resembles a man, but it's more beast than man. It seems to take great pleasure in causing fear rather than anything else, though it will attack and cause injury. I've never heard of it killing anyone, but it can and will cause severe injury, that I can attest to. I don't think it ventures out much at night, as I've experienced. Sometimes at night you can hear it weep and wail somewhere off in the distance." He paused to watch the isolated distant storm, for it was growing more colorful and dramatic as the sky turned to a more royal blue. Aegeus went on, "It has the strength of ten men; I've seen it break iron fetters and chains with its bare hands. It moves more like a twisted animal than a man. My experience with it so many years ago still gives me nightmares. You know, I was a part of a group of men that went out to capture the beast...so was your father."

"He was?" Dimitri asked and was astonished. "He never told us anything about it," he said while anxious to hear more.

"Your father was a brave man, but we were unsuccessful that day," Aegeus said as his eyes trailed off in recollection.

The young man had been sitting on the rock listening intently to his companion. He looked around nervously as his eyes grew wider, then reached down to pick up his staff and held it tightly. He slowly looked over his shoulder, then back at his friend.

"Go on," the young herdsman requested.

"We should start a fire...it will be getting dark soon," the old man responded while trying to change the subject.

The men went about their business for a while, as they gathered firewood and checked the herd one last time before nightfall. A three-quarter moon was rising with a promise of fair visibility through the night. The elder herdsman produced a large tattered cloth from his bag, and with it the two men built an improvised tent. It was held up by two long heavy sticks in the front and secured by stones in the back; a very simple but effective shelter to keep the night dampness away. They had a shelter, a large sitting stone, a place for the fire, and a good view of the herd from their slightly elevated position; also appealing was a picturesque view of the Sea of Galilee. Dimitri thought to himself that they had chosen the spot well.

"I'll start the fire," the young man volunteered as he reached into his tunic and pulled out a small leather pouch. He opened the pouch and dumped the contents on the ground next to a logical place for the fire.

"I see you got a new one," observed the elder herdsman as he watched. He didn't like to admit it, but Dimitri was much faster at starting fires than he was.

"Yeah, I bought two of them from a trader in Gadara," Dimitri said as he held up his shiny new fire ring.

"Let's see how it works; it's getting dark," the old man said as he gazed back at the tomb openings which were still visible in the waning last vestiges of sunlight.

Dimitri picked up one of several pieces of blackened cloth and a good-sized piece of flint. He arranged the charred cloth next to the edge of the flint and gripped it with his left hand. The young herdsman picked up the C shaped ring, then slipped the fingers of his right hand through and started striking the edge of the flint. Bright sparks were produced, then a small glowing ember appeared on the blackened cloth after just a few strikes. He quickly blew on the ember, while simultaneously setting it down and applied small bits of dry tinder. Dimitri continued to put down dry tinder and blew on the small smoking pile until flames burst forth. Then both men started putting small pieces of wood upon it until they had a growing, comforting fire.

"Not bad, that's a lot faster than I can do it," the elder herdsman said. "What have you to eat?" he asked as he started to root through his bag.

"Just some bread," the young man replied.

Aegeus smiled and said, "I have a few dried fish, as well as some bread, and a little wine. I'm more than happy to share it with you, but you must learn not to travel so lightly. I know you hunger, for we've put in a full day; now is the time to rest, and to eat."

Darkness enveloped the scene. It was a clear and starry night, except for the distant weather disturbance that didn't seem to affect the weather at their location. The moon had risen high in the sky and provided good visibility, but without much detail. The moonlight was glistening off the ripples of water upon the sea adding to the dramatic splendor of the distant storm. The two herdsmen sat on their stone by the fire as they enjoyed a nice meal and watched the remainder of sunlight disappear behind the western horizon. The strange weather mass appeared to be holding right in the middle of the Sea of Galilee. The storm was growing in intensity and the men could see flashes of lightning and hear thunder. The dark clouds were swirling as under high wind, but the breeze that had been blowing off the sea earlier had calmed; it didn't make sense to either of the men. They watched for a while, then the young man spoke:

"Tell me more about this *beast*...and my father," Dimitri requested as he sat by the fire which cast a flickering light upon his face. He began to stroke his beard, which was something he often did while listening to Aegeus's stories.

The elder herdsman continued to observe the storm; almost entranced by it. "That's very peculiar," he offered, but knew that he must once again tell the tale.

Aegeus spoke, "Of your father, I can only say that along with myself and many others volunteered for a very dangerous and difficult task. Many ran away, but he was not among them. He was not seriously injured but shared with all of us in our miserable defeat. Your father was a very brave man. It was several years ago, when you were just a little boy. We joined with a group of men from Emmatha, Gadara, Hippos, and throughout the Decapolis

Region. Our goal was to capture and deal with this menace once and for all after the Romans failed."

"The Romans failed?" Dimitri asked with an expression of shock.

Aegeus replied, "It wasn't much of an effort. A few of us had decided to deal with this beast. Our first choice was to have professional soldiers, the Romans, capture it. That freak of nature has been disrupting travel routes and trade in this area for years. There was one among us who knew a Centurion at the Tenth Legion Camp; his response was to send a handful of soldiers to *arrest* it." Aegeus paused and chuckled a bit, then continued, "They found it in a tomb not far from here and demanded that it come out and surrender. I wasn't there, but the story I've been told is that the beast came out right away and immediately attacked. It broke their weapons, then stole pieces of their armor and beat them with the chains they were going to confine it with." The old man paused again, reflecting. He continued, "I don't like to think of what happened to them when they returned. A larger force was sent after that but was unable to find it after an exhaustive search. The beast seems to have instincts to preserve itself when it knows superior strength is coming against it. The word we received afterward was that Rome didn't have time to deal with every petty local problem, and to deal with the matter ourselves."

"So that's when you, my father, and all these other men gathered against it?" Dimitri asked as he gazed up into the hills in the direction the elder herdsman had gestured to.

"Yeah," Aegeus answered as he sat down by the fire while warming his hands.

Dimitri threw some of the larger pieces of wood they had collected on the fire, then crawled under the shelter and settled in to listen to the story.

The elder herdsman looked up from the fire and spoke, "It was such a long time ago, but I remember it clearly...."

We gathered thirty men. Some came with swords and spears; others brought heavy chains and fetters that were strong enough to hold a lion. We thought that through our numbers we could overpower this beast. Our plan was to approach quietly and take it by surprise. We arrived near a small row of tombs up in the hills, for we were sure it was hiding there. Our group waited for a long time but saw no movement. One man finally peered into the darkness of the tomb, but it was empty. There were signs of some occupation, but impossible to determine how long ago.

So, we began our search; all of us agreed that we were not to give up easily as the Romans had. We went from one place to another waiting and watching. Hours turned into days, then some of us had to leave due to family commitments or business. Yet we still felt confident that our group had sufficient numbers to accomplish the task. Twice we encountered what appeared to be a wild man but determined that it was not the beast. He wore tattered clothing and demonstrated fear when approached; we could only get so close to him and he would bolt away. We figured him to be just an outcast; perhaps a fugitive, or a hermit. He didn't seem very dangerous, so we kept looking for the true beast. We would find a cave or a tomb, then approach cautiously and ready. Someone would then look in only to find it empty, except for the bones of the dead. The process was taking its toll on the men, as well as myself; the building of anticipation and fear, then the empty hand and disappointment. There was a growing sentiment among the men to give up the search, or build a trap, but where?

The weather had turned bad with light rain the night before and it was foggy. We were on our way to a cluster of tombs way up in the hills we thought it may be hiding in. Our group was passing through a dense stand of oak trees; a truly eerie environment as much of the detail was obscured. Suddenly, it ran up before us so fast that we couldn't see or hear it coming. Its body was contorted, like I said before; it used its arms and legs to move around, like an animal but strange. The beast had claws on its hands and feet, which appeared formidable. The odd creature sat or perched with its legs folded at the sides, and its arms straight in front with fists on the ground. Its face was grossly twisted as if a representation of great pain within. It had very long hair and beard, which was filthy and disgusting. The beast wore no clothing, for its hair covered much of its body. One could clearly see, however, that the beast was covered with scars all over, as well as a few fresh, bleeding wounds. I've been told that it cuts itself with sharp stones because it enjoys the pain, but who knows. It had an otherworldly cry that would chill your blood. Some say that the cry comes from the part of the beast that's human. I find it difficult to accept that thing as human. The most striking thing about the beast that I recall was its eyes: very dark and sinister...you can see the evil in its eyes.

We were surprised and shocked. Many ran away; the rest of us just stood there for a moment, as we were stunned by the sight of the beast. We later determined that our numbers at that point were eleven men. It slowly crouched down while sniffing the air, then growled and hissed. We were astonished as it straightened up its head and spoke!

"You have come to capture us? By whose authority do you come?" it asked. Its voice was very strange, like a chorus of deep voices speaking in unison with a kind of ethereal echo to it, but very eloquent and clear. It dropped its head back down before growling and glaring at us as it scanned the face of each man and awaited a response. A very long, very tense moment thickly filled the air.

Then, one man growing angry spoke out, "We come on behalf of all those you've terrorized for years!"

"NOT GOOD ENOUGH!" the beast shouted in response, then released an inhuman, hair-raising, cackling laughter.

The two men that were closest to it jumped on the beast. They were quickly joined by others, only to find that it had slipped away. It reappeared behind us and started attacking one after another; swiping, scratching, kicking, and biting in a flurry of unbridled violence. One man drew a sword and the beast promptly grabbed the blade, then broke it off with one hand and hurled it off into the distance. A spear was thrown, only to be caught by the beast and broken. It continued its cackling laughter as it moved with frightening speed; not only attacking men but ripping garments and breaking everything we had. We realized we would be overcome if we didn't get control of the beast fast. One man yelled, "Hold it down, EVERYONE!" First one, then another, then the rest of us started piling on top of it. With all the strength we could muster we struggled to contain the beast in a writhing mass of sweat, blood, and determination. The smell of the beast was worse than any swine smell; I'll never forget it.

The man who had been carrying the chains moved in and managed to grab one of its feet but lost his grip and was kicked very hard in the face. I remember seeing him come back with a severely swollen nose, bruised face, and blood running down his face and chest. The man regained a grip on the leg and managed to get the restraining device in place amid various pleas to hurry. He wiped the blood out of his eyes and focused on putting the bolt in the device. It seemed like a very long time, as we were starting to lose our precarious hold on the beast. The bloody-faced man jumped off and ran to secure the other end of the chain to a nearby tree. I realized that I was bleeding profusely from my left shoulder and saw that the slippery hold we had was fleeting. The whole time we were being beaten and injured continuously as we struggled and wrestled with this wild beast. Finally, that was it, and the whole pile of us trying to hold it down exploded. Men were flung into the air like dolls by the freakish strength of the vicious creature. We found ourselves scattered all over the hillside.

The beast just sat there as it sniffed the air, then looked over its shoulder at the tree with the chain wrapped around it and secured. The brave man who secured it lay unconscious beneath the tree; he had held on until the task was accomplished, but apparently succumbed to his kick in the face. The scattered men were slowly rising, while moaning and grunting.

Everyone went still when the beast let loose with that blood-curdling, cackling laughter again, then it paused and straightened its head. It had a mock sorrowful expression on its hideous face while shaking its head, then it proclaimed, "You caught us!" It sat there motionless for a few moments while looking down at the chain, then followed it to the tree and the man beneath it. A couple of the men softly called out to him; just about that time he started coming around. The man came to his senses and realized that he was in a dangerous place. He began to crawl away slowly, as well as other men who realized that they were within reach of the chain. The beast just sat there, as if trying to instill the appearance of compliance with its capture. Then, suddenly, the beast jumped straight up in the air and pounced near the man under the tree, as he quickly tried to run. The creature grabbed the man's foot, as it snapped the straps of his sandal and injured his foot in the process. The beast then sat down under the tree with the sandal in its hand and glared at us once more. Its face was twisted and evil; its hatred for us was clearly demonstrated in its expressions. The beast began to sniff the sandal while staring at the owner, then took a bite from the sandal and ate it. We watched in horror and disgust as the creature consumed the entire sandal, then belched as it glared at us.

We had begun to gather ourselves, while tending to the more seriously wounded. The wooded hillside looked like a battlefield; there were wounded men, clothing, broken weapons and belongings scattered everywhere. One man had a broken arm, and the man who had been attacked under the tree had a dislocated ankle, so he was having trouble walking. I looked myself over and had deep cuts, like claw marks across my left shoulder, which I managed to wrap up; a few others had similar injuries. I had a lot of scrapes and bruises which seemed to be all over most of us.

Someone spoke up and suggested that we stone the beast, which brought a fervor of enthusiasm and agreement among some of the men. The beast jumped up and shouted with an even greater enthusiasm of its own, "Stone us! Stone us!" It jumped up and down, while flailing about in exaggerated excitement. Just then a man picked up a stone and hurled it at the beast. I and a few others had already thought that it probably wasn't a great idea, but the objections were ignored. The beast caught the stone, as a child catches a ball, then threw it back at the man. He almost jumped out of the way, but the stone caught him by the arm and left a gash as the force of it sent him to the ground. Then the beast hurled itself at us with intense speed, as it ran to the reach of the chain and strained it. Over and over it ran toward us in slightly different directions; it seemed to target a different man each time. Every time the beast pulled the chain tight as a bowstring. The force would flip the beast in the air, then it would come crashing down, only to get back up and repeat the attempt. It was like watching pure madness on display; the whole time that insane, cackling laughter permeated the experience.

Then, it quieted and sat back down in its perched position. The beast stared at the chain and fetter around its ankle while grumbling something indecipherable under its breath. It then straightened its head as it did when it was about to speak.

"You no longer amuse us you pathetic creatures! We destroyed your kind in the old time! BE GONE WITH YOU!" it shouted and then growled and scanned our reactions.

To our collective shock the beast reached down, then we heard a loud CRACK as it broke the fetter off its ankle as if it were a piece of bread. An audible gasp of fear could be heard from the men, but it simply got up, then turned and trotted away in its usual manner.

"We were both defeated and humiliated," the old man said regretfully as he stood up from the fire, then stretched his back and looked over at his friend. "The beast had only been playing with us," he lamented.

"Can you tell me what my father did?" Dimitri asked as he was disappointed that his father had not been mentioned more prominently in the story.

Aegeus responded, "I'm sorry, but I can't think of anything specifically that he did; he was there, sustained some minor injuries and was a great help with the injured afterward. He was the one who helped the man with the injured ankle the most on the way back to Gadara. Your father handled himself well. I think all of the men were narrowly focused during the ordeal. It was the most horrendous event of my life; I imagine it's the same for the others. I would rather fight a lion than face that creature again."

"I know that you're telling me the truth…but it's so hard to believe," Dimitri said as he gazed into the fire, then glanced up at Aegeus. He wasn't sure he wanted to believe.

The old man smiled at his friend and knelt by the fire. He set down his staff and pulled aside his outer garment, then loosened his tunic and pulled it aside to reveal his bare left shoulder. Aegeus leaned forward to illuminate himself by the fire; there were four very distinct deep scars across and over the top of his shoulder. He glanced at Dimitri and noticed his mouth opened a bit.

"Took a long time for that to heal," the old man said as he put his clothing back in order, then covered his head and slowly rose back to his feet.

"How did the beast come to be?" Dimitri asked as he wanted to engage in a deep conversation.

"Freak of nature I suppose," Aegeus said as he returned his gaze toward the distant storm. It had maintained its intensity while holding right in the middle of the Sea of Galilee.

"Do you think it's because of evil spirits?" Dimitri asked as he stared into the fire.

"I don't think in terms like that," the old man proclaimed. "I've learned to trust in what I see with my own two eyes. Seen a lot of strange things with animals giving birth to freaks. We, as Greek have heard all kinds of fantastic stories about the gods and the heroes of the legends of our people; I've never seen proof of such. The Jews believe in spirits and things, as I understand. They don't have much use for us *Gentiles*," Aegeus said.

"So, you don't believe as they do, that their God is the one true God?" Dimitri asked as he shifted position while seeking comfort and indicating that he wanted Aegeus to take the first watch.

"I would believe if something came along to show me strong evidence of such a God," the old man said as he continued to observe the storm and occasionally glance at the herd. "I don't see it by observing the Pharisees," he added.

"Yeah, I feel the same way. I've heard a lot of stories from the Jewish traditions," the young man said as his speech was getting a bit slower, for the night was wearing on. The herd was settled down and the tired young herdsman's thoughts were giving way to sleep.

"I'll take the first watch," Aegeus said as he smiled at his young companion, then added more wood to the fire. "I'm sending you to the marketplace in the morning to get some more food for us; I want to keep the herd up here for another day or two," he instructed.

"First thing in the morning," Dimitri mumbled as he drifted off to sleep.

The old man was now alone with his thoughts. Something inside was tugging at his heart. He really wanted to believe in the God of the Hebrews; one that watched over men as he watched over his animals. The storytelling and the conversation had led Aegeus into deep thoughts about his life, so he decided to voice some of his thoughts under his breath. He glanced over at his young friend, now sound asleep and pulled his blanket up over his hands. Dimitri shifted slightly and breathed deeply in silent appreciation. The elder herdsman sat on the rock close to the fire and watched the distant storm. He thought of what Dimitri had said about the stories from the Hebrew scriptures, which he himself had heard many times. The old man didn't know how to pray, so he just spoke from his heart, while double checking to make sure his young friend was asleep.

Aegeus spoke, "God of the Hebrews, reveal yourself to me if you really exist, so that I might believe. I would learn your ways and live my life by your ways. If I could see with my own two eyes, then I would believe!"

The elder herdsman sat quietly while leaning on his staff and warming himself by the fire. He was lost in thought as he continued to watch the distant storm, when suddenly the storm vanished right before his eyes! He rubbed his eyes in disbelief, for he had never seen such a thing. Aegeus tried to reason within his mind of what he had just witnessed. The storm didn't move off, nor did it dissipate normally; it just melted away into a perfectly clear, starry, moonlit night. The old man couldn't help but wonder about what he had said under his breath moments before. Then he said to himself out loud, "No, just a very strange weather event; just because I've never seen such doesn't mean it was because of that."

Yet he sat and watched, as he contemplated these things throughout the rest of the night. He didn't even awaken Dimitri when the time came time for his watch. A time or two the elder herdsman heard the unmistakable cry of the beast off in the distance. He paid it little mind, though startled a bit. He knew it was out there but knew there was little threat at night. Still, nothing wrong with keeping a close watch. He pondered deeply what Dimitri had said about the beast coming to be through evil spirits. Aegeus realized that some of what he had witnessed was beyond reason, as he had told the story again. The elder man reviewed his life. He had many friends and looked after Dimitri and his family after his friend had died, but he was lonely at times. His wife had died when they were young, so he had no children of his own. He looked over at Dimitri and realized that he had sort of adopted him and his brother, Argus, as sons. He was very proud of them. Aegeus was fond of their mother, Calista, but kept his distance out of respect. Perhaps there was something more for the life of this old man. The experience of the storm vanishing left Aegeus restless. He shifted to sitting even closer to the fire with his back rested against the sitting rock. He pondered his thoughts way into the night, until finally the old man dozed off.

The Storm

The late afternoon sun cast a warm amber glow upon the ship and the men as they rowed away from the west coast of the Sea of Galilee. They left behind the multitudes that had gathered there to hear the teaching of their Master. It was a clear, warm, pleasant afternoon with a gentle westerly breeze blowing. They lowered the dingy white sail, as it billowed and pushed the little ship toward their destination. The voyage to the other side, as their Master had requested, seemed as it was going to be an easy trip with lots of good fellowship. Simon looked around the ship as he guided her along at the helm. He thought about their mission and the other men on their journey.

There were himself and his brother Andrew, who owned the ship; the brothers James and John, as well as Philip, all fishermen. The other disciples were Matthew the tax collector, Nathaniel Bartholomew, Thomas Didymus, James the son of Alphaeus, Jude Thaddaeus, Judas Iscariot the treasurer, and Simon the Canaanite. And, of course, Jesus of Nazareth, their Master; the men had a full ship. Jesus had been standing near the bow as they had set off, while making his way to the stern slowly as he spoke to all on board. He ended up sitting at the rear of the ship between Simon and Andrew. Jesus went below the stern deck as the afternoon sun waned, for Simon had told him about the ballast sacks being a good place to take rest. The men were all happy to see their Master lying down, for they had been walking all over the Galilee Region; Jesus had been teaching and performing miracles almost nonstop for days. The men settled in for the evening as they sailed across the Sea of Galilee.

What had been a calm and very pleasant evening had changed to a brisk and damp night. Darkness fell, but the stars and rising moon were obscured by an approaching mass of threatening dark clouds. The surface of the sea had been still, but now had become a bit choppy and there was spray and light rain in the air. They continued on, but the men who had been joyfully conversing with

27

one another were quiet as they became aware of the coming storm. Most had set about adjusting their garments and covering their heads to prepare for the change in the weather. The brothers Simon and Andrew remained on the rear deck. Simon was sitting on the starboard side, as he guided the little ship along with the fixed helm oar, while Andrew was on the port side with an oar as well. James and John were handling the center oars. They had set sail from the west side in fair weather and had not expected a storm. Still, the men felt confident in their ship. She was new and even after two seasons still had the aroma of fresh cut wood seasoned with fish. All of the rigging, fittings, as well as the sail were in top condition.

Simon was thinking to himself, as he scanned the ship and her passengers. He realized that it would be difficult to return to life as it was before. The excitement of following Jesus had far outmatched any of his experiences in life. The far-reaching importance of their mission had superseded anything else, as it was instantly evident upon the Master's call: '*Follow me.*' Simon secured the helm for a moment and jumped down to speak with his Master about the approaching storm. He found him curled up asleep while using his outer garment as a blanket. He didn't want to disturb him, for the time being. He knew he was exhausted.

Simon returned to his position at the helm. He guided the ship along, as he recalled his visits to the boat builders when he had commissioned the ship a couple of seasons before....

She was a fine specimen of the Galilean lake boats, as they had been built for many generations. She was big enough to carry fifteen passengers, or huge loads of fish. The little ship had one mast and yard with a square-rigged sail. A very sturdy wooden hull was fitted together with mortise and tenon joints; thus, making the need for an internal frame structure unnecessary. Instead, there was a series of lateral pieces applied to the inside of the planking to provide extra strength and were rounded to be walked on. The well-fitted joints of the hull had no need of caulking, for the water would swell the joints making them watertight. A straight keel rose at either end of the ship by way of bow and stern posts, as well as the hull planking, and the posts rose higher and curved inward. The bow post was a wave splitter, which sloped forward at the base. The stern post had a slope as well forming a kind of tail or stationary rudder. She had five oars and had oarlocks on the rail of the ship. A sixth fixed oar, or helm was attached to the starboard side of the ship at the stern and had a broader end to steer by. There were two decks at the bow and stern with spaces beneath, but open at the center of the ship. She had a shallow draft, which was excellent for getting close to shore for fishing; not so good in rough seas. The small ships would typically put in at the onset of bad weather.

The disciples found themselves right in the middle of the Sea of Galilee. The two men on the stern deck exchanged glances of concern.

"Not too bad yet; perhaps it will blow over," Andrew stated as he looked up at the ominous, dark sky.

"Yes, perhaps," Simon responded as he also looked up, then at the men in his boat, as they were faintly visible in the dim light of the two lamps burning on board.

Simon realized that there was nothing he could do to improve their situation, for he felt responsible for everyone on board. Deep down he wondered how anything bad could happen to them with Jesus on board, so he decided to focus on that and not the storm. It still wasn't that bad, as the westerly wind had picked up a bit to their advantage; they were moving along at a good pace. Simon was thinking to himself how fortunate they were that he had invested in a new boat for his family's fishing business. Their old large boat had been around since before he was born. He had grown up and learned to fish on that boat, but there came a time when it just couldn't be repaired anymore. He remembered how sad he felt when he let it go to the boat builders, but they had made a more than fair offer for it. It did help with the final payment when he took possession of the new boat. Watching it go was like losing a friend. He knew, however, that times being what they were under heavy Roman taxation, that parts from the old boat would help other struggling fishermen keep their boats in service. There were now more serious things to consider, as it all seemed like such a long time ago. Their ship had a new much more important mission than catching fish; Jesus had told them they were now fishers of men.

Gradually, the ship began to creak and groan, as the wave action increased. The men started to hunker down and hold onto something. Suddenly, a big gust of wind hit from the south tossing the ship slightly as it began to rain harder. The men looked up, for there were traces of lightning mingled in the dark clouds; the rumble of thunder was adding to the anxiety of the men facing the growing threat. There was a bit of murmuring among the disciples as they covered themselves the best they could. The powerful wind gusts started to come from all directions it seemed. The waves were breaking over the sides and pouring water into the little ship.

Simon found himself struggling increasingly with the helm to keep the ship perpendicular to the waves and keep her from rolling over. The waves had become whitecaps the height of a man and growing. Andrew was struggling himself and called out to man all the oars. The brothers James and John remained at the center oars; the men at the bow got their oars in the water as well. Now, they were fighting for their lives as the little ship pitched and rolled like a toy.

"Pull up the sail!" Simon shouted as he continued to wrestle with the helm.

Nathaniel and Judas took the task, as Judas untied the rope to pull up the sail by way of a pulley at the top of the mast. They fought to hoist the heavy, rain-soaked sail, then a very strong gust of wind blasted them from the southwest. The rope holding the end of the yard steady on the starboard side snapped and torqued the sail sideways. The men gathered themselves and continued the attempt to raise the sail, but they found the rope was jammed in the pulley and was unable to free it. The sail was less than halfway up, and the wind was tossing the ship about violently. The others not involved with fighting the storm with the oars were busy bailing water with empty clay jars that had been stowed beneath the bow deck.

Thomas was bailing water, but he saw the trouble his friends were having with the sail and acted. He grabbed the dangling, broken rope hanging from the yard, then tied it around his waist and shimmied up the mast. The man hung on for his life and wrapped his legs around the mast as he tugged the rope with both hands back and forth until managing to pull the snag free. He started to descend, but the ship abruptly rolled over to a very steep angle on the port side. Thomas lost his grip, then flew off the mast out over the sea. He quickly clutched the rope, for the man was staring death in the face; he didn't know how to swim. Fear began to creep into his mind, but the ship quickly righted itself. The motion slung him back into the ship, and he landed on his feet. He was stunned and looked around for a moment at the faces of the men on the stern of the ship, for they had witnessed what happened and were all astonished. Thomas looked at the other men with a very curious expression as he collected his senses, then staggered back to find a jar and started to bail water again.

Those who were bailing water seemed to be fighting a losing battle. They would gain a little, only to see another wave crash over the side of the ship and dump more water in than they had fought to remove. The effort was beginning to seem hopeless, as there was a growing fear and frustration among the men. The disciples realized that they would likely be lost if the storm continued much longer. The storm had grown to a greater intensity than any of the men had ever encountered at least while at sea. The thunder and lightning were becoming more intense than ever, as well as the wind gusts. The little ship was pitching and rolling to such a degree that the men thought at any moment the ship would capsize or fill up with water and sink. Despite all of this the ship kept righting itself, and the battle continued.

Simon was straining to see as the lamps on board had gone out; the rain and spray were constantly blowing in his face. He was thinking of how he had failed his Master and all the men who had come aboard his boat. His thoughts went toward Jesus, now more than ever they needed to look to him. They had been preoccupied with the storm and dealing with the emergency by their own efforts. It had all developed so quickly that the disciples had failed to believe and have faith in him. Simon wondered how anyone could sleep through all of this.

The ship had taken on a lot of water despite the efforts of the men constantly bailing. The rain had been coming down very heavy and they were all soaked, cold and growing more and more weary from battling the storm. Suddenly, the ship rose up at a very steep angle by the stern. It simultaneously rolled over on the starboard side, while creaking violently as the ship was not designed for such stresses. The men let out a collective gasp as they found themselves looking down at the water, while holding on to keep from falling out of the ship. They were expecting to crash down sideways and sink. The water that had filled the ship rushed out over the starboard side by the bow, and over the men clinging to whatever they could. One man, Philip, was washed out, but miraculously the ship slipped back and righted itself once again. Philip ended up near the stern, then quickly swam up and grabbed an oar as the others pulled him from the water.

Simon secured the helm and jumped down. He entered the space beneath the deck and was joined by two other men outside the space as they had decided to wake their Master. One said, "I don't know how much longer we're going to last out here!"

The space beneath the deck was dark, since the lamps on board had been extinguished by the wind and the rain. The men's eyes adjusted as they could barely see that the space had been swamped, but the top of the ballast sacks had remained dry. The now frequent lightning flashes allowed brief glimpses of their Master, as he was still curled up sleeping. Simon firmly touched him.

"Master, we perish!" he said rather loudly as he tried to wake him.

"The storm is overwhelming us!" shouted one of the men close by.

The only response was Jesus pulling his cover over his head.

"Master, we perish!" Simon shouted louder this time while pushing vigorously on his Master's shoulder.

Slowly he awoke, then sat up and stretched his arms a little as he ran his hands through his hair to push it out of his face. He opened his eyes, then looked down realizing that he had put his feet in water.

"Master, don't you care that we're going to drown?" one of the frightened men pleaded.

Another said, "The water is overtaking us again!"

Jesus stood up, then put on his outer garment and covered his head. He gently parted the men clinging to the edge of the stern deck and emerged from below.

The scene on the ship was frantic: men bailing water and fighting the storm to keep the ship steady with the oars. All went silent upon the appearance of Jesus.

"Why are you fearful, O you of little faith?" their Master shouted with a stern and authoritative voice.

He stood there for a moment as he looked out at the sea and up at the storm. The ship was violently swaying, for the men were unable to stand without clinging onto something. Most had been hunkered down or bracing their bodies to keep from falling over. Jesus was just standing there, as he seemed unaffected by the reality that they had been immersed in. Everyone on board was amazed by this, so much so that they all stopped whatever they were doing, and all eyes were upon him.

Jesus then raised his arms as he shouted out over the sea and up at the storm with thunderous authority:

"PEACE BE STILL!" he commanded.

Instantly, there was no movement anywhere. The dark clouds that had been so menacing simply melted away into a clear, starry sky with a bright three-quarter moon. The scene was bathed in soft moonlight revealing an unusual stillness upon the surface of the water. All the men were intensely and thoroughly shocked. Jesus lowered his arms and turned to his disciples. His countenance had returned to his compassionate and loving way.

"Why are you so fearful? How is it that you have no faith?" he asked as he scanned the faces of his chosen companions. He smiled and then turned to view the distant, now visible shoreline and hills beyond. A very small flicker of light could be seen near the shore on one of the lower hills. Jesus pointed to it while glancing at Simon, as he acknowledged his direction. Jesus then bent down and returned to the space beneath the stern deck. The men could see their Master, once the lamps on board were lit again, as he knelt upon the ballast sacks and prayed as he often did. Most of the men couldn't take their eyes off of him, until finally he climbed back upon the ballast sacks and went back to sleep.

Murmuring began to slowly develop among the men as they tried to come to grips with what had just happened.

One asked, *"What manner of man is this, that even the wind and the sea obey him?"*

No one responded. Quiet resumed as some of the men went about bailing the remainder of the water out of their little ship. Simon sat at his place on the stern deck, where he had been fighting for their lives a very short time ago. Now, he sat there guiding the ship effortlessly and felt very foolish. Why hadn't they awakened Jesus sooner? Why had they doubted? Where was their faith? A gentle westerly breeze began to blow, as it had at the beginning of their journey. Simon asked Andrew to help him lower the sail once more. The sail caught the breeze and billowed as it pushed them forward. Andrew got up and grabbed a spare piece of rope from below, then tied it to the broken rope on the yard and secured it to its place on the rail of the ship. He told Simon that it was the only damage he knew of.

The men continued on, as they quietly reflected on what they had been through together. Simon once again gazed at the faces of the other disciples softly lit by the ship's lamps. He knew that they had all grown in faith and stronger fellowship. He looked out at the Sea of Galilee as the moonlight glistening off the gentle ripples of the water. Then he looked up at the tiny flicker of light that his Master had pointed to. Simon continued to guide the ship along and introspected just how the experience had impacted him personally. He drifted into a time of silent prayer, as he recalled what had been spoken of Jesus. What manner of man was this? He watched the men who were exhausted from their ordeal, as they slowly settled in and dozed off. Simon felt a blessing wash over him. He knew what manner of man Jesus was. He was much more than a man.

The Tomb

Darkness had fallen upon the rocky bluff. The pale moonlight revealed only a slight suggestion of the grassy slopes, trees, and rock formations overlooking the Sea of Galilee. The area was typically only visited during the daylight hours, for the rocky bluffs contained many tombs. It had become very quiet, and it was a lonely, desolate place. Very few ventured into the area to honor the dead anymore. People had been frightened and attacked. Stories were told of something evil lurking there. The tombs had become overgrown and neglected as a result.

One of the tombs, however, was not abandoned. In the dark recesses of the ancient tomb there was a dim glow, and movement. He made his nest behind a large stone sarcophagus shrouded in cobwebs. It was near the back wall of the tomb beneath a row of carved niches, where he kept his treasures. Legion slept on a pile of old, dirty clothing and things that he had stolen over the years. He liked the spot due to the steady availability of vermin and insects to eat. There were symbols and depictions on the wall around his nest; depictions of an ancient world known only to him, and those within. Spirals, horned gods, giants, hideous beasts, and long forgotten languages that only had meaning to Legion; all written in his own blood.

They liked keeping things that reminded them of their exploits; bits of cloth, strands of hair, broken pieces of pottery, and broken weapons all made them feel alive. They would relive the moment; the fear, the pain, and the shame their victims would feel intoxicated them. Legion also kept a collection of swords, daggers, pieces of armor, and even arrows from the many attempts to capture him. His lamp was a badly dented Roman helmet, which had been filled with animal fat with a bit of cloth stuck in for a wick. They needed none of these things, except to feel alive.

They referred to themselves as Legion. Multitudes of ancient evil spirits had entered the poor unfortunate man early in life, for he had been left vulnerable through the worship of false gods and witchcraft. Legion had no understanding of what it was like to be alone; therefore, the demoniac had no concept of loneliness. He was a complete hermit and defended his solitude with vigor. What was left of the man was deeply buried beneath layer upon layer of demonic entities. The man was no longer allowed to think, or remember his name, or where he came from. This *Legion*, as they called themselves had very simple objectives: To kill, steal, destroy, to cause misery; and to wait for a time in the distant future when they would have free reign in the world, for a time.

Legion jumped upon the ornate lid of the stone sarcophagus and let out a screeching wail to welcome the night, which was followed by crying. Something deep inside brought an intense sadness; an inner conflict never resolved, and crying was the only way to release it. Legion perched upon his roost and had a clear view of the tomb entrance, so he could look out for a possible meal, or perhaps something or someone to torment. Legion didn't usually venture out much at night; not out of fear, which was an emotion that had become meaningless to them, but simply the lack of visibility. Legion preferred to stalk during the day, so they could see clearly all the nuances of the horror they would perpetuate. They refrained from killing anyone; not because they didn't want to, but for self-preservation. Legion understood that murder would bring a more determined quest for their capture. They knew better than to exceed their limitations, for the survival of the host was a higher priority.

The top of the sarcophagus was stained with Legions own blood. There were several pieces of flint scattered about fashioned into blades to cut himself with. Through doing this, Legion would feel powerful and at times would see images or visions of things to come. These evil spirits had driven the man into the wilderness and driven the humanity out of the man. Even the animals of God's creation have a code of behavior according to their kind. What Legion had become was a creature devoid of any virtue; a creature that just shouldn't be.

Legion was rather short in stature, because of the twisted, contorted nature of his development from the demonic possession and the way he carried himself. His muscles were bulged and rippled abnormally, as well as his face. His eyes were unusually dark and piercing. He folded his legs on either side and put his arms in front, like an animal when he sat or perched. He never wore clothing, which was something all people did. They had an intense hatred for anything human. Legion was covered with filth, for they didn't like water to touch them. To Legion, water represented cleanliness and purity; they found the concept repulsive. His hair had grown very long and was tangled, matted, and full of debris. His finger and toenails had grown into thick, sharp claws.

The most frightening thing about his appearance was that his entire body was covered with horrible scars following years of mutilating himself. Legion would cut himself and the wounds wouldn't heal properly, then they would fester. They would be gratified by the pain, which was reflected in his overall appearance. He never cut his face or neck for some reason, but his arms, legs, torso, and his back as far as he could reach all showed evidence of his long-term self-abuse.

Legion perched, as a memory of an exploit long ago emerged in his mind....

It was early afternoon. Legion had just returned to the tomb seeking the cool darkness. They felt it wise to hide, for they had witnessed a few Roman soldiers in the area searching. They conversed within his mind. Were they looking for us? Legion sought insight by making a small cut upon his leg. Yes, they were looking for Legion. Would they find us? The demoniac wanted to avoid an encounter with the Romans, if possible. Legion decided that if they found them, this group of Romans would curse the day because of it. They didn't want to leave this tomb, for it suited their needs. Legion could sit in the darkness all day and watch from within. Many creatures shared the tomb with Legion; tasty creatures. The demoniac heard sounds from outside: the sounds of beasts and men. Legion could see outside the tomb entrance as the soldiers dismounted their horses. The Romans then tied them to some trees and approached the entrance of another tomb. They knew the soldiers were coming, so Legion moved to the entrance, for they were prepared to defend their lair.

The Roman soldiers were done searching the other tomb quickly, then approached. Legion was visible just inside the tomb entrance, which startled a couple of the soldiers. The one in charge: a large, muscular, young man, stepped up and pulled a small scroll from under his armor. He opened the scroll and read the proclamation in Latin:

He shouted, "By order of the Commander of the Tenth Legion Camp at Gadara, I hereby announce this order to place you under arrest for various crimes against the Roman Empire. Disrupting trade routes, hindering free travel and various accusations of attack, theft, and injury. You are to come with us." He finished speaking, then two of the soldiers approached with chains they had brought from the horses.

Legion moved up to the entrance. The sunlight caught his hideous appearance as he sniffed the air. From Legion's point of view men appeared to move in slow motion. He viewed them as clumsy, lumbering creatures despite their shiny armor and well-fitted apparel. Legion issued a proclamation of his own in a deep, echoing voice in Latin:

"I will not go with you, you stinking dung beetles. I live by the authority of the god of this world. Your empire has no authority over us. Go back and tell this *commander* of yours to stop annoying us. You are outnumbered. We may not harm you, if you leave quickly. Now, BE GONE WITH YOU!" he commanded.

The large soldier threw the scroll to the ground and drew his sword. The other soldiers followed his lead. Legion ran up and grabbed the sword away from the large man before any of them knew what had happened. Lightning fast, Legion ran over to where the horses were tied and frightened them. He cut the reigns and swatted them on the rear with the flat side of the sword, then chased them away. The demoniac began to release an insane laughter; a cackling that wrought fear to those who heard it. Legion ran up to face the soldiers, for they now had swords drawn. Sword fighting ensued until the demon-filled man grew tired of it and complained about how slow they were. He then began breaking the blades of the swords as they came at him and threw them into the distance. Legion went at the large man, as he ripped his breastplate off with his left clawed hand. The man yelled out as the motion left deep wounds across his torso from Legion's claws. The demoniac kept going after the large man; beating him, ripping and tearing at his clothing and equipment all with his left hand. The soldiers were attempting to help their commander, but Legion flipped the sword around in his right hand and began knocking helmets off with the handle. This either severely stunned the men or left them unconscious. The soldiers were completely unprepared for the supernatural strength and speed of Legion.

The battle continued, but the large man was down and unconscious. The others kept trying to confine Legion with the chains, as the demoniac kicked and swiped with his claws. One of the soldiers came at Legion with the chain, which resulted in the demoniac kicking him in the face and taking the heavy device. Greatly amused, Legion began swinging it over his head, while he continued cackling. The chain had quickly become a very effective weapon and the remaining soldiers were simply trying to survive the battle. The large man rose up and shouted an order to retreat. The beaten and bloody soldiers ran away in different directions, as they cried out to their pagan gods to protect them.

Legion looked around still snickering a bit. The demoniac ended up glad they had found them. Legion once again retreated to the cool darkness of his tomb, after gathering some of the more useful bits of armor and weapons. The memory began to fade, as they sensed a disturbance....

Legion heard a slight noise outside of the tomb. He glared at the tomb entrance, then sniffed the air like a snake sensing prey. He saw nothing but knew that someone was there. He quickly scurried back behind his perch into his nest, then peeked out from around the corner of the sarcophagus. He waited some time, then a human head appeared around the side of the entrance and peered in. The figure cautiously crept in through the entrance and sniffed the air. Legion had encountered this one before.

He was another demon-possessed man. The man was filthy like Legion, and wore an old, tattered cloak. For years he had shadowed Legion, for reasons only known to him. The man would attempt to sneak up on them but was always unsuccessful. They shared a mutual obsession with places of death. This one was far less powerful, wicked, or cunning as Legion. Having but a few demons, this man's struggle was closer to the surface as he fought to retain selective attributes of his humanity. He had been rejected by society; an outcast, and was seeking interaction, or some sort of acceptance. Legion considered this man unworthy to share space or anything else with. They had all the companionship they needed within.

The man crept closer to his lair. Legion suddenly jumped up in the air and landed on top of his perch. He released a loud, cackling laughter that continued as he glared at the man with his dark, sinister eyes. The man jumped only a slight bit in surprise as he slowly backed up toward the tomb entrance. Legion's laughter died away for the moment, but he continued glaring at the intruder. He hurled an old dagger unexpectantly that he had picked up while lying in wait. The weapon shot across the tomb and grazed the man's ear. The mysterious man didn't move but stood there and grunted a little under his breath, as a trickle of blood ran down his neck. Legion released his insane laughter once more, then jumped down and ran up to the man with frightening speed. Legion stood in front of the weaker possessed man and sniffed him up and down, then let out a blood-curdling screech right in the man's face. The intruder continued to stand there, for he knew better than to fight; Legion could easily tear him to pieces. The demoniac retrieved the dagger, then returned to his perch with it in his clawed hand and jumped up. Legion calmly licked the blood from the old rusty weapon as he glared at his intruder, then threw the dagger back at the man. It stuck it in the ground between his feet.

He then shouted with his deep, echoing voice, "Be gone with you! You have no place with us! We are Legion, we are many, we are the mighty ones from the old time before the waters came and took our world away! We are here to destroy this creation of God! How dare you come in here seeking us! BE GONE WITH YOU!"

Legion reached behind his back, where he had laid a large human leg bone on the edge of the sarcophagus lid. The man had turned to run. He barely cleared the entrance of the tomb, then the bone flew against the lintel of the entrance and smashed into a thousand pieces. The cackling laughter of Legion followed the man as he ran off into the darkness of the night.

Legion looked down, only slightly distracted by the intrusion, and picked up one of the flint blades laying on top of his perch. He held it up, while looking at it in the dim light from his lamp. He turned and held it, so the flame of the lamp was behind it. They admired the thinness and translucence of the blade, as well as the incredible sharpness. He sniffed the blade and then tasted it; the taste of the dried blood brought back prior experiences. Legion closed his eyes in a moment of euphoria.

The demoniac made a long cut on the underside of his left forearm. He perched quietly awaiting a vision as the blood flowed out. He began to pass into a light trance, as he recalled many past exploits, and sought ways to have even greater ones. They had occasional dim memories of the times of old and the mighty ones. A vision slowly began to manifest in his mind....

Legion began to see a boat on the water. They had grown accustomed to living with little fear of anything; suddenly, they found themselves filled with terror. The vision ended because of the shock. There was something about that boat that threatened them, but how could a boat threaten Legion in these hills on dry ground? They couldn't make sense of it, as much as they tried. He made a similar cut on the other arm and called upon powerful dark entities for greater understanding. He became motionless, as they awaited a vision once more.

A long time passed, then Legion saw the boat on the water again, like the boats they had seen on the Sea of Galilee. There was a man on the boat with many others, but this man was different than the rest. The spirits within started to feel very troubled. They thought at first it was because of their disdain for water. Then, the man who was unique began to glow and transformed into a blinding white light, until the brightness was all they could see. Legion tried to open his eyes, but the vision continued, for all he could see was white. Then a strange new image emerged from the whiteness: it was the Son of God sitting upon a throne with honor and glory and his name was Jesus! Legion lost consciousness as he fell back off of his perch and into his nest. He slowly came around, then they went into a complete panic.

Legion ran out of the tomb and around the bluff to survey the Sea of Galilee. It was a clear night, except for a strange looking storm over the sea. They decided that the storm was there because of the boat. Legion raised his hands as he called upon powerful spirits to destroy it. He scanned the sea and strained his eyes trying to see the boat but knew he wouldn't unless it was close. They assumed it was there based on the panic boiling in his gut. He scanned the coast but saw no boats, only the glimmer of a small fire off in the distance; up the coast to the north. Legion figured it was the swine herders they had watched earlier in the day. They had thought about attacking them and stealing one of the animals, but now had more serious matters to deal with.

Legion began to collect stones in the darkness and made a circle in a place that couldn't be seen by the swine herders, but still in view of the sea. The demoniac started collecting leaves, sticks, small pieces of wood and threw them into the circle. Legion perched by the circle and drew symbols in the dirt with his claw next to each stone. He got up and started to dance around the circle, while calling upon demonic spirits as he danced. Legion called out for fire. The pile he had created within the circle started to smoke, then burst into flames. The demoniac let out his laughter which eased the panic.

Legion continued to dance, while calling upon wicked spirits of the earth to bring up a whirlwind to stop and destroy the boat they had seen. The demon host danced, as he could hear distant thunder and paused for a moment. Legion looked out over the Sea of Galilee, and could see the dark, swirling clouds that were laced with fingers of lightning. He let out his cackling laughter once again, but deep inside the panic remained, for the demons within knew the vision to be true. Legion resumed dancing frantically way into the night. He stopped to see that the storm had disappeared; they tried to convince themselves that the storm had destroyed the boat. The gut-wrenching reality was that the fear and panic endured. Legion continued to dance. He danced for there was fear within they couldn't cope with. He danced due to there being a very small part of them, which opposed everything that they were, and Legion could never understand it. He danced because there was a very annoying emotion which kept rising that Legion had not dealt with for a long time. They kept subduing it with their twisted logic. That emotion was hope.

Chapter Two

The Deliverance

It was a clear and beautiful morning as the rays of the sun were breaking over the hills and rocky bluffs on the southeast coast of the Sea of Galilee. Many features of the landscape were still in shadow, but the morning sun shone down on what appeared to be a beach straight ahead. Simon let go of the helm and asked Andrew to help him raise the sail. Everyone had been dozing off until daybreak, for they had been worn out from the storm. Even Simon had fallen asleep at the helm a couple of times but woke to find the ship was still on course. The morning had brought good feelings among the men as they sat around Jesus, while talking and laughing. There was an undeniable joy and confidence in the men and their mission; these men would follow their Master to the ends of the earth.

The sail was raised, and those who had been rowing grabbed the oars and started working their way to the shore. Simon knew how fortunate they were, since much of the coast in the area was rocky and steep; too rough to land a boat. He thought they might have to travel up and down the coast to find a suitable place to land. He had steered in the direction of the flickering speck of light his Master had pointed to until it was no longer visible, then used landmarks after that. He took no credit for any navigational expertise; somehow, he knew they were exactly where they needed to be. Simon figured they were near the northern portion of the harbor of Gadara.

The men rowed enthusiastically toward the beach. It was bathed in the early morning warm sunlight and was a welcome sight to all, after the storm of the previous night. Simon stood up and strained his eyes as he shaded them with his hand against the intense morning sun. He was trying to make out the details of the shoreline as they approached. Simon noticed what appeared to be a very large herd of animals to the left upon a steep grassy slope with trees. He saw what appeared to be caves in the rocky bluffs. He was unable to make anything out distinctly, so he sat down and went back to rowing. They were getting close within a short time. The men not occupied with the oars stood and prepared to disembark. Nathaniel was holding a rope attached to the bow to help pull the boat up onto the beach. Simon secured the helm and stood up again to survey the landscape.

Simon scanned to the left and up the slope while shading his eyes from the intense sunlight, then grimaced. He looked away toward his fellow disciples, as many had noticed the same thing. He again turned his shielded gaze toward the slope and muttered under his breath, "Swine." This was not something the Jewish men found appealing; they considered swine unclean animals that they wanted nothing to do with. He thought to himself that at least the breeze seemed to be taking the stench up into the hills. Simon also noticed a column of smoke rising from within the herd. He identified it as, most likely, the source of the flickering light he had followed last night. A gentle swoosh brought the little ship to a stop. The men eagerly jumped off into the shallow water and pulled the boat up onto the beach. Jesus jumped out and walked across the beach with many of his disciples following. He scanned the landscape for himself while paying particular attention to the rocky bluff above....

The elder herdsman awoke and found his young companion had already left for Emmatha to obtain needed supplies for a prolonged stay in the area. Aegeus took a drink from his waterskin and washed his face, then dug through his bag for something to eat. He was unsatisfied with the remnants of dried out bread that he found, so he decided to walk around the herd and round up strays. He got up and grabbed his staff, then immediately noticed that a ship had landed down on the beach. He was curious, so he walked a bit closer to see the group of men that had gathered there. A few of them were tying off the ship to some rocks. "They must have just arrived," he mumbled to himself.

As he moved closer, Aegeus determined they appeared to be Jewish fishermen with passengers, so he held his place. He was herding swine and smelled like swine. Everyone knew that Jewish people considered swine unclean and had a disdain for them. Still, he was compelled to watch these men, but didn't think he would be received well. Aegeus noticed one of the men was looking up at the rocky bluff. He had determined the day before that the beast was possibly hiding there, for he had tried to avoid it when they passed through. He was a tall man, and his clothing was definitely Jewish. He was intrigued by this man somehow; probably because he felt like warning him not to go up there. Aegeus wondered if they had landed here to travel to Hippos, for he would offer to move the herd and let them pass. A couple of the men noticed Aegeus and waved, which left him surprised at their friendly gesture. The elder herdsman hastily returned the wave.

For now, the men were just standing around talking, so the old man went back to check on his herd and the other herdsmen. He determined there were minimal strays, as the forage in the area was plentiful. There were also low spots here and there with mud for the swine to wallow in. He decided that they would move the herd farther up into the hills for fresh forage when Dimitri returned. After a good meal, as the elder herdsman thought to himself.

There was now little movement at the site of Legion's ritual that lasted through the night. The fire that had been raging the night before was reduced to a small pile of ashes, still smoldering and sending out wisps of smoke. Legion had collapsed from exhaustion and overwhelming panic from the vision they had seen, as well as seeing the storm vanish. It all brought about fervent, intense dancing. The morning sun was beating down and causing him to stir a bit. His first waking thought was to retreat to the cool, dark recesses of the tomb. The memories of the previous night came crashing back as he awoke; was the ship destroyed?

The demoniac jumped up suddenly, then looked around and sniffed the air. They realized their worst fear, as Legion let out an ear-splitting screech that echoed throughout the landscape. He jumped upon a large rock that was obstructing his view of the coastline below, and what they saw invoked a panic like they had never experienced before. It was the ship they had seen! They had projected and imagined it destroyed in a myriad of ways through their magic, yet there it was. They saw the men standing on the beach, and one was staring straight up at them!

Legion's countenance began to change; the fear, rage, and defiance that had permeated their existence the night before melted away into acceptance. They knew this was the Son of God; for the first time there was no escape. A strange curiosity was developing among them: why was he here, now? They knew the end of days were far off, and they would have their time before the judgment. He perched upon the rock for a moment while preparing for the inevitable surrender. Legion then jumped down. The demoniac looked around while sniffing the air, then ran down the slope toward the men on the beach in their usual animal-like way.

One of the disciples noticed him approaching and proclaimed, "Behold Master, a wild man!"

He ran to within a short distance before Jesus, then dropped to his knees and bowed his head in worship. The disciples of Jesus drew near to their Master on either side ready to defend him in case this wild beast decided to attack. Simon rested his hand on the pommel of his sword; Jesus didn't move at all.

Then Legion spoke in their deep, guttural, echoing voice, *"What have I to do with you, Jesus, Son of the most high God? I adjure you by God, that you torment me not."*

Jesus calmly asked him, *"What is your name?"*

Legion responded, *"My name is Legion: for we are many."*

Jesus slowly raised his right hand, and in a booming voice of authority commanded, *"COME OUT OF THE MAN, UNCLEAN SPIRITS!"*

The demoniac instantly recoiled, then let out a screeching wail. Panic once again consumed Legion, for he had been extremely weakened and disoriented by the command of Jesus. Thinking quickly, they formulated a negotiation:

"We adjure you, Lord, that you would not cast us into the abyss, but allow us to enter the swine nearby," Legion pleaded in a weakened state.

Jesus glanced up at the vast herd of swine for a moment, then looked back at Legion and responded with the same voice of authority, *"GO!"*

The beast at the feet of Jesus collapsed with his head down, while covering his head with his clawed hands. Immediately, the men noticed changes taking place in the strange man. His contorted, abnormal body began to re-shape. It was only a short time, and his appearance became that of a normal man. He appeared to be a bit thin, but muscular; however, it was apparent that his body was, and remained covered with horrible scars. One of the disciples took off his outer garment and put it around him. He remained motionless for the moment.

Peace and absolute serenity. How can one be thrust into an entirely new reality so quickly? The Holy One, the Son of God has had mercy and compassion upon me, but why? How can he be flesh? I am filled with an overwhelming love that has extinguished everything I had come to be. The only remnant left is a spark of humanity I thought to be long dead. I can feel his love for me, this Jesus, and my love for him...it defies explanation. My love for him is growing like a raging fire unbridled from the darkness that had destroyed me. Me, not us, but me! I feel like a seed long hidden in the recesses of a dark cave; a seed brought forth into the sunlight, then planted by a beautiful stream and instantly flourishing. The feeling of being born must be this way; I have been blessed to receive a second birth. I'm overwhelmed by the freedom to choose, to think, to express. All the oppression that has overshadowed my miserable existence for so long has vanished. I've been set free by the Son of God! He loves me more than I can understand! I want to hold this moment forever, like a precious treasure, but already I feel it slipping away. Memories are flooding in with the emotions. Memories of a life snuffed out early by wickedness. The entities that had enslaved me would not allow acknowledgment of wickedness. Through twisted logic they would translate evil into feelings of strength, superiority, and a kind of dark virtue. The knowledge of having done every foul thing under the sun has begun to filter in and crush the joy I have experienced. I am at the feet of Jesus: the personification of love, compassion, and truth. There must be a reason he saved me. Can I reconcile? I must reconcile. I must confess. The things that have made up my life are incompatible with his kingdom. I confess, as my sins are like the grains of sand upon this beach. I am a sinner! I know the Lord Jesus is aware of every thought in my mind...but I can no longer contain myself!

"I HAVE SINNED LORD!" the former beast shouted, then proceeded to weep.

The elder herdsman was watching the men on the beach, then heard the unmistakable screech of the beast. He was very startled, for he had been lost in thought; that terrifying sound cut right through to his memories. He was immediately concerned about the men below and began to scan the hillside, for the sound wasn't that far away. Aegeus instinctively grabbed his staff with both hands. He spotted the beast, as he had jumped up and perched upon a huge rock at the top of the slope. Without a second thought he shouted as loud as he could, "RUN!" He was afraid he was too far for them to hear. Aegeus slowly started off toward the men, as he walked down the slope toward the beach. The herdsman looked up again at the beast but noticed it had vanished from its rocky perch. He quickly surveyed the hillside, then saw the beast loping down the slope toward the men.

"RUN!" he shouted over and over, "RUN!" The old man quickened his pace as the beast drew near to the men. The elder herdsman saw the beast drop to its knees at the feet of the tall man. The herdsman watched, as he saw this horrific beast bow its head before him in worship! Aegeus could not believe his eyes; he stopped dead in his tracks and just stared. Beyond the group of men on the beach the elder herdsman could see his young companion. Dimitri had just rounded the bend on the road from Emmatha and witnessed the same thing Aegeus had. The young herdsman was just standing there, as he was, and they were both staring at what was happening before them. Dimitri was holding a sack of supplies over his shoulder; just as Aegeus saw him the sack fell to the ground. The elder herdsman could see even at a distance that the young man was looking at the men, then at him, and wasn't sure what to do. Aegeus thought to himself that it was too late to do anything to help the men, so they just kept watching for the moment to see what would happen. Aegeus hadn't noticed, but a couple of the larger swine had walked up behind the elder herdsman and moved up on either side of him.

A deep voice grunted to his left, "Leave us."

A quickly growing commotion erupted within the vast herd behind him. He slowly turned to his left, after almost responding to the voice, and met the glare of the swine standing beside him. Its eyes were very dark and sinister; something the old man had encountered before, long ago. Fear rushed through every fiber of his being as he involuntarily fell backward into a seated position. The second swine that had been to his right joined with the other, as both animals glared at the herdsman; they seemed to be feeding on the old man's fear. He noticed the second swine's eyes were dark also, as it moved in closer to Aegeus's face.

It spoke with a similar deep grunting voice, "I would run if I were you."

In response, and quite by instinct, the old man quickly brought his staff around and jabbed at the second swine. The swine promptly grabbed onto the end of his staff with its mouth as it bit down and broke it off, then spit the piece into the herdsman's lap. Aegeus looked down at the piece, then back at the evil faces of the two swine. The elder herdsman was unable to get up, so he began kicking his feet as he tried to scoot himself away from the horror before him. From his low perspective Aegeus couldn't see much of the herd, but there behind him was absolute chaos.

The swine were not just acting out violently, but they appeared to be trying to kill each other! Aegeus saw them biting and ramming each other hard enough to draw blood. Some were jumping straight up in the air, then attacking. Some were hurling profane insults at each other before attacking. Just then, one of the swine crashed to the ground beside him with a bloody face. It immediately scrambling up to run at another, then violently rammed into it. The instinct to survive slowly began to battle with the fear in the old man's mind, as he managed to get up to his feet.

The herdsman arose and could see over a good portion of the herd. A few of the other herdsmen that he could see were running away. The pandemonium taking place around him was spread throughout the entire herd! Almost as far as he could see was a herdsman's hellish worst nightmare. He was frozen with fear and shock, as the old man could see a massive movement off in the distance. The swine started to stampede down the slope right into the sea, like a vast flock of migrating birds. Aegeus felt a sharp pain on the backside of his calf, then looked back to see a trickle of blood running down to the heel of his foot as he realized he had been bitten. The last thing the elder herdsman saw was an enormous disturbance at the foot of the slope where the land met the sea. Drowning swine were flailing about, as more were running in on top of them!

Aegeus simply couldn't take anymore; he turned around and ran as fast as he could down the slope toward the beach. His staff was still in his hand, though quite a bit shorter. The herdsman ran by the men on the beach, as a few of them glanced at him curiously. He saw a brief glimpse of the beast who now appeared normal, while on its knees with its head down. This frightened the old man even more, as he continued to run toward Dimitri. Aegeus kept shouting, "RUN" over and over. Aegeus reached the younger herdsman who could see the terror in the old man's face. He ran also; however, Dimitri could not keep up with his elder companion. They kept running until they were half-way to Emmatha. They stopped and collapsed alongside the road, for they were completely out of breath. Both men dropped to their hands and knees gasping for air.

"The swine! The swine!" he cried. It was all the elder herdsman could get out.

"There is a Great One among them," the young herdsman proclaimed while gasping, as he had been closer to the men on the beach. He was able to see the exchange and heard the beast submit to Jesus. He continued, "The beast called him the Son of the most high God. Then, this *Jesus* turned the beast into a man; I saw it!" He continued to gasp for air.

"The swine! The swine must be stopped!" the elder man said as he had more difficulty speaking between gasps. "I know it sounds crazy, but they want to kill us!" Aegeus shouted the best he could.

The two herdsmen continued on over the stone bridge on the Yarmuk River, as soon as they caught their breath. The road changed to cobblestone there before reaching the marketplace just outside the small City of Emmatha. Rows of tents and small structures where all manner of trade goods and food were sold. The marketplace was bustling with activity; carts and animals, merchants hawking their wares, and many people from Emmatha and Gadara browsing. None of the other herdsmen seemed to have arrived yet. Aegeus and Dimitri had seen a few scatter but were unsure of their current whereabouts. The men didn't hesitate as they made their way down through the main street of the marketplace.

"THE SWINE HAVE GONE MAD! THE BEAST HAS BEEN TAMED! COME AND SEE!" they shouted.

One man, a Greek named Alexander, well-groomed and wearing costly apparel was shopping for fresh produce. He heard the men and took notice when hearing the elder herdsman shout about the swine. He was one of the more prominent members of the community: a local merchant and landowner. Alexander decided he was going to find out what had happened, for he was invested in that herd. A few had gathered around the herdsmen that were curious and wanted to see something exciting. The elder herdsman saw the well-dressed merchant, then looked at him and said humbly, "Come and see." Alexander had been joined by Eustace: business owner and another of the community leaders.

Only thirty or so gathered to go with them, for many had refused to believe the men. It had become popular opinion that the herdsmen were drunk; one of the wine merchants disclosed that the young man had purchased wine early in the morning. There was one among them who was particularly curious about the claim that the beast had been tamed. A woman who had attended the marketplace with friends coaxed them into walking to the beach with her.

One asked her, "Alethea, why do you want to see that creature?"

She replied, "Somehow, I just want to see it again, if it's been tamed."

The group walked to the end of the open-air marketplace and started down the road toward the beach.

The man who had previously declared his identity as Legion was still motionless at the feet of Jesus. He had been curled up with his head down for some time. The swine herdsmen had run away. The disciples of Jesus were amazed at the violent behavior of the swine. There had been as many demons in this man as there were swine; perhaps more. They had been acting out quite violently but showed no signs of coming their way. The swine herdsmen had fled, for they were full of fear. No one had ever seen anything like this before. The entire vast herd in a veil of increasing dust had all turned at once and started to run straight into the sea. Some of the men moved closer to observe the spectacle; others stayed by the side of Jesus, for he never took his focus off of the man.

The commotion on the slope went silent after a short time. The horrified men watched, as the last bit of movement died down at the water's edge with the dust still in the air. There had been two thousand or so swine feeding upon the slope and under the trees, now reduced to a floating mass of lifeless carcasses upon the surface of the Sea of Galilee. The enormous loss of life was somewhat disturbing to the men, even though they were swine. However, they knew that given the state of the beasts, what had happened was understood as merciful.

The man at the feet of Jesus began to weep, which grew into deep, mournful wailing. He lifted his head to reveal a handsome man's face. The man appeared to be a Greek with deep blue eyes. Despite the horrible appearance of his hair and beard, now he looked nothing like the wild man that had run up to them a short time ago. The disciples had witnessed their Master cast out demons before, but never with this dramatic of a physical change. He cried, as he fumbled with the garment that had been put around him. He carefully wrapped the garment around his body exhibiting modesty. Suddenly, he almost startled some of the men as he let out a cry in a very human voice:

"I HAVE SINNED LORD!" he cried loudly, then proceeded to weep again while lowering his head.

Jesus dropped down right in front of the man, as if this was the moment he had been waiting for. Jesus embraced him despite the filth and held him for a long time. He was then ministered to by the Master, and slowly the weeping stopped. The disciples of Jesus were amazed; not by the casting out of the demons, but the level of love and compassion demonstrated by Jesus.

Simon touched him on the arm and gestured for the man to come with him. He arose to his feet slowly and accompanied Simon to the boat. The man stood much taller and straighter than before. He moved strangely and slowly at first, for he hadn't walked as a man for many years. Philip and Andrew followed. The men stopped for a moment at the water's edge, for the man was afraid and very hesitant to enter the water. Philip waded into the shallow water followed by Andrew. The disciples gave the man a look of encouragement as they beckoned him to follow. Simon smiled and gestured forward, then the men slowly waded into the shallow water of the beach. Simon grabbed the side of the boat, then swung a leg up and jumped into the boat. He quickly returned with a piece of cloth and a small cake of goat soap, then gestured for the man to take off his garment. Andrew held it for him, as Simon and Philip helped the man start washing; he seemed somewhat disoriented. Simon jumped back into the boat, then quickly returned with a cloth sack and set it on the stern deck. The former beast had taken over, for he appeared to enjoy ridding himself of the years of filth. Philip and Simon disrobed themselves, then handed their garments to Andrew. Simon gestured for the man to go into deeper water. After washing the former demoniac eagerly went forward with his new companions into the waist-deep water beyond the boat.

Simon looked at the man in the eyes and said, "This is for your baptism; you leave the old man behind in the waters, then come out clean, renewed, and living for God." He looked at the former demoniac and asked, "Do you understand?" The man looked Simon in the eyes and smiled while nodding in agreement.

"I baptize you for the remission of sins," Simon proclaimed as he gently put his hand on the man's back and gestured for him to submerge. He was a little hesitant but nodded and allowed Simon to lay him back in the water. He emerged and was smiling broadly. The three men returned to the stern of the little ship. Simon reached into the cloth sack and pulled out a long clean cloth, which was an undergarment. He handed it to the former demoniac who watched the other men, then he wrapped it around himself and secured it in the appropriate fashion. Simon picked up the sack from the stern deck, then the four men walked up onto the beach. Andrew distributed the men's garments, then Simon reached into the sack and pulled out a slightly frayed old tunic. He handed it to the former demoniac, then watched and smiled as he slipped it on.

He looked at Simon and said, "Thank you." He spoke in Aramaic, and his response was very emotional and sincere.

"Just some spare clothing I keep on the ship," Simon told him as he handed him the sack. It also contained an old pair of sandals, two pieces of cloth to be used as a head covering or a sash, smaller pieces of cloth, and the sack had a strap for carrying. The four men walked across the beach and joined the others.

"You can keep the coat as well," James spoke out as he had been the one who lent the garment to the man.

The former beast spoke again as he warmly said, "Thank you." He looked at James and smiled. Andrew handed him the outer garment and he put it on, then sat down quietly at the feet of Jesus as before.

Simon asked, "What's your name?"

The man's face became troubled, then he closed his eyes. He was doing the best he could to function, but everything was new and strange. He was unaccustomed to the freedom he now enjoyed, as well as the overwhelming sensation of peace. The man had been heavily oppressed for so long that remembering his name, family, or anything else from the original man would bring emotional torment. The former demoniac was beginning to feel a new strength coming through an inner peace that had enveloped him more completely than his new garments. He had been forgiven. He could feel the love Jesus had for him and he loved Jesus and his disciples like a new family. They had accepted him, even though he had come from a very dark place.

He suddenly spoke out boldly, as if his newfound strength wished to make an appearance, "Jason, my name is Jason! I'm Greek! I'm from Gadara!"

The time passed quickly when the communication picked up, as they were able to overcome the language barriers. Jesus and his disciples spoke mostly Aramaic but understood Greek. Most men spoke Greek, as it was necessary for conducting business in the region. Jason's primary language was Greek, although he understood Aramaic somewhat, as well as Hebrew. He understood Latin very well, he just couldn't remember how. The former demoniac also had knowledge of forgotten languages, which he had to disregard, for they added confusion to his now clear mind. As time went on, Jason was surprisingly well-spoken as his long-subdued spirit emerged. He was asking the men many questions about how they came to follow Jesus, and about their mission. He wanted to know all their names, as well as a little about them. He was amazed at the diversity of the stories, as it began with Matthew the tax collector. They shared a laugh when the brothers James and John, the sons of Zebedee and burly fishermen were telling their story. Jesus referred to them as Boanerges, which meant the sons of thunder. Jason felt a bit awkward when he spoke with Judas Iscariot, but he couldn't understand why. He just smiled and listened, while keeping the matter to himself. Jason knew Jesus was aware of his thoughts. Just a misrepresentation of character, as he thought to himself. When he glanced at Jesus, however, his expression was that of acknowledgment. He had done well to keep his thoughts to himself. It was becoming obvious that Jason wished to go with Jesus and his disciples.

The sun was high in the sky and the day was growing warm. There was talk of moving on toward the city and possibly finding a shady spot to eat a meal before continuing. Just then, the voices of many people could be heard approaching. They began to appear, and Jesus, as well as Simon, James, and John went forth to meet them. Jesus and his disciples approached the people and most of them stopped. A few continued on to see the slope, as well as the water's edge and the expanding mass of dead swine upon the waters of the Galilee. The remainder of the disciples stayed with Jason, for he had become very quiet and reserved. He recognized some of those who had come from Emmatha.

They watched the meeting, as one of the more prominent looking men from town could be heard saying, *"Depart from us!"* He was a large man with a strong presence and spoke in Greek. His well-dressed counterpart seemed to be having an argument with the elder herdsman who had run by them earlier. A handful of people walked closer to Jason and his new friends; they seemed shocked and amazed but fearing to get too close.

Jason couldn't help feeling annoyed, for he could hear Jesus being rejected as five men and women were staring at him. He sensed mostly fear from the people; however, one of the women seemed to be looking upon him with a measure of compassion and curiosity, and even smiling once. It was enough to set her apart from the rest. She was quite beautiful; wearing what appeared to be a very fine outer garment made of deep blue linen with white clothing underneath. Her head was covered with the outer garment and a white covering, but he could see her dark wavy hair a little. Still, these people had no idea of who Jesus was, or what had taken place. Jesus had performed a great miracle; he realized that he himself needed to tell and demonstrate what Jesus had done for him. Jesus and his disciples turned and slowly walked back to join them. The people from Emmatha held their place, and the few that had come closer retreated to the main group. The elder herdsman and the well-dressed man from the city were still engaged in an argument by the sea. They seemed oblivious to everything else at the moment.

Jesus returned and looked at Jason with a serious but peaceful expression. He then informed Jason and the disciples that they were to leave the area immediately.

Jason had the immediate impulse to plead with him to stay but understood the authority of Jesus and held his place. He began to hope.

"I want to go with you!" Jason exclaimed.

Jesus responded, *"Go home to all those you knew, and throughout the city, and tell them what great things the Lord has done for you and has had compassion on you."* He then embraced Jason once more.

Jesus looked around at his disciples, then gestured toward the ship. The men quickly gathered themselves and started to board. Many of the disciples expressed regret to Jason that they couldn't spend more time with him and encouraged him. Jesus was the last to walk toward the ship but veered off to approach the two herdsmen standing by the water's edge. They had been discussing the exchange with the merchant, as well as surveying the floating mass of swine. Jesus walked straight to the elder herdsman and looked at him for a moment. Tears started to form in the old man's eyes. Jesus embraced him. Aegeus then dropped to his knees and said, "My Lord." Jesus looked him in the eyes and smiled. He embraced Dimitri as well, then turned and walked to the ship just past the bow and jumped aboard.

The men who remained off the ship untied the bow rope, then pushed her off the beach. Jesus could be seen speaking to Judas. They called out to Jason and tossed to him a small leather pouch, which he caught. Within a few moments the little ship was underway. The men swung the ship around with the oars, then slowly rowed away from the beach. Jason walked up to the water's edge and raised his hand in a gesture of farewell. Jesus and his disciples returned the gesture; waving at Jason, the herdsmen, and the others on the beach.

Jason stood there as he intended to watch the ship until he couldn't see it anymore. He watched as the men lowered the sail of the ship, then it quickly became difficult to see any detail. A short distance away the two herdsmen were watching Jason, as were the rest of the people on the beach. Slowly, the elder herdsman walked over to Jason while leaving his younger companion behind. All eyes were upon Aegeus as he attempted contact with the former beast. Jason sensed the fear and uncertainty of his approach, so he spoke first while keeping his eyes upon the ship. He now spoke in Greek:

"My name is Jason. I'm very sorry to have caused you pain and fear. Jesus has restored me from a long captivity of demonic spirits. I deeply regret your loss," he said as he looked over at Aegeus.

"My name is Aegeus," he responded while astounded by the calm, well-spoken man. He had looked right into the face of the beast many years earlier with its black eyes and twisted features. He was shocked when Jason looked at him, for his blue eyes spoke genuine sincerity. He searched for the appropriate response, then simply said, "I forgive you."

Jason smiled and held eye contact with Aegeus for a long moment. "I really do regret your loss, what are you going to do?" he asked with authentic concern.

"Something different," the elder herdsman responded. "I've lost everything. The man I was speaking with was heavily invested in that herd, so they're going to take my house as compensation," he lamented.

"If there was some way I could help," Jason offered.

"You already have," the old man replied as he smiled and extended his hand. Jason was surprised, then glanced down and took it slowly and carefully with his clawed hand in a friendly gesture. The herdsman smiled at Jason, then turned and walked back toward Dimitri.

"What are you going to do?" asked the young herdsman.

"I'm going to the other side," Aegeus replied. "I'm going to follow Jesus. I spoke a prayer last night while you were sleeping, and it was just answered. I made a promise; I intend to spend the rest of my life trying to keep that promise," he stated.

"Can I come with you?" Dimitri asked.

"You have to come. I need you to start the fires!" Aegeus said as he faced Dimitri and placed his hands upon his shoulders.

The two men laughed at each other and started back toward Gadara together. They reached the sack Dimitri had dropped earlier, then the young man picked it up and ran over to Jason. They didn't exchange any words; Dimitri set the sack close to Jason, as well as his waterskin. They smiled at each other, then the young man ran back to join Aegeus.

Jason stood at the water's edge and looked off in the distance as the ship passed from view. He was alone except for a diminishing group of people. Among them was the representative from the city who had spoken with Jesus and was now walking toward him. He was expecting to be told to depart as well. The man walked close and stopped.

He cautiously spoke, "I come on behalf of the others. They're still very frightened of you. Jesus told us you've been set free, and in your right mind; I wanted to see for myself."

Jason responded, "I'm very sorry for all the things I've done, but you must understand who it is that you've chased away. Jesus is the Son of God, and he gave my life back to me; I will forever be in his service. The one true God has had mercy and compassion upon me. I have no intentions of causing harm ever again. I intend to go throughout this region and proclaim this." Jason paused for a moment, then continued, "I'm still trying to arrange my thoughts; I haven't had any of my own for a very long time."

The man stood there studying Jason. The men made eye contact. Eustace couldn't help feeling compassion for Jason and could see his sincerity. He spoke, "Some of us have heard of this *Jesus*; it is feared that our city is not worthy of his presence. Rumors abound that our society is not compatible with his teaching. Our city could be cursed, for there are stories from Chorazin and Bethsaida of such."

Jason responded, "Yes, when the Lord teaches the truth, and sin is preferred over the truth with no repentance, then a curse could be necessary to bring about such repentance."

Eustace was intrigued with Jason, as he acknowledged within himself that this wisdom was coming from a man who, hours ago, would have bitten him. There was no question Jesus was directly responsible for this transformation. Eustace bore responsibilities for his community, but he felt increasingly troubled; he felt as though he had made a terrible mistake.

"I want to help," he said. "I own a caravansary just outside Emmatha, on the eastern side of the city. My name is Eustace: everyone in the city knows me; come, and I will give you a place to stay for a while," he offered with a voice of compassion.

"My name is Jason. I thank you," Jason responded as he was very surprised. "I need some time alone first to gather my thoughts and do a few things. I would be honored to accept your generous offer. I'll be along in a day or two," he said.

Eustace replied, "Very well, I must return to my affairs. I'm very happy to have met you, Jason."

Jason responded, "I'm very happy to meet you as well, Eustace. Peace be with you."

Eustace smiled and turned to walk back to the remnant of people that had watched from a distance. He rejoined the group, then they departed and disappeared around the bend of the road.

Jason was alone now with his thoughts, and with his past. Alone with a new inner strength that he felt assured would help him cope with this strange, wonderful, new existence. He knew that very soon he would be seeking his family, and perhaps friends that he hadn't seen for most of his life. What would they think of him? It was all such a very long time ago. He raised his garments and looked down at his legs, then his arms, which had the heaviest scarring on his body. Jason was experiencing a new self-awareness that had been previously absent. He found himself absolutely disgusted by his claw-like finger and toenails, as well as his long, matted hair and beard. Simon, Philip, and Andrew had helped immensely with his washing and the experience of the baptism was even more cleansing to the spirit. However, he determined that he had a lot to do before he would voluntarily present himself to anyone again.

It was late afternoon as Jason turned to face the slope that he, as Legion, had previously run down to meet Jesus. It was a surreal sight to him, as he came to the obvious conclusion that if he ran down like that now he would most likely kill himself. It was as if he had been transplanted into a new body, so strange. He looked up at the huge rock he had perched on before descending; it took his breath away and frightened him. Legion had easily jumped upon that rock and then jumped down just hours before. It seemed like something from a dream, or very long ago. The new sensations were overwhelming him until a different aspect of the sight offered a new perspective. The waning sun was casting a slightly amber color to the landscape, as well as the many fluffy clouds that had accumulated across the sky. He paused for a moment to appreciate the color as if he had never seen it before. He turned to view the Sea of Galilee, then back to the slope; the grass, flowers, trees, and even the rocks were so vivid and rich with color. He then closed his eyes and offered a prayer of thanksgiving to God.

Jason decided to return to the only home he knew and temporarily abide there. He was thinking of the flint blades and visualizing a new use for them. He gathered his new belongings, then started to make his way up the slope to the tombs above.

This was beyond a strange feeling for Jason. He thought to himself as he ascended the slope, that in many ways he didn't know what he would find. Slowly he climbed, as he second-guessed his decision when he got closer to the rocky bluff. Jason first encountered the circle and ash heap from the wicked ritual the night before. He took a deep breath and felt as though he had been a spectator. What struck him the most was he was looking at his own footprints in the dirt. The site brought back vague memories of the evil, fervent dance. He stood there for a moment, as he reflected upon his moments of deep repentance. Jason then spit upon the pile of ashes and walked on. He prayed on the way that God would be with him in what he was about to do. "It all seems like it was such a long time ago, even though it was just this morning," he mumbled under his breath. Jason walked around the bluff and approached the entrance of the dark, foreboding tomb.

He was a bit apprehensive about going inside and chuckled to himself, "This is how one is supposed to feel about this." He forced himself to go in. To Jason, it was somehow very important to face what was within. He felt a surge of spiritual strength as he passed through the entrance. He sniffed the air, then felt a presence; an ugly manifestation of doubt and fear attempted to enter his mind. Jason sniffed the air again; a habit that would be hard to break. He kept detecting movement as shadowy specters in the corner of his eye that seemed to be evading direct visual contact. Jason was unimpressed, and in confidence he spoke boldly, "In the name of Jesus, be gone from this place. The Lord rebuke you!" Almost instantly, he felt only peace and tranquil quiet. It was at that moment that Jason demonstrated to himself that the name of Jesus, spoken in faith, was authority over such entities; they had to obey. Jason was wise about their ways and the things these wicked principalities intended for his inevitable destruction. He realized that his knowledge, through God, could be used against them.

Jason approached the sarcophagus where Legion used to perch and gathered all of the flint blades they had accumulated, then took out his waterskin and poured a little water on them. Jason grabbed a piece of cloth from the floor, then cleaned the blades and dropped them into his sack. He looked over the surface of the sarcophagus and poured out more water, then looked around and saw the symbols upon the walls around the bedding. They were written in blood and were unknown to man; Jason wanted to keep it that way. Some time passed as the tomb grew darker. He scrubbed the blood stains from wherever he knew them to be until none remained. Jason gathered all the junk they had accumulated over the years and made a pile outside the tomb entrance, then dusted out the niches and surfaces the best he could. He attempted to move things back into place where they had been when he first started dwelling there.

Jason went outside and knelt to pray; he asked God to forgive him for desecrating a place of the dead, and that the families would return and be comforted. He went about and picked some flowers, then took them into the tomb and laid them on top of the sarcophagus. Jason walked out, and he intended never to set foot in there again.

Once outside, Jason walked over to a grove of oak trees where a shallow pit was located and looked into it. Legion had used it from time to time to have clandestine fires. He carried all the items that he had brought out of the tomb and threw them into the pit. Jason was tossing things in but paused a moment and picked up a Roman short sword from the many old weapons they had collected. Some had rusted, but the sword was still in fair condition, as it was still in its original scabbard. Jason threw the scabbard back and chose a sheepskin one instead with a leather belt. He then gathered some tinder and pulled one of the larger flint blades out of his sack. Jason looked through the pile and chose an old broken dagger to strike on. He retrieved a piece of charred material from the bottom of the pit, then held it next to the flint. Jason managed to get an ember started after many strikes, and in a short time had a small fire. Within moments a raging fire slowly consumed the pile of his tormenting memories.

It was truly a healing moment for Jason as he prayed and deeply repented, while asking God for help adjusting to his new life. He settled back against a tree near the fire as he feasted his eyes on what turned out to be a gorgeous sunset. He felt as if it was God responding to his prayer. The sun passed behind the bluffs, as the sky and the clouds became alive with a deep rich crimson and violet of every shade. Jason couldn't remember ever seeing anything so beautiful, except when he opened his eyes and beheld his deliverer. He sat there for a long time and watched the fire, as well as the wondrous colors of the sky until darkness fell. He reviewed the day and wanted to relive every moment, as he thought about how much he loved Jesus.

Two things were becoming apparent to Jason: he was getting tired and hungry. He suddenly remembered the sack that the young man had left for him, then picked it up and brought it beside the fire. Jason opened the sack and looked inside; there were four loaves of fresh bread, many dried fish, a small sack of dried figs, another small sack of dates, a bundle of lintels and a skin of new wine. It had been many years since Jason had a good meal. He had to fight off the memories of the disgusting things the demons had caused him to grow accustomed to eating. Jason feasted as he sat and watched the fire dwindle down, for it had turned the remnants of his past into ashes, embers, and red glowing metal. Jason threw some large wood on the fire; thus, crushing the remnants of his memories to oblivion and replacing them with a simple warm fire.

Jason settled back into his comfortable place beneath the tree, as he felt a good honest weariness that comes at the end of the day. All Legion had known was pushing himself to unconsciousness, for there had been no peace in his life. He hadn't been able to fall asleep like most people, since there had been chaos in his spirit constantly. A new sensation of peace his Lord had bestowed upon him, as well as the weariness was very pleasant. He closed his eyes and enjoyed every moment until he drifted off....

Jason dreamed of building a house. He was arranging a chaotic mass of stones into a structure. Each stone was like a lost memory, as some were flawed and couldn't be used; some were great but too large to lift by himself. He was frustrated, so he called upon Jesus. He suddenly appeared, and with a wave of his hand the structure was completed. The discarded stones were still lying around, however. Jason marveled at the organization and beauty of the structure. The Lord was pointing to the base and the stone upon which the structure stood. Jason realized that Jesus was his rock, his foundation, his stone footing. He remained troubled by the disorganized, flawed stones scattered about the structure. Jesus smiled and picked up one of the stones, then cast it away. He picked up a stone and handed it to Jason. Jesus then began to glow as he had in Legion's vision and became a bright white light....

He awoke with the morning sun breaking over the ridge as it beamed down upon his face. He sat up a little but stayed in place contemplating the dream. Eventually, he had to get up. Jason spoke a proclamation out loud when he returned, "Lord Jesus, I will always trust in you no matter what! You are my rock! My stone foundation! I will trust you no matter the circumstance!"

Jason had the knowledge and faith to believe. His interpretation of the dream was that Jesus had given him the power and authority to rid his own life of these unwanted memories and traits, but it would take time. Jason realized he had knowledge that most did not have; knowledge of spiritual wickedness and entities bent on the destruction of mankind. He thought of a time far off when this evil would inevitably rise once more. An attempt to destroy mankind as in the old world, before the great flood would come in the last days. Most would not understand or believe, but Jason knew that those who believe in Jesus and hold to his teaching would be able to stand against this evil.

He considered his wounds. Jason knew he had two fresh bleeding wounds on his arms. After his encounter with Jesus they were healed just like the older of the scars. There were festering sores in diverse places also, but for the first time in his recent memory all had been healed. The absolute power of Jesus to restore and heal was his, through God, to demonstrate; his testimony was his own body and spirit. He knew that if he held on to Jesus, this wicked multitude of spirits that had been his former masters would not be able to take control again. They would attempt to harass, intimidate, persuade, and twist the truth, which had already been demonstrated in the tomb. Jason did not take his new life for granted, as he acknowledged that he had received a very precious gift; all he could do was share that gift. He knew that others face the same dismal fate that could have been his. How could he not be eternally grateful?

Jason decided the first task of the day was to complete the burial of his former life. He picked up a large cloth he had set aside to drag material with. Jason then began to remove some of the loose dirt and rocks at the base of the bluff and transported it to the still smoldering pit. He filled the pit until it was slightly mounded, then dug a small hole in the center for the cloth he had used and buried it. Jason stood for a moment and looked upon the grave he had created.

He spoke, "Here lies Legion. They still roam in the dry places, but their manifestation in this man has ended. May they wander aimlessly in the darkness, as I have, until the judgment. Let this moment mark the end and a new beginning in the name of Jesus."

He returned to his comfortable place beneath the oak tree. Jason pulled his bag over, then removed the flint blades and lined them up. He picked up one of the blades, then drew his feet in as close as he could and started cutting the huge claw-like growth off each toe. Jason completed the cutting, then went back and trimmed until they looked human again. His feet now appeared to be normal, except for the rough, dry callous on his feet from years of walking barefoot. He got up and walked around a bit, while flexing his toes into the ground. It felt good.

Jason sat back down beneath the tree and started on his hands. The blade slipped when he cut his left thumb claw and sliced deep into the cuticle. He experienced a waking nightmare as the blood flowed out. Jason immediately flashed back to the bloodstained perch in the tomb. The bloodletting ritual was in progress, as they were searching for visions and dark spiritual power; he had inadvertently fallen into a demonic trap. The influence of powerful evil that rushed into his mind attempted to arrest his freedom and independence. Jason was absolutely paralyzed with fear, as he desperately clutched the recent memory of his deliverance within his spirit. He gathered all his strength, then managed to speak the name: "Jesus." The vision instantly stopped. The first thing he did was cover the wound with his other hand. Jason was trembling from the experience, so close after the burial. Doubt tried to creep into his mind.

Recognizing it for the foul spirit it was he cried out, "The Lord rebuke this spirit of doubt; make this bleeding stop in the name of Jesus!"

Jason sat there for a while, as he clutched his hand with his eyes closed. He knew he had to wrap the wound to avoid another festering problem, so he opened his eyes and looked down. Jason slowly released his left hand and was quickly overwhelmed with emotion. The blood was gone! What was a very deep cut was reduced to a tiny scar as if it had healed years ago! He closed his eyes and bowed his head in prayer, thanking God. He had been shown that, in the name of Jesus, he had the authority to heal; it had been demonstrated to him with his own body! It took time to contemplate this before he could resume the effort; his confidence had been restored even stronger than before.

Jason finally completed his claw-cutting task while sitting beneath the tree. He held out his hands and was rather pleased with the new appearance. Jason reached into his bag, then pulled out the old pair of sandals Simon had given him and put them on. Easy enough to figure out, but they felt a little awkward. Jason could walk just fine without coverings on his feet, which had become toughened; he wanted to get used to them for appearance.

Jason sat beneath the tree once again and ran his hands through his hair. He Picked up one of the blades, then began to pull some hair with his left hand and cut with the right. He worked his way around until the excessive length, as well as most of the mats were cut off. Then he started pulling hair from either side and cut to match the length, as he worked his way around his head. He did the same thing by feel where he couldn't see. Jason performed the same practice with his beard, as he touched to check the consistency of the length. Finally, he ran his fingers through his hair looking for any remaining mats, then removed a couple of small ones. Jason had no surface to see his reflection, but knew his appearance had to have greatly improved. He remembered a few isolated pools of water at the beach and decided to see how he looked later.

Jason gathered the huge amount of hair and debris, as well as all of the flint blades and took them over to Legion's grave. He dug a deep hole, then dropped everything in and buried it. That was the last remnants of his past of a physical nature, except for his scars. Jason knew there were many people whose lives had been affected by Legion's abuse. All he could do was pray about it. He would share what God had done for him and pray for these people whenever he would encounter them, as Jesus had instructed. His sorrow and remorse were great, but his new inner peace overcame it. The guilt and shame from his previous life would always be there, for his inner scars were as bad as the ones on the outside. Jason realized he had been given a supernatural peace from Jesus that transcended his understanding of the things of this world. He knew he would never have to carry the burden alone.

He scanned the area for any further evidence of Legion's presence, then spotted a familiar figure. It was the same demon-possessed man who had crept into his tomb the night before last. The man peeked around a large stone but froze when he noticed he had been spotted. "Come here!" Jason called out, but there was no response. Jason felt compelled to reach out to him, since he was aware of how Legion had treated him. He took one step in his direction, then the man bolted off. He knew to chase him was a waste of time; the man was fast, as fast as legion had been. Jason prayed that the man would be delivered also. Jason felt very grieved in his spirit, for he knew the power of Jesus could heal him and deliver him. "That man has a strong spirit of fear; I'm coming back for him soon," Jason said as he realized that he spoke out loud, even though he was alone. He concluded that he was never alone. He was learning to pray without ceasing; to speak to God who was always with him.

Jason decided he was going to stay another night, as the midday sun waned a bit. He still had things to do, so he decided to take a walk. Jason went around the bluff and down to where Legion had danced. He stood by the circle with the ash pile in the center as he contemplated his transformation. The stark contrast of the spot to his new life inspired Jason to spend some time discovering who he was. He prayed and asked forgiveness for the evil that Legion had performed there. He then proceeded to throw the stones from the circle down the slope. Jason discovered that the strength he had as Legion was gone, for the effort involved in throwing the heavy stones was challenging. Also, the work he had performed in the tomb, as well as at the pit had left him feeling tired. He realized, however, that his strength was more than adequate to live as a normal man. Jason looked at the rock that he, as Legion, had jumped upon effortlessly yesterday morning. He found he had to climb with great difficulty to get to the top, then sat in the exact spot where he had beheld his deliverer and remembered the submission. Jason had been there, but only as a tiny inert portion of Legion. He again identified the fact that these powerful wicked spirits had no choice but to submit to and obey Jesus. He was the example; there was no place in the world so deep, or dark, that Jesus could not reach into and save that which was lost.

He sat upon the rocky outcrop and looked out over the Sea of Galilee. Jason could also see the land of the Galilee beyond. He imagined Jesus and his disciples were out there, somewhere. He longed to be with them, but understood he was to be his representative in a land that had feared and rejected Jesus. Jason smiled and accepted his new identity and vocation.

The afternoon sun was developing the amber tones that warmed Jason's heart as he continued to sit and retrospect. Who was Jason, as a man? He tried to remember back to an earlier time, while calculating the seasons and years. After some time, Jason concluded that he had been seventeen years old when the demons had taken control and forced him into the wilderness. He was fourteen or fifteen at his first recollection of their presence. A bit of sadness passed through his mind as he concluded his age: Jason had been a prisoner of multitudes of demonic entities for twenty-five years! His last memories as a normal human being were those of a boy, now he was a man of forty-two years! Jason silently lamented all those wasted years. He didn't know how much life was left to him, only God knows, but he wanted to spend the remainder of his life in the service of his Lord.

Jason imagined his role in society as he was. He thought about the woman he had noticed at the beach. The result was a realization that a normal life had passed him by. The inescapable fact was that he had a mutilated body with scars on his mind as well. Jason was free of the demons that had tormented him, but the memories remained. He remembered the dream and encouraged himself with the hope that it provided. Another aspect, however, was the accumulated knowledge was also there. Jason had come away with a unique understanding of a great many things. What would his role in all this mean? Would he be able to convince people of the evil in this world, and Jesus being the only way to stand against it? Jason was going to dedicate the rest of his life to this cause.

He climbed down from the rock, as afternoon transformed into evening and prepared to go back to his place under the oak tree. Jason paused to enjoy another sunset. Not as colorful as yesterday, for the sky was clear. He grabbed a fallen limb near a tree, then went about brushing the ground where the fire had been to remove the footprints and all traces of the ritual. He picked up a few fragments of charred wood, then proceeded back to his campsite. Jason walked by his old tomb and picked up a large piece of flint from the base of the bluff, as well as gathering a bit of tinder. He walked over to the tree, then dropped down and placed a thin, flat piece of charred wood on top of the flint he had picked up and held it in his left hand. Jason drew his sword, then stuck the tip of the blade into the ground and began striking the side of the blade with the flint, which produced sparks. It took some effort, but he soon had a glowing ember. He had a fire quickly, for there was fire material set aside from the previous night.

Jason was curious. He drew his sword once more and held it for a moment feeling the weight and the balance. He tried a couple of moves, as he slashed and Jabbed at the air; it seemed very natural. He stood there, then flipped the sword over the back of his hand and caught the handle securely. Then he did it again perfectly, and it was easy. In the diminishing light he set a piece of firewood next to the tree, as it was illuminated by the fire. He returned his sword to its sheath and walked several paces. Quickly he turned, then he drew his sword lightning fast and threw it with one fluid motion. The sword sunk into the wood dead center and knocked it over. Then he did it again, perfectly. Jason picked up a piece of charred wood, then made a small mark on the firewood. He set it against the tree and walked twice as far. He turned quickly, then drew his sword and threw it. The sword sunk deep into the wood within the small mark. He retrieved his sword and returned it to its sheath. Jason was a little stunned and afraid. He discovered that this thing that had developed in Legion remained, and the thought disturbed him. He prayed that his ability would never be needed, except by the will of God. Jason knelt by the fire, then drew his sword and held it out with both hands.

He prayed, "Lord God, in the name of Jesus, I ask that you take that which the demons intended for destruction and turn it for good. Not only this thing but all things. I pray that this weapon is for the protection of the innocent and of righteousness. Let it never be used in anger or hatred. Keep my mind at peace and let no temptation enter therein. Thank you, Lord."

Jason settled back into the comfortable spot beneath the tree, as he enjoyed another nice meal from the sack the young herdsman had blessed him with. He was Feeling much more adjusted to his new existence, as he prepared for tomorrow by going through his belongings. He placed the piece of flint in his bag. Legion had made blades from it, but it was just a useful piece of stone. He pulled out the small leather bag that Judas had tossed to him and opened it. It contained several coins: mostly silver with a couple of gold ones. Jason knew nothing about money and would need some help managing it. He thought about Eustace and wondered if he could trust him. He thought about the people he would encounter in Gadara. Jason felt almost overwhelmed by these thoughts, but his faith and confidence overruled. He fell into a peaceful sleep, after stoking the fire for the night.

Morning came early for Jason, so he gathered his belongings and prepared to leave the only home he had known for years. Jason pulled a piece of cloth out of his bag and tied it around his waist for a sash, as he wanted to cover the leather belt and conceal the sword a bit. It was a clear and sunny morning that promised a warm day. He was disappointed that he didn't have a vivid dream as he had the night before, for he slept so soundly that the night seemed very brief. Jason stopped and stood in front of the tomb one last time before leaving the memories of this place behind. Jason was pleased there were no signs the ritual had ever taken place when he passed the site.

The morning sun was breaking over the ridge as Jason started down the slope toward the beach. He couldn't help remembering running down to submit to Jesus, for even then the human remnant within did so joyfully. Jason never took for granted how fortunate he was, that in no other way could he have been salvaged. The demons had no choice but to submit to the authority of Jesus. Jason now had a rock-solid understanding of how that name, spoken in faith, was authority. He was praying that he would get another opportunity to engage the mysterious man, for Jason felt confident he could see him delivered as well.

He walked down the slope with joy in his step, and a partial smile on his face that just wouldn't go away. Jason arrived at the beach where he found even more reason to be joyful. Jason set down his bags, then walked over to a pool of water nearby and looked in. He had been prepared to see a mess, for he was unsure what his grooming efforts had produced.

"Not bad," he observed as he beheld his reflection. His dark, now curly and slightly graying hair turned out just shy of shoulder length. It looked well groomed, even and clean. His beard also looked much shorter and appeared normal. Jason's joy was short-lived, however, as he considered his scars. His clothing effectively covered most of them, until he raised an arm, or lifted his leg a certain way. What would people think? Jason remembered the group of people that had approached him but kept their distance. They stared at him like a caged wild animal for the theater, except one. Jason couldn't forget the woman that had looked upon him with curiosity, and her smile. Jason realized he had been sitting with an outer garment wrapped around him, and his scars were hidden. He accepted that he would try to be a blessing to others, but he would, most likely, be alone. He would be satisfied with a daily meal and a place to sleep, so long as he could effectively fulfill what Jesus had asked him to do.

Jason sat down in the same place where Jesus had ministered to him, as he contemplated his own ministry. Jesus had told him to tell people throughout the city about what God had done for him, but he was very concerned about how he would be received. Jesus himself had been rejected, after all. Jason had spent most of his life in darkness, and he would need help adjusting to life as a man. Was it even possible? Jason thought again about Eustace: the man who had nervously offered to help him. Could he trust him? He decided he was going to try.

Jason looked around at all the faded footprints, as well as the marks the ship had left on the beach. He had so many questions he would ask if they were still here, only disappearing marks of the event that saved his life remained. He looked around and sniffed the air. A few of the swine remained and were floating near the northernmost portion of the beach. One appeared to have been drug partially out of the water and left. Jason approached it, and it was quickly evident as to why. The swine had a grotesque appearance upon its face that was shocking; the pungent smell of death was in the air. Jason took that as the moment to depart and start his new life. He gathered his belongings, then arranged his bags for walking and left the beach behind. He looked up at the ridge and scanned the rocky bluffs one last time for a sign of the mysterious demoniac. Jason was shielding his eyes from the intense morning sun, as he prayed to get a glimpse of the man. He remembered the way Legion dealt with him in the tomb, so it wasn't difficult to understand why he may be hiding. He would return and devise a cunning method to attract him. Jason started down the road to Emmatha and Gadara. He prayed as he walked asking for strength and wisdom. He also asked for greater humility, and to never lose sight of where his new life flows from.

Jason decided to stop before going too far down the road and pray for the man hiding in the hills. He could sense that he was up there, somewhere, watching him. There was a burden on his heart for the man, as he realized his compassion for others was growing. Jason suddenly felt a need to offer praise to God, for he knew of the majesty and beauty of the most high God. He had never been able to behold the knowledge through worship, but instead through fear and resentment. This ended up being quite an experience for Jason, as he could feel a growing strength within his spirit. Jason bowed his head and imagined the seraphim above the throne. They were in steady continual worship, and crying *holy, holy, holy, is the Lord of hosts: the whole earth is full of his glory!* Jason felt a cleansing within his soul, like purification as with fire; he remained there for some time. He prayed once more that he would encounter the mysterious man before rising, but there was no sign. He gathered his things and walked on.

Walking the wide path to Emmatha was a welcome experience in many ways. Legion would never use paths or roads but would watch them for potential victims. It felt good to walk down the road like a normal man in contrast to creeping around and lying in wait. The feeling of joy and anticipation was returning stronger than ever as he walked along. Jason couldn't help imagining if Jesus had not departed. He would be walking with Jesus and his disciples, as opposed to walking alone. Then a thought entered his mind, that through the power of his testimony Jesus was very much walking with Jason. This profound reality greatly encouraged him and increased his sense of purpose as he walked. Jason found himself at an arched stone bridge passing over the Yarmuk River, after walking for some distance. He gazed down at the crystal-clear water as faded boyhood memories emerged in his mind that brought a smile to his face. The road also changed to cobblestone at that point; all sure signs of Roman engineering and civilization.

Jason looked up, after some time of walking, and in the distance saw a busy marketplace. There were tents, smaller mud-brick structures, carts, animals, and lots of people. He could also see the striking edifices of buildings beyond the marketplace. The temples impressive columns rising to hold friezes and cornices depicting the legends of the gods and heroes of old, as celebrated in finely crafted statuary and relief. The grandeur and the distant memories made his mission clear, as Jason identified the concepts behind these temples as the thing he was there to oppose. He reflected on his distant past, and how these concepts were instrumental in him putting his faith in false gods. Jason now walked with the one true God; he walked in authority over deceptive and wicked spirits in the name of Jesus. He knew that many of these people would be unwilling to listen to the truth, for the sake of their long traditions. Jason understood what these false gods really were, as well as the heroes, the mighty men, the men of renown; he was very aware of them.

Jason arranged his outer garment to cover his head and body as much as possible. He entered the marketplace, then he looked up and unexpectantly a young girl ran up to him holding a chicken by the feet. He instinctively sniffed the air. She looked at him a bit strangely, then asked in very bad Aramaic if he wanted to purchase the bird. Jason smiled, for he immediately realized that she had mistaken him for a Jew because of his clothing. He answered her in Greek, "No, but thank you and God bless you." The little girl smiled and skipped off. She looked back at him once with a curious expression, then disappeared into one of the booths.

Jason looked up once more to behold the City of Gadara, which sat upon a flat hill just to the south of Emmatha. The buildings, the theater, and all the memories were flooding in. Memories of what he now knew to be sin. He remembered his last moment in the presence of Jesus and what he had been instructed to do. "I'm home," he said as he wiped a tear from his eye.

Jason heard a man shouting, though the noise and activity of the marketplace was loud and distracting. He looked to his left and saw a withered-looking figure emerge from the crowd. The old man was very thin and gaunt; with long white hair, long white beard, and dark eyes. His clothing was old and tattered, but most notable was his outer garment; dark, dusty, rotten fabric covering everything except his wrinkled hands and face. His posture was very poor, as he walked hunched over. He appeared weak and feeble, for he walked slowly and carefully with a stubby, crooked stick. Jason had noticed the old man briefly when he had arrived as he appeared to be begging but paid little attention at the time. As the two men made eye contact, now Jason was giving full attention to the mysterious old man as he hobbled his way toward him. Jason sniffed the air as he drew near and stopped.

"We know who you are!" the old man shouted as he glared at Jason.

Jason was taken by surprise with the deep, strong, guttural voice coming from such a frail-looking old man. He quickly identified the nature of the verbal assault, then closed his eyes for a moment and responded:

"Be silent, old man," Jason said calmly, which seemed to infuriate the man. He raised his stick and pointed it at Jason.

"Leave this place! We don't want you here!" the withered old man yelled even louder as he shook his stick at Jason in a threatening manner. The confrontation had attracted the attention of just about everyone in the marketplace. Jason, thinking quickly, saw this as his moment and responded:

"In the name of Jesus, be silent!" he said. His voice emerged calm but commanding with authority; he shocked himself. He was astonished even more as the old man instantly dropped his stick and sat down. He lowered his head and refused to look up at Jason. Again, he recognized the opportunity and spoke, "IN THE NAME OF JESUS, COME OUT OF HIM!" Jason shouted boldly, loudly, and not so calm this time.

Suddenly, the old man threw his head back and let out an ear-splitting scream, then lowered his head again and started to weep. Jason threw off his bags and dropped to his knees before the man, then embraced him. The old man responded by returning the embrace and continued weeping.

"Today, the one true God has had mercy and compassion upon you," Jason said softly to the old man. He continued, "You are free from the wickedness that has consumed you in the name of Jesus."

The two men arose. The old man looked at Jason and he could see that his eyes had changed from almost black to a normal gray color. His overall appearance was not quite as withered, and his face seemed more vibrant and healthier. The old man attempted to refrain from weeping as he smiled at Jason, then looked into his eyes. He spoke in a normal voice:

"What must I do?" he asked.

Jason responded, "Seek the one, true, living God with all your heart; seek the teachings of the Lord Jesus, the Son of God, for he is the only way to eternal life. I was as you were, but much worse just a short time ago. The Lord Jesus himself found me and set me free. He told me to tell of this throughout the city, that's why I'm here. I once dwelled in the City of Gadara long ago. I've come home to share this." He then asked him, "What's your name?"

"I am Orpheus...can I come with you?" the old man asked with hope in his eyes.

"My name is Jason," he responded, and thought to himself that a short time ago he was in a similar situation. It filled Jason with compassion for the old man. He then asked, "Do you have a place to sleep, my friend?"

Orpheus responded, "Yes, the entire world is where I sleep," he said while grinning. "But I don't currently have a place with a roof, if that's what you mean," he added as his grin grew into a smile.

Jason smiled at old Orpheus as he immediately realized he had a new friend. He said, "Right now, I'm as you are, for I have no place to dwell. Go your way and tell all those you know what God has done for you. I'll be around, and perhaps we will meet again if God wills it." As the men were standing there, Jason noticed that Orpheus was standing straighter, appeared taller, and didn't bother to pick up his stick. He smiled broadly at Jason as he initiated an embrace.

"I will do as you say. Thank you, Jason, thank you!" Orpheus exclaimed.

"Thank God, for I am but the messenger," Jason replied while smiling at the old man. He watched as Orpheus disappeared into the crowd.

He had to pause for a moment as he gave thanks to God and praised him. He acknowledged that without God he would still be Legion and condemned to an eternity of darkness. He was now Jason of Gadara: servant of the one true God, and disciple of Jesus.

Jason picked up his bags, then covered his head and walked away. He realized that he and Orpheus had become quite a spectacle. All eyes were upon him as he made his way through the marketplace. Jason recognized one person right away as the woman he had noticed at the beach. She appeared to be browsing some of the fine fabrics on display. His eyes met hers as she smiled at him and he returned the smile. He thought to himself that she probably didn't recognize him. He was almost compelled to speak with her but realized that if she knew about the scars concealed within his garments she would be repulsed. Unknown to Jason there was someone else who had taken interest in the name spoken, as well as what was said and done. A young Rabbi from the local synagogue hurried away to report what he had seen; one anxious for recognition.

Jason continued into the city upon the cobblestone street, as he sought the man who had offered to help him. His joy and purpose were strong. He felt that Jesus was walking with him after the encounter in the marketplace. Jason looked around and thought to himself that his adventures were just beginning....

Chapter Three

A Gathering of Friends

The early afternoon sun was bearing down on a perfectly clear summer day as Jason left the marketplace and entered the City of Emmatha. He arranged his outer garment to provide as much obscurity as possible, as on the road from the beach. In his new environment Jason felt much more comfortable concealing himself somewhat. He counted it fortunate that James was a big man; his donated garment covered his scars very effectively. He decided that one of the first things to do was to purchase new clothing, as well as getting his hair and beard trimmed a bit. It wasn't a matter of trying to hide, for Jason had an important message to share; he didn't want to shock anyone before he had a chance to speak.

The marketplace had been full of activity, but the streets of the city had only a scattered presence of people. Jason looked around to pick out someone to, perhaps, direct him to the establishment of Eustace. He saw a group of people gathered on the steps of a nearby temple and decided to approach them. Eight or nine people were scattered about on the steps listening to a scholarly looking elder man. He had a long gray beard, short hair, and was wearing a costly white garment. The man seemed to be teaching philosophy of some kind. Jason stood for a bit and listened. He whispered to a man standing next to him asking who this was.

"That is Theophanes, who studied the writings of Philodemus: a native of Gadara. He is quoting Epicurus," the man whispered back quickly, as he was listening intently.

Jason also listened, for he had only scant distant memories of such things. He had vague recollections of his youth starting to become clearer; things he had been taught as a boy. At first, the teaching sounded practical, as to the way he, perhaps, wanted to live his own life. The philosopher spoke:

"Live your life without attracting attention. The pleasant life is not produced by continual drinking and dancing, nor sexual intercourse, nor rare dishes of seafood and other delicacies of a luxurious table. On the contrary, it is produced by sober reasoning which examines the motives for every choice and avoidance, driving away beliefs which are the source of mental disturbances. The things you really need are few and easy to come by, but the things you can imagine you need are infinite, and you will never be satisfied," the philosopher said, then paused briefly.

Jason was about to ask the man next to him if he could direct him to the establishment of Eustace, when he heard the words that shocked him. The philosopher spoke again:

"Is God willing to prevent evil, but not able? Then he is not omnipotent. Is he able, but not willing? Then he is malevolent. Is he both able and willing? Then whence comes evil? Is he neither able or willing? Then why call him God? God is all-powerful. God is perfectly good. Evil exists. If God exists, there would be no evil. Therefore, God does not exist," Theophanes taught proudly as he glanced around the crowd.

"You are a fool," Jason proclaimed loudly as he stood glaring at the philosopher. The people around him let out little vocal expressions and gasps. Theophanes stared back as he was at a loss for what to say, for he wasn't used to such criticism. After a very uncomfortable moment with murmuring among the people, the philosopher spoke:

"By what authority and by what knowledge do you say such a thing? I have been educated by some of the greatest minds in the known world. Do you realize who it is that you're speaking to? Who are you?" he asked Jason

"My authority comes from the God who you just said doesn't exist," Jason responded with boldness. "My name is Jason. The Lord Jesus, the Son of God, has personally saved me from eternal darkness," he proclaimed. He pointed his finger at the impressive looking philosopher, then said, "I am living proof that you are teaching lies."

"Well, I've never heard of you," Theophanes responded, which incited snickers from the crowd. He arrogantly continued, "But this Jesus I have heard of. He is a wandering magician who is trying to convince people that he's some kind of deity through tricks, as I've been told. His kind comes and goes all the time." The philosopher's last statement invoked even more snickering.

Jason immediately saw this as not only a confrontation of ideology, but a spiritual one as well. The need for caution arose in his mind doing battle with the fact that he was livid. This time, Jason was at a loss for what to say. He decided, rather impulsively, to let actions speak. Jason threw aside his outer garment; thus, exposing his forearms, as well as his scars. The instant result was a gasping reaction from the small crowd including Theophanes. He then spoke with boldness but maintained his composure:

"Let me reintroduce myself. My name is Jason, and I'm originally from Gadara. Formerly, I have been known as Legion. Some of you may know Legion as *the beast*," he said. Jason calmly moved his arms to conceal them once again as he put his hands together in a peaceful stance.

A couple of people screamed, then quickly turned and ran away; everyone else slowly backed away from his immediate location. Jason realized he had brought fear among the people as he quickly regretted his actions.

Jason quickly spoke, "I mean you no harm. I'm here to share that God has had mercy and compassion upon me. I have been instructed by Jesus himself to share this miracle throughout the Decapolis. Jesus is not a magician; he is the Son of God. As I said before, I'm living proof that the one, true, living God does exist. As for you, Theophanes, you must repent and ask God's forgiveness. Seek the teachings of Jesus, for he is the only way to stand against the evil in this world full of darkness."

"I think you have come into this city to terrorize us," Theophanes responded with a very shaky voice. "What is it that you want from us?" he inquired sheepishly.

"I'm looking for the establishment of Eustace. Can you tell me where it is?" Jason asked casually.

"I thought you said you were from Gadara," the philosopher said. "How is it you don't know where Eustace is? Why are you looking for him? Are you going to murder him?" Theophanes asked while getting more sarcastic.

"Never mind," Jason replied as he turned and walked away. He walked to the west a little way, but in the wrong direction. Suddenly, he heard a voice from behind call his name.

"Jason!" a man shouted. He turned and saw one of the men from the crowd approaching him. He quickly sniffed the air.

"Are you really the beast?" the man asked as he stopped short of getting too close; he was cautious but curious.

"I was," Jason responded as he was equally curious about the man. "What can I do for you?" he asked, while a little suspicious about the intentions of the approach.

The man responded, "My name is Symeon. I will take you to the establishment of Eustace, if you tell me about Jesus on the way."

Symeon appeared to Jason as a man who had spent his life in peaceful pursuits; mild-mannered and well spoken, well-groomed light brown hair with a shaved face, and he wore a white tunic with an off-white linen outer garment. Symeon carried a small scroll under his arm that suggested higher education. He seemed to have a way about him that indicated intelligence.

Jason just stood there for a moment and was pleased at the expression of genuine curiosity upon the face of Symeon. He smiled and said, "Of course." The two men turned and headed east. Jason told Symeon all he could about Jesus as they walked along the cobblestone street among the temples and buildings of Emmatha. Jason enjoyed giving a detailed account of his recent experiences as the story unfolded. Symeon was very intrigued by Jason and made mention that he would like to have more conversations with him. He also expressed interest in learning the teachings of Jesus, after hearing the testimony. They arrived at the eastern edge of the city. Symeon gestured to a large stone building across the cobblestone street with an inner courtyard.

Symeon smiled and said, "That is the caravansary of Eustace. I'm sorry we're here; I want to hear more."

"I'm most likely going to be dwelling here for a while. I would be honored if you would come and visit me," Jason responded with a smile and extended his hand. Symeon grabbed his hand and smiled as well, then turned and departed.

Jason watched as his new acquaintance walked away. He had a feeling he would learn a lot from the man if he had the chance. He turned and shielded his view from the sun as he took in a better look at the establishment. Quite impressive, as he thought to himself. Jason walked across the street and beheld the large stone building. From his vantage point he could see that the street in front of the building seemed to join with the main road. The well-used eastern thoroughfare continued up through the hills toward Gadara and connecting to the road he had come in on as well. The facility appeared to be there to serve caravans and travelers. The side of the building faced him, so he followed the cobblestone side street that went around the front to get a better view of the huge courtyard. He entered the open space and saw a well which was surrounded by stonework in the center of the U-shaped structure. There were six large arched openings on the left side; within were several camels in two of them, a few asses in another, and the remainder were empty. The other side of the building consisted of normal doorways and windows. Jason assumed the doors across from the huge, arched stalls were rooms for the guests, as the double doorway on the back wall of the structure was larger and more ornate. There was a protruding porch with carved stonework around the doors, which suggested large spaces within. He walked up and knocked on the large double door entry. A pretty middle-aged woman opened the door and smiled at him. She was well dressed in a medium blue garment with a white head covering.

"Can I help you?" she asked as she gestured for him to come inside. Jason smiled and nodded as he entered the establishment and uncovered his head.

"My name is Jason, and I'm here seeking Eustace. We spoke a couple of days ago and he offered me a place to stay," Jason said as he looked around. There wasn't anyone there except him and the woman, although the large room appeared to be a gathering place. Well-constructed smooth cut stone walls and floor with a wooden beam and plank ceiling overhead, which indicated rooms above. There were niches built into the walls to hold lamps, and the room was furnished with eight standard short tables, which were surrounded by plenty of pillows to recline on. Two large west-facing open windows in the back of the room allowed ample lighting, and there were closed doors on either side. Overall, a very welcoming environment.

"Master Eustace is out right now, but your welcome to wait here until he returns," she said while studying Jason, not with fear, but curiosity. Her smile had faded, but her demeanor was very friendly and professional. "Can I get you anything?" she asked.

"No but thank you. I'll just sit here and wait," Jason responded as he smiled and carefully removed his bags from under his outer garment. He was trying not to reveal his scars to the woman. He sensed she was aware of who he was; his intuition was correct.

"Are you the man from the beach?" she asked as she gestured toward the nearest table for him to sit and picked up his bags for him. She obviously had been prepared for his arrival.

"Yes, I'm that man," Jason answered. He felt suddenly awkward and decided to seize the opportunity. He proclaimed, "The Lord Jesus has saved me from a lifetime of darkness. The one true God has had mercy and compassion upon me; I'm here to share this." After pausing for a moment, he asked, "What is your name?"

"My name is Lydia. Master Eustace told us about his encounter with Jesus and a little about what happened with you and the herd of swine. He was quite moved by speaking with Jesus; he's been taking a lot of long walks. Please excuse me. I'll be right back," she said while smiling and quickly disappeared through the left back door. It was surrounded by a short wall with a flat surface on the top, which seemed to be there for serving food and drink, and it was open at the side to access the door.

Jason was a bit overwhelmed by the luxury of the environment and he couldn't help feeling out of place; however, he had foreseen a substantial adjustment period. He was a little unprepared to be treated so kindly. He anticipated Lydia's return and looked forward to meeting with Eustace, after spending most of his life alone. Jesus must have had an impact on the life of Eustace, as he had just heard. Jason was about to reach into his sack to get a morsel of food to eat, for he was growing hungry. The door Lydia had gone through opened, then she emerged with full hands while accompanied by another younger woman bearing a goblet. The room was instantly filled with the aroma of freshly baked bread. The two women approached Jason with smiles and set everything on the table beside him. His senses were overwhelmed by the array of delightful food before him; a loaf of bread, a large bowl of fresh fruit, and a bowl of dates. The goblet was filled with an abundance of wine mixed with water, which was a standard to have with meals. Jason tasted it and wonderful flavors exploded in his mouth. He realized he was in danger of tearing up, as the former demoniac had no recollection of this level of kindness. Jason decided to focus on the new arrival.

"What is your name?" he asked in the friendliest way he could manage. He noticed that she was dressed in a similar fashion as Lydia, except her garment was a pleasant pale green color. He saw indications of dark, silky hair beneath her head covering in contrast to Lydia's curly reddish-brown hair. The pleasant appearance of the two women, as well as their friendly personalities were very enjoyable to Jason.

"I am Melina," she said with a genuine smile, and a friendly with not so subtle curiosity like the demeanor of Lydia. "We were hoping you could tell us about Jesus," she added.

A huge involuntary smile grew on Jason's face as he gestured for the women to join him. He hated to delay his testimony even for a moment, but he had to tear off a small piece of bread and eat some; the aroma of the bread was irresistible. The women seemed to sense his comfort and were pleased.

"I really want to thank you for your hospitality," Jason said after he swallowed the bread and reached for a small cluster of grapes from the bowl. He then spoke, "Jesus is the Son of God, manifest in the flesh and has come to seek and to save that which was lost. I am a living example of the grace and mercy of God. Jesus himself has sent me to be among you, and to share the miracle he has performed." He quickly realized that Eustace was the one who had told Jesus to depart; he didn't want to say anything derogatory. "Jesus had to leave abruptly; I'm afraid there was a misunderstanding," he said.

"What's Jesus like?" Lydia asked Jason with great curiosity as she sought a greater understanding due to the limited knowledge that she had of him.

Jason responded, "In appearance, you could say he looks like a typical Jewish scholar, or teacher if you will. But I can tell you, that to be in his presence is like being in the presence of God."

The two women looked at each other with astonishment, then looked back at Jason. "What is his teaching?" Melina asked.

Jason replied, "He ministered to me for some time. To summarize, he taught, '*Love God with all your heart and all your mind; love your neighbor as yourself.*' He said there are no commandments greater than these."

The women looked at each other again as their smiles grew wider. Just then, the large front door opened, and Eustace entered the room. He was a big man, and his strong presence filled the room; well-groomed, full head of brown hair and full beard, rugged but handsome features, and was wearing a white tunic with a light brown outer garment. He looked up at them and smiled.

"I see you've met some of my helpers," he said in a friendly voice as he walked over and rested his hand on Jason's shoulder. He looked at Jason and smiled, then looked over at the women and asked them to leave for a bit. They smiled and quickly departed through the back-left door behind the serving area.

"I want to begin by saying how much I regret the way things worked out at the beach," Eustace said. Lydia quickly returned with a goblet for Eustace, then hurried away. "Thank you, Lydia," he said while smiling at her.

"I want to start by thanking you with all my heart for the help you have graciously offered me," Jason said as he extended his hand; Eustace took it with both hands. He was smiling at Jason as a friend. The two men sat at the table reclining on the pillows.

"What do you need and how can I help?" Eustace offered as he showed a genuine concern for Jason's well-being. He continued, "I want you to know that I've been through somewhat of a transformation myself. I remember the first time I saw you at the feet of Jesus; I've found myself envious of you as the last two days have passed. I have started praying and I long to be where you were. By the way, you look great!"

Jason was amazed at the fortunate situation he found himself in, and there was a growing joy in his heart. He didn't know what to say for a moment, then thought of an important matter. Jason reached into his tunic and pulled out a small leather pouch. He opened it, then dumped a pile of coins on the table and spread them out. He said, rather awkwardly, "I need help with this; I have a unique collection of knowledge, but I don't know anything about this."

Eustace looked at him for a moment as he was somewhat puzzled, then let loose with healthy laughter. "No, I don't suppose that you would," he said, then leaned forward to examine the coins. "Let's see what you have here. Where did you get this?" he asked.

"One of the disciples of Jesus gave it to me as the ship was leaving; Judas Iscariot tossed it to me," Jason responded.

"Ahh yes, I remember that, but I didn't know what it was," Eustace said as he continued to look at the coins. He picked up one of the silver coins. "This is a denarius; for a lot of people, this is a day's wage," he said as he set the coin down and picked up one of the gold ones. "This is worth twenty-five of those. You were given the equivalent of about two months wages; Jesus wanted you to have a good start!" Eustace said as he smiled at him.

Jason was overwhelmed with emotion as tears welled up in his eyes a bit. He looked over the coins, then put his finger on one of the gold coins and slid it over to Eustace. He proclaimed, "This is to pay my way here; I want you to know how much all of this means to me."

Eustace looked at Jason seriously for a moment, then his smile returned. He put his hand on the valuable gold coin. To Jason's astonishment he slid the coin back to him.

Eustace said, "Your money is no good here. I offered to help you; not to solicit commerce. I'm doing this for you and I'm doing this for *Him*. I've realized there are very few that know the true nature of who you are now, for there are many who hold great contempt for you. I advise caution when moving around the city; stay in the open when you're alone."

Jason suspected as much. It was unlikely that some of the people that had encountered him as Legion would soon forget. He had contemplated these things before he came. "I understand," he responded. "I have to ask…would you do the same thing with Jesus now?" he inquired.

Eustace replied, "That is a difficult question. You see, there are some who have heard of Jesus, though I'm afraid most would reject him. The people of this culture either worship the pantheon of gods, or they've shifted to the self-absorbed philosophies being taught everywhere. I'm concerned about how he would be received, as I spoke at the beach. Some of us have discussed the issue; there's hope that your coming will change some people's minds."

"Yes, that is exactly why I'm here. I've already experienced some of this philosophy you speak of," Jason said while glancing west in the direction of his encounter earlier in the day.

"Oh really, explain," Eustace inquired with curiosity.

"I listened to Theophanes for a few moments," Jason responded.

"What did you think?" Eustace asked with even more curiosity; he didn't like Theophanes.

Jason looked Eustace in the eye and said, "Well, I called him a fool."

Eustace erupted in uncontrollable laughter and was unable to speak. So fervent was his laughter that Jason started laughing too. This went on for several moments. "I like you more and more," he finally got out between laughs. "Come, let me show you your room," he said as he gathered himself. Jason took a quick sip from his goblet and set it down. He patted Jason on the back as he gestured to the back door on the right side of the room.

Eustace opened the door and the two men ascended a wooden stairway within a vertical space in the building that led to a hallway. There appeared to be another stairway at the other end coming from the large room below. He opened the first door across from the top of the stairway and the men entered. Jason couldn't believe the size of the room, and it had a large window facing west with wooden shutters; the view was spectacular! A beautiful view of the City of Emmatha and surrounding hills, as well as the southern tip of the Sea of Galilee. Through this, Jason could watch the sunset every evening. The ceiling had beams, and roof stones could be seen above. There were two wall niches the same as below for lamps, and the room was furnished with two very comfortable looking beds made of iron with stuffed mattresses. A short table sat on the other side, which was surrounded by plenty of pillows; enough to entertain several guests. Again, Jason was overwhelmed. Everything smelled fresh and clean.

"This is my room? Will there be others as well?" Jason asked. He was shocked that a room this size was for him only.

Eustace chuckled and said, "Yes, this is your room. There will be no others, unless you invite them. Consider this your home, for as long as you desire. I only wish I could offer accommodations for Jesus and his disciples as well. This is a room that I reserve for my special guests. We bar the doors at night, so you know. The housemaid's quarters windows are on the west side in the back.

Toss a pebble at their shutters if you're out late, and they will let you in; I have to do that occasionally myself."

Jason embraced Eustace and said, "I'm very happy to be here. I'm having trouble comprehending the fortune I've walked into."

Eustace said, "You have the favor of God upon you, Jason. I feel it, don't you?"

"Yes, I do," Jason said. He paused and suddenly experienced a renewed urge; compassion for the mysterious demoniac still in the hills. He continued, "I still have something I must do; I'm going to have to leave for a day or two. I was going to put it off for a few days, but I'm feeling an urgency somehow. I think God is leading me, so I'm going to set out first thing in the morning; a bit of unfinished business."

"You know what you need to do much better than I do, Jason. I have a bit of business I must attend to this evening myself, so I'm going to be leaving in a short while. I will instruct Lydia and Melina to prepare a special meal this evening. Make sure you get plenty of rest tonight," Eustace said. Jason looked over at the beds and smiled.

The two men returned to the community room, as Eustace called it, and talked throughout the remainder of the afternoon until early evening. Eustace had to depart and bid farewell as he left Jason to attend to his affairs. Melina had made an appearance and told Jason the evening meal would be some time off, but not too long. Jason decided he would take a walk, so he gathered his belongings and took them up to his room. He opened the door and felt blessed as he beheld the late afternoon sun bathing the room in the warm amber color which he recently had grown to love. Jason set his bags by one of the beds and took off his outer garment. He removed his sash, then his sword and slid it under the bed. He had to try the bed, so he lay back on the inviting comfort. Heaven must feel a little like this, as he thought to himself, for he had no memory of anything so restful and pleasant. Jason got up and threw on his outer garment, after almost drifting off, and walked over to the window. He stood there for several moments and gave thanks to God.

Jason took off walking, as he made mental notes of the landmarks. He didn't want to get lost trying to find his way back in the dark, as he was still a little disoriented at times from the massive transformation. He felt like walking to Gadara, but the evening meal spoken of gave him a time restraint; he didn't want to miss it. He set off to the west with no destination in mind, and he hoped to run into someone to have a conversation with. The early evening was cool after a warm day. Jason covered his head with his outer garment, as he walked along and took in the sights. He prayed for the city as he walked and recalled the conversation with Eustace, that most were not ready to receive Jesus. Jason was not feeling led to speak with any of the people he passed; he would nod, and either be ignored altogether, or a return nod with no pause. He continued walking as he prayed and enjoyed the evening. The daylight began to wane, so Jason turned and faced west as he beheld another beautiful sunset; a few scant clouds were exhibiting brilliant color. After a few moments he walked back to the east. The columns and building edifices were coming to life from the myriad of colors generated by the setting sun. Jason decided to let his memory guide him back, as he felt confident in his direction by sighting one of the landmarks. He continued to pray for the city and for the hearts of men, when he sensed something behind him....

The men had seen Jason walking at a distance as they sat on the steps of a public eating establishment just moments prior. They passed a wineskin of strong drink among themselves. The leader of the little group had been a young man when he had joined an effort to capture the beast. The big, burly man always took charge of his younger, smaller companions; they were working men and were rough and weathered with well-worn clothing and banded head coverings. They met often at the end of the day to drink and look for anything exciting. The leader was full of liquid grandeur as well as a lust for revenge; he quickly decided what the excitement of the evening would be. He had heard the description and the gossip around the city of the reformed beast, so he convinced himself, and his friends, that they were to perform a public service. He had told the story of the humiliation and defeat regarding the attempted capture many times. The drunken men crossed the cobblestone street, then quickly creeped up the walkway behind Jason.

Jason sniffed the air a couple of times, then turned his head slightly and saw a group close behind him in the corner of his eye. Very quickly, he felt strong hands grab his arms from both sides and lifted his feet slightly off the ground. Unexpectedly, Jason felt a hard blow on top of his head and was stunned. He was unable to fight or escape, as he was dragged off the street and into a space between two buildings with no exit. There he was violently thrown against the wall. The small group of men backed off a little to view their quarry. Jason's head was throbbing with pain as he struggled to get up on his feet. His vision was fuzzy, but he could see four men, so he thought. He fell once, then managed to stand up and speak:

"Who are you?" he managed to get out with his voice wavering and squinting his eyes while trying to make out the men's faces.

There was one who stood closer to Jason than the rest, as he was obviously the leader of the small horde.

"Why, I'm Prometheus! I bring you fire from the gods!" the leader proclaimed.

A chorus of laughter erupted from the men, but not the leader.

Jason spoke with sincerity, "I'm very sorry for anything I have done to you or your friends. I have been set free by...." He began but was cut short.

"Shut up, you lying piece of dung! You open your foul mouth one more time and I'll shut it for you!" the leader shouted in Jason's face.

Jason's vision was returning somewhat, and the throbbing was beginning to subside a little. He saw the leader draw a sword. Jason followed his instinct to go for his sword for a brief moment, but quickly realized that it was laying beneath his bed. He closed his eyes and prayed silently for God to receive his spirit.

The leader spoke, "I'm going to kill you now, for you just tried to attack us. You should know better than that. Many have been waiting for that to happen since you arrived this morning." The other men continued to laugh and snicker as he spoke. The man shouted questions, "Do you remember me, beast? Do you remember kicking me? Do you...." He was distracted and stopped.

Jason heard a strange noise, like rapid swoosh and thump sounds. He couldn't see anything past the leader of the horde, as he had moved in very close. The leader turned his head slightly to see what the distraction was. Jason heard a very distinct swoosh and a loud thump. The murderous man in front of him seemed stunned, as he turned back and looked right into Jason's eyes. He slowly raised his sword. Another swoosh, then followed by a loud thump, and the leader's eyes went into a blank stare. His sword fell to the ground, then the large man fell flat on his face.

There behind him was Aegeus, the elder herdsman, whirling his staff over his head and turning to see if his younger companion needed any assistance. One man was trying to get up; Dimitri whirled his staff and brought it down upon the man's head, which knocked him out cold. The herdsmen returned to holding their staffs normally as Aegeus reached out his hand to Jason, and he eagerly grabbed it.

"Let us get you out of here before they wake up and blame you for their headaches as well," Aegeus suggested as the three men made haste back to the street. There they met up with a young adolescent boy holding Aegeus and Dimitri's outer garments. He looked like a smaller version of Dimitri; similar clothing, the same shoulder length dark brown hair, and of course, no beard. He looked at Jason and smiled.

"My name is Argus. I would have gone in there too, but I didn't have a staff," he proclaimed as he handed the coats back to the herdsmen. "Aegeus has been telling us about you, and about Jesus. You know him?" the young man asked.

"Yes, I do, young Argus. I bet you would have taken them by yourself, if you would have had a staff," Jason said as he took an immediate liking to the boy. Then he staggered a bit, as he was having to keep himself from falling. He felt the top of his head and brought back blood on his hand.

"Are you alright?" Aegeus asked as he moved closer to Jason. He then asked, "Do you have a place to stay?"

"I'm staying at the caravansary of Eustace," Jason said as he spoke slowly and slurred his words a bit. He pointed to the east.

Aegeus and Dimitri moved to either side of Jason and held his arms as they walked. Jason was having increasing difficulty walking and feeling very dizzy at times. His head was bleeding, as a trickle of blood appeared and ran down his face. Jason recognized the temple where he had the encounter with Theophanes earlier in the day, then a thought came to him. He asked the men to take him to rest upon the steps of the temple. Dimitri produced a cloth and wiped the blood from Jason's face, once there. They were concerned as they stood and observed him. His condition was getting worse rapidly. Jason did the best he could to gather himself.

"Aegeus, do you believe that Jesus is the Son of God?" Jason asked as he continued to slur his words.

Aegeus knelt in front of Jason and said, "As confident as I am of my own existence. Yes, I do believe."

"Lay your hand upon my head and pray that God would heal me in the name of Jesus," Jason spoke very slowly as his eyes were beginning to close.

Aegeus did exactly as Jason instructed him and prayed, "Lord God, in the name of Jesus, I pray you would restore this man, that you would heal him of this injury wrought by those wicked men!"

Jason closed his eyes and went motionless. Aegeus and his young companions were horrified, for the man they just rescued had died right before their eyes. Dimitri and Argus began to weep. Aegeus grabbed Jason's wrist trying to detect a sign of life. With his old, calloused hands he couldn't feel anything and began to weep as well. The men turned away and stood as the sun was setting on the horizon while sniffing and fighting back tears. A few scattered people had noticed what had happened, so they watched from a distance as darkness was beginning to fall. A couple of onlookers suddenly gasped and pointed, which brought an annoyed glance from Aegeus. They had turned away and didn't notice that Jason had sprung to his feet!

"I was on my way to a special evening meal; do you men want to join me?" Jason asked very clearly.

Aegeus, Dimitri, and Argus slowly turned around to behold Jason standing on the steps of the temple. He stepped down to join them with a huge smile on his face. The men quickly took turns embracing him. Aegeus was especially astonished, as he looked at the hand he had laid upon Jason's head: there was no blood. Four others who had witnessed what happened walked up.

One woman spoke, "I saw this man's head bleeding." She reached up and laid her hand on Jason's head. "There's no blood!" she exclaimed.

The man with her concurred, "I saw it too! Who is this *Jesus*, in whose name I heard this old man speak?" he asked.

Jason seized the moment, as several others were beginning to gather to see what all the commotion was about. He stepped back up to the exact spot where Theophanes had taught earlier in the day and spoke with boldness, "My name is Jason. I am here as living proof that Jesus has come to this world to seek and save that which was lost. These men you see here witnessed Jesus deliver me from a lifetime of demonic possession." He gestured to Aegeus and said, "These men have just rescued me from the hands of wicked men, as they sought to murder me. You have witnessed the mighty power of God to heal in the name of Jesus, who is the Son of God. Jesus came here to the shores of the Decapolis but was told to depart due to this city's reliance on false gods made of stone, and false teaching built upon lies. I am here to oppose these things in the name of Jesus!"

"What must we do?" one from the crowd asked.

Jason responded with a shout, "REPENT! Repent of your sins and God will forgive you! Seek the word of the one true God and the teaching of Jesus, the Son of God, for he is the only way to eternal life! Make God the Lord of your life! Forget the false teaching that comes from the limited wisdom of men, or false gods made of stone that neither see nor hear! Seek God! Love God with all your heart! Love your neighbor as yourself! Stop seeking pleasure only and trust God, for he will fulfill the desires of your heart!"

The crowd had listened intently but now had erupted in a buzz of conversation. Jason once again stepped down to join the herdsmen.

He heard one say, "I've never heard anyone speak that way before."

The woman and her companion who had witnessed the healing approached Jason with tears in their eyes. "Thank you for your wonderful words, Jason!" the woman said.

Jason smiled and embraced them both. Then came another, and another....

The excitement finally began to die down, so the men departed and walked to the caravansary. The courtyard was illuminated by two urns burning on either side of the porch with the double doors, and large lamps hanging from the walls. Jason knocked upon the huge doors. They were greeted by Lydia, as she gestured for them to come inside. They entered and uncovered their heads.

"Jason, Aegeus, Dimitri, Argus; welcome!" Lydia announced as she smiled at the men. Jason was pleased that his friends were well known at the establishment.

Many people had gathered in the community room for the meal. Aegeus stood and told the tale of their adventure, then Lydia gestured to an empty table as the men sat down and reclined. Jason arose to offer a prayer of thanksgiving and praise to God; for the meal, the fellowship, and deliverance from the hands of wicked men. Argus moved after the prayer, so he could sit next to Jason. Melina brought goblets, then the two women brought a steady procession of delicious blessings.

"How did you end up here, Jason?" Aegeus asked.

Jason responded, "Eustace spoke with me, after you and Dimitri departed from the beach. He offered me a place to stay for a while to help me get started back into society. I just arrived today; he's been treating me very well."

"Eustace is a good man. I've known him for many years," Aegeus said.

"So, Aegeus, how did you happen to be there for me like that?" Jason asked.

Aegeus explained, "We were on our way home after securing supplies at the marketplace. We normally would have taken the main road around, but for some reason we decided to cut through the city. I saw you walking at a distance and pointed you out to Dimitri and Argus. We wondered if it was you; we weren't sure, but we recognized your clothing. You look different, but in a good way! Anyway, we saw those men approach you, then we got to you as quickly as we could."

"It was God!" Argus said in a very matter of fact way. He looked at Jason and smiled. "God was looking out for you, Jason," the young man stated.

"You're a very insightful young man, Argus," Jason said as he put his arm around the boy for a moment. He realized why he thought the boy was so special. Argus was of a slightly younger age than he was when he started to be influenced by demons. Aegeus had mentioned that he was eleven years old. He had been born just before his father died.

Jason spoke a prayer, "Lord God, I pray that you always watch over this one, as well as the whole family in the name of Jesus."

"Thank you, Jason," Dimitri said. "I want to thank you for a lot of things. A couple of days ago, I didn't know what I believed. I couldn't deny what I had seen after the beach incident, or who Jesus is, but I was afraid of you. I deeply regret setting the food sack down and leaving without introducing myself or sharing a moment with you. I say this because tonight I saw your heart. You brought everything that's important into focus for me," he said with emotion.

Jason got up from the table and went around to Dimitri. He dropped to his knees and embraced him. Then he asked, "You're not afraid of me now?"

"I would trust you with my life, Jason," Dimitri said with genuine affection. The former demoniac smiled.

Jason returned to his spot and spoke to Aegeus. "So, you were securing supplies. Herding again?" he asked.

Aegeus responded, "No, I'm going to do something different, like I told you at the beach. I'll be honest with you; I never want to see another swine as long as I live!"

Laughter erupted from the table, indeed, around the whole room! The story of the swine was destined to become a local legend.

"But what are you going to do?" Jason asked.

"We're going to the Galilee to seek Jesus and follow him wherever that may lead. We're going as a family. It was decided yesterday that Calista, Dimitri and Argus's mother, and I have more in common than we thought. I asked her to become my wife; we're to be married immediately!" Aegeus proclaimed.

Everyone at the table was smiling. Jason said, "I'm so happy for you!"

Everyone around the room shouted good tidings of joy for Aegeus, as he got up and waved at everyone. Jason, deep down, couldn't help but be a little envious of Aegeus, but he had been sent by Jesus himself. He was not to be as other men. He felt more confident than ever of his mission, after what had taken place this evening. The evening wore down as Aegeus and his new sons were preparing to leave and made all the farewell gestures. Jason called out to Aegeus before he left and extended his hand. The old man took his hand and withdrew it, then he realized that Jason had passed something to him. Aegeus opened his hand to behold a gold coin.

"A wedding gift," Jason said. Aegeus embraced him once more. He looked Jason in the eyes and smiled, then departed.

Jason remained at the table for a while, as the others in the room would stop and speak with him before they departed. The merchant with the caravan sat with Jason and asked a lot of questions; he said he collected stories to tell around the campfire as he traveled. Jason was pleased that he was able to share the truth about Jesus with him, for he would spread the good news far and wide. He was preparing to depart himself as the entry door opened. Eustace entered and immediately walked toward Jason.

"I've heard you had a bit of excitement this evening, Jason. Are you alright?" Eustace asked as he walked up to Jason, then knelt and looked him over.

"I'm fine. It was fortunate that I had friends there to help me and pray for me," Jason responded as he reviewed the events in his mind. "Aegeus, the herdsman and his new sons rescued me," he informed Eustace.

"Yes, I know. I met them on the road coming home. He's getting married; good for him! He's been looking out for that family for a long time. Unfortunate things have worked out for him the way they did," Eustace said as his thoughts trailed off about Aegeus and his new family.

"I think there was a reason for it; God has brought his new family together. He seems very happy," Jason said while reflecting.

"You know, I told you to be careful walking around. Perhaps you need someone to go with you. There's a lot of talk about you and a lot of speculation. People are afraid of things they don't understand; in their minds you're a mysterious character," Eustace advised.

"Yeah, maybe I do need someone to go with me. It may be why I feel an urgency to go and take care of the task I'm headed off to tomorrow. I'll let it go at that, for now," Jason said. He was staring off as he spoke while deep in thought.

Eustace stood up and offered a hand to help Jason up. "Are you sure you're alright?" he asked as he looked Jason up and down.

"Yeah, I just need a good night's rest; I can't wait to try out that bed," he said with a big smile.

Eustace chuckled. "Goodnight, my friend," he said as he exited through the first left side door. Jason exited himself and went to his room.

He opened the door, then noticed the two lamp niches in the wall had lamps that had been lit for him. He smiled and appreciated the thoughtfulness; however, he blew them out soon after entering as he planned to go to sleep right away. He was tired but couldn't stop thinking about how well he was received. He had seized the moment to speak following the prayer of Aegeus and the healing. Such things get the attention of people. The comfort of the bed was unbelievable, and in a short time he drifted off to sleep....

In a dream, Jason found himself walking on a road, like the one he came to Emmatha on. He was alone, but something seemed different. He came to a bend in the road. He stopped for a moment, then decided to take a drink from his waterskin. He raised it to drink, as he could see his arms in his side vision and then dropped the waterskin. Jason looked himself over and couldn't believe his eyes. He pulled up his garments and almost lost his balance as he was overcome with emotion; his scars were gone! His skin was perfectly clear! He couldn't remember ever seeing himself this way even in his most distant memories. He knelt, wept, and after a while noticed a glow progressively getting brighter. Jason looked up and there standing before him was Jesus! Not as he had seen him before, for his clothing was like something not of this world. A brilliant white, but more than that; the cloth itself appeared to shimmer with an iridescence. Jason fell at his feet, but Jesus reached down and helped him up. He stood in his presence for some time worshipping him. Jesus smiled at him, then moved beside Jason and rested his hand upon his shoulder. He waved his other hand and they beheld Gadara and the entire Decapolis region as from a great height. Jesus turned to him and was smiling but with tears streaming down his face. Suddenly, whiteness overcame Jason's sight....

Jason awoke abruptly, and immediately looked himself over. He was very disappointed to see that his scars remained. It was early, but he decided to get started with his plans. He had to go to the marketplace to purchase some things he would need. Jason walked over to the window and opened the shutters. He stood there for several moments, for the view of the landscape was bathed in the colorful auburn sunlight of the dawn. He gazed out to the distant land beyond the Sea of Galilee and had deep thoughts about Jesus.

Old Orpheus curled up within one of his regular sleeping spots. It was a space between two buildings, which was concealed behind various bushes that had managed to grow there. Sleep was slow in coming, even though he was tired. He was a new man, but his painful memories endured. He couldn't stop thinking about Jason, and what he had done for him. Somehow, he loved Jason as if he were his brother, and he loved God with all his heart. He knew that he had been forgiven despite the pain that remained. This *Jason* had demonstrated the power of Jesus to change a life. He had been set free from wicked spirits that had taken over his soul, and his mind. He felt, somehow, that he was getting a second chance. Orpheus was overwhelmed, but what could he do? He prayed for God to lead him. He decided he was going to seek out Jason in the morning, for he just couldn't continue his life as it has been. He struggled to find comfort upon the hard ground. Finally, the old man drifted off....

Orpheus was cold as he fell asleep but awakened beside a warm fire. He came to his senses and arose quickly to realize he was inside of a vast cave. There was a figure on the other side of the fire and was sitting and facing his direction. The strange figure wore a long outer garment with his head covered; he could see no face, only darkness. The old man recognized the spirit as something evil but felt no threat. Orpheus sat across the fire as the strange entity did in silence for a moment.

The figure spoke in a deep, echoing voice, "So, you have a new life now, eh? You have nothing. You are nothing. You had a chance at a good life once, and you burned it down. You did it to yourself. There is no hope for one as wretched as you. Your family and everyone you knew hates you. Honestly, it would have been better if you had never been born. Take my advice and kill yourself, since you were. Put an end to your miserable existence. You've thought about it, haven't you? I know you have. This *Jason* is no better, for everyone wants to kill him. He has been attacked; he lies bleeding even now. Forget about him. Do you really think God has any use of you? Your nothing but old garbage, that needs to be burned. Your only hope is to welcome back the spirits that were keeping you alive; they, at least, gave you some worth."

Orpheus sat quietly listening to the condemnation and enduring the pain. He had been delivered and recognized the voice as one that had been with him for some time. One thing the spirit had underestimated, however, was that old Orpheus had been given a restored, sound mind by God.

Orpheus responded, "I don't dispute the things you've said about me. I've failed at life. I also know the truth. The Son of God has come to seek out and save that which was lost. The reason for this encounter you've orchestrated is, within itself, proof that you feel threatened by what I have become. I've begun to pray, and I know that God loves me. Jason is my friend, and I feel there will be more in my new life. God will deliver him, if he has been attacked; he has an important mission. I intend to stand with him, that means I stand against the likes of you!" Orpheus raised his hand and shouted, "IN THE NAME OF JESUS...."

Orpheus awoke to the cold dampness of early morning. It was a stark contrast to the warm fire in the dream, as he was shivering. He immediately arose and started walking, for he knew movement was the best way to knock the chill off. Orpheus decided to walk to the marketplace, but he didn't want to seek alms; he wanted to find Jason. Orpheus decided to sit and wait, after receiving a free piece of bread from a benevolent vendor. He prayed that God would facilitate another meeting with Jason. He contemplated the nightmare, and realized he now had a powerful weapon to use against the onslaught of guilt: it was hope. He also knew that the name of Jesus had a powerful effect upon wicked, harassing spirits. One mention of that name put an end to that ugly experience. He was unable to finish his command, for it would have sent the demonic spirit into the abyss. He would now evoke that name readily, before sleeping especially. Orpheus bowed his head and prayed as he gave praise to God. After a while he felt a hand upon his shoulder. He looked up and smiled: it was Jason! He offered a hand and helped the old man to his feet.

Jason said, "I was hoping to find you this morning, and here you are! I'm doing some browsing; I want you to come with me."

Orpheus responded, "Praise God!" Then he asked, "Are you alright?"

Jason looked at him curiously and said, "Yes, I'm quite alright. I was attacked last night, but I was healed in the name of Jesus. God is glorious!"

Orpheus just smiled and embraced Jason. The two men then walked through the marketplace together. The morning sun warmed them as they headed for a vast clothing display....

The morning wore into afternoon as Jason pulled some remnants of bread from his bag to nibble on. He had second thoughts about not asking for two loaves from Lydia when he approached her before leaving. He had found her baking bread at an earthen tannur behind the building. It was a large tannur, or bread oven, for producing bread to supply the caravansary as well as selling the surplus in the marketplace. A fire was built in the base, and the dough was stuck to the walls within. The bread would bake very quickly. He saw many loaves baking within the walls of the dome-shaped tannur, as well as a large basket full of delicious smelling, freshly baked loaves. He explained that he had need of it, and she was more than happy to help him with his plan. So happy, in fact, that he was sure she wouldn't have minded giving him two loaves. He could smell the fresh bread even from his hiding place. Jason was surrounded by rocks, trees and concealed within some bushes. He sat and patiently waited, while watching the delicious looking loaf of bread he had placed upon the rock near the tombs. He sat and nibbled but was trying to take in the aroma of the fresh bread as he tasted his three-day-old remnants. He spoke under his breath, "Idiot! I'm sure she would have given me another one." Jason watched and waited.

He thought about the dream last night and how it had impacted him. His mission was now in sharp focus. Jason imagined himself standing on the stage in the Great Amphitheater of Gadara and sharing his testimony. He longed to see the stone idolatry crumble into ruin, and to see the minds of men cleansed with the truth. Jason was troubled by the part of the dream that allowed him a glimpse of life without his scars. What seemed like a great blessing in the dream played out as a cruel joke in real life. Jason wanted to be as other men but knew that for the rest of his life he would be covering and hiding his true appearance. He thought of Aegeus and how blessed he was. Jason questioned himself: was he being obsessed with vanity? No, he was a man with feelings like a man. He thought of the mysterious woman that had caught his eye, for he knew that the appalling appearance of his flesh would disgust any woman. He decided there were more important things to consider, and he had to master his flesh. He then silently asked God to forgive him. He was not to be as other men, but to walk in the spirit of truth. He was to help others and disregard himself. Perhaps someday he may find himself in God's kingdom, that's what was represented in the dream. "Yes, that's how I will look after I pass from this world! That's it!" Jason exclaimed. He realized he had spoken out loud and thought to himself that he needed to be quiet; he was hunting for a lost soul. His peace was restored as he continued to focus on the bait. The wonderful aroma of the bait.

A little time passed, then Jason detected a different scent: a pungent one. He couldn't see anything yet but sensed a presence. This time he caught himself and did not sniff the air; he didn't need to. The demon possessed man slowly hobbled into view and he looked terrible. The man was holding himself up with an improvised staff and leaning on it heavily. He had a ghostly, pale appearance as he stopped and sniffed the air. Jason kept quiet and still. The man continued on to Jason's bait after a few moments. The demoniac arrived at the rock, then picked up the bread and began to eat. Very slowly, Jason crept out of his hiding place, and quietly approached his target. He was surprised by how close he came undetected.

"Greetings!" Jason announced loudly as he decided to use the element of surprise. He sniffed the air as he detected more than just a filthy man; something was wrong. The demon possessed man instantly panicked. He Spit the bread out of his mouth, then turned to run but fell over. Jason quickly pounced on him and held him down. He soon realized what the problem was, as the man's dirty, ruddy brown hair fell to one side. Jason was horrified to see that the man's right ear was swollen and inflamed, as was the whole side of his head. He looked up at Jason in complete disorientation, then closed his dark eyes. The man managed to whisper two words in Greek, "Kill me."

Jason immediately laid his hand on the man's head and began pleading to God in prayer. He knew that Legion was responsible for this man's injury that was about to kill him. Jason at that moment developed a more intense righteous indignation against the wicked spirits than ever before. He laid his hand upon him and prayed boldly and loudly, "THE LORD REBUKE THIS SPIRIT OF DEATH IN THE NAME OF JESUS!"

The man lay motionless and had fallen into unconsciousness. Jason removed his hand, then watched as the ghastly appearance of the swollen injury dissolved away. He collapsed and lay his head upon the man's chest as he gave thanksgiving and praise to God. The two men lay there for some time, then Jason began to feel movement. He lifted his head with a smile on his face, and the man promptly punched Jason in the nose! He then squirmed violently, while trying to escape. Jason was going to have none of that and held him firmly to the ground.

"You were Legion; we don't know what you are now. Let us go!" the demoniac shouted in a deep echoing voice as he continued to struggle violently.

"IN THE NAME OF JESUS, COME OUT OF HIM!" Jason shouted loudly with authority.

The man screamed, then went limp and began to weep. Jason took a moment to wipe the blood from his face. The man sat up, then Jason embraced him and held him for a long time. Jason ministered to him, as well as asking him to repent of his sins. The former demoniac readily did so in a normal human voice. Jason shared his knowledge of the assurances and forgiveness of God, then the weeping ceased. Jason further comforted the man by telling of his recent deliverance.

"What is your name?" Jason asked.

The man thought for a moment, then said, "I am Lukas."

Jason noticed a change in the man's face, which now appeared peaceful with pleasant features. Most notable was his strong, pronounced nose and what had been dark eyes were now a striking green. His reddish-brown straight hair and beard were filthy and disgusting, but not as thickly matted as Jason's had been. He was a slighter build than Jason, but Legion had known him to be quick and agile. His body had not been distorted as Jason's had, so there was little change there.

"My name is Jason. I'm very pleased to meet you, Lukas. God sent me back for you. I give him great thanks, for I was going to wait a few days. You would be dead in your sins if I would have," Jason said with a voice of compassion.

Lukas felt his right ear and a look of astonishment fell upon his face. He looked at Jason and raised his eyebrows. "What happened?" he asked with great curiosity. "I had intense pain in my head, that's all I remember. The pain is gone, so is all of the torment in my mind," he said. A smile appeared on his face, then he told Jason it was the first time he had smiled in years.

Jason responded, "You've been healed in the name of Jesus!"

Lukas shouted, "I'm free! I'M FREE!" He jumped to his feet, when Jason got up Lukas embraced him. Then he started jumping up and down repeating, "I'm free! I'm free!" Jason started jumping with him. The two men were laughing, jumping, and giving glory to God.

The afternoon sun was beginning to turn to its yellowish warm tones. The two settled down and rested from the ordeal, as Jason looked Lukas over with his tattered, rotten outer garment and nothing else. He walked over to the place where he had laid in wait and gathered his bags. Jason returned, then set them down and walked over to the loaf of bread on the ground. He picked it up and grimaced, for the bread was covered with ants.

"How was the bread, Lukas?" Jason asked with a tinge of disappointment in his voice.

Lukas replied asking, "What bread, Jason? Do you have bread? I'm hungry."

"He doesn't remember," Jason said under his breath while tossing the bread to the ground. "Let's go for a walk, Lukas," he said.

The two men set off around the bluff, down the grassy slope and on toward the Sea of Galilee. The colors of the late afternoon were becoming striking. Lukas stopped for a moment and smiled, once in view of the sea.

"What is it?" Jason asked.

"It's like I've never seen it before!" Lukas responded. Jason put his hand on Lukas's shoulder, and they enjoyed the moment together.

The two men made their way down to the beach. Jason didn't see the swine carcass that had been there when he left. He was glad it was gone, as he sniffed the air and smiled. He thought to himself that perhaps it was dragged off by a predator, or someone pulled it back into the water. Jason set his bags down and began digging into his large sack. He produced several pieces of clean cloth and a cake of goat soap. Jason stood up, shed his outer garment, then reached down to untie his sandals and kicked them off. He noticed Lukas was nervous and reassured him.

"It's alright, Lukas. The water will not hurt you," Jason assured his new friend.

"It's not being afraid of the water...I can't remember washing, ever. It's like I can't remember being that way; it's all so strange," Lukas said as he looked to Jason for guidance.

Jason was suddenly a bit nervous himself as he found himself hesitant to remove his tunic. He slowly removed his sash, as well as his sword and lay them by his sack. He pulled off his tunic and set it down with his other things, then looked over at Lukas as he stood there smiling at him.

"You're not shocked?" Jason asked.

Lukas responded, "Of course not, Jason. You're my friend. I've seen your scars before, but you're no longer the terrifying monster you were before; this is a new day!"

Jason smiled at his friend and gestured for him to disrobe. He grabbed two pieces of cloth with the goat soap, then the two men entered the water. Jason waded out to deeper water after washing and waved to Lukas to join him.

"Lukas, this is something that needs to be done. Even Jesus went to be baptized," Jason said as he noticed that Lukas was looking at him curiously.

"What is baptized?" Lukas asked.

"You leave the old man behind in the waters and come out new. You said it yourself a few moments ago, this is a new day. It's a way to make a statement to God that you're starting over and living for him," Jason informed the formerly demon-possessed man.

Lukas responded, "Baptize me, Jason."

Jason spoke boldly, "I baptize you for the remission of sins. Today, the Lord God has had mercy and compassion upon you."

Jason placed his hand on Lukas's back and laid him back in the water. He came out smiling, as Jason had. They left the water and Jason walked over to his sack. He tossed a new, clean undergarment to Lukas, and put a new one on himself. Lukas watched how he put it on, for it had been a long time. Jason dug into his sack, then pulled out two new tunics and a cord belt. He handed one to Lukas and he slipped it on. Jason handed him the belt and watched with joy as his friend smiled while tying the belt around his waist.

"You look great!" Jason said as he looked at Lukas, then saw him reach for his old, rotten outer garment. "No, wait," he said. He went to his sack and pulled out a new outer garment: a light brown one; he liked the way Eustace looked in his. Jason reached into the sack one last time and pulled out two new pairs of sandals. He gave a pair to Lukas, then Jason slipped on his new tunic. It had long sleeves, and he was very happy with the fit. He put on his sword and sash, then started collecting the remainder of the items scattered about. Jason left Lukas for a moment, then returned with a large piece of wood he dragged up from the water's edge. He dropped it as he walked up to Lukas and looked him over, while examining his hair and beard. Jason then spread out his old tunic upon the ground next to the wood.

Jason touched Lukas's hair, and said, "Not as thick and curly as mine; most of the mats are down lower...lay down." He then drew his sword and gestured to the old tunic.

"What are you going to do?" Lukas asked while very concerned.

Jason said again, "Lay down, and put your head here." He pointed at the base of the large piece of wood with his sword. "Trust me," he said with a grin.

Lukas complied, although a little nervous. Jason gathered his hair and pulled it up over the top of his head. He held the hair with his left hand, then took aim. One chop, then Jason told Lukas to stand up. He got up and his hair was free of mats, even, clean, and fell to shoulder length. Jason then touched Lukas's beard, which was thinner than his. He swiped it a few times with the blade, as he held with his left hand and cut with the right.

"Not bad," he said as he pulled and cut here and there to touch up the grooming job. "Your finger and toes aren't that bad. How did you manage it?" Jason asked.

"Well, I developed a habit of biting my fingernails, and I got fairly good at cutting my toenails with my dagger," Lukas said. He walked over to his old garment and pulled out a large dagger, then quickly tucked it beneath his new cord belt on his left side and covered it with his outer garment. "I never liked the way it felt to walk if I let them grow," Lukas added. Jason grinned at his new friend.

"We'll use that old coat of yours to start a fire with," Jason said as he put on his new sandals. He threw on his outer garment, then the two men sat on the beach as they watched a beautiful sunset and talked about Jesus.

Later, Jason and Lukas settled down beneath the oak tree near the tombs, after sharing the remainder of food scraps. The risen full moon provided a soft glow, which was enough light to see the details of the landscape somewhat. Jason leaned back into his favorite spot against the trunk of the large tree, and Lukas found a spot next to him. The two men began to talk as they gazed into the fire.

"Why did you come back for me, Jason?" Lukas inquired while having deeper thoughts about his new life.

"You were unfinished business. I tried to call out to you before I left for Emmatha, but you ran away," Jason said as he reflected. "I felt a need to get away from here, yet, here I am. God somehow impressed upon me to return quickly to find you. You were near death when I did so. You are very important to God, Lukas, we all are. I quickly developed compassion for all people once delivered by Jesus, but you're something special," he said as he looked over at Lukas.

"Why is that?" Lukas asked, intrigued.

Jason responded, "You and I are going to face challenges that most would never dream of or understand. There is another: his name is Orpheus, and I intend to seek him out when we return to Emmatha. I think it's important that we form a fellowship. We need to strengthen ourselves; to pray for one another and to stand against the familiar spirits that will try to ensnare us. We can help each other, since we have a common point of reference. You were just delivered; I have only been delivered four days. The contrast makes it seem longer, but in many ways we're babes in the wilderness and it really intimidates me sometimes. That's why an intimate relationship with God is so very important for us. I realized my first day that we can never take a step back, for utter destruction will result." Jason went silent as he stared into the fire.

Lukas spoke, "I'm glad you came back for me, Jason. Everything you just said makes perfect sense to me. You're my friend, but I feel more like we're brothers. I have already experienced the familiar spirits you spoke of; the temptation of what seems right and comforting, and it's all a lie. I know you haven't been at it for very long either, but you seem to have a strong grip on it."

Jason replied, "I take no credit for anything, except being fortunate enough to have found myself in the presence of Jesus himself. I've been touched by the Master's hand; I could never forget that experience." Jason looked up at the moon. "Perhaps someday I'll get to see him again," he said.

"I only saw him at a distance; I saw everything that day," Lukas said.

"Ahh, so you were watching," Jason responded. "That explains why Matthew asked me if I had a companion. He must have seen you up on the ridge watching. It's too bad you didn't come down. We could have started out together; you wouldn't have had to deal with the sickness and pain," Jason said with compassion.

"It was the spirit of fear," Lukas said. "It seemed to rule over everything I did. It all goes back to the experiences I had as a child, for I never had parents that I can remember. I grew up on the streets of Gadara, as an orphan. I learned to fear men...I was abused in many ways. I sought the power of darkness to strengthen myself and got involved with a witch. The evil drove me into the wilderness, as you've known me for many years," Lukas confessed.

Jason put his hand on Lukas's shoulder for a moment, then said, "I was compromised by wickedness at a very early age. My parents worshipped Zeus and the other worthless stone *gods*. I was introduced to temple prostitutes by my father. I never saw a problem with the way I behaved, so I thought if it felt good to my flesh it must be the right thing to do. I sought alternative spiritual experiences as well, like you. Witches seemed to have a tangible power that, in my mind, was undeniable at the time. The mind-altering potions and spells opened doorways. I'm sure you know what I'm talking about. I understand the source from where that power flows, now. Somehow, powerful entities began to influence me at only fourteen or fifteen years old, perhaps earlier. I was out here by the time I was seventeen. I was the dwelling place for thousands of very ancient evil spirits who have roamed the earth since God destroyed them with a great flood. They were the Nephilim. They were not men and they were not gods, but something that should never have been. They were giants sired by the fallen ones. They spread throughout the world; building massive structures, cities, giant temples, and demanding worship. They devoured men, then each other, and sought to corrupt and destroy everything God had created. God has cursed them to wander the earth as evil spirits."

Jason paused while looking at Lukas, then continued, "Their immense intelligence was used only for evil, as they sought to alter both man and beast, for they mocked the wonderful creation of God. I could tell you more, but even I can't understand all the ways they manipulated nature. I became a prisoner and was dwarfed by the overwhelming presence and wicked desires of these evil entities. I think a tiny shred of hope that I tenaciously clung to is what brought Jesus to me. I've often wondered how many more are out there like I was, since my deliverance. I pray to God there are no more with the depth of evil that was contained within my skin. But we cooperate, as you know; we allow it through ignorance of God. We have an inherent sin nature that can be readily exploited by the spiritual wickedness of this world. The Lord God is always willing to forgive us, but we must take that step toward him and walk in his ways. The spirit of ignorance has destined many to eternal darkness; it would have been our fate if not for Jesus, the Son of God. He is the way, the truth, and the life, and came to seek and save that which was lost. That's why he came for me; that's why I came for you."

Lukas stared into the fire for a long moment, then said, "I was a little older than you when I ended up out here, but close. I think I was eighteen. I figure I'm thirty-three or thirty-four years old now. Such a waste." Then he asked, "Does the regret and shame ever pass?"

Jason responded, "Focus on Jesus and he will give you peace. Not in the way of men, but in a wonderful way. Trust God. love God. Seek his ways and he will fulfill the desires of your heart. We are going to carry our scars, but Jesus can and will carry that burden for us. He will give us rest. Jesus is walking with me in a very real way: through my testimony. What he has done for me has a presence of its own. He has appeared to me twice already in my dreams. Just last night I was about to be murdered. The herdsmen who lost the swine, that were on the beach that day were sent by God to rescue me. If God is for us, who can stand against us?"

Lukas spoke with excitement, "I want you to know that the spirit of fear is gone from me. The words you just spoke has driven away the doubt that was eating at me. I feel a boldness like I never thought possible, now all I want to do is share what I have. You have explained these things in a way that I can understand. I will trust God and I will trust Jesus; I really want to meet him!"

"Perhaps he will return someday. My mission is to prepare the way. Gadara is a den of wickedness; I've already been opposing such in just one day. They tried to murder me, as I told you. It's not going to be easy. Will you join me in my mission?" Jason asked.

Lukas answered Jason by extending his hand and Jason eagerly grabbed it. A very firm grasp in silhouette against the roaring fire. A new fellowship was born.

Early morning at the marketplace was bustling as usual as the two men entered the main street. They headed straight for a booth that was selling freshly baked bread.

"JASON!" a loud voice shouted. Jason looked around and saw an old man with long white hair and beard waving. He was sitting on sacks of grain, and a few people were sitting around him. Jason and Lukas walked over to the man who Jason had immediately recognized, for he was wearing a new outer garment. "JASON! See, this is the man I was telling you about!" Orpheus exclaimed as he arose and embraced Jason. "This is the man who walks with God!" he shouted.

The men uncovered their heads, then Jason introduced Orpheus to Lukas. Jason spoke to the people who had gathered to listen to the testimony of Orpheus. He confirmed Orpheus's experience, then Lukas spoke as well, as he briefly shared his testimony. The crowd grew; among them were two Pharisees....

Chapter Four

Love Conquers All

The clear, beautiful morning meant there were a lot of people in the marketplace of Emmatha. The local people often met in the marketplace to share information, as well as the social interaction. Many seemed to be drawn to join a growing crowd. They were gathering to listen to the testimonies of Jason, Orpheus, and Lukas, although there were a lot of competing distractions. The men were speaking to the people as two Pharisees stepped forward. Jason noticed they wore the same type of prayer cloth as Jesus: white with blue stripes and tassels on the borders. Both wore costly garments; colorful stripes with embroidery, fine clothing beneath, and turbans upon their heads covered by the luxurious outer garments. One walked with an elegant staff, and the other stood with his hands together. Both were elder men with long gray beards. Jason and Lukas smiled at the impressive looking men; Orpheus did not. Jason assumed the men were going to ask questions and give glory to God. This time his intuition was incorrect. Jason stepped forward, then extended his hand. Both Pharisees took a step backward and glanced at Jason's extended hand as if it were a scorpion, then glared at him. Jason slowly withdrew his hand as his smile faded into a look of confusion; he had never felt so awkward. The silence that had overtaken the small crowd made his heart sink, even though the noise of the marketplace filled the air. Jason directed his attention to the one nearest to him and spoke, as an attempt to put an end to the tension.

"My name is Jason, what are your names?" he asked. The men remained silent. The Pharisees stared at Jason as if he were a rodent. A brief but very uncomfortable moment ensued, then one of them spoke:

"It is enough for you to know that we represent the Sanhedrin," the man holding the staff said with arrogant authority.

"What is the *Sanhedrin*?" Jason asked honestly. The Pharisees both erupted with mocking laughter and incited others in the crowd to chuckle also. Jason blushed as he realized he had been made to appear foolish.

The Pharisee with the staff spoke again, "This *Jesus* you speak of; you claim he is the *Son of God*. By what authority do you speak such nonsense?" His expression returned to a stern glare as he stood and awaited an answer.

Another man approached from the crowd in the street of the marketplace. He wore a white robe with a tan outer garment: it was Theophanes. He stepped up beside the Pharisees as he pointed his finger at Jason.

"The day before yesterday, this *beast* threatened my students and chased them away! Then, he announced a plan to murder Eustace! He is a threat to us all! He is a demon who has come to infiltrate our city, then gain our trust and murder us in our sleep!" the philosopher shouted while drunk with retribution.

The Pharisees had listened to the false accusations of Theophanes intently. Both men were grinning as having received a gift.

The Pharisee without a staff spoke this time, "People of Emmatha and Gadara, hear me! These men are not what they claim to be. This *Jesus,* as he calls himself, casts out devils by the power of Beelzebub! He has been spreading his false teaching throughout the Galilee, Samaria, and Judea. He has obviously recruited these *men,* or whatever they are, so he may proliferate his false teaching to your communities! These men know nothing of the laws given to us by God!" He pointed his finger at Jason and waved it at the other men as well, then shouted, "HEATHENS! DEVILS! BLASPHEMERS!"

Murmuring among the crowd, which had swelled following the wild accusations, then grew to a fever pitch and attracted the attention of the entire marketplace. Jason looked back at his two friends and saw that they were wide-eyed and flushed.

Jason spoke to the crowd the best he could, "People of Emmatha and Gadara, hear me! We are not telling lies; we are speaking of our experiences. We have not been educated in the ways of their laws, but by what we've seen with our eyes." Jason pointed his finger at the Pharisees, shouting, "THESE MEN KNOW NOTHING OF JESUS! I know that Jesus is the Son of God! He has come to bring truth and to lead men in the path of righteousness!"

"You claim to know that Jesus is the Son of God. How do you know this?" the first Pharisee asked Jason.

Jason realized the man had led him into a trap this time. He wasn't going to say that the demonic entities had no choice but to submit to the Son of God, after all of the accusations. He wasn't going to say he had a vision of Jesus prior to his deliverance, before the arrival of the ship.

Thinking quickly, Jason spoke, "The power and authority of his name spoken by those who believe can heal the sick. Many have witnessed his miracles! Many have been healed by his touch!" Jason read the smirk on the faces of the Pharisees. There was no choice but to speak the truth. He spoke with boldness, "Jesus set me free from a lifetime of demonic possession, and I delivered these two men by speaking in the authority of his name. Lukas here was near death yesterday; I laid my hand upon him and he was healed in the name of Jesus!"

Lukas stepped up and spoke, "Yes, it's true! I'm here and would be dead in my sins if not for Jason and his faith in the Lord Jesus!"

"BLASPHEMY!" The first Pharisee shouted. "How dare you call this false teacher *Lord!* These men cast out devils by the power of devils as I have said!" he exclaimed.

Jason asked, "What sense does it make for devils to cast out devils?"

Jason noticed Theophanes had slipped away. He looked up through the marketplace and saw him making his way straight to the booth that he and Lukas were headed to when they arrived. There he saw a couple of Roman soldiers purchasing bread. Instinctively, Jason no longer saw even the slightest chance of a good outcome from this whole ordeal. The Pharisees had turned their backs on the men, likely discussing how best to continue their attack. The people around them were deeply conversing with one another. The Pharisees turned around as one started to speak with his finger in the air, then abruptly stopped. Jason, Lukas, and Orpheus had vanished.

"Well, Jason, you told me it wouldn't be easy," Lukas said as the three men walked on the eastern road around the city heading south.

Jason spoke with indignation, "They have rejected Jesus. I can't believe it. They are Jewish leaders of the Temple of God; I know that much. They are no better than Theophanes!" He shouted questions after pausing for a moment, "What kind of misguided world is this? How can they not know who Jesus is?"

Orpheus spoke, "The Pharisees have become self-absorbed politicians; I've seen those men before. They dwell in Jerusalem but visit the synagogue here occasionally. I knew there would be trouble as soon as I saw them. They have much power and influence where they come from, as well as some persuasion with the Romans. The High Priest Caiaphas is who they serve. Jesus threatens their system, which is full of greed and corruption. They are self-righteous and think that everyone else is beneath them."

Jason and Lukas both looked at Orpheus and were amazed. "How is it you know so much about them?" Jason asked.

The old man responded, "I've been around for a very long time, Jason. You and Lukas were in the wilderness, but I've walked the streets of Gadara, Hippos, Gergesa, Gerasa, Bethsaida, Gamala, Abila; I've been around. In the past I used to travel all over: Jerusalem, Petra, Athens, Rome, around the Mediterranean and Aegean Seas, as well as destinations to the far east. Listening to people talk you learn a lot. I was a merchant once before the darkness fell upon my life. I had a lot of bad habits...one of which was strong drink. Wicked spirits entered my life through my mouth; I started treating my friends badly, then lost my family and became known as a liar." Tears started welling up in the old man's eyes. He continued, "Demons began to deceive me, and blinded me from seeing what I was doing. They destroy you, once they have you. When I approached you that day, Jason, they wanted to kill you. They sensed the anointing of Jesus upon you. God knew that deep down I was crying for help." The old white-haired man began to weep. First Lukas embraced Orpheus, then Jason.

"Welcome to our fellowship Orpheus," Lukas said as he extended his hand; Orpheus grabbed it eagerly and grasped it firmly.

Jason was smiling and grabbed the men's clasped hands with both of his. He said, "You shall always find understanding with us, Orpheus, and you will always find peace with Jesus. We know where you've been. We intend to spread our message throughout the Decapolis." Jason then asked, "Will you join us in our mission?" He added, "It won't be easy, as you've seen."

Without hesitating Orpheus shouted, "Yes, yes, of course I will join you!" The old man smiled widely with tears still streaming down his face. He seemed even more full of life; almost abnormal for a man of his age.

The men were ascending a hill, and Jason could see the caravansary with its cobblestone side street. He smiled thinking of the warm hospitality, the friendly conversation, the comfort, and the delicious fresh bread. He stopped, then the other two men stopped as well. Jason turned and surveyed the landscape to the north. He could see from their vantage point the Roman built arched bridge over the Yarmuk River, as well as the road they had traveled from the beach.

Jason looked at Orpheus and spoke, "We left unfinished business behind, Orpheus. I was letting my flesh guide me; please forgive me. Considering the confession and commitment you have made to us and to God, this is important."

Jason began walking back down the hill while gesturing to Lukas and Orpheus to follow. Lukas smiled as he had figured out what Jason had in mind, but Orpheus didn't know.

"Where are we going?" the old man asked.

"You'll see," Lukas responded as he patted his elder companion on the back. The men set off for a trip to the river. The younger men were not slowed down by the old man, for he was keeping a good pace with a spring in his step.

It was early afternoon when the three men reached the bridge. They veered off the road and headed down the escarpment to the water. The heavily forested terrain around the river was a shadowy contrast to the open area around the bridge. The midday sunlight penetrated the clear water of the river, which revealed the sandy riverbed with strewn rocks and a few fish swimming by. The men disrobed and prepared to enter the water. Orpheus couldn't help looking at his friend's scars.

Orpheus quickly spoke, "We all have them, Jason. Mine are there too, but you can't see them." Jason smiled at the old man as he was revealing even more surprising wisdom. Jason was at ease around his new companions; he felt accepted.

Lukas slowly waded in first. He studied the river as he looked through the transparent crystal-clear water. He looked up and smiled at Jason and Orpheus as they looked at each other with curious expressions.

The men waded out into waist deep water. Jason spoke to Orpheus, "This is to leave the old man behind, and commit to God that you will walk with him from this day forward, like being born again." Jason asked, "Do you understand?"

Orpheus responded, "Yes, I do understand; I've heard of John who baptizes people in the Jordan River. I never thought I would be baptized. Yes, please, baptize me!"

Jason spoke with boldness, "I baptize you for the remission of sins." He placed his hand on the back of Orpheus and submerged him. The old man raised his arms and shouted when he emerged. Old Orpheus took off swimming like a fish, to the astonishment of the younger men. The two men looked at each other; Lukas shrugged his shoulders and joined him. The three men swam around for some time, for they were filled with joy. It was a warm afternoon and the water was cool and refreshing. The men thoroughly enjoyed themselves.

Jason and Orpheus left the water and returned to the bank to dress. Orpheus wasn't in need of grooming, as he had kept his appearance up somewhat. His white hair and beard were long but clean and the look suited him. He explained to Jason that asking alms was more profitable if one didn't look like an animal. Jason had never thought about it, for he had been living alone most of his life, but it made sense. The two men finished dressing and sat on the bank of the river watching Lukas. He had returned to the same spot as when he first entered the water. Lukas was bent over slightly with his hands extended, as he appeared to be studying the river.

"What are you doing?" Jason asked, very curious.

"SSSHHHHH," was the only response from Lukas.

The two men remained quiet and watched their friend, for he seemed to them as acting peculiar. They exchanged puzzled glances and continued watching intently. Lukas froze and slowly dipped his hands into the water. Suddenly, to the utter amazement of Jason and Orpheus there was a violent splash. A fish came sailing through the air and landed right next to Jason!

"Don't let it go! I'll get another!" Lukas shouted as he immediately went back to his peculiar stance. Within moments there were three fish in the men's possession. Lukas emerged from the river and smiled at his friends.

"I was hungry. God just supplied us with a meal; all I did was grab 'em! One of the ways I learned in the wilderness," Lukas said as he proceeded to get dressed. Jason and Orpheus were very impressed with the resourcefulness of Lukas.

Jason set about starting a fire. The men sat back on the bank of the river giving thanks to God for their fellowship, and the unique skills assembled from each man. The three men acknowledged that each of them contributed something valuable, and together they made a much stronger whole. The men prayed giving praise and thanksgiving to God and the Lord Jesus. They stayed until early evening and enjoyed a fine meal of roasted fish. Orpheus told fascinating stories about his travels as a younger man and continued his tales as they returned to the road. They began to walk back toward the city.

The three new friends veered off the main road and walked up the cobblestone street in front of the caravansary. Lukas commented on how impressive it was. Orpheus was accustomed to living in the streets; Lukas had been living in tombs and caves, as Jason had. Jason stepped into the courtyard and beckoned his two companions to follow him. He had intentionally not spoken of where he was staying. Jason had planned since last night by the campfire that he was going to surprise Lukas; now, Orpheus as well. They passed the large arched stalls, as Jason noticed more camels had arrived and all the spaces were full, except one. Perfect, Jason thought to himself as he gestured to the open space.

"What do you think? It's a roof over our heads," Jason asked as he desperately tried to keep from chuckling. He was enjoying his playful joke.

"It's a lot better than a tomb," Lukas responded.

"This is a perfect place to sleep, Jason. They let you sleep here?" Orpheus asked as he walked over and looked around. "Do you suppose they could spare a blanket?" he asked.

Jason started laughing, then gestured for his two friends to come with him. He walked over to the impressive double door entry and knocked. Melina opened the door and smiled broadly.

She expressed a very friendly greeting, "Jason! We missed you! And you've brought guests! Welcome!" She stepped aside and gestured for the men to come in. The men entered and when Jason uncovered his head a voice from across the huge room shouted, "Jason!" He looked and saw the merchant he had spoken to a couple of nights before and waved. There were four others reclining around one of the back tables who waved as well, although Jason had never met them. He felt warm in his heart after the morning encounter with the Pharisees and Theophanes.

"We'll be serving a meal in a while. I hope you and your friends are hungry," Melina said as the back door opened and Lydia appeared, then waved and smiled.

"Is this who the bread was for, Jason?" Lydia asked as she looked at Lukas and Orpheus. They were in a mild state of shock, for neither of the men had been treated kindly in a very long time.

Jason sensed their awkwardness and performed the introductions. He gestured to his younger friend and said, "Lydia, Melina, this is Lukas: he's the one the bread was for." He then put his hand on the old man's shoulder and said, "This is Orpheus. They are very dear friends of mine...like brothers."

Both women gestured to the nearest table. Jason said, "I want to show them my room first, but we'll be back shortly."

Lydia said, "Very well. We'll bring refreshments and put them on the table, Jason. It's good to see you! Master Eustace is out, but we expect him to return any moment. He was asking if we had seen you earlier."

"Thank you, Lydia, Melina, we'll be back down in a few moments," Jason said as he walked toward the back-right door and gestured for his companions to follow. The men ascended the wooden stairway and crossed the hall, then Jason opened the door. The window shutters were open, and the picturesque view of the setting sun beyond the Sea of Galilee was breathtaking. The room was saturated with warm, auburn, fading sunlight. Jason dropped his bags near the table and turned to his friends. Melina appeared and knocked slightly upon the open door, then smiled with a small lamp in her hand. Jason nodded and gestured for her to enter. She quickly lit the lamps in the wall niches, then turned to the men and spoke:

"Master Eustace has just arrived, and he wants to sit with you for the meal," she said as she smiled and departed.

Lukas walked over to the window and asked, "How did you end up here? This is like a dream!" He gazed out the window with a look of wonder on his face.

"Eustace is having a meal with us? The same Eustace that Theophanes accused you of plotting to murder?" Orpheus asked. He walked over to stand by Lukas as they looked out of the window. They were both trying to process everything.

Jason said, "The favor of God through our devotion to the Lord Jesus rests upon us in this place; it shall be our refuge. Eustace spoke that to me himself the night before last." Jason paused as he glanced out the window himself. "I think Eustace will be very interested in what Theophanes said," he added.

Lukas and Orpheus looked around the room and were shocked. Lukas sat on one of the beds with a huge grin on his face, as Orpheus tried the other; the men were amazed. "Jesus and his disciples could lodge in here along with us!" Lukas exclaimed.

"Come, let us go back down to the community room. Eustace is most likely waiting for us," Jason said as he gestured toward the door.

Just as the men entered the large community room Eustace entered from the other side as he smiled and waved. They met at the table that had been prepared for them. Eustace embraced Jason as if he were his brother. Then Jason introduced Lukas, and he was warmly greeted by Eustace. He introduced Orpheus, then Eustace paused, and his smile faded. Jason quickly told of the encounter when he first arrived in the city, as well as the events of the morning. Eustace stood for a moment looking over the now clean and well-dressed Orpheus. A smile returned to his face, and he extended his hand. Orpheus eagerly grasped it.

"I apologize for that reaction, but I've seen you around for some time, Orpheus. What I see now is the power of Jesus to transform a life. I'm looking forward to getting to know who you really are," Eustace said as he gestured for everyone to recline.

The table was set with four Goblets, two small bowls of dates, a large bowl of fresh fruit and two loaves of bread. Jason immediately reached for a loaf of the bread and broke it. Eustace broke the other loaf as Jason offered a prayer of thanksgiving. He then tore off a large piece of the fresh bread and started eating. Orpheus and Lukas eagerly indulged as well. Although they had eaten a fish earlier the spread on the table was, in their eyes, a blessing from heaven.

"I've heard about the commotion at the marketplace this morning and I was told of the words spoken by Theophanes. He accused you of plotting to murder me?" Eustace asked with raised eyebrows while looking at Jason.

"I asked him for directions to your establishment when he asked me what I wanted of him. That was after I called him a fool and advised him to repent," Jason said in a very matter of fact way, for the truth in his voice cut through the confusion. "He then accused me of finding you to murder you," he added.

Eustace looked Jason in the eye for a long moment as a bit of tension built around the table. He then looked away and stared into space. A smile grew on his face followed by chuckling and then laughter. Eustace had a joyful nature to his laughter that was contagious, as everyone at the table began laughing.

Jason brought up a concern after calming down, "I saw Theophanes approach a couple of Roman soldiers in the marketplace, which inspired us to remove ourselves from the attacks we were experiencing. He seized the opportunity that presented itself, for we were being verbally assaulted by two Pharisees. They were trying to make us look foolish and insincere following our testimonies," he said.

"Actually, I just came from the Tenth Legion Camp; I know one of the magistrates there. You won't have any trouble from the Romans, as far as this issue," Eustace said as he looked at Jason with concern. He continued, "You may have some matters to settle with them eventually, Jason. They were involved with trying to capture you over the years. People have said things; be careful what you say and do in public. They know you're here, but I have spoken on your behalf. The Romans are the authority over us all. They want peace; they want the people of their empire to behave themselves. I advise you, as your friend; don't give them a reason to take notice of you. You are Jason: a follower of Jesus; you are no longer *Legion,* for the Romans would be very interested in arresting and executing that creature."

Jason now knew that Eustace was truly looking out for him. He was lost in thought for a moment, while Eustace engaged the other men in conversation. Would the Romans arrest him? He knew that if they did and held him to account for the years of Legion's activities; the penalties were widely known and brutal: beating, torture, and crucifixion. Undaunted, he silently concluded that he would avoid them as much as possible and continue with his mission. Then a thought came to him. He waited for a lapse in the conversation, then spoke:

"What of Theophanes, Eustace?" Jason asked as he was curious about his reaction to the false accusation.

Eustace looked at Jason and said, "Tomorrow, I'm going to confront him; I want all of you men to join me."

The four smiled as a large plate of meat was served to them and they feasted.

"Tell me more of this *fellowship* Lukas spoke of, Jason," Eustace requested.

Jason told Eustace of the prayers and commitments made by them, as well as the baptisms. They all had been mightily impacted by Jesus and felt that God has brought them together to accomplish the mission Jesus had set upon him. He discussed the trouble he had already encountered and that the mission would not be easy.

Eustace responded, "I have a business to run here, Jason, but I would be honored if you would welcome me into your fellowship. I have spent much time contemplating the experience I had with Jesus. I would be very honored to be a part of your mission, if you find me worthy."

The men were astonished that such a prominent man questioned whether he was worthy, but Jason understood. Lukas and Orpheus were very impressed with the man's humility despite his wealth. They smiled at each other, then joined hands across the table and invited Eustace to join. Jason spoke a prayer as he thanked God for continuing to bless their fellowship. They continued to talk way into the night. Eustace said he would have his stablemen bring another bed to their room tomorrow. The men grew tired, so they finally retired to their room. Jason told Lukas and Orpheus to take the beds, as he settled comfortably into the ample pillows by his table. Jason pulled out a half loaf of bread he had tucked into his tunic and set it upon the table. He nibbled a little before he drifted off to sleep....

In a dream, Jason found himself alone once again traveling upon a road. The road seemed familiar, but strangely the landscape was not. The weather had been cloudy, and it was starting to rain while growing more and more threatening. He noticed a large cave above on a hillside beyond the escarpment. Jason began to climb, as he sought shelter from the storm. With some difficulty he made it to the cave, then entered and sat down. He wondered what had happened to his friends. His self-confidence seemed to have diminished. Although out of the weather Jason disliked the cave; it reminded him of the dark tomb: the lair of Legion. He began to flash back to the attack from the horde of drunken men when he thought he was going to die. He relived the encounter with the Pharisees and Theophanes with the hate-filled faces hurling false accusations. He sensed doubt in the minds of the people who had heard their testimonies; all of these things were making him feel diminished. He began to doubt how effective his ministry could be, for he was a scarred former demoniac. The storm intensified, so

Jason settled in for a long wait. He pulled some bread out of his sack to nibble on.

Suddenly, Jason felt a presence. He didn't feel threatened; he felt no need to pray, or call out to Jesus, so he continued to sit and chew on a piece of bread. Jason was already aware of an impending confrontation, when a cloaked figure emerged from the depths of the cave and approached. He moved his hand near the handle of his sword just in case. The figure walked up and stood before him, but the face was in the shadow of the head covering. Then, delicate hands reached up and pushed back the shroud of the outer garment. The face of a beautiful woman was revealed; the same mysterious woman that had been on the beach and the marketplace when he first arrived in the city. She smiled at him but remained silent. Jason was shocked as he found he was unable to speak. He opened his mouth, but no words emerged. Then he realized he couldn't move either, which distressed him greatly.

"We want to come home, Legion," she said in a very friendly, loving way. She knelt before him and repeated, "We want to come home."

Jason desperately tried to speak or move. He found himself as a dead man, except for his eyes and ears. He became aware that it was a dream, but he couldn't wake himself up. Cold terror enveloped his mind as he realized he was once again a prisoner, like he had been as Legion. The woman in front of him continued to smile, then began to laugh. Her voice changed from a pleasant woman's voice to the deeper, hollow sounding voices he was more familiar with. His spirit thrashed about inside, but his flesh remained dormant. Then, more figures emerged from the depths of the cave, as well as hideous, animal-like creatures. The giants were enormous in stature and spoke in their deep, guttural voices the same as the woman; over and over they spoke, "We want to come home." Jason was terrified as the woman covered her head once again. He looked to see her face, but there was only darkness.

The spirit that had disguised itself as the woman spoke in a deep, echoing voice, "We want to come home, Gadarene!" Jason continued to try every way to break the paralysis of his body. He began to see brief, faded visions of Lukas and Orpheus come in and out of his sight as the giants approached. The creatures started pushing him against the wall of the cave and attacking him with their huge hands and claws. He couldn't speak and he couldn't move. Jason began to silently pray and cried out to Jesus in his mind. Finally, he gathered every bit of strength he could muster and managed to whisper the name, "Jesus." The images of his friend's faces faded in and out, then a distant voice Jason recognized as Lukas called out his name. The storm outside the cave stopped. An immense beam of light shone into the cave. All of the hideous giants and creatures shouted and screamed violently as they fled back into the bowels of the earth. The faces of Orpheus and Lukas came into sharper view and remained. The opening of the cave transformed into the open window of Jason's room.

Lukas and Orpheus were on either side of Jason, for they had been frantically trying to wake him for some time. Jason was at last calm but found himself deeply full of fear. The dream had been so terrifying he was afraid to find himself still in it. The sweat had run profusely down his face; he could feel the dampness in his clothing as well. Jason flexed his fingers, then raised his arms a little and moved his legs. The dream was over, but some of the horror remained. Orpheus and Lukas looked at their friend with concern.

"Are you alright?" Lukas asked as he put his hand on Jason's shoulder. "Had a bad dream, huh," he added.

"I had one the first night after I was delivered, Jason, but I don't think it was as bad as yours. Do you want to talk about it?" Orpheus asked.

Jason responded weakly, "I don't think talking about it will help, Orpheus, but I appreciate you both being there. I feel the same as when Aegeus and his sons rescued me from those drunken fools the other night. No, I'm afraid it was perhaps more than a dream. I need to spend some time alone with God, I think. We have plans with Eustace today; I smell food being prepared. You both get something to eat and see if Eustace is about. I'll be along in a little while."

"Are you sure you're alright, Jason?" Lukas asked as he looked intently at his friend.

"Yeah, I'm well. I Just need some time to pray," Jason said as he forced a smile.

The two men smiled back, then left the room and closed the door. Jason walked over to the window and looked out at the land beyond the Sea of Galilee seeking comfort, as he gazed upon the land where Jesus was most likely walking. Jason would love to be able to seek his advice. He began to pray, and asked God to help him with the scrambled emotions whirling within his heart. The dream was a vicious attack on him in a very personal way. The wicked spirits had revealed they know what hurts, and they made it clear they intend to use it against him. Only God, and apparently these entities were aware of the affection he held deep within his heart for his mystery woman. In his dream he felt as though he belonged in the darkness, even though it was filled with horror and disgust. The most frightening thing about it was the appeal of what was familiar. He couldn't understand it, for it seemed to be something of a deeply spiritual nature. It was all a lie. Jason now had a new life; he had been forgiven. The incredible awkwardness made him feel unworthy.

He cried out to God, then closed his eyes and went silent. Jason dropped to his knees right there beneath the window and stayed there for a long time. He lowered his head as he had done in the presence of Jesus. The room was very quiet, for there was no activity outside. Thoughts began to enter his mind: assurances. He felt confidence begin to take over the gloom. Suddenly, there seemed to be a knowledge that he would never be tempted beyond his ability to withstand it or escape. His friends had been there; friends that he somehow knew God had brought together for his good. From this day forward he would always pray before going to sleep and ask God to protect him. Not having control during the dream showed Jason he couldn't rely upon himself.

He was new at all of this. Jason had learned that if he tried doing things by his own power he would fail quickly. Everything he did henceforth would be done in the name of Jesus. The war he was to wage was not for the minds of men, but their hearts. The battles he was to fight was not against flesh, but powerful spiritual entities and their realms. Jason felt a great burden lifted from him as he continued to pray, and a great relief it was. The dream had taken its toll with a couple of new inward scars added to his collection. He gave thanks to God and rose to his feet. He splashed a bit of water on his face, then ran his fingers through his hair. Jason now felt refreshed and ready to start another day, as he left the room and walked downstairs.

Jason found his two friends sitting with Eustace eating a morning meal; a bowl of hard-boiled eggs, fresh bread, a bowl of chopped vegetables mixed with olive oil to dip in, and bowls of fruit and dates were spread out upon the table. Not only was the food very appetizing, but Jason admired the bowls and plates themselves: dark with geometric patterns. The contrast from his former life enriched him, for the dream had brought back unwanted memories. Jason reclined with his friends. After the greetings he began to partake in the wonderful meal. Jason listened to Eustace continue a conversation he was having with Orpheus and Lukas.

"We were talking about taking a walk into the city later this morning, Jason, but I heard you had a rough night; are you alright?" Eustace asked while looking at Jason with concern.

"I'm fine now, as soon as I came down and sat here it all just seemed to pass away," Jason said with a growing smile. "How would you feel about taking a walk to the river later, Eustace?" Jason asked while looking at his friend across the table.

Orpheus and Lukas smiled at each other, then looked back at Eustace.

"This is a serious matter, Eustace. This is a decision only you can make. Do you wish to accept Jesus as the Son of God and accept the ways of God?" Jason asked and paused briefly. "This is your chance to make that commitment to him," Jason said as he continued to look at Eustace.

Eustace looked away for a moment as he considered the gravity of the decision. He looked back at Jason and said, "I set this day aside for you. Yes, I'm prepared to make this commitment." He again let his gaze trail away, as a look of seriousness slowly turned into a smile.

The four men left the building but paused so Jason could fill his waterskin with fresh water from the well. They left the caravansary compound and walked west along the cobblestone streets into the heart of the City of Emmatha. Jason glanced up at the flat hill on which Gadara stood as he was longing to take a walk up there, but a little apprehensive. He thought to himself that in the next couple of days he would make the trip and face his past. He once again indulged in his daydream of sharing his testimony in the Great Amphitheater of Gadara. Jason thought about the growing fellowship consisting of witnesses to the majesty and authority of Jesus, which made the possibility seem more realistic.

Jason felt very encouraged. A few scattered people the men passed greeted them with waves and smiles, as Eustace was very well known and popular. Jason couldn't help thinking this could benefit his ministry in many ways. It didn't take long to spot a small crowd gathered upon the steps of the Temple of Artemus. They had come to hear the Philosopher Theophanes, for he typically taught daily in the city. The men approached, but Eustace had the idea of walking around the temple to approach from behind the crowd unnoticed. He waited for the long-winded teacher to pause, then shouted a question loud enough to be heard by the crowd, as well as anyone else within a respectable distance.

"What would Epicurus say about false witness?" Eustace shouted as the gathered people turned to look, then parted to clear a visual path between Eustace and Theophanes. The impressive philosopher stood in silence as his face blushed. He looked at the men with no response. Murmuring erupted from the crowd, then went silent upon Jason appearing from behind Eustace. He stepped forward and approached Theophanes while raising his hand and pointing at him.

"Why did you tell all those people in the marketplace that I was going to murder my friend, Eustace? This man is like family to me! How dare you lie, while attempting to cause trouble for me!" Jason shouted with indignation. The confrontation had the entire crowd looking back and forth between him and the philosopher. The murmuring was growing intense, as more of a crowd was gathering. Eustace stepped up beside Jason and put his hand on his shoulder.

Eustace spoke, "This man is my good friend. I trust him a lot more than I trust you, Theophanes! What do your students think of you now? You are a liar!"

The commotion within the growing crowd reached an intensity that brought desperation within Theophanes. Fumbling for something to say, he shouted, "How can you trust these men? You haven't known them that long! This *Jason* is a devil; the Jewish Pharisees said so!"

One man from the crowd shouted, "I remember the morning Jason arrived. He didn't say anything about murdering Eustace, but you did! He asked where to find his establishment, that's what I heard!"

This brought even more commotion from the crowd, which had reached fifty or sixty people.

A woman spoke out. "I've heard of Jason. He was the beast; Jesus healed him! That old man with them was that filthy, crazy beggar from the marketplace! Look at him! He's been restored like Jason! We've seen this with our own eyes! These men are telling the truth!" she shouted which brought more murmuring.

Another man spoke, "I saw Jason healed from a bleeding head wound. The old herdsman, Aegeus, laid his hand on him, then spoke in the name of Jesus and he was healed! The blood disappeared! Jason, we believe you!"

The crowd was still growing, as many were calling out for Jason to tell about Jesus. The chaotic murmuring and shouting were mostly directed at the now disgraced philosopher. He suddenly left and walked at a quick pace down the cobblestone street to the west. A few followed after him, as they ridiculed and shouted profanities at him.

He began to publish in the Decapolis how great things Jesus had done for him: and all men did marvel.

Jason climbed the steps and began to speak, "People of Emmatha and Gadara, hear me! It's all true; Jesus found me, cast multitudes of demons from me and healed me! He walks with me now, in spirit! Jesus is the Son of the one true God! We are going to the river after we leave here, so Eustace can be baptized. Anyone who wants to can be baptized in the name of Jesus for the remission of sins! Don't be fooled any longer by gods made of stone, or teachers that tell lies. Follow us and discover the way to everlasting life! FOLLOW US!" Jason shouted as he descended the steps.

Suddenly, a few people came running up. One said, "Theophanes has fallen! He can't breathe! He's clutching his chest and rolling on the ground!"

147

Without hesitation, Jason ran as fast as he could down the cobblestone street to the west with Lukas close behind. Theophanes didn't make it that far; Jason found him laid out in the street and was struggling to breathe. His face, as well as his hands and feet were turning blue. Jason instantly knelt by the man, then laid hands upon him and cried out for God to restore him in the name of Jesus. The entire crowd had followed and was watching intently. All went silent, except for the fervent prayer of Jason. Theophanes ceased all movement and closed his eyes. Many thought he was dead.

All at once, Theophanes opened his eyes as the normal color returned to his face, and everyone gasped. He looked at Jason with a very confused and troubled expression.

Jason stood up and spoke to Theophanes with compassion, "You've been given another chance, Theophanes. The Lord your God has had mercy and compassion upon you this day; you must repent!" He stood there for a long moment and waited for a response from the disgraced philosopher. Theophanes just lay there avoiding eye contact with anyone. "I pray you think about the opportunity God has placed before you. He will forgive you, if you repent," Jason said, then turned and walked away.

A couple of people stayed with Theophanes. He sat up and looked down at the ground with a very forlorn expression. The rest followed Jason and the other men as they walked down the street to the east.

Lukas walked beside Jason and said, "I think things may have become a bit easier; the truth prevails."

"A few have seen the truth, but there are many we must reach both here and in Gadara," Jason said as he glanced back over his shoulder for a moment.

Jason was stunned, then he turned and walked backward for a moment. He couldn't believe his eyes! There were at least a hundred people following them! Orpheus and Eustace were right behind them, while looking back and smiling themselves. It seemed that the large group was growing exponentially, as there were people joining as he watched. The word was spreading throughout the city! They continued toward the bridge over the Yarmuk River and the spot where Orpheus was baptized. Now, many more were following; Jason's heart was soaring! He thought to himself that the dream last night was intended to hinder him. The Lord God and his truth prevailed. He remembered a thought that manifested at his rebirth: feeling like a seed hidden in a dark cave; Jason was brought forth into the sunlight and flourishing. He thought about the realization of Jesus walking with him in spirit, now more convinced than ever. This scarred, former demoniac was leading a large group into the knowledge of Jesus and eternal life!

Jason was very thankful and offered praise to God. He was thankful for the choice of clothing he made, as his new long-sleeve tunic would cover his scars very effectively. He was prepared to baptize Eustace, but he knew that Lydia and Melina had been invited; therefore, disrobing would not be appropriate. Having prepared for women to be present worked out very well; given the huge crowd of men, women, and children. Jason looked over at Lukas and smiled, then glanced back at Eustace and Orpheus as he gestured for them to come close so they could talk.

"I want you both to join me to baptize all these people," Jason requested.

Orpheus smiled and said, "I thank you for the opportunity to do this, but I hardly feel worthy."

"None of us are worthy without Jesus," Lukas said while looking at Orpheus with a look of sincerity and a touch of newfound wisdom.

Jason looked at Eustace and said, "We may need your help as well, once you're baptized." He chuckled and proclaimed, "There's a lot of people here!"

Eustace responded, "Jason, I've never done this before."

Orpheus spoke, "Lukas and I never have either. You'll have the same experience as us, once you're baptized." He then smiled at Eustace.

Eustace started laughing, which caught on to the other men. Once they calmed, Jason spoke:

"We shall baptize them in the name of Jesus for the remission of sins. Ask each one if they accept Jesus as the Son of God, and that they live for the one true God," Jason instructed them, as he had already thought about what to say to baptize Eustace. He had prayed about it and decided everything he was to do henceforth was to be in the name of Jesus...wisdom he had obtained from a dream.

Something wonderful was happening. The ever-growing crowd had arrived at the escarpment by the arched stone bridge. Jason and his companions looked back upon the large mass that had followed them. It extended all the way back to the last bend in the road! From what the men could see there must have been a crowd of two hundred people that extended beyond the bend, so it was impossible to count. Tears welled up in Jason's eyes as he dropped to his knees and praised God. He didn't realize how the many public demonstrations had affected the hearts and minds of the people, and it spread like wildfire! Jason climbed upon a rock and beheld the people.

He addressed the crowd with a shout, "People of Emmatha and Gadara, welcome! We are here to proclaim to God that we wish to follow him and accept Jesus as his Son! You leave your sins in the water and come out new, like being born again! Eustace is to be the first; follow us!"

The four men led the way, as they treaded down the well-established path to the river; it appeared sparkling and beautiful in the midday sun. Jason and Lukas immediately sat on the bank of the river and removed their outer garments and sandals. Orpheus and Eustace did the same, then all four men waded into the water. The people of the crowd seemed to be organizing themselves to walk down single file upon the narrow path. The majority remained on the road until space was available.

"Looks like we're going to be busy for a while; I don't think you'll have much time for fishing now," Jason said while looking at Lukas with a grin.

Lukas let out a healthy laugh saying, "Yeah, it's like you told me of the disciples of Jesus; he made them fishers of men!"

Eustace was first. The people waited on the bank, for they weren't sure how to proceed, so they waited and watched. Jason got into position beside Eustace.

"Eustace, do you accept Jesus as the Son of God, and agree to follow the one, true, living God from this day forward?" Jason asked.

"Yes, I do," Eustace proclaimed boldly.

"Then I baptize you in the name of Jesus for the remission of sins," Jason said and laid Eustace back into the water. He emerged with a broad smile on his face and raised his arms in praise to God. Everyone that witnessed it applauded and cheered. Following the example of the respected community leader; they came, and they kept coming!

Before long there was a mass of very wet, joyful people. The work continued, but even with Eustace helping they just kept coming. Jason tried to have a personal interaction with each one; men, women, and children. Then, one approached Jason that made him smile and tear up a bit. He said the same as to the others:

"Do you accept Jesus as the Son of God, and agree to follow the one, true, living God from this day forward?" Jason asked.

"Yes, and I repent. I'm very sorry. Just call upon me if there is ever anything I can do to help you," Theophanes said humbly.

"Thank you, my friend. I baptize you in the name of Jesus for the remission of sins," Jason said as he laid the man back into the water. He emerged with a huge smile upon his face, then Jason embraced him. A roaring response of joy, cheering, and applause erupted from all who witnessed it; even more than they offered for Eustace. Theophanes walked away a changed man that day.

Lydia and Melina came also, as Eustace had told them they could take a little time to join them by the river. They were both excited to be baptized. They didn't stay long but enjoyed the time they spent there. Symeon, the man who helped Jason find the caravansary, came also; Lukas baptized him. He greeted Jason, then said he was coming for a visit soon. He told Jason he had writings to show him; something he had been working on. Jason was intrigued and anticipated his visit.

Jason could see after a while that the crowd at the top of the escarpment was thinning out a bit. He had taken a moment to discuss with Lukas how many had come, then asked Orpheus and Eustace as well. They figured roughly three hundred and fifty or so had been baptized that day! Jason was intensely amazed, for he knew it was God. He had touched the hearts of these people. He took a moment to pray and give thanks to God, for he felt like Jesus was there with them.

Jason came to his senses, then realized someone had been waiting for him. He noticed the clothing first, as white flowing fabric caught his eye. He smiled and looked up to greet the person, then was a bit stunned. It was the woman from the beach! She had a big grin on her face as she realized she had surprised him.

"My name is Alethea. I'm glad to finally get a chance to speak with you, Jason. I was hoping you would stop that day in the marketplace, but you seemed preoccupied," she said in a very friendly way.

Jason gulped. She knew his name. Not knowing quite how to respond and with awkwardness to his voice, he said, "Greetings. Are you here to be baptized?"

She giggled a little. "I'm standing in the water next to you, Jason. Yes, I would like very much to be baptized by you," she said while smiling.

"Do you accept Jesus as the Son of God, and agree to follow the one, true, living God from this day forward?" Jason asked as he was a little embarrassed that his voice was wavering slightly.

Althea responded with a smile, "Yes. There's no doubt in my mind from what I saw at the beach and in the marketplace that Jesus is the Son of God. I've defied my family and refused to pay homage to these stone idols. The stories of Jesus that had reached our city made some fearful, but I was hoping he would come. I'm a friend of Melina's; she's my cousin. I've heard all about you, and some of the trouble you've had. You look much better by the way."

Jason was shocked, and in the back of his mind, troubled. He desperately hoped she didn't see his scars. He gently laid his hand on her back and said, "I baptize you in the name of Jesus for the remission of sins." He then laid her back into the water. She smiled and embraced Jason when she emerged.

"I'll be seeing you," she said as she waded back to the riverbank. A friend was there waiting with her dry outer garment.

He watched as they walked away and didn't know what to think. Jason had resigned himself to the belief that a normal life had passed him by. Now, there was more emotional turmoil than he had experienced since his deliverance. He had to admit to himself, that along with his turmoil the encounter left him with great joy in his heart. Jason looked over at his friends. Although he had never shared his innermost feelings about this woman, Alethea, they all grinned at him.

Finally, the last of the eager local people had all been baptized. The four men waded out of the water, then put on their sandals and outer garments. They all sat down for a little while and conversed with a few that had lingered about. It had been a blessed day for all involved.

Lukas said, "I don't feel like fishing. I feel like I would become a fish if I were in there any longer."

Orpheus started laughing and proclaimed, "We've become fishers of men!" He looked at Jason while still chuckling and said, "Jason may have brought in more of a catch than that!"

Eustace said, "We saw what was going on, Jason. I think Alethea's taken an interest in you. She comes to the caravansary occasionally to visit Melina and Lydia; they're all friends. I suspect she might be coming more frequently now based on what I saw."

Jason responded, "I don't know what you're all talking about. I've seen her around, and she seems to know a little about me, so I spoke to her a bit."

Eustace started laughing and said, "We'll see." He continued to chuckle as he got up and prepared to walk back to the caravansary.

The afternoon sun cast a warm glow and long shadows upon the tree-lined road as the men climbed up the escarpment from the river. Eustace seemed more joyful than usual; the baptism had a powerful, life-changing effect upon him. He said it looked like four hundred people had been baptized in the name of Jesus. They all broke into prayer and took turns praising God as they walked.

Jason said, "If God is with us, who could possibly stand against us."

Lukas spoke, "I was taken out of my miserable existence and near death just a couple of days ago. Now I feel truly blessed as I walk with good friends and with God."

Orpheus offered, "My heart has been healed, now I'm walking in power and authority from God, in the name of Jesus."

Eustace said, "I thank God for blessing me and I'm praying to be a blessing to others."

The men walked in true fellowship as they arrived at the caravansary. They entered the courtyard and found themselves hungry and tired. Eustace said, "The evening meal should be coming soon."

The four men were still a bit damp when they entered the community room, so they decided to change before the meal. Eustace invited his new friends into his residence, then supplied clean, dry undergarments for the three other men for he knew they had limited clothing. He supplied Lukas and Orpheus with off-white tunics. Jason had an extra long sleeve tunic he had purchased upstairs in his room. They met back in the community room just as Lydia appeared saying the meal would be ready soon. They returned to their usual table, then reclined and sipped wine until the meal was brought out. Jason was very satisfied, as Lydia had brought the wine and Melina brought two loaves of freshly baked bread.

During the meal, Jason expressed a desire to go into Gadara, since there had been a great success locally. "I feel a need to see my family; it's been a very long time. Perhaps I should go alone, since I'm not sure what I'll find," he said.

Eustace spoke out, "I don't agree with you, Jason. Do you remember a couple of nights ago, what happened when you went out alone? I know we had great success today, but there are still those who fear you and have revenge in their hearts. You've made a lot of friends here, but even in Emmatha I think you should have someone with you."

Lukas said, "I agree, Jason. I would be offended if you wanted to go without me. I'll wait for you outside wherever you go, if you want me to."

Orpheus commented, "I would like to stay around here and build upon what the Lord has begun today. When you and Lukas are in Gadara; Eustace and I will do what we can here. I'm very well acquainted with walking these streets alone. A few of the people today mentioned my testimony. Think of it as spreading out the blessing."

"It's settled then, Jason. All your friends are making good sense. When you're ready, that's the way we'll do it," Eustace said as he returned his focus to his food.

Jason said, "Symeon told me today he's been working on something; I think it's of interest to all of us. He said he would come for a visit soon and I don't want to miss it. I have a feeling it's writings to give us greater understanding. I spoke with him quite a bit when I first arrived; he's a scholar and studies ancient texts."

Eustace quickly swallowed. "You may have another visitor as well," he quipped, then smiled and went back to eating.

Everyone around the table chuckled. Melina was nearby and walked over. "I think you can count on it, Jason," she said, then smiled and walked away.

All of his friends smiled at him, but Jason pretended not to notice as he blushed and continued to eat.

The men decided to walk out into the courtyard after the meal, so they sat around the well to share inner thoughts. The beautiful, clear, starry night provided an excellent forum for their discussion.

The reality had set in that they were being used by God, and a great change was coming to their region. Some had hoped for a miracle, and it seemed to be coming to pass.

Eustace said, "Jason, you not only received a miracle; you bring it with you. Jesus looked me in the eye and told me you were restored, but I was skeptical at first. He not only restored you; I believe he equipped you for this mission. I'm a little overwhelmed by it, but I'm deeply honored to be a part of it."

Orpheus mused, "I heard Jesus was a carpenter's apprentice, then he became a wandering teacher, yet, he is the Son of God. The Lord seems to take the weaker, simple things of this world and uses them to accomplish his will. I'm still trying to comprehend what happened today, and it was led by three former demoniacs and a businessman."

Everyone went silent for a moment, then Eustace started chuckling. They all busted out in laughter.

Lukas proclaimed, "Who cares what we were; it's who we are now!"

"Do you really think she will come and see me?" Jason asked his friends.

Everyone again broke out in fervent laughter as they all got up and prepared to go inside. They reclined around the table and conversed way into the night. Eustace excused himself to go to bed, then the other men retired to their room as well. There were now three beds lined up and all with a view of the large window. The three men were all tired from the day's many activities. Orpheus extinguished the lamps as Jason spoke a prayer asking for God's protection in the name of Jesus. In no time they were all fast asleep. The open window provided a soft glow from the full moon.

Morning came quickly for Jason. He realized he had slept into late morning and was very pleased that no significant dreams came during the night. The horrible nightmare from the previous night had robbed him of rest and was followed by the busy day yesterday. Now, Jason lay there looking at the sunlight beaming in the window and feeling more joy as his thoughts organized; he felt very refreshed. Lukas and Orpheus had already left the room and he was alone. Suddenly, a light knock came upon the door.

"Jason, you have a visitor," a soft female voice announced through the door. It sounded like Lydia.

"I'll be right down," Jason responded as he jumped up and began to gather himself.

Everyone had been poking fun at him the previous night, which made him excited to receive his visitor. He did the best he could to prepare his appearance, then Jason quickly exited the room and descended the stairway. He entered the community room, then saw his friends enjoying the remainder of a morning meal; they waved and greeted him. Then he looked over at the double door entry and beheld his visitor: it was Theophanes. Jason smiled and tried desperately not to show disappointment. He walked over and warmly greeted the now humble man, then gestured to the table so they could join the others. Eustace greeted the visitor with as much grace as he could muster, as did the other two. They had just about finished eating, then Lydia and Melina brought more food and drink for Jason and Theophanes. Shortly after, Eustace announced that the three of them had planned to walk to the marketplace.

"I think you should stay here today, Jason, since your days have been very busy. As your friend, I suggest you take a day of rest," Eustace advised. Orpheus smiled; Lukas nodded and grinned at his friend. They all rose and departed shortly thereafter.

Jason couldn't deny that he had mixed emotions about Theophanes. Some things just take time to overcome. However, he was elated about the apparent transformation; something he could surely relate to. The encounter gave him insight as to the reservations Eustace had regarding him at the beach. The two men were alone, except for a couple of travelers in the far corner.

Theophanes said, "I want to apologize to you personally, Jason, for I did bear false witness against you. My fear led me to assume the worst. I now realize that you're a changed man, as I too have changed. I've made the decision to abandon my studies. I'm seeking wisdom from the ancient scriptures of the Hebrews, for the knowledge of the one, true, living God. You have demonstrated his awesome power; I shouldn't be here. From the bottom of my heart, I thank you."

"I forgive you without reservation Theophanes," Jason replied as he reached out across the table and offered his hand in friendship. "I'm expecting a visit from Symeon soon regarding the scriptures. Do you know him?" he asked.

Theophanes replied, "Yes, I do somewhat, for he has attended a few of my lectures. He's a very bright young man." He asked, "You say he's studying the Hebrew scriptures?"

Jason responded, "Yes, and Symeon said he had something to show me. My friends and I are anticipating his visit. I would like to invite you to come as well; I'm not sure when he's coming, however."

"I will seek him and perhaps join him when he comes," Theophanes reasoned as the two men began eating more than talking.

The remainder of the morning passed quickly. Jason spoke with Theophanes, as well as ministered to him. He was a very intelligent man and curious about his newfound faith. The former philosopher was asking a lot of questions about new emotions and confessing inward struggles with his trained mind. Jason noticed the back-left door open as he listened. He thought it was Lydia or Melina, but it was Alethea. She smiled at Jason, for he was facing that direction. He smiled in return while listening to Theophanes, as he kept talking continuously. Jason felt mixed emotions, since he was very happy with the change in Theophanes; however, a comfort level had been reached, so the intelligent philosopher went from being a wellspring to a deluge. Jason found himself listening only, as Alethea sat quietly at the nearest table to the back-left door. It became apparent through eye communication that Jason and Alethea were patiently waiting for Theophanes to go away. Jason waited for a lapse in his new friend's monologue, which was a long time coming.

Finally, Jason interjected, "You know, I have some things I must attend to. You'll have to excuse me."

The two men arose, but Theophanes just kept talking. Now they were standing, and the monologue continued. Jason glanced over at Alethea, as she seemed to be enjoying his dilemma. Jason slowly moved toward the door, but Theophanes stayed put. Jason tried slowly walking over to face Theophanes closely, then end the encounter with an embrace. When he paused, Jason quickly embraced him and said, "I really have to go."

Theophanes very slowly started making his way to the double door entry, while talking as he moved. Jason was alongside with his hand on Theophane's shoulder while nodding and smiling. He couldn't help but wonder if it were possible to move any slower. At last, the men reached the doors. Jason opened the door for Theophanes. He stepped through but kept talking outside the door. Jason could hear a very faint giggle from within the room, which caused him to struggle to not do the same. At long last, Theophanes promised to return with Symeon as he waved and set off through the courtyard. Jason closed the door, then fell back against it and smiled at Alethea.

She arose and walked over to him. She was wearing the same costly blue outer garment as when he first saw her. They were alone in the community room now. She approached as Jason reached out his hand in a friendly gesture. Alethea ignored it and embraced Jason warmly instead. He never wanted the moment to end. She withdrew, then Jason looked into her big brown eyes and realized his life would never be the same. He sensed she felt the same way. A long moment of silent communication passed. Jason turned, then opened the door a little to peek out and see if anyone was in the courtyard. He opened the door, while gesturing outside as he looked at Alethea. She smiled, then covered her head and passed through the door. Jason followed close behind and suggested they sit by the well to have a conversation.

Jason started with a trace of awkwardness, "So, you recognized me in the marketplace that day? I remember thinking you probably didn't."

"What struck me the most that day at the beach was your eyes," Alethea said as she looked into them. "They are reborn eyes; I'll never forget that. I saw you sitting there with the disciples of Jesus. I could see your heart through your eyes...a pure one," she said.

Jason responded, "I was a bit annoyed, for I could hear my Master being rejected while your companions were looking upon me with fear. You were different; from you I felt compassion and curiosity. I have to tell you that you've been on my mind a lot since then."

"That makes me happy, Jason. I'd like to stay there. You've been touched by the Master's hand, that makes you very unusual and special in this city. I've been hoping to meet someone like you for a long time," she said.

Alethea spoke softly but in a very matter of fact way. Jason was impressed by her insight; her presence was taking his breath away a little. He had a sudden reality check. He wasn't like other men. There was way too much respect for this woman to let it go any further. He had to be honest about his shortcomings.

"I must reveal that I may not be what you think I am," Jason said as he pulled up his sleeves. He then stuck his leg out and pulled up his garments a bit. He looked over at Alethea as he expected to see her grimace. Her smile faded and look of sadness was expressed.

Alethea spoke with compassion, "Oh Jason, I'm so sorry you had to endure the hell you must have had to live with. I've known about your scars from the beginning; you're not as good at hiding them as you think." She reached over and laid her hand upon his. "It's not your scars that brought me here today, but your heart," she said as her smile returned.

Jason was shocked and elated. Could the Lord God be blessing him beyond any expectations? He had never felt so accepted, except in the presence of Jesus. This was different. For the first time ever in Jason's memory he felt like a normal man.

They sat for a long time while conversing and looking into one another's eyes. Then Alethea spoke, "Let me tell you a story. I was a young girl, and my parents and I were traveling back to Gadara from Hippos. We were using an oxcart. My parents were involved in temple worship; they had purchased stone figures there and were transporting them home. On the way back, as my father was driving the ox, my mother and I were riding in the cart. Suddenly, you appeared. Not who you are now, but who we used to refer to as the beast. I've known about your scars since then. Anyway, you didn't hurt anyone, but you totally humiliated my father. I'm not going into any details; I don't remember much. The point is I saw you then, and I saw you at the beach. The sharp contrast demonstrated to me the awesome power of God to restore and to heal. I know you've committed the rest of your life to Jesus; I want to as well. I'm thankful to God and his Son Jesus for bringing you to me. There's no one I would rather spend time with."

Jason quickly looked around to see if anyone was in the courtyard, then leaned over and kissed Alethea on the cheek as tears streamed down his face. Then they embraced for a long time.

Alethea pulled away and said, "Now, I need to be honest with you. I have never in my entire life worshipped these false gods. I can't explain it, but from a very early age I've had knowledge of the one, true, living God. My father's name is Andris. He used to beat me on a regular basis while trying to change my mind, until a few years ago. My parents had my marriage arranged with the High Priest of the Temple of Zeus in Gadara. The wedding was cancelled, since my defiance and my increasing age made me less desirable. I'm thirty-two years old, by the way. My father lost a lot of social status over the matter. My mother died a couple of years ago, and he blames me for that too. As if that wasn't enough, he knows you're here and has a hatred for you like no other. He's my father, but I stopped loving him long ago. I do honor him, but what I'm trying to tell you is I have a lot of scars on the inside as you do, as well as on my back. Now you know all about me. My father, Andris, will try to kill you if he gets the chance."

Jason looked into Alethea's eyes and said, "Nothing could ever tear me from you, now that I've found you. I accept the challenge of your father and pray to see him delivered from the wicked spirits that torment his soul."

Alethea smiled, this time leaning over to kiss Jason on the cheek. She didn't bother to see if anyone was looking. "I love you...I know it sounds strange, but I feel that I always have," she said with a curious expression.

"I love you too," Jason said as he arose, then took Alethea by the hand and she stood up as well. They strolled out of the courtyard and out to the walkway beside the cobblestone street to take a walk together. "I want you to know that I feel the same way; I feel that God has brought us together. It just feels right, like speaking the truth," he said with his voice full of wonder.

Unknown to the happy couple there was someone watching them. Upon a nearby rooftop was one who observed them with sinister eyes; one with deep bitterness in his soul. His name was Andris....

Chapter Five

The Lord Is My Shepherd

It was a typical sunny afternoon in the City of Emmatha for most of its inhabitants, but the lives of one couple had just changed forever. For them the sky was more beautiful, the colors were a bit richer, and the future looked brighter. Jason and Alethea walked along the cobblestone street in front of the caravansary with no destination. The conversation ran deep as they shared their innermost thoughts and feelings. Alethea learned more of the darkness Jason had lived with, as well as the details of his miraculous deliverance. Jason learned of the unhappy life Alethea was living at home, for her father scarcely spoke to her. She would spend as much time away from home as possible; at the marketplace, walking with friends, or an occasional event at the amphitheater. She was hated by many who worshipped in the Greek Temples, for she was seen as an enemy of the gods and cursed. She shared her worst experience with Jason: she was once forced by her father to partake in the festival of Dionysus. The temple priestess and others forced her to drink huge amounts of wine, as well as other activities that went against her nature and beliefs. She cried continuously and was unwilling to partake in the pagan festivities. She was shunned after that, but at least they left her alone. Alethea had never spoken of it until now. Jason had the impulse to be full of anger but sought comforting words for this woman that he loved. He put both hands upon her shoulders and looked into her eyes.

"Your life has changed now. You have Jesus in your life; I think you're stuck with me too," Jason said as he smiled and did his best to reassure Alethea.

"I'm afraid of what my father might do if he finds out about us. Right now, I don't care. I just want to be here...with you," Alethea said as she managed a smile.

"I want you to leave home. I want you to come here and stay with us," Jason said bluntly. He knew about the social requirements of Greek society, but God was above it all. He continued, "I know this is very sudden, but at this moment all I know is God has brought us together. Would you consider becoming my wife?"

Alethea looked at Jason, and she was shocked. Then a huge smile appeared upon her face with tears welling up in her eyes. She jumped at Jason, then wrapped her arms so tightly around him he couldn't breathe. They held each other for a long time. Reality began to set in on Alethea's mind, so she withdrew and spoke:

"My father will never consent to the marriage. He would rather kill us both," she said with great concern, but the joy was overcoming it. She continued to smile.

"I will ask him," Jason said as his commitment came through in his voice. There was no obstacle he was unwilling to face for her. "I will share the truth with him as well!" he said with confidence.

"Be careful, Jason. Take your friends with you. My father is not a good man; I've seen his adversaries disappear. He was of the Temple Guard and has a strong connection with them. He's retired, but still quite active. He's surrounded by them usually; I don't like them at all. They're as rude to me as he is. His house is on the northern side of Gadara. Be careful, Jason; promise me you'll be careful," Alethea said as she took his hands and looked up into his eyes.

Jason responded with great joy, "If God is for us, who can stand against us? Of course, I'll be careful. My good friend Lukas has committed to going with me everywhere. I've been wanting to go to Gadara to seek my family, now I have more business there. I want you to stay here with us; I don't want you to live that way any longer. I don't care what anybody thinks. I'll talk to Eustace and we'll work something out," Jason said. He was so preoccupied with Alethea that he didn't notice Symeon approach.

Symeon smiled and said, "Jason, greetings! I just wanted to come over to see if you were around; I want to come for a visit tomorrow. I need to set a time, for I have things to show you and it will take some time to go through it." It was obvious he wanted to talk about it right there, but he could sense the couple wanted to be alone. "Are you busy tomorrow afternoon?" Symeon asked as he was brimming with enthusiasm.

Jason responded, "Symeon, this is Alethea: a very special friend of mine."

Symeon took her hand and bowed to Alethea. He smiled and said, "Nice to meet you. I've seen you around."

"Yes, I try to stay active around the city," Alethea responded while smiling at his friendly gestures and mild manner.

"Tomorrow afternoon would be fine. I'll be busy for the next couple of days after that," Jason said as he looked over at Alethea and smiled.

"I perceive I've interrupted you; I just wanted to set up a time to meet. I've got a couple of things to do before dark, so I'll see you tomorrow," Symeon said as he waved and bowed a little again in respect to Alethea, then turned and set off to the west.

"I'm glad he set that up for tomorrow. I want to go to Gadara as soon as possible now, but I didn't want to miss an opportunity to learn more about the Hebrew scriptures. The day after tomorrow I'm off to Gadara," Jason said as he smiled at Alethea.

They were at the northwest corner of the building with a perfect view of the Sea of Galilee and what promised to be an awesome sunset. There were a lot of fluffy white clouds which assumed the colors granted them by the orange sun low upon the horizon. The couple was delighted by the colors; yellow, orange, and magenta with traces of crimson upon the crisp edges of the clouds. Alethea told Jason she often escaped the house to watch the sunsets and how she had grown to love them. He smiled at her as he put his arm around her shoulders. She moved as close as possible, then put her head upon his chest. They enjoyed the sunset together. Jason walked her home after that, as darkness quickly approached.

The last vestiges of sunlight illuminated the trees and buildings, while presenting lovely pastel shades of color upon everything as they walked. He wanted to see her safely home, and to see exactly where the house was. Alethea said she would leave and call it an extended stay with Melina; Jason wanted this to be her last night under Andris's roof. Alethea turned and kissed Jason when they arrived close to the house. He held her hands and prayed for God's protection upon her in the name of Jesus. She smiled and said, "Until tomorrow," then turned as she quickly departed and entered the house. Jason hated to see her go in there after what she shared with him. He stood watching for a moment and put the matter in God's hands, then turned and headed back to the caravansary.

The walk back was full of thoughts about Alethea, but also about the meeting tomorrow. He also contemplated a talk he needed to have immediately with Eustace. His life had grown very complex in just one day, but he went forth in confidence for he knew God was with him. He knew that God had brought Alethea into his life. He was very grateful and praised God continuously as he walked. Jason arrived just in time for the evening meal; Eustace, Lukas, and Orpheus were reclining around their usual table and waved. Jason joined them. He didn't know where to start.

"Symeon is coming tomorrow afternoon, and I want all of us to meet with him," Jason said with a huge smile upon his face.

"Also, I had a long conversation with Theophanes, then spent the day with Alethea," he added.

"Well, I said we'll see what happens. We didn't have to wait very long," Eustace said while chuckling as he reached over and patted Jason on the back.

Lukas smiled and said, "I'm glad to see you so happy."

Orpheus nodded to Jason and jokingly asked, "When's the wedding?"

Jason couldn't believe he said that. He looked at Orpheus with a curious expression, then turned his look toward Eustace and said, "As soon as possible." His smile remained, but his eyes were very serious.

Eustace was taking a drink at the time and almost started choking. He set his goblet down as he looked at Jason and thought about what he had just said. Then he started laughing and smacked Jason's shoulder saying, "He's getting us back for poking at him!"

"No, actually I'm dead serious!" Jason said as he was laughing along with Eustace.

Eustace stopped laughing, but his smile remained. "You are serious!" he said as he got up and embraced Jason, then his other friends got up and embraced him also. The evening meal was now a celebration. All of Jason's friends wanted to know what happened. Lydia and Melina walked over and shared in the joy; Melina broke out in tears. Jason looked at her with acknowledgment, for he knew she must be aware of Alethea's troubled life. Jason engaged Eustace in a serious conversation when the excitement faded a bit.

He spoke with determination, "Eustace, I know you must be doubting my reasoning, but there are things in this world that I'm sure of. Jesus is the Son of God. I've been delivered from demonic possession by Jesus himself. Four hundred people were baptized in the name of Jesus yesterday. Now, I'm telling you that God has brought Alethea and I together; I'm as sure of that as these other things. As you know, I'm still trying to learn how to live as a normal man, for there are many things I haven't worked out. I'm asking for your help. The day after tomorrow I'm going to the house of Andris to ask for his daughter's hand; Alethea told me he wants to kill me."

Eustace stated, "Andris is a dangerous man. The Temple Guard have their own society and their own way of doing things. I would have advised you to avoid this situation, but I see it's too late for that." He trailed off for a moment while thinking things over. Then he said, "Of course I will help you; I want to go with you to the house of Andris!" He thought for a moment, then asked, "Have you thought about taking care of a wife?"

Jason responded, "I'm also going to visit my family in Gadara when I go. I have no idea what I will find; I was thinking there may be some help there. I haven't seen them for most of my life. I was wondering if you have something I could do here, but so far my only vocation is to share the message of Jesus."

Eustace said, "You've been quite successful at that, Jason. Perhaps you could become my assistant, since I've thought about hiring one." Eustace was grinning at Jason as he continued, "Yes, I like the idea of you helping me. The business here is quite profitable, but with my responsibilities to the city I get very busy at times. Go and see what your family can do, then we'll talk."

Jason was elated, for his friend was going to help in very tangible ways. "I don't know where to begin to thank you, Eustace. You are a true brother, as with you two," Jason said with a lot of emotion as he looked over at his other two friends.

Lukas and Orpheus had been listening to the conversation and talking among themselves, while trying to think of helpful ideas.

Lukas proclaimed, "One thing I know for sure: I'm going with you to see this *Andris*; I'm not letting you out of my sight. I would have no life had you not been obedient to God and come back for me. I will lay down my life defending you, Jason." Lukas stood up and pulled his garment aside slightly: a new sword hung by his side.

"The same goes for me, Jason!" Orpheus stood up and revealed a new weapon as well.

Eustace explained, "Yes, I've equipped Lukas and Orpheus to protect themselves and you, Jason, that's one of the reasons we went to the marketplace today. I also want you to know that I'm aware of the way Andris has treated Alethea over the years. I want her to come here to the caravansary and stay with us. She can stay with Melina in her residence until the wedding, then we'll figure it out from there."

Jason was absolutely shocked. Lydia and Melina were listening with smiles and tears. They embraced each other, then came over and took turns embracing Jason.

Jason said sheepishly, "Uh, she'll be here tomorrow. She's calling it an extended visit with Melina; I couldn't let her continue to live in that house."

Eustace let loose with his healthy laughter and said, "Of course you couldn't! It means a lot to me that you felt comfortable enough to invite her. You are my true brother!" Eustace got up and embraced Jason again. Lukas and Orpheus got up also and extended their hands. The four men locked hands in a four-way handshake, which had become a symbol among themselves of their fellowship.

Jason spoke a prayer and asked for protection and assistance to go against the spiritual wickedness they were to face. All the men joined in agreement, then offered thanksgiving and praise to God that went on for some time. No one noticed Eustace disappear briefly. He returned from his residence and handed Jason a leather pouch, which contained twelve gold coins. Jason didn't know what to say.

Eustace said, "Remember your first day here, Jason? You said there was something you had to do; you felt God was leading you. That's what this is: it's a wedding gift from your new family."

Jason began to weep. Eustace, Lukas, Orpheus, Melina, and Lydia stood around him, as they placed their hands upon his head and back. Jason felt another presence there as well. Some time passed with no words spoken, for the love in the room was beyond words. The cares wrought by the day faded, and everyone fell into a very peaceful sleep that night....

Jason awoke in the middle of the night and walked over to the window. It was a dark night, for the moon had not risen and the stars were shining brightly. He glanced over at his friends sleeping, then realized he was in a dream; his bed was occupied also. Jason instantly cried out to God, in the name of Jesus for protection. Suddenly, there was a dim light in the room, though no lamps were lit. There was a strange figure by the door with his head covered and the face obscured. He was wearing a typical outer garment, but nothing unusual. Jason once again invoked the name of Jesus to stand against wickedness. The figure walked over to stand next to Jason by the window and looked out. Jason was not afraid, however, and looked out of the window as well. He felt as though the strange uninvited guest belonged there.

"Nice view," the stranger commented while looking out across the darkened landscape. His voice was very soothing but powerful. "Keep speaking the name of Jesus, as you always do," he said.

"Who are you?" Jason asked the stranger as he glanced over but was unable to see his face.

The stranger responded, "I am one who is concerned with the spirits of men. Your beautiful repentance has given you a bit of distinction. The Almighty God is with you. Pave the way for the Lord Jesus to return." The stranger continued to look out of the window as he spoke to Jason.

"I'm facing a lot of challenges," Jason said as he simply gazed out of the window with the stranger as if passing the time with a friend.

The stranger spoke, "Do not fear men, or what they can do to you; fear God! He is with you. I cannot tell you much of what is to come. A few days ago, you made the decision to disregard your personal feelings and be a blessing to others. I will tell you that Alethea is your chosen helper. She will always be a comfort and a blessing to you. God has given you your heart's desire, for you were willing to abandon it. You already knew that. The people God has put into your life truly love you; they are your new family. You already knew that too. You are seeking the ways of God; not the ways of men, nor the things they seek. You have knowledge most men do not have, and it is a burden upon you. Ask God to help you carry it. Use it wisely. The words you are to receive this day will strengthen you."

"What will I find in Gadara?" Jason asked, for he was unashamed to take advantage of the incredible insight of the stranger.

"You will find your immediate future, but I can tell you no more. Trust in the Lord God always no matter the circumstance," the stranger said.

Suddenly, Orpheus walked up to Jason and put his hand on his shoulder. The level of light began to increase in the room. The stranger faded as the light increased.

"Remember, trust God no matter the circumstance!" the stranger said before he faded from view....

It was morning, as Orpheus gently pushed on Jason's shoulder to wake him. He said, "Something smells very good downstairs; just waking you to see if you wanted to go down with us."

Jason opened his eyes and was surprised he hadn't seemed to have left his bed all night. He needed a little time to process the dream while it was still fresh in his mind. "Let me lay here a few moments...I'll be along shortly," he said as he smiled at Orpheus, and also acknowledged Lukas across the room with a wave.

"Did you have a good night's sleep? I think we both did, that was the best I've slept ever!" Lukas said as he walked over to Jason's bed and put his hand on his shoulder.

"Yeah, I did sleep well since you mention it; I feel very refreshed," Jason commented. He didn't share the dream, as he felt it was something for him only. "Yeah, I'm getting up; I'll go down with you," he said as he sat up. Jason decided he didn't need a lot of time, that dream would be with him always. The refreshed feeling made him anxious to start the day.

The three men got themselves together and went down to the community room, where the morning meal was in progress. There were a lot of people, for all the tables were occupied except for their usual table. Before the men settled down a call came from across the room, "Jason!" All three men looked over toward the corner by the back-left door, and familiar faces smiled back. It was Aegeus, his sons, and a very beautiful elder woman. They walked over to the table, as Aegeus stood up and embraced Jason. He then introduced his new bride.

"Jason, meet Calista, my wife," Aegeus said as he stepped aside to reveal Calista standing behind him. She appeared to be the epitome of a wealthy Greek woman with status and sophistication. Her appearance was very pleasant; dark dressed hair with hints of gray, beautiful brown eyes and a hearty, friendly smile. She wore a light blue chiton and a very ornate darker blue outer garment with a lot of embroideries. She had beautiful rings upon her fingers, as well as necklaces and earrings. Jason bowed while gently touching her hand, as did his friends. They were all very impressed by the wife of Aegeus. Jason introduced Lukas and Orpheus to the family as well. Aegeus suggested they join them, so they all reclined around the back table as Melina brought more food and drink. She smiled at Jason in a special way, then disappeared through the back door. Jason sat next to Argus, as he playfully wrestled with him a bit.

Aegeus spoke, "We're on our way out to the Galilee beyond the sea; just arrived early this morning. I decided camels were the best way to travel, for a family camp is a lot more than a herdsman's camp. We're set to travel long distances for some time if need be. All of us are yearning to be in the presence of Jesus and hear his teaching."

Jason was anxious to tell Aegeus about his betrothal, when suddenly the back door opened. Alethea appeared with two loaves of bread, followed by Melina and Lydia. Jason was blessed to see her, as she wore the same white head covering as the other women. To Jason she was the most beautiful woman in the world. She walked around the table to him and set the bread on the table.

Jason stood up, then put his hand on her shoulder and said, "Aegeus, everyone, I want you to meet Alethea. We're going to be married." Alethea looked at Jason with a big smile.

Aegeus stood up, as did all, then took her hand gently and greeted her with a bow. "I'm very happy for you Jason; it seems God is richly blessing you!" he exclaimed with joy.

"Yes, I think he is," Jason said as everyone at the table showed affection toward Alethea with embraces and bows. She then excused herself, as she told Jason that she was now working there.

"Enjoy yourself. I'll be back," Alethea said as she disappeared through the back door.

Calista spoke, "I've been wanting to meet you, Jason, ever since Aegeus told me the tale. You're becoming famous; I can see that you have truly been touched by the Master's hand. I, like many others have waited a long time for the truth to come to Gadara. You see, I believe in the one, true, living God. When Aegeus came to faith it was a blessed answer to prayer. I loved him, and I trusted him to turn my sons into men, but his spiritual emptiness made a deep relationship impossible. That is until Jesus cast your demons into that dreadful herd of swine. Your demonstration of the power of God to heal and restore has brought this family together."

"Jesus is the blessing, for I am nothing," Jason said as the words of Calista brought back the origins of his new life as if it were yesterday. "All glory and honor belong to God," he added.

Calista responded, "Yes, I know, but I want you to know how special you will always be to this family; I want to show you something." She pulled out a gold chain from around her neck with a gold coin affixed to it. Calista continued, "When you gave this it came out of your heart; I know you don't have much. It has become one of my most prized possessions." She put the necklace back beneath her clothing, then said, "I'm a very wealthy woman, Jason, but that gift transcends earthly value. Since you've announced your wedding, what I'm going to do is even more appropriate." Aegeus smiled, then reached into his bag and pulled out a small leather pouch. He set it down in front of Jason. Everyone at the table looked at him, smiling. He picked up the pouch, and it was very heavy. Calista smiled broadly and said, "I think you will find you no longer have to worry about how to fund your ministry, Jason. We're here for you, if you ever need anything."

Jason was, again, at a loss for words; his tears said it all. "Thank you, so very much!" he managed to get out. Calista stood up, then came around and embraced Jason, as well as the rest of the new family.

Most of the morning crowd began to thin out, but the group at the back table remained. Lukas and Dimitri were involved in a deep conversation, as they seemed to have become fast friends. Orpheus and Aegeus were having a conversation as well. Jason wondered where Eustace was, then Alethea told him he was off on business as she passed by. Calista asked Jason to walk with her in the courtyard, and Argus joined them.

"I want you to pray for our journey, and over our camels and supplies," Calista requested as she gestured to the arched stall which contained their animals.

Jason smiled, then walked up to the camels and pet one on the neck. He prayed, "Lord God, in the name of Jesus, I pray you would protect and bless this wonderful family as they go to seek your Son and his teaching. I pray you would drive away any wickedness that would hinder their devotion to you and bring them back safely in the name of Jesus." He put his hand on Argus's head and prayed, "Again, Lord, I pray protection upon this one, that his heart is guarded against any deception, that the spirit of wisdom and discernment come into his mind and his heart in the name of Jesus." Jason continued to pray until he saw Symeon and Theophanes enter the courtyard. They were both carrying scrolls.

"Behold, these men bring the word of God," Jason proclaimed to Calista and Argus as the two men approached.

Symeon and Theophanes smiled and greeted the best they could, for both had full arms. Jason sought to relieve their burden a bit by taking some of the scrolls from Symeon who seemed to have the most. They quickly went into the community room. Jason gestured to the first right table, as it had been unused. The men unloaded their scrolls and reclined. The room was empty for the moment, except for Aegeus, Dimitri, Lukas, and Orpheus still conversing at the back table. The room had mostly been put in order. Jason excused himself for a few moments, then stopped at the back table to invite Aegeus and Dimitri to the meeting. He then slipped through the back-left door. He found the women in the back room as they were washing things and preparing food. Melina saw Jason coming and told Alethea to take a rest. She smiled at Jason and the two went out back.

Alethea embraced Jason, then spoke, "I no longer have a home with my father. He saw us together yesterday; he must have followed me. I left early this morning, and he told me never to come back. I'm a little frightened, but I trust God and I trust you." She embraced Jason again, then continued, "You said yesterday I was stuck with you; looks like you're stuck with me too."

"Consider this the first day of your new life; with me and your new family," Jason said as he pulled away just enough to look into her eyes, then kissed her.

She started to weep and said, "Andris said he would never give his blessing. He called me an old maid; he called you a beast." Alethea looked Jason in the eyes and said, "My father is convinced that Zeus had empowered him to take revenge upon you; I'm afraid for you...for us!"

Jason spoke with boldness, "Zeus was nothing more than a hybrid freak that never should have been, as well as these other *gods.* They're dead and exist only as evil spirits upon the earth. I carry the knowledge and authority of Jesus to trample on such entities. Fear not, dear Alethea, what God has put together let no man put asunder. We will be married soon, whether we have your father's blessing or not."

Alethea responded without words. She gave Jason a huge smile and then kissed him. Jason then indicated he needed to get back to his guests, so they went back in. Jason returned to the community room, after a little light conversation with the women. He entered the room as Eustace came in through the front doors and waved. Everyone had congregated around the front table.

Symeon addressed the gathering, "I'm very happy that so many of you have gathered to hear this. I became aware of Jesus visiting our shores, then began to search the ancient Hebrew scriptures. I think you'll agree, what I found is amazing. I'm going to start with the book of Enoch. He was the seventh generation from Adam and Noah's great-grandfather. This is a section of the text called *The Book of Parables:* "

"There I beheld the Ancient of days whose head was like white wool, and with him another, whose countenance resembled that of a man. His countenance was full of grace, like that of one of the holy angels. Then I inquired of one of the angels, who went with me, and who showed me every secret thing, concerning the Son of man; who he was; whence he was; and why he accompanied the Ancient of days. He answered and said to me, this is the Son of man, to whom righteousness belongs; to whom righteousness has dwelt; and who will reveal all the treasures of that which is concealed: for the Lord of spirits has chosen him; and his portion has surpassed all before the Lord of spirits in everlasting uprightness. "

Symeon then said, "I believe that Jesus is the Son of man, as spoken of in this ancient text. I understand he refers to himself as the *Son of man.* There's more, this is the book of the Prophet Isaiah. He lived seven hundred years ago. There are several prophecies here about the Messiah." He continued to read many passages:

"Therefore, the Lord himself will give you a sign; Behold, a virgin shall conceive, and bear a son, and shall call his name Immanuel. "

"For unto us a child is born, unto us, a son is given: and the government shall be upon his shoulder: and his name shall be called Wonderful, Counselor, The mighty God, The everlasting Father, The Prince of Peace. "

"And therefore, shall come forth a rod out of the stem of Jesse, and a Branch shall grow out of his roots: And the spirit of the Lord shall rest upon him, the spirit of wisdom and understanding, the spirit of counsel and might, the spirit of knowledge and of fear of the lord."

Symeon read the scroll, then paused for a moment and said, "There's a story I've heard a few times out of Nazareth. Jesus was reading the scroll in the synagogue there. They read systematically and were reading from the prophet Isaiah. He stepped up to read, and the set place was as follows:"

"The Spirit of the Lord is upon me, because he hath anointed me to preach the gospel to the poor; he hath sent me to heal the brokenhearted, to preach deliverance to the captives, and recovering of sight to the blind, to set at liberty them that are bruised, to preach the acceptable year of the Lord."

Symeon continued, "Jesus closed the book and sat down, after he had read this. He then said unto them, *'This day is the scripture is fulfilled in your ears.'* Nazareth is the hometown of Jesus. Many there would not accept his authority, for they had known him as a boy, I suppose. Anyway, here comes the good part. After accusing Jesus of blasphemy; a group of men laid hands upon him, then carried him out of the Synagogue, and went to throw him off a cliff. He disappeared! I don't know how, but he vanished when they got to the edge of the cliff. I've heard this from many unrelated sources. This *Jesus* is the Son of God, and the proof is right here in the scriptures! I've been going through this for days. I've found many references; way too many to be by chance. Some of these scrolls I'm leaving with you, Jason."

Jason had been listening intently, but also examining a scroll. He looked up, then smiled and walked over to embrace Symeon. He said, "Thank you so much. I have a good idea of how valuable these are." Jason quickly realized the word of God contained within the scrolls could help demonstrate what he knew to be true. An obvious question arose in Jason's mind. He asked, "If all this evidence is available within these texts, then why do the Pharisees deny Jesus as the Son of God?"

Symeon responded, "That is a good question, my friend…I don't have an answer, but that's a good question."

The reading of the scrolls went on throughout the afternoon. Everyone was deeply enthralled with interest as they learned more and more. The two scholars attempted to introduce as many topics as possible. The Prophecies of Jesus; the stories of Abraham, Moses, Elijah, and the Babylonian conquest through the writings of the Prophets Daniel and Jeremiah. Alethea was there also, as she was told to take the remainder of the day and spend time with Jason. They were soaking up all that they could, as they sat together both listening and reading for themselves. Jason's friends were quite impressed with his knowledge and understanding. He engaged with Theophanes and Symeon in several deep conversations about interpretation. Both men had very disciplined minds and were thrilled by Jason's point of view.

He had knowledge from years of living with wicked entities that were, however, extremely intelligent. It was a heavy burden that Jason relied upon God to help him carry. Also blessed were Aegeus and his family, as they felt God had planned for them to be there to receive the word before they departed to seek Jesus. Orpheus and Lukas were listening intently. Lukas confided in Jason that he couldn't read, but Jason said he would teach him. Orpheus could read Greek and was examining some of the scrolls for himself. Eustace seemed to be blessed that this sharing of knowledge was taking place in his establishment, so he asked Symeon if they could meet regularly. Symeon was excited and said certainly, whenever they could get everyone together.

It came time for the evening meal. Alethea excused herself to help prepare the food, then returned and said Melina and Lydia wanted her to sit with Jason and enjoy, for there was a light presence for the meal. Aegeus and his family were the only patrons at the caravansary currently. Symeon and Theophanes wanted to stay for the meal and the fellowship; still, there were only three tables in use. Jason indicated that he wanted to walk out into the courtyard with Alethea, then the two slipped out to have a few quiet moments. The sunset was approaching and the colors in the sky warmed their hearts. There was a scant amount of white clouds that assumed color, but it was beautiful. It was one of the first things they discovered they had in common.

"I want you to know that my faith has grown today, Jason. I'm very happy and I feel good about you going to see my father; I'm trusting God to keep you safe. I'll be praying for you going to see your family. It must be difficult for you," Alethea said as they sat down by the well. The spot was special to them, for it was there that both realized they were in love.

Jason spoke, "I'm a bit apprehensive about my family. I don't know what to expect. Something inside tells me I will find something pertinent to our future, but I'm not sure what that means. It's been twenty-five years; my parents will be old. Even my sister was several years older than I. I'll be glad to go, so I can find out. The house and property are just outside Gadara to the south a bit. I'm going there first, then to see your father. Lukas, as well as Eustace and Orpheus are going with me. I'd ask Aegeus and Dimitri to go too, but they're leaving in the morning."

"That makes me feel a lot better," Alethea said as she reached over and took Jason's hand. Then she continued, "I would go with you if I could; Andris told me never to come back, so I don't think my presence there would help." She thought for a moment, then asked, "You said his permission didn't matter, but our culture would question the legitimacy of our marriage if he doesn't consent; you know that don't you?"

"What is our culture?" Jason asked. "We are members of a new culture. God has brought us together, so I could care less what

Pagan Greek culture has to say about that," he stated. "Are you concerned?" he asked.

"No, and for the same reasons you just said," Alethea replied. She smiled, then leaned over and kissed Jason on the cheek. "I feel as strongly as you that God has brought us together. Whatever this new culture, as long as the followers of Jesus would recognize us, that's all that matters," she said.

Jason proclaimed, "As long as God approves, that's all that matters. I want to do it as soon as possible; I want us to be married right here in the community room. Eustace is a city official, so he can perform the ceremony." Jason was getting excited, as was Alethea.

Alethea said, "I still feel good that you're going tomorrow; to try to talk to my father and do what's right for our traditions. But if things don't work out it doesn't matter…I love you."

"I love you too," Jason said as he gave Alethea a kiss on the cheek. He continued, "We should get back in; I'm hungry." He stood up and offered Alethea a hand, then sniffed the air a couple of times which made her giggle. "Yeah, I think they're serving the meal just about now," he said with a grin.

Alethea giggled again when they walked through the entry doors, for Jason was correct. It would always be a private joke between them. Aegeus waved and gestured to space at his family's table, then Alethea and Jason joined them. Symeon and Theophanes sat at his usual table and were engaged in conversation with Eustace, Orpheus, and Lukas.

Calista spoke to Alethea, "You're going to be a very beautiful bride, Alethea. I pray that God richly blesses you and Jason as you start out together. We're just starting out too, but we've both been married before. It's obvious that you two love each other; I've been watching." Calista looked at the couple with a big smile.

Alethea responded, "I thank you, for everything. I think I'm very fortunate; I've been waiting for him all of my life." She held Jason's hand, then looked over and smiled at him.

Aegeus spoke, "I want you to know how much knowing you has blessed me, Jason. Jesus performed the miracle, but you've demonstrated the miracle to me over and over with your *humanity*." A tear welled up in Jason's eye. Aegeus continued, "I owe where I am now to you, for I saw you and fought you before; it wasn't you, as I now know. I will tell you this: I think anyone who encountered the *beast* would be at a loss if they tried to identify you. There is absolutely no similarity. I know you carry scars, so do a lot of people, but I was unwilling to acknowledge you as a human before your deliverance. Now, you're an example to us all," Aegeus said as he put his hand upon Jason's shoulder.

Argus came around to sit between Aegeus and Jason saying, "I want you to come with us. I want you to become part of our family, Jason." He looked up at Jason with hope in his eyes. Alethea was touched, as she looked around Jason to smile at Argus, for he was speaking directly from his heart.

Jason spoke, "You know, Argus, Jesus has given me work to do here, but I want you to know something. Your father and I are spiritual brothers, that makes me your uncle. That won't change just because you're going away for a while; you're going to meet Jesus!"

Argus smiled broadly, and from that moment on Jason would always be *Uncle Jason* to the boy.

Jason said, "Aegeus, I know you're leaving in the morning, but I want you to be a part of our fellowship here. If you get to speak to Jesus face to face; tell him that I'm doing the best I can to fulfill what he asked me to do. Tell him that he would be received differently, if he came back. Tell him I'm learning." Jason extended his hand and Aegeus clasped it firmly.

Aegeus said, "Thank you, Jason, for I'm very honored to be a part of your fellowship. I shall carry your words to the Lord himself. I heard of the baptisms; I would have come, if I had known."

Jason responded, "I recommend you go to the Yarmuk River before you depart the Decapolis. I want to baptize you and your family in the name of Jesus for the remission of sins. I can do it in the morning before you leave, if you want me to."

Aegeus quickly agreed, "We will do it, what a wonderful way to start our Journey! Now, I'm glad we missed the large baptism. I feel very good about you doing it personally." Aegeus looked around the table and received nods and smiles from his family.

The evening wore on until everyone was ready to get a good night's sleep, for tomorrow was to be a very busy day for all of them. Symeon and Theophanes departed; Aegeus, Calista, and their sons retired to their rooms, and Alethea went to sleep in Melina's room. The four men sat a bit longer to discuss the day ahead. Jason informed them he wanted to find his family first. Eustace assured him that they were there for him, whatever came their way. Eustace retired to his residence; Jason and the others to theirs. The men were tired and went to bed right away. Jason lay there for a while, as he wrestled with distant memories and wondering what to expect. He pondered what his encounter with Andris would be like as well. He prayed, while trusting God as he had been advised. Jason gave God thanks for a great many things, then fell asleep.

The morning sun was breaking over the ridgeline, which sparked dramatic colors in the sky. There were still a few clouds as there had been at sunset the night before. Jason cherished the sight even though he was quite preoccupied with the day's events ahead. They went back to the caravansary briefly, so Jason could change out of his wet tunic. He wore the old tunic that he had received from Simon to baptize Aegeus and his family, then changed into one of his newer ones. Jason prayed for the safe journey of the family again, and it was an emotional farewell. Aegeus and his new family also prayed for Jason and the others, for Jason had shared with Aegeus what they were facing. He and Dimitri offered to help, but Jason said they had enough; more might be trouble.

The four men walked the eastern road into Gadara. It didn't take long to ascend the hill; the first building was the huge Roman bath house just up the street from the amphitheater on the east side of the city. It seemed to be a popular meeting place in the morning, as there was many walking around it and lounging on the steps. Jason had distant memories of going to this one with his family. He didn't think much of it at the time, but now he felt a bit awkward. Many of the people lounging on the steps were completely unclothed and smiling at the men as they walked by. Jason could only think of his natural state before his deliverance. Now, he was quite modest, which came instantly when Jesus cast out the demons. He couldn't resist the opportunity.

Jason addressed the people loudly, "I have come to share my testimony. Several days ago, the Lord Jesus delivered me and healed me from a lifetime of demonic possession. Now, I seek to follow his ways: the path of righteousness! God will cleanse you of all wickedness and heal your mind, if you repent of your sins. You can be set free; God will restore within you a right spirit! Seek the way of the one, true, living God, and he will fulfill the desires of your heart! Repent, and God will forgive you!"

Many of the people jeered him, while hurling insults and defending their gods. Two women and a man started dancing and smiling at the men who refused to look. A small group covered themselves and listened. Jason told them about the scripture reading that would soon be available at the caravansary. He also spoke about the four hundred who were baptized a couple of days ago. One of the women listening asked when the scriptures would be read. Jason told her a time wasn't determined yet but ask at the establishment in a few days for a time. She said she would, for she was intrigued with Jason's sincerity and bold statements. Five or six showed interest in what Jason was speaking. The remainder were increasingly belligerent and lewd, so the men walked on.

"That was interesting," Lukas commented while glancing back as the fading insults followed them down the street.

"At least you didn't have to worry about concealed weapons, Jason," Orpheus said, then chuckled as he walked.

Eustace spoke, "They are set in their cultural traditions; naturally they're going to resist new ideas. I must confess, Jason, I was a bit embarrassed when you began to speak. I'm a civic leader, and my mind automatically shifts to the status quo. I'm embarrassed at myself for thinking that way, now that it's behind us. I haven't developed the boldness you operate in."

Jason responded, "Yeah, six or so seem to have been reached. It would be worth the effort if only one repents. My boldness comes from Jesus; something that set in when I sat at his feet. He is the only way to eternal life. I'm finding that people's spirits seem to be yearning for something more, so it's their spirits I speak to. I try to, anyway, that group was sort of distracting." Jason looked over at Eustace with a grin. "Alright, I'll try to preach to people that have clothes on in the future," he added. That made Eustace break out in laughter, as well as the other two.

The men decided to stop at the amphitheater to the right, as a scant number of people were sitting on the seats of the quiet theater. It was a good place to take a rest and a small morning meal. Eustace, Lukas, and Orpheus sat nibbling on dates, while Jason pulled out a half loaf of bread.

"What is it with you and bread?" Lukas asked.

Jason responded, "It goes back to your new day! I've been craving fresh bread ever since I lay in wait to pounce upon you and pray for you. The bread I used for bait was ruined, that's why we ate dried out remnants that night. Also, Alethea baked this special for me to bring today."

"Why didn't you just bring two loaves that day, Jason?" Lukas asked.

Jason didn't answer; he just looked at Lukas with a curious expression.

Suddenly, a young couple approached the four men. "Jason!" the man shouted his name in greeting. "We were at the baptism; we're very happy to see you!" he said. The couple were warmly greeted by the four men, then sat with them. Jason told them they were planning to have scripture reading at the caravansary, but no time had been set up yet. The couple seemed to be excited about it. They were spoken to by all the men and were greatly encouraged. The woman said they had been sharing the experience, which pleased Jason. Before long, Jason stood up and requested they move on, for he was anxious to see the home he left so long ago. They bid the couple farewell, then Jason led the men off to the south. They walked away from the City of Gadara into an area of small farms and houses.

"It's not much farther; just over this hill," Jason said. He walked toward what he hoped was an aging couple ready to receive the truth. When they reached the top of the hill, what Jason saw made his heart sink. There was the house, as well as the orchard and the vineyard in an obvious state of long-term neglect. The four men approached an arched entryway to what was a garden in front of the house. It was covered in creeping vines, as was the house and the stone walls around the property. The stone house seemed intact, though in a state of disrepair. The front door was open, so they entered and found the residence was occupied. A startled young man was sitting in an improvised camp in the main room. Jason knelt to speak with him:

"Who are you?" Jason asked.

"I was told by Damon that this house was vacant," he responded while pointing to the adjacent property. Jason remembered Damon: a neighbor and an acquaintance of his father when he was a boy.

"What is your name?" Jason asked again trying not to frighten the man.

He replied, "I am Linus. I've been working for Damon sometimes. He told me this house has been vacant for a long time and that it would be alright to sleep here."

"What of the people that lived here?" Jason asked.

"I don't know. Damon said nobody lived here. I don't know anything about people living here," Linus answered. It was obvious he was concerned about being thrown out; it was also clear he didn't know anything about Jason's family.

"Don't worry. You're not in any trouble; we're trying to find out what happened. I used to live here long ago. We'll go speak to Damon," Jason said as he looked up at the other men.

Jason and his companions walked through a meadow and over to the house of Damon. Jason knocked upon the door. An elderly man answered flanked by his wife. He looked the men over, then asked what business they had with him.

Jason inquired, "I'm here to ask about the property next to you. What happened to the family that lived there?"

"What business is that of yours?" the man asked as he seemed bit suspicious of their intentions.

"That was my family; I've been gone for twenty-five years," Jason responded.

"You're Jason?" the man asked and seemed a little shocked. "I remember you. You became troubled and left. Your parents grieved for you a long time, that I remember," he added.

"What happened to them?" Jason asked firmly.

Damon responded, "They both died. Your mother died about fifteen years ago; your father about seven years back. Your sister got married and moved to Athens while your mother was still alive, and she's never been back. Your father died a lonely old man; he blamed himself for what happened to you. In the end, I think I was the only person he confided in. They stopped worshipping in the temples shortly before your mother died."

Jason said nothing. He walked over where he could see his former house. Tears welled up in his eyes as his friends gathered around him.

Damon spoke again, "Are you really Jason? I've heard some awful stories."

Jason turned and responded, "Yes, I'm Jason. I've been delivered from a lifetime of demonic possession by Jesus of Nazareth who is the Son of God. I've returned home to share this, as requested by Jesus himself."

"I've heard of Jesus; I've been curious about him. You know him?" Damon asked.

"Yes, I do. I would love to share knowledge with you, but my friends and I have a very busy day; I will return to speak with you about it if you desire," Jason offered.

Damon answered, "Well, yes, that would be wonderful. I suppose we're neighbors, if you're here to stay. Your father told me before he died, that if you ever returned the property is yours. You are the sole heir, for he recorded it so."

Jason was speechless. He asked Damon if his friends could linger a while so he could walk back to the house. He wanted to spend some time alone with his memories, so Jason slowly walked back to say goodbye. He asked Linus to take a walk when he encountered him, so he could be alone. Jason informed him that he was the owner of the house. Linus didn't speak; he just nodded and quickly departed. Jason walked through the house and chose to dwell on the memories he had as a young child, but not the troubled years. He stood and looked around the house; the large main room, as well as the wooden stairway to the upper level, where the bedchambers were. The side and front windows, where he used to look out; the back rooms, where he spent time with his mother. He now knew that his parents loved him, although when he became demon possessed there seemed to be no love between them. Oh, how he wanted to be able to go back in time, if only for a moment.

Jason remembered helping his mother prepare food and taking long walks with his father. Walking through the rooms brought the memories back into sharp focus. He would smile, then start weeping uncontrollably. He was told by Damon that his father blamed himself. He spoke out loud, "No, father, it wasn't your fault; the wicked spirits you worshipped were at fault." He thought of his sister and prayed for her. He spent some time walking through, as he realized everything would have to be removed. One thing that encouraged him: there were no idols in the house. He clearly remembered many, as well as in the garden around the house, but he saw none. "Mother, father, did you find truth in the midst of your sorrow?" he asked out loud, as if he somehow expected an answer. He cried out for God's mercy, for himself and his family. He found himself grieving deeply but understood that he had other concerns of the here and now; not the long-dead past. He gathered himself and started walking back to Damon's house. Jason saw Linus standing beyond the arched stone gate and called him over.

"You can go back in, Linus. Wait there, and I will come and speak with you before I leave," Jason said as he detected a look of hope upon the face of Linus. Jason smiled at him and walked away.

His companions stepped up and took turns embracing him. All were expressing condolences for his loss. Jason had just found out he is a property owner, although deeply saddened by the demise of his family. While Orpheus and Lukas were embracing him and patting him on the back, Eustace spoke:

"Jason, that property has a lot of potentials. We can all help you get it in order. It has an orchard as well as a vineyard, and the house just needs a little fixing," Eustace said while looking toward the house and property.

"There's a winepress in back of the house as well, or so there used to be," Jason commented.

"I can't wait to get started on it, Jason," Lukas said while looking over at the property.

"The blessings continue, Jason. What are the chances of inheriting a nice property like that right after proposing marriage to Alethea?" Orpheus asked as he looked over at the property also.

"Your absolutely right," Jason said as he knelt and offered a prayer of thanksgiving and praise to God.

"What of Linus?" Damon asked. "I have a man temporarily sleeping in the house. He's been a great help to my wife and I, since we're older. He's a good man and a good worker," he commented.

Jason said, "Linus can stay for the time being. I'll pay him to start cleaning the place up and allow him to stay until I move to the house." Then Jason thought for a moment and asked, "I have a question for you…what did my parents believe before they died?"

Damon responded, "All I know is they abandoned temple worship and the gods of our people; they felt the gods had abandoned them. What did they believe? I'm not sure. I know they grieved, when your sister left especially."

Jason gave Damon and his wife, Letha, a brief rendition of his testimony. They were moved by his story and offered to help in any way they could. They wanted to know more about Jesus. Jason assured them he would return and speak with them more, much more. He wanted Damon to take him to the tomb where his parents were laid; Damon promised he would.

"We need to be going for now. We have further business to attend to, but I will stop by and speak to Linus," Jason said as he offered his hand to Damon and bowed to Letha, as did the other men. "I'll be seeing you, neighbor," he said as they departed.

The four men walked over to Jason's house and entered the main room, where Linus was nervously waiting. He seemed to be a hardworking, sensible young man, as he was dressed in frayed work attire with a banded head covering. Jason re-assured him he could stay, then laid out some work needing to be done. Jason then handed him a couple of silver coins. Linus was extremely grateful and promised to do good work for Jason. The men spoke with Linus, then walked around to the back of the house and had a look at the winepress. Afterward, they stood in front of the property for a bit. Jason was more than overwhelmed. He now had property, as well as plenty of money to invest in it. He found himself a bit suspicious; things seemed to be going too well. He felt guilty for feeling so and decided to trust God, for he was extremely happy with his good fortune. Jason shifted his thoughts to the business at hand: Andris. The men walked over the hill and back to the eastern road around the city toward the north side of town.

The men approached the house of Andris and were impressed by the grandeur of the two-level stone house. Columns with capitals in front supporting a porch roof featuring carved friezes and cornices. Around the house were carved stone depictions of the pagan gods among the trees. Jason stopped for a moment, then looked at his companions and requested they remain silent except for social, and hopefully friendly gestures.

Eustace spoke, "I don't know Andris personally, but what I do know is we should be alert. I agree that this exchange is for Jason; make sure your weapons are well concealed and maintain a humble stance."

Lukas said, "I agree, but I'm ready!" Orpheus nodded in agreement as well.

Jason and his friends drew near and noticed two large men were in front. They appeared to smile, then casually walked into the elegant stone house. It appeared that Andris knew they were coming, if he was in there. Jason walked up and knocked upon the door, then looked at the finely carved architectural motif as he waited. It seemed odd to him that two men saw them coming, yet there was an incredibly slow response to their arrival. The door finally opened, and a man who was at least a head and a half taller than Jason stood there silently. His weapon was not concealed.

"I'm here to speak with Andris," Jason said with an intentional meekness to his voice. He was, however, staring into the eyes of the large man and sought a response. It was obvious he was there to intimidate Jason and his companions.

The huge man stepped aside after a long, uncomfortable moment, then gestured for the men to come in. Jason and his friends entered into a large room, and immediately noticed several men standing in a group. The men parted to reveal a table beyond with one man lounging behind it. The room was adorned with columns and statuary depicting the Greek gods, as well as painted walls which also depicted scenes of the legends. An intricate mosaic tile floor and luxurious cloth window dressings completed the lavish atmosphere. Altogether, the house seemed the epitome of pagan Greek culture. Jason could actually feel the pain Alethea had to endure in this house.

Jason looked at who he assumed to be Andris reclining at the table. He had a half-smile upon his face, but there was hatred in his eyes. He took a drink from his goblet, then stood up and walked around the table to stand face to face with Jason. His companions stayed back near the door. There were eight men besides Andris, as two of them walked to the door to stand on either side of it; thus, blocking an easy exit. Andris wore no outer garment, only an off-white tunic and was boldly displaying a sword hanging on his left side. He was a tall man; with graying short hair, full beard, a bit fat but muscular, and an arrogant demeanor. His eyes were not dark, but sinister, nonetheless.

Andris spoke as he glared at Jason, "I'm going to have to speak to the man who let you in. I don't like animals in my house, except when they're to be eaten." He then looked back at Jason's companions and asked, "Eustace, I understand you to be an important man in Emmatha; why are you associated with these beasts?" Andris returned his glare at Jason, for there was no response from Eustace.

Jason spoke up in a gentle voice, "I have come to ask for Alethea's hand in marriage."

Andris continued to glare at Jason, as he displayed a wicked grin and chuckled. He then started laughing, as did his cohorts. While still laughing Andris said, "He wants that old maid's hand in marriage, did you all hear that? The beast wants to marry my daughter!" He stopped laughing and glared at Jason. In a very sinister voice Andris asked, "What makes you think you're going to get out of here alive?"

"I think we'll get out alive for the one, true, living God is with us," Jason proclaimed as he continued to look right into Andris's eyes and was stone-faced.

"I don't think your Hebrew God is going to help you now, beast. I've been waiting for this a long time," Andris said as he continued to stare at Jason. He nodded at his men; the two by the door stepped in front of the door. Jason heard swords drawn. Andris shouted, "Kill these animals, but spare Eustace; I'm going to kill this beast myself!" Andris drew his sword. Jason had remained motionless up to that moment. As soon as Andris cleared his sword from its scabbard; Jason drew his sword lightning fast. The point of his blade was pressing into the throat of Andris.

"Tell your men to drop their weapons in the center of the room, NOW!" Jason demanded with his voice no longer gentle.

"Do as he says!" Andris said while struggling to get the words out as Jason's blade was breaking the skin of his throat. "Do it now!" he repeated with a voice of panic.

Eustace, Orpheus, and Lukas had all drawn swords and stood back to back. They made sure the men by the door complied; Jason could hear swords hitting the floor.

Orpheus spoke loudly, "I think it would be a good idea to take a rest. All of you men back off; go to the sides of the room and sit down!" All eight men left their swords in the center of the room and complied.

Andris still had his sword in his hand but was frozen in place.

Jason warned Andris, "Drop your sword, or your head will hit the floor instead."

Jason immediately heard the sword fall between the men's feet. A man suddenly jumped up from the left side of the room with a dagger and ran toward Jason. Lukas leaped into his path, then swiped his right arm and laid it open. The dagger hit the floor and Lukas glared at him, then gestured to the side of the room with his sword. The man went back to his place, while wrapping his wound with his garment. Jason kicked the sword of Andris away. He never broke away from eye contact during the event; Andris displayed intense hatred with his eyes. Suddenly, Jason pulled away and quickly returned his sword to its sheath.

Jason then spoke in a calm manner, "Now, I hope we can conduct ourselves like civilized men. I came here to ask for Alethea's hand in marriage. This is an opportunity for you to do the right thing, for once in her life."

Andris responded very angrily while holding his throat and asked, "You come in here, then threaten my men and I, and you call yourself civilized? You ask for my permission at the point of a sword?"

Jason spoke boldly, "You lie! You ordered your men to kill us." He looked Andris in the eye and stated, "You were going to kill me yourself, remember?"

"I said nothing like that," Andris replied as his half smile returned. He went on, "I feel that you have entered my house to force me to consent to my daughter's marriage. Be that as it may, I give you my permission to marry my daughter. Far be it from me to stand in the way of her happiness. You men are all witnesses! I give my consent!" He gave Jason a piercing glare and asked, "Are you satisfied now, beast?"

Jason responded, "My name is Jason, and yes, that is the reason I came into your house. We came in peace, and we shall now go in peace. If you or your men try to follow us, then we will defend ourselves, as we did here. I must tell you the truth before I go: Jesus, the Son of God, has healed and delivered me from years of demonic possession. I am no longer the beast. I am very sorry about what I have done in the past; now, I live for God. Alethea is like-minded. I have no reason to hate you, but I strongly recommend you seek the truth about the one, true, living God. Confess your sins to him and repent. He will forgive you and heal you."

Andris responded sarcastically, "Now that's real good advice, beast. You hear that men? All I must do is turn to this Hebrew God and all my problems are over. I'm so glad that you came in here and straightened me out, beast!"

Jason looked upon Andris with pity. "Let us go," he said as he turned and walked toward the door. "I will pray for you, Andris," he said as he walked between his companions and out through the door followed by Lukas and Eustace with their swords were still in their hands. Orpheus was the last one out.

"God bless you all, and peace be with you!" Orpheus shouted as he passed through the door.

The men walked in silence until they were a good distance away from the house. They made their way back to the eastern road at the edge of Gadara, then stopped for a bit.

Eustace was looking curiously at Jason and spoke, "That was a den of murderous, evil men. We came out of it quite well thanks to you. I must ask you about it, for I've been around and seen a lot; I've never seen anyone that fast with a sword." He looked intently at Jason and asked, "Can you explain where that comes from?"

"I've been around longer than you, Eustace. I've never seen the like either," Orpheus commented with a slight grin.

Lukas spoke up, "I was ruled by the spirit of fear. I felt it was gone from my life, but now I'm sure. That man was going to kill Jason; I had the calmness of mind to not only stop it, but I did it without taking his life. The man can be saved, but the arm holding the dagger was the threat."

Jason said, "Lukas is right. Those men are not the problem, but the wicked spirits they serve is what was opposing us in that house. God was with us, and I never thought otherwise. As far as my abilities, that's something I've already worked out with God, which happened right after my deliverance. I found that most of the strength and abilities I had as Legion were gone. I destroyed all the things Legion had accumulated over the years, except for this sword I'm carrying. I discovered my skill by accident; not only speed but accuracy. It is a remnant of a being long dead; a spirit thousands of years old. Somehow, the skill remains even though the spirit is gone. I took it to God in prayer as soon as I made the discovery and asked that it be turned for righteousness. I think we saw that prayer answered today. We got out and none were killed with only one injury." Jason paused, then continued with a slight grin, "I'm not counting the small cut on Andris's throat; it was necessary."

Eustace responded, "I wasn't accusing you of anything, Jason. It's just the fact that if you hadn't been there with that ability; well, we were outnumbered and none of us are professionals. I remember Andris instructing his men to spare me, for there would be a lot of questions asked if I were murdered. His men are professionals. I have no doubt they've killed before and they will try to kill again. Yes, he gave his consent for the marriage...that really shocked me."

Orpheus said, "A man like that has hidden meanings to everything he does. I think it would have been better if he had not given consent."

"Yeah, I would be very surprised if he quietly accepts it, Jason," Lukas commented.

Jason said, "Andris gave consent as a curse. I agree with Orpheus; I read it in his eyes. He wants revenge against me and Alethea. There's nothing I can do about it, but there's a lot God can do. I'm going to trust God, then proceed with the wedding and believe things are going to work out. I'm not giving into fear of this man. God has brought Alethea and I together, as well as made provision for a fruitful life with her and given me a treasury of good friends. Why would God allow a pagan like Andris to destroy that?"

Lukas smiled, then stood up and extended his hand. Jason grabbed it firmly, then Eustace and Orpheus. The four-way hand clasp renewed the men's commitment to each other and to God. The men then prepared to walk back to the east side of Emmatha and the caravansary.

Jason spoke, "I want you all to know there are no secrets I'm withholding from you. That was the only thing different about me. I wasn't trying to hide it, but I could see it shocked you, Eustace. I can assure you there are no others, that I know of. I am tormented in my sleep occasionally, but God is helping me with that. I think God has equipped us all in different ways to forge a stronger fellowship. It was God that saved us a while ago. I would not have been able to get out of there, if not for you men no matter how fast I am. I would have been killed with a dagger in my back, if not for Lukas. We couldn't have held that many back, if not for Eustace and Orpheus. I think we all have a great many things to be grateful for."

The four men walked down the hill from the City of Gadara and enjoyed the early evening. The plentiful white fluffy clouds presented a breathtaking display of color as the sun waned. A gentle breeze from the west made for a pleasant walk following a very busy and eventful day. Jason's thoughts were drifting toward his inheritance and the loss of his parents. He wondered what his mother and father believed before they died. He was thinking about what Damon had told him, of how his father finished out his life. Did he repent? Jason had to resign himself to the fact that in this life he would never know. He was, however, looking forward to telling Alethea they were landowners. He thought about Linus, that he already had someone to watch over his estate in his absence; God even supplied that. He figured one of the first things to do was to purchase an oxcart, for there was a lot of work to do. The men were in sight of the caravansary before long. Even at a distance they could see a lone figure standing by the southeast corner of the building: it was Alethea. She saw the men approaching and came running to meet them.

"Looks like someone's eager to see you, Jason," Orpheus observed.

Jason responded by starting to run; thus, leaving his companions temporarily to meet his Alethea. The two slammed together in an embrace. They continued to hold each other until the three men caught up with them.

"I was so worried about you, Jason! I'm so glad your back!" Alethea said with an expression of joy. "Did you find your family? How did things go with my father?" she asked. It was obvious that she had been worried sick.

Jason responded, "Calm down, dear Alethea. Everything's fine; God was with us. Your father gave consent, and we're going to be married as soon as we can arrange it!" That brought a huge hug from Alethea, then she embraced the other men as well. She thanked them for going with Jason and being good friends. Jason added, "That's not all; I've inherited my family's estate. My parents have both passed away and left me the property." Alethea became a bit solemn and expressed sorrow for Jason's loss; she also demonstrated a concerned look.

"How did things go with my father? did he really give consent?" Alethea asked. She was apparently having a difficult time excepting the news.

Jason assured her, "We'll discuss it later, but he did give consent; witnessed by three of my friends and eight of his." Alethea looked at Jason as her concerned expression remained.

They arrived at the caravansary. The group walked through the courtyard and into the community room, which was empty. There were no patrons at the time, nor were there any for the meal yet. Eustace was usually concerned about a lack of business but given the events of the day he was rather pleased that it was quiet. The men immediately reclined around their preferred table. Lydia and Melina came out and greeted the men, then brought goblets, bowls of dates, and bread. Alethea waited a little while, then asked Jason to walk with her in the courtyard. The couple walked outside and sat down by the well.

"Tell me what happened, Jason. I know there was trouble, for I could read it in the faces of the others. You, not so much; your faith overcomes a lot of your concern," Alethea inquired with great curiosity.

Jason confessed, "There's no hiding anything from you, for your insight is correct. Your father tried to kill us; he was unsuccessful, however. He had surrounded himself with eight large men with swords and ordered them to kill us. No one was hurt; well, not seriously anyway."

Alethea was astonished and asked, "He had eight Temple Guards there, and you all got out? That's four against nine. They're all swordsmen. Jason, I had no Idea it would be that dangerous; he usually doesn't have that many around him! He must have been expecting you! How did you get away with no one getting killed?" She was shocked with panic in her voice.

Jason proclaimed, "God was with us! I went in calmly and made my request known right away. Your father just wanted to kill us; he gave the order, then I responded by holding my sword to his throat and demanded that he and his men disarm. One came at me with a dagger, but Lukas stopped him with a sword blow to the arm. That was the only injury, except a small cut on Andris's throat. The consent was given to mock us; I gave my testimony, and he continued to mock us. Alethea, we must trust God in this. Please, don't live in fear; God was with us in the house of Andris, and he will be with us forever after. Promise me, that you will trust God no matter the circumstance"

Alethea laid her head upon Jason's chest and said, "Yes, I will trust God no matter what. I promise. I have an even stronger faith since I saw the four of you approaching. There wasn't much work to do around here; I was very worried and needed to pray. Melina told me to focus on that, so I prayed for you and your friends all afternoon. I waited to see you coming. I would have been out there all night had you not arrived. I'm so sorry you walked into danger, for I should have known. And all this after you found out your parents are gone; I feel your sorrow with you. Andris is no longer my father in any way. I'm just happy that God brought you all back safely."

"We have a vineyard, an orchard, and a good-sized house," Jason said as he changed the subject. He went on, "I want you to oversee fixing up the house; make it any way you want. I want it to be an expression of you. There was a beautiful garden all around the house when I lived there as a boy. We already have a man staying there and watching things. His name is Linus, and he's going to start cleaning it up for it's been neglected. I heard my father died seven years ago; my mother fifteen. I was told they gave up temple worship. I'll probably never know if they acknowledged God or not, but there is reason to be hopeful."

"I can't wait to see it, Jason, when can we go see it?" Alethea asked with a warm smile as she looked up at him. Thinking about it had chased away the concern, as well as stronger faith. There was no doubt in her mind that God was with them.

The next morning, Jason, Lukas, and Orpheus decided to go out into the City of Gadara. The men were full of confidence and faith following the events of the previous day. Jason knew where he wanted to go, what better place to proclaim the awesome majesty of God than the pagan Temple of Zeus. They had no intention to set foot inside the temple, but to speak to people outside. Jason wanted to confront the misplaced devotion to the false god; one displayed most prominently in the house of Andris. A few people who recognized them from the baptism greeted them warmly on the way. They spoke with others as well and were quite successful. It was early afternoon by the time the men reached the temple. There were a few people coming and going, and group of worshippers engaged the men as they were leaving the temple. Jason began to give his testimony:

"I walked in darkness most of my life. Jesus, the Son of God, delivered me from a lifetime of demonic possession. God has had compassion and mercy upon me, as he will to all who call upon him!" Jason spoke boldly.

"Why do you trouble us with this Hebrew God?" one of the men asked angrily. "Zeus has a son also: his name is Herakles. His legends speak of power and greatness; proof that Zeus is the ruler of the gods," he boasted.

Lukas spoke, "These gods you speak of are not what you think they are. They're nothing but meaningless images carved in stone."

"How dare you speak this way, and right outside his temple!" one of the women cried out. "He will strike you down!" she shouted.

Lukas looked up for a bit, then shrugged his shoulders as he returned eye contact upon the angry woman. "My God is greater," he said.

"All three of us have experienced his compassion and mercy," Orpheus said calmly while trying to restore an intelligent debate, but it was not forthcoming.

The woman who had shouted at Lukas swiped Orpheus in the face with the outer garment she was carrying. Jason received the same when he attempted to speak. Lukas backed away from the angry woman, while looking around at the other hateful faces. All three were then backing away from the disagreeable Pagan worshippers.

Four men appeared in the temple entrance, for they had heard the disturbance. One was the high priest, as well as three of the

Temple Guard. Two of them had been in the house of Andris. They disappeared into the temple but returned quickly with many more people. The angry crowd approached the three men as Jason sniffed the air. Suddenly, the threat of violence had become very real, since they recognized the guards. Jason couldn't see anything good coming out of the encounter once again. This time, however, there was no easy escape. The men began to walk away, but the increasing crowd followed. Some picked up stones and began to pelt the men. They increased their pace until they were running. The people ran after them while screaming foul and profane insults and continuing to throw rocks. Finally, the crowd in pursuit diminished. The men stopped and turned around once there were only a few, then the angry mob retreated. Jason and the others looked themselves over; a few cuts and scrapes, but nothing serious.

"That was interesting," Lukas said as he pulled a piece of cloth from his bag to wipe away a little blood from a wound upon his left arm.

"I don't regret it, but I'm sorry about the injuries; you two alright?" Jason asked as he looked at Lukas's arm. It was just a scrape.

"I'm fine," Orpheus reported. "I heartily agree in confronting the false gods, but perhaps picking a fight with them just outside their temple is not the preferred method," he said, then began to chuckle. "I don't regret it either," he added.

After a couple of days, it was time to take Alethea to see the property Jason had inherited. They had spent the day yesterday at the marketplace. Alethea had picked out fabrics to be used in the home but wanted to see it before purchasing too much. Jason purchased two asses. He set about loading the bundle of colored cloth upon one and the other was for Alethea to ride. Jason was apprehensive to ride his and content to lead it, as well as Alethea's animal. Jason was a bit saddened, for he was convinced his ass sensed his prior spiritual state. Alethea thought it all nonsense and was playfully telling Jason he just needed to get to know it, for both asses seemed to like her. They headed up the eastern road to the south side of Gadara. Jason heard something that completely took him by surprise once they started traveling. He looked back at Alethea and she was playing a double aulos; her skilled music was absolutely beautiful.

"What a pleasant surprise!" Jason exclaimed as he smiled at his future bride. "You didn't tell me you could play music," he added.

Alethea paused and said, "You didn't ask me." She stopped just long enough to comment and give a warm smile back at Jason, then went back to playing.

"What other wonderful surprises am I in for, sweet Alethea?" Jason asked while unable to stop smiling.

She stopped briefly once more and said, "I'm a fairly good cook; I don't shy away from responsibility, nor am I afraid of hard work, and I'm a very passionate person when it comes to things that I love." Alethea then smiled at Jason.

Jason felt like picking her up off her animal and kissing her, but that wouldn't get them to their destination. They continued on a very happy couple indeed. It was a peaceful little trip until they passed the huge bathhouse on the corner where they turned off the main road. Many patrons were out front in various stages of dress. Some beckoned to Alethea to bring her music and entertain them. Alethea just kept playing, undaunted. Jason waved and prayed for them under his breath. He thought he recognized a couple of them from two days ago as they passed by. At least this time there weren't naked people following and hurling insults.

At last, they approached the arched entry gate of Jason's house. Linus was working at clearing unwanted vegetation from the stone outer wall. He saw them approach and came running to the gate.

"Greetings Jason!" Linus shouted as they drew near to the gate and stopped. "Been working on it ever since you left. Everything seems intact, except for being grown over and dusty. A few repairs needed here and there, but nothing serious," he said as he was very excited to see Jason and his companion.

Jason approached Linus and embraced him, for he was happy to see him enthusiastically doing what they had discussed. "Linus, this is Alethea, my future bride," he said as he walked over to her and offered a hand as she slipped off her animal. Linus walked up as he hastily wiped his hands on his garment. He took her hand gently and bowed.

"Very happy to meet you, Alethea. I'm here fixing up your new home for you. Looking forward to bringing some of this garden back," Linus said as he gestured around the jumble of growth in front of the house.

"Nice to meet you, Linus. Jason said we have someone working on it already; looks like you've been working hard," Alethea responded while looking beyond at the house. It was obvious she couldn't wait to see the inside. It was a good-sized stone house; taller than most, and there was a stairway on the north side to access the roof. There was a simple but well-built porch in front with a small roof supported by two columns at the front door, and there were windows on either side. The house was surrounded with a stone short wall featuring the distinctively arched gateway in front, which faced east. Alethea indicated she wanted to see the inside. Linus went back to work; Jason took Alethea by the hand as they entered.

The front door was a bit stuck as it dragged on the floor. Alethea was struck by the spaciousness of the main room. She tried to imagine it cleaned out; there were broken pots, an old table, and other debris strewn about. The improvised camp of Linus was evident, but it was a large room with a high ceiling. The floor was difficult to see with all of the clutter, but Alethea could see a well-fitted stone floor. The stone walls rose to the thick wooden beams holding the roof stones. In the back there were two stone columns holding the wooden floor platform for the upper bedchambers. Wooden columns stood on top of them in front of the upper level, which helped support the roof. A wooden stairway to the right led up to an open walkway with a wooden rail and two doors. There were three additional rooms in the back beneath the upper rooms. Alethea was pleased with the two hearths. One for the main room, which had the stones for the chimney joining the side wall on the left. The back room for food preparation had one as well and was built into the wall with the chimney on the outside. The bedchambers all had windows facing west.

Alethea looked at Jason with a huge smile after looking around for a bit and embraced him. She said, "This is beyond what I expected, Jason. It will be a beautiful home. The rising sun will light the main room every morning, and the setting sun can be observed from all the back rooms. I can visualize it in my mind, for it will be beautiful; a true blessing from God."

Jason responded, "I want you to have full control over it, Alethea. There are many memories for me here; I want you to make it something new. The more different the better. Some of my memories I cherish; others I wish to forget." He kissed her as they were making their way to the front door. They heard voices in front of the house: familiar voices.

Upon exiting the house, Alethea was pleasantly surprised to see Lukas and Orpheus talking to Linus. Jason wasn't surprised, for he knew they had followed them. Lukas had already started assisting with the clearing and cleaning effort. Damon and Letha had also come to visit, for they had seen them arrive. After the brief greetings, Jason unloaded Alethea's bundle and stowed it in one of the upper bedchambers, then he took Damon aside.

Jason asked, "Could you show me where my parents are laid? Is it nearby?" He was seeking further closure of his distant past. Unwanted memories were swirling in his mind mixed with the blessings of the present.

Damon responded, "Yes, of course. It's not far; just to the southeast of here. There's a large stone face just over that hill," he said while pointing off in the distance. "Many tombs there, that's where they were laid; they're together," he said.

Jason smiled. Alethea approached, and he asked her, "Do you want to go with us? I'm going to see my parent's tomb."

Alethea responded, "Of course I do. I only wish I could have met them previously. We're to be a family, so they're my family too."

Old Orpheus walked over. Having overheard the conversation he asked, "Do you mind if I come as well? What's important to you is important to me."

Jason just smiled at his old friend, and the five of them announced they were going for a walk. Lukas had struck up a friendship with Linus already. He felt a foreboding about tombs, and decided he was of more use to Jason by helping with the work.

"No offense, Jason, but I would prefer to stay away from tombs for now; you can show me later. We'll get the whole front cleared by the end of the day if I stay and help Linus," Lukas said as he continued working. "Were you surprised to see us?" he asked as he glanced up at his friend.

"No," Jason replied.

"How did you know we were following you?" Lukas asked.

Jason walked up close to Lukas and sniffed the air. Lukas smiled, then went back to work.

They walked for a little while, then Damon pointed out the rock face he had described. There were many cut openings which suggested tombs within. Suddenly, Jason felt what Lukas had wanted to avoid. Damon led the group to the entrance where the remains of Jason's parents were, and Jason knelt to pray. Alethea Joined him, as Orpheus stood with Damon and Letha observing silence.

He prayed, "Father, in the name of Jesus I ask for strength. I ask you to be with me, as you were in the tomb of Legion. I pray that Jesus walk with me, for I now go into the darkness. If there be any wicked spirits within; the Lord rebuke them, in Jesus name."

Jason and Alethea stood up, then he gestured for Damon to lead the way. There was only quiet and peace when they entered the large tomb. There was a carved motif over the entrance, as well as a couple of Greek-style columns within. Many sarcophagi lay in the large tomb chamber with many carved niches in the walls. Damon walked over to two long niches not far from the entrance, and they were well illuminated by the natural light from the opening. He held out his hand as he presented them to Jason.

Jason walked up and saw the bodies as they had been laid. The rotted burial shrouds were still covering the bones somewhat. There hadn't been anyone to collect the bones to put them in an ossuary, as Jason thought to himself that soon he would do so. He determined his father was the highest one, for his name was faintly inscribed just above it. He brushed the dust away from the inscription and spoke it: "Jarvis." There didn't seem to be a name upon his mother's niche, so Jason spoke it: "My mother, Nora." Jason stood motionless and silent for a bit as Alethea stood by his side. Then Jason said, "Mother, father, I came to say goodbye. I want you to know that the curse upon my life was broken away by Jesus, the Son of God. I know you both grieved, but now you are both at peace. I pray that somehow you found the one, true, living God, as I have. I pray that someday…we will meet again."

Jason was about to turn and walk away. He noticed what appeared to be an object that seemed out of place. Upon further examination he saw that his father had something in what was left of his hands. He easily opened the degraded fabric, then Jason saw what appeared to be a small scroll within his finger bones. He removed it carefully, as the fingerbones collapsed into a pile. It was very dry and brittle. He wrapped the tiny scroll in a cloth carefully and placed it in his bag.

Jason asked Damon, "Do you know anything about this scroll that my father was holding?"

Damon responded, "No, it must have been something in his possession. If those preparing the body found it, they may have placed it within his hands. Looks like you have something of a mystery to examine, Jason."

They all quietly exited the tomb.

The next day, Jason reclined at the table in the community room after the morning meal, and the scroll sat in front of him. Alethea, as well as Lukas and Orpheus sat with him. Everyone was almost as curious as he was, so he decided to try to unroll it. The parchment fell into small pieces. He began to lay some of the pieces out; all he could tell was that it was written in Greek. He put together the top of the scroll, then suddenly put his head down and began to weep. Alethea put her arm around him asking what it said, but he didn't answer. Orpheus walked around and carefully examined what was laid out upon the table. Lukas went around to comfort Jason the best he could.

"What was so terrible about it, Jason?" Lukas asked.

"What does it say, Jason?" Alethea asked while trying to comfort her future husband.

"Those are not tears of sorrow, Alethea," Orpheus said as a smile began to appear upon his face. He continued, "I know what the entire scroll says. The fragment Jason has assembled is faint, but it reads: *The Lord is my shepherd.*"

Chapter Six

Blessings and Curses

Orpheus sat alone at the front table in the community room. He had adopted the habit of reading in the morning and was currently focused the scroll of the Prophet Isaiah. He was content to sit and contemplate some of the deeper meanings of the prophecies he had found therein. A pleasant distraction broke his thoughts as he pondered: Alethea approached and asked if she could get him anything.

Orpheus responded, "Well, I've already eaten; the only thing I can think of is, perhaps, a little conversation." He then smiled at her.

Alethea smiled and spoke across the room to Lydia, "I have a request for a conversation; I'm sitting for a bit." Lydia smiled and giggled.

Orpheus started, "I've had a good night's sleep, then read the word of God, and ate a nice meal; now I'm sitting in the company of a beautiful woman. My day's going great so far, but how are you doing?" He looked at Alethea with a sincere expression. "The big day is tomorrow; are you excited?" he asked.

"I'm more than excited. I just hope I can sleep tonight. It's been two weeks since Jason confronted my father. He hasn't made an appearance, nor sent word. I don't think he will come, which makes me a little nervous," Alethea confided in the old man.

"Do you want him to come?" Orpheus asked, for he was concerned about anything that would interfere with her happiness.

"No, I don't. My concern is that he will show up unannounced and cause trouble," she said with a bit of silent fear, but overruled by joy.

Orpheus changed the subject and said, "You know, I lost my family when I was overcome by evil. I had a daughter that would be about your age. You remind me of her, though you're prettier."

Alethea smiled at the old man. "Why couldn't I have had a father like you?" she asked as she looked at Orpheus with genuine affection.

Orpheus looked at Alethea seriously for a moment and said, "Why can't you? I would love to have you as my adopted daughter; Jason is very special to me as well, for I love him too."

A very special relationship was born that morning. Orpheus was to be the father that Alethea never had. Alethea was to be the daughter that Orpheus had lost. A healing had taken place in the hearts of both; a new family was taking shape. The two embraced as father and daughter, which brought mutual tears of joy. Before long the two were having deep discussions, as well as laughing together.

Jason looked around and was pleased with the appearance. The only problem with the house now was the emptiness. It seemed like an empty shell after removing the old furnishings; however, the unwanted memories were taken out and burned, which left behind endless possibilities. Lukas and Linus were working behind the house. He went out to find them completing the task of removing debris out of the winepress. Jason jumped in to help, as he wondered how long it had been since it was used.

"It was close to being buried, but we took it back," Lukas said to Jason as he hoisted a basket of dirt and leaves up to the rim. "It's all intact, and there sure was a lot of debris from things that fell or crawled in there. How did things go with the door?" he asked.

"It works fine now," Jason responded. "Had to take it off and reset it. The house overall was still in good shape; I think the repairs are done inside," he said as he looked back at the house.

The men finished hauling out baskets and bundles of debris, then took them to the burn site to dispose of it.

After starting the fire, Linus spoke, "I can continue to clean up around the outer wall, for there's still a lot of growth with vines and debris. The place is in good shape now; I suppose you want me to leave soon."

"I've been thinking about that, Linus," Jason said while looking him in the eye. "A hired hand should be trustworthy and a good worker; you have proven to be both. You have accepted Jesus as Lord, and have begun to follow the ways of God, so we are like-minded. You can stay if you want to; Damon has offered you work as well." He smiled as he saw Linus's face light up and asked, "What do you say?"

"Yes! I will stay! Thank you, Jason! I'll finish cleaning up the outer wall, then I'll start pruning the trees in the orchard to see what we can salvage. I've worked in vineyards as well, and I know all about cultivating and harvesting. I won't let you down!" Linus said as he was very excited.

Jason said, "I want you to come with us. Lukas and I are heading back to the caravansary, and I have something for you," Jason said as he put his hand upon Linus's shoulder.

The men waited a bit until the debris fire had burned down, then set off down the eastern road around the City of Gadara. On the way, Linus was impressing Jason and Lukas with his agricultural knowledge. Again, Jason gave praise to God for bringing yet another helpful member to his growing family. He liked Linus; he was a young man, saying at one point he was twenty-six, average in appearance, with medium brown hair and beard that was well groomed. He had no family, for he had been on his own since he was a boy. Lukas could relate to him, for he was the one who shared the truth with Linus and prayed with him. Jason wanted to run in and see Alethea as the men approached the caravansary. They had business to attend to, however, and proceeded down to the Yarmuk River. The men followed Jason's example and disrobed, then waded into the water waist deep.

Jason spoke, "This is what I have for you, Linus: a new life. You leave the old man behind in the waters and come out living for God. Do you accept Jesus as the Son of God, and follow the ways of God from now on?"

"Yes, I do," Linus responded.

"Then I baptize you in the name of Jesus for the remission of sins," Jason said as he laid Linus back into the water. He came out smiling as most people do.

Not only was the baptism of Linus a blessing, but Jason and Lukas also enjoyed an opportunity to wash up after a lot of labor-intensive activity. Linus exited the water first, while Jason and Lukas remained for a bit. Linus thought they were acting strangely as they were looking into the water and standing bent over with their hands extended. He soon found out why, when Jason threw a fish beside him onto the bank.

"Don't let them get away!" Lukas shouted as he threw one out also.

In no time they had caught six fish, then Jason and Lukas exited the water. Jason pulled a cord out of his bag and strung the fish together. He strung two separately before handing them to a surprised Linus.

"Your welcome to return to the caravansary with us, or you can return to the house; either way you have a meal for the evening," Jason said to his new friend.

"I would like to share a meal with you all, but aren't you busy? Tomorrow's your big day, right?" Linus asked. He obviously wanted to go with them, but he didn't want to impose.

Jason responded, "The preparations have already been made; we're having a simple ceremony with family and friends. You can come if you want to."

"Yes, I will come, but I've never been to a wedding. What must I do?" Linus asked.

"Just wear your best clothing and be there, that's all," Jason answered as he smiled at Linus.

The men dressed and gathered themselves, then climbed up the escarpment from the river and headed down the road toward the caravansary. Jason had grown to appreciate the walk between the caravansary and the river; the tree-lined road always filtered the sunlight in various ways, this day the afternoon sun was particularly beautiful. Jason always appreciated the color and beauty around him, since his deliverance, and praised God for the new heart created within him. Linus had never been to the caravansary and was impressed as the three men entered the courtyard. They noticed many camels in the arched stalls, for a caravan had arrived since morning. Jason opened the large entry door, and the men entered the community room. A few people had already gathered for the evening meal and social interaction. Jason immediately saw Alethea and Orpheus at the front table, so he handed the fish to Lukas, then reclined at the table with them. They were happy to see Linus, as Alethea and Orpheus greeted him warmly. Linus sat down as well, while Lukas volunteered to take the fish to be prepared.

Alethea smiled at Jason. "Your hair's wet, and so is his. I can guess what you've been doing," she said as she scooted a little closer to Jason and took his hand.

Linus spoke, "Yeah, Jason baptized me; I feel brand new! I want to be a blessing to you both; just wait until you see that orchard and vineyard next year!"

Jason explained, "I've hired Linus to help us grow things, for he seems to know a lot about it." He asked, "What have you two been up to?"

Alethea proclaimed, "We've adopted each other! Orpheus is my new adopted father, and I'm his adopted daughter. We were having family discussions."

Jason looked at Alethea with a broad smile, then at old Orpheus. He patted his shoulder and said, "I guess that makes you my father as well! I love the idea! There's plenty of room in the house, and there shall always be a place for you. We're more like family already; I think God is at work here."

Lukas came back from delivering the fish to Lydia and Melina. He offered to clean the fish, but they said they would prepare them special for the three men's evening meal. He was a bit disappointed, for he was looking for an excuse to flirt with Melina. Lukas hadn't said anything, but there was a desire growing in his heart for the cousin of his friend's future bride. He had no idea how to express it, so he kept it to himself. He sat at the table and joined the conversation.

"So, if Orpheus is the father of the house, what am I?" Lukas joked and received glances of adoration mixed with a playful need for an appropriate response. Jason delivered it:

"You're to be the problem child!" Jason responded with a serious expression, which brought roars of laughter from around the table.

Alethea spoke with affection after recovering from the laughter, "You're to be the faithful brother. I never had a brother. It didn't need to be spoken, for you have been made so by God. You belong by Jason's side, and now mine. In the future you may even be the uncle!" That comment brought an unusual expression upon Jason's face, which brought another round of laughter around the table.

Everyone looked up when the entry door opened, as Eustace entered the room. He looked over and smiled at his friends, then scanned the room. He seemed pleased that many were there. He disappeared for a moment into his residence, then quickly returned and reclined at the table. The conversation went toward filling him in on the day's events, and the family designations.

"What am I to be in all of this?" He asked in a lighthearted way.

Jason said, "You are to be my special brother who will always be welcome in my house. Your generosity and kindness, as well as your love has brought all of us together. You are the patriarch." When Jason said this, he got up and walked around to Eustace, as did everyone else, so they could lay hands upon him. Jason offered a prayer for him and his business, which put a smile upon Eustace's face.

"I have plans for us after the meal; just us men," Eustace announced. Alethea had an unusual expression this time. Eustace reassured her, "Don't worry, I'll bring him back to you in time for the wedding." She smiled at him, then looked at Jason as he smiled and leaned over closer to her.

"I think Lydia and Melina have something planned for you as well," Eustace informed Alethea. He continued, "By the way, I'm letting you go. You can stay as long as you like, but I recommend you move in with your new husband after tomorrow." Eustace was learning from Jason, as he spoke with a serious expression. When everyone started laughing, however, he joined in.

Following the meal, Lydia announced they would all be leaving for a while, and all were welcome to stay. Eustace had made plans for his stable help to watch the place, but there would be no one to serve them. Everyone from the city was leaving anyway. The people of the caravan just requested enough wine to last them. Eustace then revealed his plan: he had reserved the steam room at one of the bathhouses in Emmatha. It was one of the few in the area that was segregated usually. He informed Jason he had made reservations for Lydia, Melina, and Alethea in the women's section. No one except Eustace had ever experienced a steam bath, so the men were excited. Melina came out and gestured for Alethea to come with her, then they disappeared into the back room. Eustace looked around at the men, then smiled and gestured to get up.

He said, "Let us go; I'm looking forward to this!"

"Tonight, we feast, for tomorrow we have a wedding to attend!" Andris shouted across the table at the many Temple Guards. All the men had eaten their fill of a whole roasted swine that had been prepared and laid out upon the huge table. They were dining in the great room, which was the largest in the impressive two floor stone house. The room featured four impressive columns; statuary depicting the gods, art upon the plastered walls depicting the legends, fine fabrics, and six bronze urns with fire burning inside. They responded with howls of laughter, for they had discussed earlier the plan to ridicule and shame the couple. Andris had sought out all the stories about the beast available throughout the city, whether true or not. He also came up with a myriad of insults for who he viewed as his disgraced daughter. She had brought shame upon him in the temple community. The three *animals,* as Andris referred to Jason and the others had shown disrespect to Zeus at the temple; Andris wanted to avenge his god.

Andris was convinced that Zeus had revealed a plan: to end the marriage before it could begin; and to goad Eustace, the beast, and those other animals into a more public fair fight. They would attack first with many witnesses, which would eliminate the need to answer questions about dispatching a few troublemakers. They had entered his house and made demands at the point of a sword, after all. Multiple witnesses, as well as a man having a stitched-up sword wound on his arm perfected the plan. Andris listened as some of the men were practicing some of the viler condemnations to shout at the freak, and the daughter he hated. His servants had brought more wine. One came to serve him, but he knocked the pitcher out of her hand and shouted, "Bring out the strong drink!" This brought loud cheers from the men. Suddenly, four musicians entered the room playing aulos, lyres, and tambores.

"Tonight's the celebration of putting to an end this scourge that has entered our city!" Andris announced, then gestured for the man to his right at the table to stand. "This is Dameon from Athens: he is the preeminent Temple Guard there, and his ability with a sword is unmatched! Show them!" he shouted.

The man arose and looked around at the guards. He was dressed in dark but elegant clothing. He unleashed a dazzling display of quick, fancy swordplay which brought applause and cheers from the many guards assembled. He sat back down, then grabbed a large chunk of meat he had cut off just prior to the introduction.

"Many of you already know Leander, for he will also join us tomorrow!" Andris exclaimed as he gestured to the man on his left. He grinned as he stood up. He was good with a sword but kept it in its place. His claim to fame was his size, for he easily stood two heads above most men and as broad as an ox. He too sat back down and picked up another large piece of swine meat from the table.

Andris himself was indulging heavily on the meat, as he swallowed a huge gulp before announcing the next feature of the evening. He Hastily wiped his mouth with his sleeve, then quickly looked around the table. Andris was satisfied with the assembly of men devoted to his cause. They were growing drunk and lustful for revenge; many of them were there two weeks ago and defeated. They would attend this wedding. All fifteen of them.

"Now, bring on the entertainment!" Andris shouted loudly.

Suddenly, three dancing girls sprung into the room twirling and flirting with the men around the table. Andris sat back watching and smiling with his half-smile, as the drunken men were thoroughly mesmerized by the display. They will do anything I say after this night, as he thought to himself. He knew his daughter; she would thrust herself forward to defend that animal. He imagined how unfortunate it would be if she were accidentally killed. Andris looked over at Dameon, as a wisp of transparent fabric passed over his face from the girl dancing around him. He returned the glance with a half-smile of his own.

The five men were thoroughly enjoying the steam bath, as Eustace got up and poured water upon the heated stones to produce more steam. The men couldn't stop looking around in wonder; the white tile floor with blue geometric patterns, finely crafted marble benches on which they sat, and the Roman engineering that made it all possible. The steam chamber even had tile walls, which were blue half-way up with white above. Jason thought to himself that he never dreamed being overheated could feel so good.

Lukas came up with an idea. "How about steam baptism? It could boil the evil out of you!" he joked, which brought a round of laughter from the men.

Orpheus responded, "That wouldn't work. The evil would still be in the steam and would get back on you." He spoke with a serious expression, which brought even more laughter.

"I want to thank you all for inviting me to join you," Linus said as he looked over at Jason.

"You're an important part of what God is doing here, Linus," Jason responded.

Eustace got up again, this time reaching outside the chamber, and retrieved something out of his sack. He brought back a small, round, alabaster vessel, then struck it against one of the heated stones as the other men watched curiously. Immediately, the chamber was filled with the most extraordinary fragrance any of the men had ever experienced.

Eustace announced, "This is spikenard. There's enough here to anoint each one of us for the wedding. It was very costly, so don't let any of it go to waste."

Jason prayed that it would be a symbol of the blessing being poured out by God upon the new family he had created; protection against any evil that would try to hinder the special day.

Eustace went up to Jason first, and poured a bit of the precious oil over his head, then Lukas, Orpheus, and Linus. He sat down and gestured for Jason to take what was left and anoint him, so Jason took the oil from Eustace and poured the remainder upon his head. The men were amazed at the luxury, as they ran their fingers through their hair to spread the oil as much as possible.

Lukas commented, "This would make you feel clean even if you're not!"

Orpheus said, "I've heard of spikenard, but I never thought I would experience it!"

Jason was smiling and said, "Thank you, Eustace. I owe you one for this!"

"It's the least I could do for my good friend, Jason. We should probably get out of here soon before the steam washes away all of the essences," Eustace advised as he got up and left the chamber. The others quickly followed, as the steam was beginning to have a draining effect on the men.

Lydia, Melina, and Alethea entered the bathhouse to find they were alone. There was an attendant who left some supplies, then vanished. The section they were in was beautiful; blue and white tile on the floor with solid blue tile going half-way up the walls, arches with plastered walls above and hanging plants on either side of the arches. At the end of the room there was a pair of dolphins painted beneath a high set window. The bathing pool was huge, and full of crystal-clear water; there were two lion sculptures at the edge beneath the window with water pouring from their mouths. The women sat on one of the many marble benches for a moment continuing the conversation began on the way. Lydia and Melina were amazed by how much Alethea was talking about Orpheus adopting her.

Alethea proclaimed, "It really means a lot to me. To have a father there for me tomorrow is much more than I had hoped for."

Melina said, "We know that, but we want to hear about Jason!"

"She can be happy about whatever she wants," Lydia said as she picked up one of the cloths left by the attendant.

Alethea responded, "I can't wait to be Jason's wife, but you must understand what I've been through; Orpheus is a blessing as well. I think about Jason all the time, if you must know, and it's private!"

"Perhaps we should talk about how Lukas sometimes looks at you, Melina," Lydia said with a playful grin, which made Melina blush.

Her comment brought laughter between them. Melina looked around, then jumped in. She reported that the water was warm and wonderful, which inspired the others to join her. Lydia winced a little when Alethea turned around. She had noticed the scars on her back from years of abuse at the hands of her father; Melina gave her a quick look of acknowledgment. The warm water was a delightful experience, as all three women relaxed for some time. Lydia and Melina both shared hopes and desires to be married and have children. The women put on new white chitons after bathing, which were purchased for the wedding. Lydia asked Alethea to pray for them, so they might receive the joy and happiness of marriage soon. Alethea did so and spoke long beautiful prayer. Lydia and Melina then started brushing Alethea's hair and produced scented oils and fragrances she had purchased for the event. She felt very loved and honored as the two women made over her to make sure everything was just right. Lydia wanted to put a few flowers in her hair, but that would have to wait until morning.

The men had waited for some time outside the bathhouse in the shadows, while waiting for the women to emerge. Jason had the impulse to greet them when they finally did, but At Eustace's request the men let them pass by; he said it was a tradition not to see the bride before the wedding. They followed at a distance and saw them safely back to the caravansary.

When the three women returned to the caravansary they decided to go to bed right away, for the night had grown late. Melina and Alethea retired to her room. Alethea expressed a desire to go to bed right away and pray. She prayed that God would help her to be a good wife, then had a strong yearning to feel God's presence at the wedding. Alethea also prayed that her father or anyone else who would hinder the joy of the special day would fail in the name of Jesus. She continued in prayer that went on for some time, then fell into a peaceful sleep.

Jason lay in bed looking out of the window and recalling the dream, or whatever it was. He worried about not being able to fall asleep but knew that prayer was the answer. He prayed that God would show him how to be a good husband, and for protection against anything that would seek to spoil what God had brought together. Secretly he had been quite concerned about Andris, and what he might try to do. Trust God no matter the circumstance; it was engraved in his heart and mind now. Jason prayed, then got lost in a desire for God to bless the wedding and his entire new family in attendance. He playfully invited God to the wedding, which put a smile upon his face. He chuckled a little to himself, then drifted off within moments.

Andris had just retired to his bedchamber but was unable to fall asleep. He didn't feel very well and thought a drink would solve the problem, so he went downstairs. Entering the great room brought back the recent memories of the depravity that had taken place there, which made Andris grin while reaching for a goblet he had left on the huge table. The fires in the urns around the room had died down but were still burning. He had ordered the servants to leave when things got wild, so the remains of the feast were still laid out upon the table. He glanced around the room, which was dimly lit by the urns, and there were several people laid out around the room on the floor.

Suddenly, Andris realized something was wrong. There was a smell in the air like rotten meat. He got very dizzy and nauseous as he hung on to a column to steady himself, then he heard one of the men rise up while vomiting all over the floor. Two others were aroused by the noise and ended up in the same state. Andris couldn't control himself any longer and began vomiting. He slightly recovered, then staggered over to grab one of the flaming urns and pulled it over to the table. There, he saw a sight that shocked him to the core, and immediately vomited again. The remains on the table were crawling with worms and maggots. The meat was completely rotten as if it had been there for days. Everyone in the house at that point was scurrying to get outside, for they were all violently ill. Andris was curled up on the floor of his great room and was unable to move while vomiting continuously. And so, this continued throughout the night.

Jason had been so bold and confident up until this morning, but now he felt jittery. Eustace had brought him into his residence to dress, for he had been forbidden to enter his own room. Lydia and Melina were working fervently decorating the community room, and his as well. Jason and Alethea would be using his room until they moved into the house; Lukas and Orpheus were given a different room. Beds were being moved and flowers were popping up everywhere. Eustace had asked the woman who cuts his hair to come. Both Jason and Lukas were getting a hair and beard trimming; however, Orpheus declined. He liked the way he was, and rightly so, for his long white hair and beard seemed an expression of the wisdom he had from all of his travels. Jason changed into a special tunic he had purchased, which had embroidery around the neck, sleeves, and bottom hem of a blue geometric pattern. He had also purchased a special outer garment, which was light brown with dark brown accents. It was embroidered on the borders as well with an organic design like leaves and flowers. Jason checked his appearance in Eustace's polished copper wall mirror. He had to admit; he had never looked this good in his life.

Alethea looked into Melina's large hand-held mirror. She was very pleased with the look of the new chitons the women had purchased. Very high-quality white fabric; opaque but soft and flowing that joined at the shoulders which required clasps. Jason had purchased special gold clasps for all the women, like leaves with the stem forming the pin. The garments were designed to hang loosely around the upper body naturally. Alethea complained a little and said she felt exposed, for she had shunned promiscuous Greek culture. She tended to wear high-quality clothing, but of a modest nature. Melina convinced her that she looked breathtaking. Alethea was not concerned with the scars on her back that showed a little. Most of the people that knew her were aware of them, and the cause. Alethea felt strongly that it was a way to honor Jason. Lydia began to decorate Alethea's hair with flowers, which started her jitters. That meant the time was approaching. She responded by weeping a little, but out of joy. Lydia was done with her hair, then came the last detail: a very sheer head covering, which Lydia carefully placed over her head. They heard music coming from the community room. Eustace had hired three musicians: two aulos players and a lyre player to provide simple, soothing melodies.

The four men walked into the community room to see a full house. Jason noticed Symeon and Theophanes sitting at one of the back tables and greeted them. He saw Linus sitting with others, but isolated. Jason called him over and introduced him to Symeon and Theophanes, then Linus sat by them and became involved in conversation, which made him smile. The men assumed positions according to plan: Lukas stood by Jason and Eustace; Orpheus stood by the back-left door waiting for the women to emerge. Jason didn't recognize all the people in attendance, but he assumed many were probably friends of Alethea. The ceremony was to take place in the back of the room between the windows. It appeared to be another beautiful, clear, late summer day; there was a gentle breeze blowing in through the windows from the west. Jason considered it a great blessing, for the breeze was coming from where Jesus most likely was. He couldn't help thinking how great it would be if Jesus and his disciples were there. He remembered praying last night and thought of how silly it was to invite the Almighty God to his wedding. He chuckled a little.

"What's so funny? Are you nervous?" Lukas asked.

Jason responded, "Yes, I'm very nervous, Lukas, and thank you for asking."

Eustace started laughing and said, "You think you're nervous? I've never done this before! it will be a very simple ceremony; I don't have much to say!"

Jason scanned the room once more and saw a few he vaguely recognized from baptisms or street ministry, as he smiled and acknowledged people. Then he noticed a man on the other side of the room; he was sitting at his usual spot. His head was covered, but Jason could see the lower half of his face. He appeared to be a younger man. The mysterious man appeared to smile as soon as Jason noticed him. Was he the stranger from his dream? Just then, the back-left door opened; Jason didn't have time to figure it out.

First Lydia emerged, then Melina, as both were dressed in white chitons and looked very elegant and beautiful. Orpheus walked up to the door and extended his hand. He led Alethea out through the door, then took her by the arm and led her to Jason with the other two women following. Jason's nervousness melted away; Alethea was the most beautiful sight of his life. She was so beautiful he had to fight back tears. The gentle music set the perfect atmosphere, as Alethea approached Jason with a huge smile upon her face. Orpheus strutted alongside of her like a proud father. They came together, as Jason extended both hands and took Alethea's. They had chosen to face each other while holding hands during the ceremony. They were following their own traditions that they felt from their hearts. The music stopped.

Eustace began, "We are gathered here today to celebrate the union of Jason and Alethea. This is my first wedding, and the couple requested it be brief and casual, so let us get started. All I've done is officiate at building dedications up to now, but in a way, this is like it, for I have never seen such a beautiful structure built on such a firm foundation. The Lord Jesus is that foundation. God has brought these beautiful souls together; let no man ever put that asunder. Does anyone here today have any objections to this marriage? If so, then speak up now, or forever be at peace with it."

A moment of silence filled the room as Jason and Alethea scanned the crowd of family and friends. They almost expected someone associated with Andris to cause trouble. Jason glanced at the mysterious man as he sat quietly with an even bigger smile upon his face. He was not concerned by the presence; actually, somewhat encouraged. Alethea looked over the crowd and saw only smiles and tears. She then turned her gaze toward Jason as her big brown eyes melted his heart.

Eustace continued. "Jason, do you take Alethea to be your wife, in the sight of God?" he asked.

"I do," Jason responded with a little waver in his voice.

Eustace then asked, "Alethea, do you take Jason to be your husband, in the sight of God?"

"I do," Alethea answered with a little waver and a tiny sniffle as well.

"Then by the authority given to me by the City of Emmatha, and in the presence of the Almighty God; I proclaim that you two are now husband and wife!" Eustace announced bringing cheers and applause.

Jason and Alethea just continued to look into each other's eyes for a moment.

"You can kiss her now, Jason; everyone's waiting!" Eustace said with his usual chuckle. Many others chuckled and giggled as well.

Jason looked over at Eustace, then back at Alethea. They embraced, then Jason lifted the transparent veil from Alethea's face and kissed her, which brought roaring applause and cheers from everyone. Afterward, they looked around the room and smiled at all those in attendance. Jason noticed the mysterious stranger was gone! He looked around trying to spot him; the doors hadn't opened, but he had vanished. Jason was so perplexed that Alethea asked him if something was wrong. "It's nothing; I'll tell you later," he responded as he looked around again. People were approaching, and soon the new couple was heavily involved with greeting guests.

What happened next would become a point of controversy in Emmatha and Gadara for years to come. The bright sunlight that had been beaming in through the windows suddenly faded, then it grew dark outside. Eustace looked out of the window to see a massive dark cloud seemingly right over Emmatha. What had been a perfectly clear day was suddenly threatening. Loud thunder started to erupt with flashes of lightning, and it was vibrating the building. People were beginning to wonder what was going on, then silence filled the room. The atmosphere changed; there seemed to be smoke, which grew denser by the moment. No one had time to be afraid, for it all happened so quickly. The smoke, or whatever it was brought with it a sweet fragrance like no other. Anyone who was standing sat down; those already sitting couldn't get up. Jason and Alethea were still in the places they were during the ceremony, and neither were afraid; they both dropped to their knees and raised their hands. The smoke had grown quite dense and it was affecting all the people. It was as if the smoke contained peace and joy. Everyone in the room was overwhelmed with a sense of well-being. Jason and Alethea bowed down. The musicians attempted to play their instruments but were unable;

some tried to speak but were unable. The one thing people could do was smile, as everyone was smiling.

Suddenly, the level of light in the room grew brighter, and all went quiet outside. The beautiful smoke began to dissipate; shouts of joy and much murmuring began to arise from the crowd. Jason and Alethea raised their heads at the same time, then looked at each other in amazement. Alethea managed to speak:

"What was that?" she asked with a trembling voice, but a look of wonder upon her face.

"That was an answer to prayer!" Jason responded as tears were streaming down his smiling face. He then got up on his feet.

Jason shouted, "Dear friends, hear me! What you have just experienced was the glory of God! Seek him while he is near! Seek him where he may be found! Seek him with all your heart! Love God, and he will fulfill the desires of your heart!"

Alethea jumped up and embraced Jason as soon as he was done speaking, then the musicians started playing their instruments again. Most were at a loss of what to say, but everyone in the room was in a mood to celebrate. Jason looked toward Eustace, where he was still sitting beneath the right window with a big smile on his face. He looked around at all of his friends. The common expression was shock and wonder. To those outside the caravansary it appeared to be just a freak weather event. However, those inside would never be the same. No one in attendance could deny that God's presence was there that day. A great joyous celebration ensued throughout the remainder of the afternoon and into the evening. All enjoyed the feast as outside help had been hired; Lydia and Melina enjoyed the festivities as well. As evening descended into night the celebration continued. Jason looked at Alethea and asked to have a private word with her. They went to an unoccupied corner and spoke:

"Have you had enough celebrating?" he asked.

"More than enough," she responded.

"Let us get out of here," he said as he looked around. Everyone was engaged in conversation following the wondrous events of the day. He opened the back-right door that they just happened to be close to. Jason gestured politely and Alethea passed through. Jason picked Alethea up in his arms, once out of view, then kissed her and carried her up the stairway. He opened the door to their room; the lamps were lit, and there were flowers everywhere. Jason kissed Alethea again and carried her through the door. Once inside, while still in his arms Alethea smiled, then raised her foot and kicked the door shut....

The scene was grim at the house of Andris. It was late in the day before a physician was called to the house. The servants had been ordered away, and no one was able to walk away to get help. By the time organized help arrived many of the guests in the house were already dead. Only Andris and four others survived the mysterious incident. The three servants worked to clean up with covered faces, as the physician and his assistant went outside to get a breath of fresh air.

"I've never seen anything like this. It appears these people intentionally ate rotten meat," the physician said as he shook his head.

"Do you think they knew it was rotten?" the assistant asked.

"They had to, for it took a long time for the meat to get to that state. The servant in charge said it was slaughtered and cooked yesterday. It doesn't make sense," the physician responded.

"Is there anything else we can do for the survivors?" the assistant asked as he prepared to go back in.

"We've already administered all the medicine we can for such a thing. Only time will tell. We may have saved more, if we had been here sooner. We should go back and ask Andris a few more questions; it just doesn't make sense," the physician said with a dismal expression.

The physician and his assistant walked back into the large room where the dead had been wrapped and laid out. There was still a foul stench in the air, although the servants had cleaned. They were currently out back and were burning everything from the feast. The two men climbed the stairway to Andris's bedchamber. He was very weak, pale, and hardly able to speak.

"We've done all we can. I'm asking you again, what happened?" the physician asked with great curiosity.

"We were having a celebration, as I told you. The meat was fresh. What happened was some kind of dark magic, and I think I know what the source of that magic may have been," Andris said faintly and slowly as he lay motionless in his bed.

"We've sent word to the people you requested; is there anyone else?" the assistant asked.

"Yeah, I have a worthless daughter living at the caravansary east of Emmatha. You can send word to her, as if she doesn't already know," Andris said as he struggled to stay conscious. It was obvious that just talking was wearing him out.

The physician responded, "It's already late in the day; we'll send word to her in the morning. Drink as much water as you can, if you've made it this far it looks like you'll live. You'll be sick for several days, as with the others."

Andris asked very weakly, "When will you get all of these bodies out of my house?"

The physician looked down at Andris with disgust and said, "We've sent word out as best we can according to the identities you and your servants provided. They should be recovered by the families starting tomorrow."

"Good, since the house smells bad enough already," Andris said as he lost consciousness.

The physician and his assistant left the house with no intention of returning unless called. They asked the servants to inform the daughter he spoke of. The two men then made haste to get back to the physician's house, for they wanted to escape the stench.

Jason and Alethea entered the community room after the morning meal was finished and found Orpheus and Lukas at the usual table. The newly married couple were smiling and holding hands, which brightened the mood of the room for everyone. They said Eustace had been there but had to leave a short time ago. Melina and Lydia were there also, as they had completed getting the room in order. Many of the flowers remained, as beautiful as they were yesterday. Alethea sat between Jason and Orpheus and placed a hand on each of the men's shoulders as she smiled.

"Yesterday I was alone; now, I have a husband, a father, and a brother. I never thought I would be so happy," Alethea proclaimed while beaming with joy.

Jason said, "I want a day of rest and fellowship." He then asked, "Do either of you know when Eustace will be returning?"

Just then, a knock came upon the entry doors. Melina answered and let in a woman that Alethea recognized: she was one of the servants of Andris. Her name was Desma and she brought a message.

Desma spoke nervously, "Master Andris has been taken very ill. He was having a celebration, but he ordered us away. Everyone in the house became very sick during the night, because the swine meat suddenly rotted. Many are dead, but your father lives. The physician requested that I come and inform you."

"What kind of a celebration was he having?" Alethea asked as she was very suspicious. It began to sink in that he was having a celebration on the eve of her wedding.

"It was the Temple Guard. A big feast with entertainment. We were sent away, that's all I know," Desma responded.

Alethea was visibly suspicious and responded, "Thank you, Desma. Go back and tell him we'll come today."

The woman bowed slightly at Alethea and departed. Jason, as well as the others, then looked at Alethea as she sat with a blank stare for a moment.

Alethea spoke, "I feel it's a trick, but I've never known Desma to lie." She then asked, "What should we do, Jason?" She was visibly expressing wild emotions.

"You told her we would come. I say we go; all of us," Jason answered. He spoke while looking at the other men, "We go, but prepared for the worst."

"So much for a day of rest and fellowship," Lukas said as he looked at Jason.

"Are you sure you're up to this?" Orpheus asked Alethea with a concerned expression.

"Yes, I'll be alright; I just want to get it over with," Alethea responded as everyone arose from the table to prepare for an unexpected trip to Gadara.

The four approached the house of Andris, as Alethea gestured for Jason to go around to the back of the house. They had decided not to knock on the door, but to enter the house secretly to avoid a trap. Alethea walked up to a wooden door at the back and opened it, then stepped back as the men entered. There were two servants working in the room preparing food; they were startled until they saw Alethea.

"Who's in the house?" Alethea asked abruptly.

Desma, the servant who had come to the caravansary answered, "Only Master Andris and four of his friends. They're upstairs in the bedchambers, and all of them are very sick. There are many dead men in the great room. We are the only other ones here."

Alethea looked Desma in the eye and asked, "Are there any guards in the house hiding?" Then with a stern voice she demanded, "Tell me the truth, Desma!"

"No, no, there are no others, Alethea!" she responded very nervously.

Alethea looked at Jason and said, "I believe her, but let us be careful, nonetheless."

Alethea led the way; through the back room, then through another door and down a corridor that led to the great room. Halfway down the corridor the foul odor of rotted meat filled the air but was much worse in the large room. There they saw that Desma was correct: there were eleven wrapped up bodies laid out along the sides of the room on the floor. Orpheus and Lukas began tapping them with a foot, one by one.

"Yeah, they're dead, Jason; all stiff," Lukas reported.

Alethea was getting very upset; Jason and Orpheus were attempting to comfort her as much as possible.

Jason said, "Let us find your father, then do what we came to do and get out of here; we can start by getting out of this room full of death."

Alethea led them to a stone stairway off the small corridor on the other side of the great room. They ascended the stairway and looked around the space at the top; the house was very quiet. All the doors to the bedchambers were half open. Alethea pointed out the one that belonged to Andris, then the men entered first followed by Alethea. Andris was motionless in his bed and appeared to be sleeping. He opened his eyes, however, when Jason and Alethea approached.

Andris spoke faintly, "Alethea, and I see you've brought your animal friends." He then asked, "Have you come to finish me off?"

Alethea responded, "I don't know what you're talking about; we came as soon as we received word of the tragedy." She asked angrily, "What happened? Why were you celebrating on the eve of my wedding that you were not planning to attend?"

"Oh, but we were going to attend. The Temple Guards and I were going to come and express our opinions about this group of beasts you've chosen to associate with," Andris said slowly while trying to maintain a half smile in his weakened state.

"You're despicable, Andris!" Alethea shouted in his face. "It looks like you'll live. I saw how many you had here; you were going to attack the wedding weren't you? Let me tell you something, *father*: I never want to see your miserable face in my life again!" Alethea shouted. She began to cry uncontrollably, then ran out of the room with Orpheus following.

Andris immediately turned his focus upon Jason. He asked weakly, "Tried to murder us with your magic, eh beast?" He spoke with hatred in his voice, "You almost succeeded too. Zeus protected me. I've sworn to him that I'm going to destroy you. One way or another I'll see you dead."

"I had nothing to do with this, except praying for protection. I believe God answered that prayer, if you have a complaint take it to him!" Jason shouted. "For some reason you've been spared; therefore, I pray for you to be healed in the name of Jesus," Jason said and then touched Andris's shoulder.

Andris pulled away as best he could. He spoke with venom in his voice, "Don't you ever try to touch me you filthy animal! One way or another I'm going to get you. All of you!" Andris managed to shout a little as some strength was returning to him.

Jason heard noise from below as some people had arrived. He said, "We're leaving now; you must repent, Andris! Seek the one true God and repent!" Jason then looked over at Lukas and nodded saying, "Let us leave this place."

Just outside Andris's bedchamber Alethea was sobbing with Orpheus embracing her. Jason touched her shoulder and she immediately shifted over to him.

"We must leave. Some people have just arrived; we may be in danger," Jason advised, then they proceeded down the stairway. There was weeping and talking from the large room where the bodies were. Alethea guided everyone to the right, then down another corridor into the room that Jason and the others recognized. They slipped out the front doors unnoticed, and quickly started back toward the caravansary. Alethea had calmed somewhat by the time they reached the eastern road and spoke:

"I'll never set foot in that house again! I don't care what kind of word comes from that monster! I hope I never see him again!" Alethea exclaimed with anger as she was fighting back tears.

Orpheus spoke, "I think what you two need is some time alone after that. You should take her away from here for a while, Jason."

Lukas said, "I agree, get away from the area for a while and go somewhere that's beautiful. You must build good memories and wipe away the filth that man spoke against you. God is with you! What happened there was not by chance, for it would have been terrible if he would have shown up at the wedding. Andris appeared to have assembled a lot of men; more than when we confronted him."

Alethea quickly broke in, "I think it's a wonderful idea, Jason. I don't care where we go; I just want to spend time with you. This was a terrible first day. I want to build beautiful memories, as Lukas said. Let us go out and enjoy ourselves." Alethea's tears changed into excitement.

Jason walked with his arm around Alethea. Deep inside he realized that going out for enjoyment was a foreign concept to him, but he was more than willing to try it. The first problem Jason faced was not knowing where to go, for a long trip would be burdensome. He decided to leave it all to Alethea.

"Where would you like to go?" Jason asked.

"I don't care, as long as we're together," Alethea responded.

That didn't help. Jason decided to, perhaps, travel around to places he was unfamiliar with. New places and experiences for both of them. Spending quality time together and getting to know each other better. He knew the hills of the Decapolis region between Gadara, Hippos, and Gergesa too well. Jason didn't want to visit his old territory, so he decided to consult with Orpheus. What he had in mind was interesting things to see, but without traveling half-way around the world. He smiled at Alethea as they arrived at the caravansary. Eustace was waiting in the community room, while speaking with Lydia. The four told him the tale of their visit to the house of Andris and what had happened.

"I would have wanted to go with you, but I understand your haste," Eustace said.

Jason reported, "There wasn't much of a physical threat, only a verbal one; Andris is convinced that I put a curse upon him and his men."

Orpheus commented, "I think God has dealt with many of his friends, for the threat has apparently been diminished."

"We've suggested these two get away for a while; they should go out somewhere and enjoy themselves," Lukas said as he walked up to the couple and stood between them while putting his hands on their shoulders.

"That's an excellent idea, Jason," Eustace said. "Where do you plan on going?" he asked.

"Actually, I wanted to speak to Orpheus about it. He's been everywhere," Jason said as he looked over at Orpheus.

Orpheus gestured to the table, and everyone reclined. He looked at Jason and Alethea, then asked, "What do you have in mind?"

"I don't want to go on an extended journey, but perhaps a week or two," Jason informed his friend.

Orpheus thought for a moment. "You two want to be alone, correct?" he asked. Jason and Alethea looked at each other with smiles and nodded. "Go south. The City of Gerasa is about a day's journey from here, then about two day's journey south of that is Mount Nebo. It is the place where Moses viewed the promised land, and where he died. Some of the most beautiful sunsets I've ever seen in my life were from up there. You can see spectacular views of Judea, as well as a good bit of the Region of Perea, and Nabataea. Travel around the mountain to the east, and you'll see some strange ruins you may find interesting," old Orpheus said as he smiled at the newlyweds.

Alethea got up, then gave Orpheus a quick embrace and said, "Thank you, it sounds like a wonderful trip. I've only been to Gerasa once, and it was long time ago; I hardly remember it."

Eustace said, "On the south side of Gerasa there's another caravansary owned by a friend of mine. His name is Ammayu, a Nabataean trader who was made wealthy dealing in copper and frankincense. Tell him I sent you and identify yourselves as my family. He speaks fluent Greek, and he can help you plot your tour. We'll miss you, for it looks like you'll miss our scripture reading in a few days."

"I regret that, but I'll be back for the next one, God willing," Jason responded.

"I suppose this is one time I can't go with you. I'll pray for you, since I can't be there to look out for you," Lukas said and received a look of genuine affection from the couple.

Jason and Alethea took a walk to enjoy the sunset together after the evening meal. They both loved this time of day. The long shadows and warm colorful displays of waning sunlight upon the buildings and landscape delighted them. The reality of all that had taken place had set in upon Alethea, as she was struggling a bit with accepting the strange events.

"Do you really think it was God that stopped my father and his men, Jason?" Alethea asked while emotional perplexity was clouding her mind.

Jason responded, "No, I don't think it was; I know it was, but your father was spared. The more I think about it the more I think of the opportunity he has. I understand how powerful it could be if he would let go of those false gods. They influence him, for he's not possessed by demons, but he walks with them. His will is intact, and he chooses to cooperate. He is heavily deceived by his admitted devotion to this *Zeus,* for he was nothing more than a

Nephilim freak. We must pray for your father, for his eyes to be open to the truth."

Alethea confessed, "I have difficulty praying for him, but I hear what you're saying. Pray for me, that I can overcome the hatred I have for that man. It's very difficult for me right now, Jason; he is my father."

Jason held his new bride and kissed her. Then he said, "You must understand, that the battles we fight aren't against men, but the spiritual evil that drives them. Somewhere, deep inside, Andris is a child of God and the Lord God loves him passionately. I know this to be true, for I am the example. The spirit within me desired to be set free. Andris must accept the truth, so the desires of his heart change. That's what we must pray for, Alethea. I sense that if he tries to destroy us; he himself will be destroyed. I pray that he has an encounter with God as Theophanes had, that example should give you hope." Alethea looked up and smiled at her husband, then laid her head upon his chest.

Darkness was falling as the couple slowly walked back to the caravansary hand in hand. They entered the community room to many shouts and greetings from those who had attended the wedding, and other well-wishers. The walk and conversation had been a blessing for Alethea as she smiled and waved to the busy room. They joined Lukas, Orpheus, and Eustace at the usual table and reclined.

"You look better, my dear," Orpheus observed as he smiled at Alethea. She smiled and gave him a peck on the cheek. "Ready for the big adventure tomorrow?" he asked.

"Yeah, even more than earlier," Alethea responded. "Jason needs prayer, however. He'll be spending a lot of time with just me and the asses. He's convinced they're conspiring against him," she said as she looked over at Jason with a grin.

"It's not that bad, Alethea," Jason responded. "The animal usually cooperates with me. I just have to watch it when I turn my back; no worse than some people," he added.

Lukas advised, "You need a persuader. A small, limber tree branch should do the trick. They'll cooperate with you one way or the other."

Jason said, "As long as the *persuader* doesn't make it want to bite me even more. I've seen others use switches like that, but I would rather have an understanding with the beast. Alethea does, and she doesn't even have to try."

Eustace mused, "That's because Alethea is what she is, and you are; well, you are what you are." He tried to keep a straight face but began to laugh. As usual everyone joined in, except Jason.

"I just don't like being bit," he said, then began laughing too.

"Have you two discussed what happened today?" Orpheus asked Jason. "I just wanted to recommend that you try to leave it behind when you go in the morning. Looks to me like you're already doing that," he said.

Alethea responded, "Yes, we have. I want to ask all of you to pray for Andris, though you may not feel like it. Jason has convinced me that God's will is for him to repent. We're going to be praying for him, but we're leaving the trouble behind. Pray for him, for if he continues...."

"If he continues, then it will be turned against him," Jason said as he completed Alethea's statement. "If God is for us, who can stand against us? For his sake we must pray for his eyes to be opened, like Theophanes," he added.

Lukas spoke, "Jason's right, for no one knows this better than repentant demoniacs. God loves him despite what this world and the things of this world would have you believe. If it were not so, this new family would not exist. Jesus demonstrates the love of God. If we truly follow Jesus, then we must follow that as well. He says to love your enemies and pray for them."

Eustace said, "It is very difficult, Lukas, for I don't have the understanding that you do. My life experience tells me that Andris will continue on his course no matter what. I'm trying to understand the level of compassion of which you speak. I will pray for him. Theophanes is a good example, if anything convinces me, that will."

Orpheus suggested, "Why don't we pray right now; for Andris, for Jason and Alethea's safety, and for the ministry God has placed in our hands."

And so, they prayed for some time. They all joined hands and prayed until the night grew old, then everyone retired to their bedchambers. Jason settled in to attempt to get a good night's sleep before starting their journey, but peaceful sleep eluded Alethea. She finally fell asleep, then immediately had a nightmare; Jason had a difficult time waking her, then held her as she cried.

"They were taking you away, Jason! Hideous creatures!" she cried as Jason comforted her.

"It was only a dream, dear wife," Jason said as he consoled her. "They don't like the fact that your faith has grown, for I must deal with it too. Did you pray for God's protection before you fell asleep, as I've recommended?" he asked.

"No, I was too tired to think of it," Alethea admitted after calming down a bit. "They were horrific monsters; animals like I've never seen, and very large, distorted men," she explained.

"Let us pray for protection, but if you find yourself in a situation like that again just remember to speak the name of Jesus. They will stop, for they cannot withstand that name," Jason said.

They laid in bed and prayed together, then fell into a peaceful sleep.

The morning brought joy and excitement within both Jason and Alethea. They had prayed for the joy of the Lord in the morning, and the prayer was answered. Jason loaded up the asses, then they said their goodbyes to everyone. They would miss their new family, but both were looking forward to some time alone. Jason helped Alethea mount her animal, then turned and saw Lukas walk up with something for his friend.

"I went out early and picked one out especially for you, Jason my friend," Lukas said as he handed Jason a switch from a tree, and it was a long, limber one.

Jason swatted his leg with it. "Ouch!" he exclaimed as his ass looked around at him. He looked at the ass and held up the switch, then raised his eyebrows. Everyone laughed as Jason mounted his animal and the newlywed couple headed out of the courtyard while waving. It was a good lighthearted moment for them to depart with, as joyful shouts and last words followed them out. They traveled a little way down the road, then Jason asked Alethea if she wanted to stop at the house on the way out of the city.

"No, I want to see new things with you, Jason. We'll have plenty of time with the house, God willing, until we are old. Let us travel and make wonderful memories for that time," Alethea proclaimed as she reached into her bag and brought out her aulos. She handed the reins of her animal to Jason and began to play a beautiful melody.

And so, Jason decided to focus on putting as much distance as possible between them and the trouble of yesterday. For now, his ass was cooperating, and the travel was going smoothly. That only lasted until Jason had to stop. He came to mount the ass once again, and it promptly bit him on the leg. He swatted the animal, then it bolted off and Jason had to chase the ass a long way. Alethea was quite amused. After that, he did things a little differently. He unloaded Alethea's animal, then put all their belongings upon his. Jason decided he was going to walk on this journey. The problem was solved, and they began to make good time throughout the remainder of the morning. Jason was determined to make up the lost time due to the trouble with his ass. He didn't want to push things to the point of discomfort, however, so he began to look for a good place to stop.

Jason walked along leading both animals. He decided it was much better to lead than ride on an ass, since his seemed to dislike him; he had been bitten twice. Having decided to make his animal for packing only; Alethea's burden was lightened and made her ride more comfortable. Both animals seemed to love Alethea. Jason was enjoying the walk as he listened to his wife play her pipe, once that was behind them. Her beautiful melodies made the travel very pleasant as they made their way through the increasing aridness of the landscape. He looked back at Alethea, as she sat sideways upon her animal with her long, dark, wavy hair peeking out from her head covering, and smiling at him as she played. Jason was getting a bit hungry and spotted a level place off the road beneath some oak trees.

"Let us stop for a small meal," Jason said as he led the animals off the road toward the spot. He looked back at Alethea as she nodded in agreement and continued to play. Jason's ass wanted to continue on the road, but a little gentle persuasion with the switch he was carrying did the trick. Jason and his ass seemed to be coming to an understanding.

Alethea stopped playing and said, "Yeah, I'm hungry too."

The two sat close to each other beneath the trees and ate bread and figs. Jason tied the animals some distance away, for he was convinced that his animal would sneak up and bite him again. Alethea thought the situation was hilarious.

"You need to share your heart with it, Jason; make friends with it," she suggested as she was fighting back giggling.

Jason got up and walked over to his ass. He began petting its neck, then embraced the animal while speaking gently to it. The ass promptly bit Jason on the arm and caused him to jump back. Alethea started laughing uncontrollably.

"Aren't you glad that I didn't respond to you that way, Jason?" she managed to ask amid laughter.

Jason couldn't help laughing as well and said, "I don't think you gave me sound advice there, Alethea. I'm going to stay with a business arrangement with this disagreeable beast!" He sat back down with Alethea and gave her a kiss on the cheek, then she kissed him back.

They spent a bit more time beneath the oak trees than Jason had planned, then headed down the road toward Gerasa. Jason wanted to make it there before nightfall, since they would have to seek out Ammayu and his establishment. The afternoon sunlight was beginning its magic, as it transformed the landscape with deepening shadows and amber hues of color. Alethea's melodies changed with the light, as Jason was both blessed and amazed. She seemed to be interpreting the color through music, while adding a new dimension to the heartwarming experience. Alethea appeared to be in possession of endless varieties of melodies. Jason looked up at the sky to see the color being portrayed by the clouds, then Alethea instantly changed her melody. The music fit the feeling that Jason was experiencing in his heart! It affected him so emotionally that he had to stop for a moment and knelt. Alethea asked him about it, then he looked up at her with tears in his eyes and said, "I was thanking God for you." She immediately jumped off her animal and embraced him.

In a short time, the couple met a heavily laden caravan with many camels heading north toward Gadara. Jason recognized one of the traders as a man he had shared his testimony with not long after arriving at Eustace's caravansary. Jason embraced him, as well as his companion. He informed them there would be a scripture reading at the caravansary in a couple of days. They spoke with the men for a few moments and Jason introduced Alethea, then they parted. Swift travelers they were not. Evening was quickly approaching, but they could see buildings in the distance.

The City of Gerasa was assuming violet and crimson shades of color as the couple drew near. They looked at each other and smiled, then continued on the road which went around the city on the east side. They passed the city walls for some time, as the crisp lines with rising columns and rooftops beyond reflected the evening shades of color. They passed the impressive south gate of the city with its high arch, which was actually at the southeast corner. A cobblestone road to the right appeared not long after, and it seemed to lead to the south side of Gerasa. Jason followed it, as Alethea played a melody that seemed to fit the urban scene at twilight perfectly. He looked upon his wife and smiled, then looked around for someone to give directions to the caravansary. In the dwindling light they could see the landscape sloped down beyond Gerasa to the south, and rather abruptly to the west. Jason stopped a man to ask him where the caravansary of Ammayu was located. He answered, "You're almost there; just ahead to the left." Jason thanked him, as the man smiled at the couple, then bowed to Alethea. Within a few moments they came upon a building similar in layout to Eustace's establishment with an inner courtyard. The couple entered the courtyard and encountered a group of three men talking by the arched stables which contained many camels. Jason approached the men, then asked about Ammayu.

"I am Ammayu," a tall Arabian man said as he offered his hand to Jason. He had an impressive violet and blue turban but was dressed in white. The men had been speaking in Aramaic among themselves, but Ammayu spoke Greek after Jason addressed the men.

"I am Jason of Gadara. I'm traveling with my wife, Alethea," he said while gesturing to her. "We were advised by Eustace of Emmatha to seek you for accommodations; we are of his family. We're on a pilgrimage to Mount Nebo," he added.

Ammayu expressed a huge smile, then embraced Jason and bowed deeply to Alethea as she jumped off her animal. "Eustace is my friend, so you are my friends as well! Welcome to my caravansary. Yes, we have plenty of room for you! Please, come inside, for the evening meal will be coming soon," he responded with very friendly gestures.

Ammayu spoke to the other two men who were his stable help. They were speaking in Aramaic; Ammayu was directing the men to tend to the animals. Jason could understand a little, as the language was Aramaic, but a different dialect than he was accustomed to with a heavy accent. It was his weakest language. Jason found Jesus and his disciples easier to understand. Ammayu gestured for the couple to join him as he placed his hand on Jason's shoulder. They entered the huge room, which was different from the one they were familiar with but similar in function. Both establishments were basically Roman construction with Greek influence, but here was a very colorful Arabian décor. There was the unmistakable aroma of frankincense enhancing the experience. There were finely woven rugs and pillows with colorful, intricate patterns around the tables. The walls were plastered and painted with colors that reflected the landscape and featured scenic depictions of caravans. There were also hanging plants and copper ornaments all around the room. The lamps and flaming urns, as well as the fragrance gave the huge room a very mystical atmosphere. Ammayu gestured to an available table, like the ones they were used to. A housemaid that appeared Arabian as well quickly brought goblets and bowls of dates with a loaf of fresh bread, which made Jason smile.

Ammayu spoke, "So, tell me about Eustace. I have not seen him for some time; is he well?"

Jason responded, "Eustace is fine; he just married us."

"You two were just married? Congratulations!" Ammayu responded with excitement. "I can see a great happiness upon you both. Tell me, what can I do for you?" he asked. Ammayu was incredibly friendly and he seemed to want to add to their joy.

"Your heartwarming hospitality has already blessed us," Alethea said while smiling at Ammayu.

"We were told you could give us information about touring Mount Nebo and the surrounding area. We've never been there before," Jason said.

Ammayu responded, "Of course I can help you! I know that region well, in fact, I know many regions well; I have traveled for a good portion of my life. I am originally from Raqmu."

Alethea was excited and curious asking, "You're from Raqmu? The city carved of stone? I've heard of it, and I would love to see it someday."

Ammayu smiled at Alethea and responded, "Perhaps you and Jason could travel with us when we visit it." He paused for a moment, then looked back at Jason and continued, "There is a place high upon the mountain memorializing Moses, and it is marked by stones at the summit. There is a legend that he was buried in an unknown valley in Moab, then angels battled for his body and it was taken away. No one knows exactly where, for it is a mystery unto this day." He was obviously excited about the opportunity to tell a good story.

"Are you familiar with strange ruins at the foot of the mountain?" Jason asked.

Ammayu's face grew a little serious. He said, "Yes, I know what you speak of. There are many mysterious ruins mostly in the southeast region at the foot of the mountain. No one knows how old, or why they were built. They are made up of very large stones and appear to have been placed there long ago."

"You are familiar with the story of Moses, so are you familiar with other stories of the Hebrew scriptures?" Jason asked as he tried to start a conversation in which he could bring up Jesus.

"No, not really. I am of the Nabataeans; our gods are Al Quam, who watches over the caravans; Al Kutbay, over wisdom and commerce, and the goddess's Al 'Uzza, Manawat, and Allat. Then there is Dushares, god of the mountains. These are the gods of my people. We depict them in stone, as faces only in squares on obelisk's or walls," Ammayu informed Jason. He gestured to a couple of examples within the room.

"Do you speak to these gods?" Jason asked.

"I do not speak anymore, for I have never seen any evidence of their influence. They are part of our culture," Ammayu said less than passionate about the subject.

"Alethea and I represent the one, true, living God and Jesus, the Son of God who walks in the flesh; he is currently teaching in the Galilee," Jason explained, then looked intently at Ammayu. "Have you heard of him?" he asked.

"Yes, I have, but only a little. What can you tell me?" Ammayu asked.

Jason smiled and said, "I was set free from a lifetime of demonic possession by Jesus himself by the Sea of Galilee, north of Gadara. Eustace was witness to this, which is how I came to be part of his family. Alethea here witnessed it as well; we fell in love and were married. Jesus has sent me to tell how God has had mercy upon me, and anyone who calls upon him." Jason awaited Ammayu's reaction.

Ammayu began to smile. He said, "I see nothing but truth in your eyes, my friend. That is a wonderful story, for you speak of a God who makes real changes; I want to know more." Then he asked, "What does Eustace say about all of this?"

Jason responded, "Eustace has become my brother, and he has accepted Jesus as the Son of God; he met him personally. We have formed a fellowship. We've seen God do some truly remarkable things. At first, Jesus was told to depart from our shores out of fear. He demands repentance from those who come to him."

Ammayu spoke with Jason and Alethea way into the night and asked a lot of questions. The couple was pushed to the point of weariness as the good news was lovingly shared with their new Nabataean friend. The journey, the good meal, the long conversation, and the wine sent Jason and Alethea to bed hardly remembering falling asleep.

Jason wanted to get an early start the next morning. He chose a banded white head covering, as the lower elevation promised warmer temperatures and dryness. Alethea chose a long white head covering to provide shade from the more intense sun as well. The couple started out with their usual outer garments but shed them quickly. They left Gerasa behind and came to a bridge over the Jabbok River, then passed quickly into a much more arid environment as they descended in elevation. Trees became sparser, and Mount Nebo loomed in the distance. Jason planned to head to the southeast near the foot of the mountain to see the mysterious ruins first. The couple traveled slowly but consistently, as Alethea provided the melodies and Jason led the animals toward their goal. The day was a serious travel day until they stopped for a late mid-day meal.

They found a small stream, then Jason and Alethea took advantage of a large growth of bushes along the stream to enjoy some shade for a while. They rested, then Jason filled up on water for them as well the animals, and they continued on. The couple noticed trees off in the distance as evening approached and made haste to reach what appeared to be an oasis. It was another stream, and even larger than the last one. Jason and Alethea both knelt and offered a prayer of thanksgiving to God, for they knew he was guiding their way. Jason set up their tent beneath a large oak tree, as Alethea gathered wood. Jason had a fire going in no time utilizing a new fire ring he had purchased, but still used his piece of flint that came from his past. That, as well as his sword was a memorial to him of how God had transformed his old life. For the rest of his days he never wanted to forget how hopeless he was, and what Jesus has done for him. Jason and Alethea cuddled together beneath the oak tree by the fire, after a satisfying evening meal

You know something about these strange ruins we're traveling to, don't you?" Alethea asked as she gazed into Jason's eyes.

Jason answered, "Well, yes and no. I have a good idea of what they are, but I want to see for myself. Many of the bits of knowledge I have is like something from a dream. What I seek is a confirmation for both of us. I believe the ruins to be of the old time before the flood; the origin of the evil that destroyed my life." Jason spoke deep in thought as he gazed into the fire, then looked back into Alethea's eyes.

"I too want to see, so I have a better understanding of what my husband sees," Alethea said. "I want to know what you know," she added.

Jason responded, "Dear Alethea, I would never burden you with all of the knowledge that I carry; secrets of the evil spirits that cause misery and destruction upon the earth. I call upon God constantly to help me carry this burden. You will, however, attain a greater understanding of many things. All you really need to know is that Jesus is the Son of God, and he is the only way to everlasting life." Jason then embraced her.

"I trust God, and I trust you. We will see these things together tomorrow. All I know is I have more right now than I ever thought possible," Alethea said as she brought her pipe from her bag and prepared to play.

Jason spoke, "I will tell you that these evil spirits are alive and at work in our world today in opposition to what Jesus is doing to redeem mankind and save us from ourselves. The agenda of the fallen ones and their demons is to kill, steal, and destroy; it always has been. What brought it all about was a rebellion against God from entities that he created, for there is nothing in existence that he did not create. Much of it is a great mystery even to me. One thing I know is the fallen ones, as well as their terrible offspring, the Nephilim, corrupted the entire earth so completely that God had to destroy it with the great flood. These ruins we are to see are remnants from that age; somehow, I know this. What was done in the past will be done again. There will come a time in the future generations that these things will rise again. I have contemplated this deeply, since I've been able to search for myself through the ancient scriptures."

Jason paused for a bit while staring into the fire. He looked up at Alethea and continued, "The fallen angels, or watchers were to instruct men in righteousness; instead, they taught of war, destruction, and sin. They abandoned their former habitation and bred with the daughters of men to produce offspring: they were the Nephilim, and I lived with these things. Their disembodied spirits are the demons that darken this world. They carried through the flood somehow and produced races of Rephaim and inhabited these lands long ago. Joshua and his forces killed them and drove out any remaining survivors, only with the help of Almighty God. Then they scattered around the world; they are accursed, unforgiven, and irredeemable. The Prophet Daniel wrote of a time when knowledge would increase, and men would travel to and fro, like the angels. It all happened before. Adam and Eve were tempted in the Garden of Eden with forbidden knowledge, and in the end, this will come to fruition. The fallen ones want men to rely upon themselves and not trust in God; they want men to become their own gods. It was the lie in the beginning; it will be the lie in the end." Jason then went silent again as he gazed into the fire.

Alethea had been listening to Jason with curiosity and asked, "When will these things be?"

Jason responded, "Only God knows, but I am reasonably sure that's why Jesus came now, so men could prepare and be equipped with the truth. To offer us tangible spiritual weapons, and to stand against the very gates of hell, for them that believe in the Son of God. Through his name we have authority over the darkness that prevails in this world." Jason finished speaking, then leaned back against the tree.

Alethea was amazed by her husband. She slowly raised her pipe and began to play a soothing melody as the couple relaxed. The flickering firelight brought a pleasant glow upon their faces as they beheld each other....

Chapter Seven

A Journey of Discovery

Dawn broke over the horizon illuminating the dry landscape; a rocky environment with dry grass, brush, and sparse trees covering the gentle hills at the foot of Mount Nebo. A small group of gazelles, which had been foraging in the pre-dawn hours settled into a bed of dry grass near the large stones. Many animals would take advantage of the shade cast by these seemingly random stone structures, for they provided concealment from predators and relief from the raging sun. The heat of the day was rising quickly as first one animal, then the rest sensed danger approaching. There was a scent carried upon the gentle warm breeze, then a sound of hooves walking across the dry, rocky ground. The sight of the approaching menace was all it took; the group jumped up and sprinted away to another, hopefully, quiet location.

"Jason, look! Gazelles!" Alethea observed as the couple made their way across the dry expanse toward their goal: a curious structure of very large stones.

Jason stopped for a moment and watched a bit of God's creation in action as they leaped off into the distance. He turned to Alethea and smiled saying, "We must have looked hungry to them."

They continued on until they reached the large stones. Jason took Alethea's hand and helped her dismount her animal, then tied them to some sturdy brush nearby. The two approached the structure and were amazed by the size of the flat stones. They were definitely placed but appeared to have always been there. There was what appeared to be a ridge of stones around the edifice that was almost buried. Other large stones, which appeared to be markers were set in a strange pattern around the area. The main structure was comprised of walls made up of three huge rock slabs, and topped with one as a roof; thus, creating a space within. The flat ground sloped down at the rear of the site. Jason stood in front of it for a few moments and watched as Alethea looked around. He could see another similar structure in the distance as he scanned the terrain. He determined there were many in the area, for he had already inspected others.

"This is fascinating, Jason, but I get a feeling of heaviness here; something very old," Alethea said.

Jason responded, "Yeah, I sense it too. I feel that I've found what I was seeking: a greater understanding. These are tombs, but more than that; they have a dark spiritual energy that remains, and I stand against it in the name of Jesus. I suspect the Rephaim held these places as sacred; possibly offering sacrifices to their elder gods. The Nephilim attempted to leave things behind to survive the flood. Based on what I know, and what I'm reading and putting together from the ancient text I know this to be true. Nimrod arose as a great leader not long after the flood, then rebelled against God and embraced the evil of old. This gave rise to the empires of the Sumerians, Babylonians, and other civilizations who have worshipped these false gods and perpetuated their evil."

Alethea walked up to Jason, then took both of his hands and suggested they pray together, which they did for some time. "I feel God is protecting us no matter what wickedness has taken place here. I also feel you need this, like you said, for a greater understanding," Alethea said.

The two walked around the structure together and examined the rim of stones surrounding it. Jason noticed the stones were exposed a little where the ground sloped down while walking around the site.

"This isn't a border of stones; it's the top of a wall!" Jason exclaimed as he knelt to clear away the loose dry rocks, sand, and dirt. Indeed, the stones continued down into the ground. He walked over to the pack animal and grabbed one of the tent posts to dig with, then returned and dug deeper. Below the surface was hewn stone blocks, and two of them seemed to have been dislodged; perhaps from an earthquake. They were large, but of a manageable size. It wasn't long before the white clothing the couple was wearing assumed the color of the landscape as they worked to reveal the top of a wall. Jason paused, as he looked at the loose stone block and said, "I should be able to remove this, but I don't know if I should." He thought about it for a moment, then worked his fingers in around the block. Jason shifted it from side to side, then the block eventually fell away. A dark opening was revealed, as cool, stale air flowed out. The intense sunlight penetrated the opening and gave a limited view of a large chamber. Jason looked at Alethea with a curious expression.

"I want to see for myself what this is; I want you to stay out here, for it may be dangerous," Jason said as he stood up from peering into the darkness.

"I respect your concern, but my curiosity is great. I want to come with you!" Alethea proclaimed while challenging Jason's statement.

"Well, alright, but be very, very careful," Jason said as he questioned his decision. Then he smiled at Alethea and said, "I shouldn't expect anything less of you, but all I want to do is protect you."

Jason went back to the pack animal and brought back a rolled-up package. He unrolled the cloth and produced the two torches he had made, then pulled out his fire making kit. He lit both torches, after starting a small tinder fire, then Jason passed his torch into the opening and saw that the chamber was full of sediment with a few rock fragments strewn about. There were other openings within but were almost buried. Only small spaces were visible, but too small to pass through. Jason crawled in after examining the chamber. He noticed the ceiling was one great stone, which seemed very stable. There were markings carved into the ceiling and Jason recognized some of them. His memory flashed back to his tomb, as he had scrubbed away the bloody evidence of Legion. He then extended a hand out through the opening for Alethea. The couple both noted that the extreme cold was very peculiar once they were inside the chamber. Their exhaled breath was visible, though it was quite warm outside.

"Are you alright?" Jason asked Alethea as he passed his torch to illuminate her face.

"Yes, I'm fine, but I don't like the feel of this place," Alethea said as she looked over at the two other small openings. She spoke, "I pray in the name of Jesus to break the evil that lingers here."

Jason put his hand upon her shoulder and said, "I agree, in the name of Jesus."

Suddenly, there was a notable rise in the temperature of the chamber. They looked at each other and smiled. Jason began to examine the walls once their eyes adjusted to the dim light of the torches. Irregular shaped very large stones fitted together perfectly; the joints between the stones were very tiny, so that a blade could not pass through.

"No man has the capability of this type of construction," Jason said as the couple looked closely at the impossible precision of the walls. He continued, "I suspect the large stones above are markers built upon much older ruins that lie buried. See, the stones on top are rougher, and more recent. I believe this to be very ancient; not built by the hands of men. The Nephilim had abilities inherited from the fallen ones. They built mighty fortresses; not to protect themselves from men, but from each other. This is but a small remnant and most likely revered by the Rephaim, so they used it as a tomb."

"Do you know the meaning of these strange symbols upon the ceiling, Jason?" Alethea asked as she passed her torch up and examined the petroglyphs.

Jason responded, "I'd rather not go into it too much, Alethea, but the spirals represent a doorway; a passage to another realm. The others present here depict diverse creatures, as well as normal animals and men. The size differences you see are, most likely, actual. See the large one with horns standing next to the spiral? It's holding a man by the foot. That's about all I wish to contemplate about these symbols."

Jason then moved over to the two visible dark voids on the opposite wall. One was very small and completely buried; the other, however, continued back. Jason scooped the sediment away until it was large enough to pass his torch in. The sediment sloped down into the smaller void and was free of sediment further back. Jason passed his torch into the chamber, then went silent for several moments. He backed out, then looked at Alethea.

"You said your curiosity was great; take a look," he said with an unusual expression. "Just don't touch anything," he added.

Alethea put her torch forward into the opening, then crawled in slightly and gasped. There was the exposed upper half of a very large skeleton. The skull, which was half buried in the sediment was more than twice the size of a normal person. There was a breastplate covering the chest area that assumed the color and texture of the sediment. Also visible was the unmistakable glint of gold rings upon the bony fingers, of which there were six on each hand. The hands rested upon the handle of a huge sword which extended into the sloping sediment that concealed the waist and legs. The sword itself was, most likely, the height of a normal man. She felt Jason's hand touch her back.

"Let us get out of here," he said calmly as he assisted her backing out of the opening. Then he began to scoop up the smooth sediment and tossed it into the opening until it was covered.

They said nothing as Jason gestured for Alethea to exit the chamber first. She handed her torch to him and crawled out, then Jason tossed the burning torches out and exited himself. He summoned all of his strength, then struggled to pick up the stone block and slide it back into place. He used the tent post again to re-bury the wall more completely than it was.

Jason sat down and rested his back against the structure. Alethea stood in front of him preparing to sit, as Jason beheld his new wife covered in dirt. He smiled and said with a grin, "I love you."

Alethea smiled as the dirt upon her face was unable to hide her natural beauty. She sat down next to Jason and looked him over. "I love you too, but we need to find a place to wash," she said.

"What we just witnessed was the reason God instructed Joshua to go into certain cities and kill every living thing. The Rephaim were not human. They, like the Nephilim, were creatures that should have never been. Now, their existence is just as real to you as to me. I'm very impressed by your bravery, for you saw it yourself. If I would have gone in alone and told you it wouldn't have been the same. You knew that, and my respect for you has grown," Jason said as he looked into Alethea's eyes.

Alethea kissed Jason on the cheek, even though they were both filthy. She said, "I can't get over the sight of that *thing,* for it had two rows of teeth! I couldn't help but wonder what just one of those rings would be worth; I could wear it as a bracelet! Your dreams and distant memories now have a very firm foundation, as well as my interpretation of what you tell me; your stories have a new dimension in my mind. Not that I ever doubted you, but physical proof provides its own establishment. My respect for you has grown also, as well as my faith. I think these sites are focal points of dark spiritual energy. I want to travel around them for the remainder of the day and pray as we did here, after we find a place to wash."

"But you look adorable covered in dirt!" Jason said as he chuckled, which inspired Alethea to smile and embrace him. He pointed to a denser concentration of olive trees in the distance and said, "I suspect there's a stream over there. Rest assured, Alethea, you wouldn't want anything from that tomb." He asked, "You didn't touch anything did you?"

"No, of course not," Alethea responded. "I felt what you're feeling, for everything in there was tainted with evil. That was a lot of gold though, Jason," she added.

"Yeah, it was a grave robbers dream," Jason said. "I thank God that we're not. I shudder to think of someone attempting to take that gold, but unaware of the curse that would accompany it, that's why I tried to conceal it. Sometime in the future men may discover such things and interpret them as a confirmation of the scriptures. Perhaps an age in which the thirst for knowledge surpasses the lust for gold; the value of such things would become precious. For now, however, it's a tomb filled with filth; better to remain buried," he concluded.

Jason gathered the torches and the post, then gave the animals water. He narrowly escaped yet another bite as his pack animal was very impatient. The couple was off again searching for one of the few small streams found in the otherwise dry land. Jason was correct, for the couple found a stream nourishing a grove of wild olive trees, as well as bushes and various plants. There Jason and Alethea washed, then changed their clothes, and worked together washing the clothes they had worn in the chamber. They hung the garments in the trees and suspected they would be dry in no time. The two settled down in a beautiful spot beneath one of the larger olive trees and felt very refreshed after washing. They enjoyed a nice mid-day meal of dried fish, bread, and dates, then laid back in a thick growth of soft grass and looked up at the sky.

Alethea spoke, "Tell me about that perplexing moment you had at the wedding, Jason. I asked you what it was, and you said you would tell me later. I think we've both been distracted after that horror of going to my father's house."

Jason responded, "I saw a *man* sitting at the table where I usually sit. I recognized him from, well, a dream, or some kind of vision. I've never seen his face completely. He gave me encouragement when I needed it; I believe him to be an angel of the Lord. He seemed to disappear right after the ceremony."

Alethea's curiosity was ignited. "What did he say to you?" she asked.

Jason arose for a moment and looked into Alethea's eyes as he smiled. He disclosed to her, "I wasn't going to share this with anyone, but you're different." He lay back down and continued, "He confirmed to me that you're my chosen helper, and you would always be a comfort and a blessing to me. I didn't hesitate when I met you, as you know; somehow, I already knew this. I couldn't get you out of my mind from the first moment I saw you."

This time, Alethea arose and looked into Jason's eyes. She had a serious look upon her face, but a pleasant one. "That would explain why I love you so much, for I knew as well," she said as she bent over and kissed Jason on the forehead. "I thought of you often too," Alethea added as she looked into Jason's eyes for a long moment, then lay back alongside her husband.

Jason continued, "He also told me about the people God has put into my life; true friends that love me. Speaking of them makes me miss them, especially Lukas. He identified himself simply as one who is concerned over the spirits of men." He looked at Alethea intently and said, "This was the night before the first scripture reading, remember? He told me the word that was coming would strengthen me and it came to pass."

Alethea lay beside Jason and was overwhelmed by the revelations coming forth as her spirit bore witness to them as truth. "What else did he say?" she asked in a very peaceful voice.

Jason responded, "Something very important, for it has become engraved upon my mind and my heart. Trust God no matter the circumstance. He said it twice; I'll never forget it. It's a little foreboding really, as it makes me wonder what's coming. But I'm confident, for I trust God daily no matter the circumstances. He commented on what he referred to as my *beautiful repentance* and that it had been noticed. You experienced what happened at the wedding; I have a great confidence that God is with us."

"I'm still coming to grips with that, Jason. Again, the distraction of Andris and what could have happened took our focus away from that tremendous blessing. I prayed the night before for a powerful presence of God at our wedding," Alethea said as she gazed up at the sky.

Jason had rolled over on his side as he smiled at Alethea and played with her hair a little. He said, "That's amazing, for I prayed also. I was thinking of how great it would have been if Jesus and his disciples could have attended. I, kind of jokingly, invited God Almighty to our wedding. I felt silly about it at the time. I even thought about it right before we were married; I was pretty nervous."

Alethea had been looking out at the sky, then looked at Jason. A smile grew upon her face and she began to giggle, as did Jason. Before long both had erupted in fervent laughter. Their joyful moment distracted the couple so that they didn't notice three men approach. They were Arabian men; wearing tattered, dusty, light-colored clothing, and all had banded head coverings with the lower portion of their faces covered. Jason noticed the men after they had already come close. One stood near the animals, as he looked them over while touching the supplies. The other two were quickly approaching Jason and Alethea. The larger of the two walked straight for Jason; the other walked toward Alethea as he was snickering. Jason sprung to his feet, which caused both men to stop. The larger one stood only a few paces away from Jason; the other was looking intently at Alethea, as a very tense moment ensued.

"What do you want? Are you hungry?" Jason asked, but knew these men only had wickedness on their minds. The larger man uttered something in a language Jason couldn't understand, which inspired the men to chuckle. Alethea was frightened, as the other of the two men moved slowly toward her and she gasped a little. She could see the evil in his eyes. The man who had been standing by the animals began to approach Alethea as well. The larger man in front of Jason drew a dagger and lunged at him.

Jason had spoken to God in the few seconds that he had and thanked him for providing the impulse to fully dress. He drew his sword and struck, which severed the hand that held the dagger. He brought the pommel of his sword down upon the man's head, which sent him crashing to the ground. The other two men stopped dead as Jason turned toward them; he noticed one had also drawn a dagger. Jason flipped his sword over the back of his hand a couple of times. The man dropped his dagger as he looked at his unconscious, dismembered companion. Suddenly, the two men ran off, while leaving the third behind.

"Jason!" Alethea shouted as she jumped at her husband and clung to him in a tight embrace. She then began to weep. Jason dropped his bloody sword and held his wife for a long time.

Jason walked over to the unfortunate criminal, once Alethea had calmed. He bent down and put his hand on his neck to see that he was alive. Alethea brought some spare cloth out of one of the bags on the pack animal, then Jason wrapped the stump of the man's right arm. He laid his hands upon him and prayed, "Father God, I pray for this man to survive and receive restoration in the name of Jesus. I pray that he be forgiven, as we forgive him in the name of Jesus." The man remained unconscious. Jason walked over to the pack animal, once again pulling out one of the tent posts. He dug a small but rather deep hole, then walked over to the dismembered hand still holding the dagger. He used his foot to kick it over into the hole, and buried it dagger and all. He retrieved the dagger the man had dropped and slid it into his sash. The Arabian man began to awaken. He opened his eyes and slowly sat up as he looked at his bandaged stump, then at Jason with both fear and hatred.

"Do you understand me?" Jason asked in Aramaic as he attempted to communicate, but the man remained silent.

"What was your intentions?" Alethea asked, which was more of a rebuke than a question.

The man just sat there and glared at Jason. He walked over to pick up his sword and held it while glancing back at the man. He then wiped the blood from the blade in the grass the couple had enjoyed and returning it to its place. Jason walked back toward the man, when he suddenly found the strength to jump up and run. He and Alethea watched as the man ran and staggered at times until he was far off; the others had disappeared.

Jason said, "I strongly suggest we depart quickly, for they may return attempting revenge; they may have friends. I say we head for the mountain."

Alethea agreed and said, "Yeah, I just want to get away from here, but it's a shame. I was going to suggest we camp here, for it's such a beautiful spot." She then looked upon the bloody grass. "At least it was," she added.

"I can't get over the feeling they're in danger," Lukas commented as he reclined at the table with Orpheus and Eustace. Lydia and Melina had joined them as well, for they had completed the preparations for the evening meal. It was the slow part of a usual day.

"Your letting your imagination run away with you, Lukas. You've been worried about them ever since they left," Orpheus responded.

"Lukas, I feel sorry for anyone who tries to harm them," Eustace said as he attempted to reassure Lukas.

Melina reached across the table while placing her hand upon Lukas's and said, "Jason and Alethea both have survived a lot of adversity, but I understand how you feel; I love them too." Lukas looked at her with a smile.

Lydia said, "I really missed them at the scripture reading yesterday. I have full confidence in Jason being more than capable to take care of them."

They sat and conversed for some time until a few people started to come in for the evening meal. Lukas and Orpheus decided to take a walk. "You really think they're alright?" Lukas asked Orpheus.

"Let us pray for them as we walk. One thing I know for sure; God is with them," Orpheus said as he looked at Lukas and smiled. They decided to walk up the hill toward Gadara, so they could look south....

Jason and Alethea traveled until dusk, so they could put as much distance between them and their previous stop as possible. Their fortune prevailed, as the couple found a larger stream that seemed to neander around the southern edge of the mountain's base. There were plenty of trees, bushes, and grass. It was a more beautiful place than the last one by far. Jason took Alethea's hand and helped her off of her animal.

"I really missed your pipe this afternoon," Jason said as he began to unload the tent and other supplies they would need. There was no problem with the asses, for they were busy drinking; Jason had tied them to have access to the stream. "Are you alright?" he asked.

"I'm fine. I'll play for you tonight. Just wasn't in the mood this afternoon. I'm sorry," Alethea said as she began pulling things out that they would need.

"I understand, that's quite alright. We'll start over tomorrow and leave that evil far behind us," Jason responded, then got busy with the tent.

"Actually, I've already left it behind," Alethea proclaimed with a smile. "I'll play my aulos for you and we can get back to enjoying ourselves after the meal," she said as she began to gather firewood.

Jason dug a pit after setting up the tent, then started a fire within. Alethea watched with curiosity.

"Why did you dig a hole for the fire?" she asked.

"So it cannot be seen from a distance. I don't want to give those men a beacon to follow if they're looking for us," he said. Jason could tell Alethea was a bit frightened, although doing a very good job of hiding it. He added, "I plan to stay awake tonight while you sleep. I'll sleep a bit in the morning."

Jason and Alethea ate a nice meal, then cuddled by the fire wrapped up in their outer garments, for the night was chilly. They watched the remainder of a beautiful sunset looking to the southwest; a bright gold display upon the high cloud layer, which descended into deep, rich hues of violet and blue. Alethea held onto Jason tightly, as the darkness enveloped them.

"Is the evil in this world getting worse, Jason?" she asked as she gazed into the fire.

Jason responded, "Yes, I believe it will keep getting worse until the end. Somehow, I know after a lot of contemplating that Jesus came to do something very important. Many will fall under the influence of the fallen ones and think they're doing righteous acts. They are great deceivers; they will seduce men to bring about their own destruction. It happened before and it will happen again." Jason's words trailed off for a moment, then he reminded Alethea she was going to play her pipe. She smiled while reaching over to her bag, then pulled out her aulos and began playing a slow soothing melody.

Alethea stopped after a while and wanted more conversation. "I can't stop thinking about that monster we saw in the tomb; it's frightening to think of that thing in life. Are they still around? I guess that, as well as the trouble we've experienced has me unsettled. Maybe I'll stay up with you tonight," she said as she cuddled with her husband.

Jason replied, "I believe they were scattered, but who knows where. I don't know of any recent reports of the Rephaim in this part of the world. I'm much more concerned with men whose spirits are compromised by such evil." Jason paused for a moment as he looked into the fire. He then continued, "Be of good cheer, dear Alethea, for God is with us. Tomorrow, we shall ascend this mountain and see where Moses stood and looked out over the promised land; I'm pretty excited about that."

Alethea smiled and said, "Thank you, Jason, for I feel much better. I am very excited about seeing the site, as well as the sunsets Orpheus spoke of. It's difficult to be very frightened with you around. Orpheus told me a bit about your *abilities*."

Jason responded, "It's not something I'm proud of. I was very disturbed by it when I first discovered it after my deliverance. I prayed fervently for God to turn what arose out of wickedness into defending the innocent. It has served me well since then. I don't rely on my ability with a sword, but in God. I did thank him for giving me the impulse to put my sword and sash on when we changed clothes; I almost left it lay." Jason looked over at Alethea as the firelight reflected as a flicker in his eyes.

"I've never seen anything like it, Jason," Alethea said as she looked at him with raised eyebrows. "Do you realize how fast you are?" she asked.

Jason responded, "I tend to look at it as being effective. The last thing I ever want to do is take someone's life, that should be reserved for the Almighty God. I could have slain those three men, but my heart's desire is to see them repent. To learn of the one true God and be forgiven. To accept Jesus as the Son of God. That's my ministry."

"Mine as well," Alethea said, then leaned over and kissed Jason. "Did you have to cut off his hand?" she asked.

Jason explained, "The hand that held the dagger was the threat; it was quite instinctive. He was holding it at such an angle that it wasn't feasible to knock it out of his hand, and I may not have had a second chance. I prayed for him, for all of them. The loss of the hand may be what saves the man; he has a permanent reminder of what's wrought by a wicked life."

Alethea looked at Jason with a serious expression and said, "My prayer tonight will include asking for a peaceful conclusion of our journey together. I will pray that no other wicked people try to take advantage of us, for their sakes." Alethea then resumed playing her pipe while resting her head upon Jason's chest.

Jason awoke late into the morning, as the relentless sun found its way through the olive trees that had provided shade earlier. He was a bit surprised that he didn't have some kind of dream after the trouble, and a little disappointed. He smelled something good, so he crawled out of the tent.

"Good morning, sleepy," Alethea said playfully. "I found an ostrich egg this morning and it's more than enough to feed both of us!" she added.

Jason smiled, then darted off. A plentiful bowl of scrambled egg awaited him when he returned. He said, "What an unexpected treat; I woke up hungry, now we have a nice break from the travel food." Jason then spoke a prayer of thanksgiving.

"I found what appears to be a path up the mountain as well. It's just to the north a little way," Alethea announced while pointing in that direction. Jason smiled at her, and she moved over and embraced him.

The couple quickly packed up and headed north along the foot of Mount Nebo, after eating the delicious morning meal. They found the path quickly and began to ascend the mountain. The winding path wasn't too steep, and Jason was pleased with how easy the ascent was. Alethea started her beautiful pipe music, which made traveling pure joy for Jason. The big meal was more than enough to get them to the top; they arrived in the early afternoon. The view was spectacular as it was a very clear day. To the west was the Dead Sea and the Jordan River, as well as Judea beyond. They could see way off in the distance to the west the outline of many buildings and towers, which they believed to be Jerusalem. Across from the Dead Sea to the west was a small settlement nestled into a rocky plateau, which rose from the Judean desert. To the south was Nabataea, which appeared as a dry landscape with wadis, canyons, and rocky mountains. To the east was the dry land they had traveled over, and the Eastern Desert beyond. To the north they could see the rise in the landscape that would lead to Gerasa and eventually, Gadara. Jason and Alethea could see all around them the hills and smaller mountains, which was the Region of Perea. It was such a beautiful place the couple was surprised that they seemed to be the only ones there.

"You know, I wanted to travel around more of the ruins and pray, Jason; we could do it from up here," Alethea said as she scanned the region that they had traversed the day before.

Jason was viewing the land of Judea and responded, "To be here where Moses stood is filling me with a desire to pray."

The couple set up camp close to where they arrived at the summit. Nearby, they discovered a pile of stones they assumed was the spot honoring Moses. The site also offered some of the best views, so Jason and Alethea decided to pray there for some time. They each prayed in their own way, as they sometimes walked around and knelt at times. Jason prayed for the Decapolis quite a bit, for the teachings of Jesus to prevail throughout the region. Alethea was focused on prayer to break the evil upon the land. Quite a bit of time passed, as it was well into late afternoon. There were high clouds, as well as some lower fluffy ones which promised a beautiful sunset. Jason and Alethea departed back to their camp to eat an early evening meal. They had set up camp within a group of pine trees, but with a clear view of the western sky. The elevation brought with it a coolness, for the night felt as it was to be a chilly one. The two donned their outer garments and shared a blanket as they settled in on a cover Alethea had spread out. The colors of the sky were breathtaking already. With a backdrop from the high clouds of gold with crimson highlights; the lower clouds began to take on a myriad of hues: gold, violet, crimson and magenta filled their hearts with delight. They spoke to each other with smiles, for no words were adequate. It was the high point of their adventure. Jason and Alethea held each other as they hoped the evening would never end. Eventually darkness came, but they kept observing until the last vestiges of sunlight disappeared into the western horizon.

"I want to stay another night, Jason," Alethea suggested as she brought out her aulos. She began to play a melody similar to one Jason had commented on earlier. He had started to tell her when she played something he really liked. Actually, he loved everything she played, but everyone has preferences.

"I agree, but we'll have to go down for water tomorrow. We can only carry enough for us and the asses to last one day; I haven't seen any water sources up here," Jason said as he reclined while listening to his wife's beautiful music. When she paused, Jason said, "Thank you, my lovely one."

"That melody was an attempt to express how much I love you," Alethea commented as she lay down and cuddled with her husband. They looked up at the sky; the clouds had dissipated. The starry sky with a half moon was so bright and beautiful that they decided to sleep outside.

The next day was exactly what Jason and Alethea desired: a non-eventful, restful time together. A lot of time was spent surveying the land. They watched a caravan way off in the distance to the east, which was almost invisible except for the dust trail. Alethea pointed out a smaller city or settlement south of Jerusalem she thought to be Bethlehem. The two made the journey for water, when they came upon a small herd of huge white animals near their previous camping spot. The encounter was exciting as they watched them gallop away; they were the Arabian Oryx. After the evening meal the couple settled back and entered into conversation.

"What was he like, Jason?" Alethea asked after being deep in thought about Jesus. "I saw him, heard him, made eye contact with him a couple of times; you were ministered to by him for some time. He embraced you. I long for the kind of interaction you had," she said.

Jason responded, "It was several weeks ago now, but in my mind it's like it was yesterday." He paused for a moment, while smiling at Alethea and gesturing to the sunset. "I think my encounter with Jesus was something hard to describe unless you're a delivered demoniac. Physically, he's no different than any other man, except I did recognize him. It's very hard to explain, as much of what recognized him within me was cast away. He knows every thought. He walks with the Father. His love for us is boundless. I spoke with him and felt his compassion wrapping me like a garment; I never wanted to leave his presence. It was a very difficult time for me, as I watched the ship leave that day. It started my journey; one I'll be on for the rest of my life," he said. Jason leaned over, then kissed Alethea and added, "You'll never know how pleased I am that you're on that journey with me now."

Alethea smiled with a tear of joy, then picked up her pipe and began to play as they enjoyed the remainder of the sunset....

The morning came, as a particularly beautiful sunrise rose from the east. It didn't take long for the warm, dry breeze to replace the chill of the night. Jason and Alethea decided to slowly start making their way back home. They descended Mount Nebo, and Jason suggested they spend one last day visiting the Great Salt Sea, for neither of them had ever been there. Alethea heartily agreed as the couple revisited the campsite at the foot of the mountain to replenish their water. The couple ate an early mid-day meal, then proceeded to the large body of water they had observed from above. They simply followed the stream that eventually flowed into it. Jason enjoyed the journey, as Alethea filled his ears and his heart. By the next day they approached the Dead Sea, as the crystalline salt structures came into view; a somewhat eerie but very interesting landscape. Jason helped Alethea off her animal, and they began to explore. He tied the asses next to the stream a good way from the salty water.

"I've been told that you can't sink if you float upon the waters of the Great Salt Sea," Alethea informed Jason, and the thought intrigued him.

"Why is this water different than any other?" Jason asked with curiosity.

"Probably because it's so salty," Alethea answered as she examined a piece of a tree that had become encrusted with salt crystals.

Jason immediately disrobed down to his undergarment. Alethea giggled as he bravely waded into the water, then lay back. "You're right!" he shouted as he effortlessly floated upon the surface of the Dead Sea.

"How's the water?" Alethea shouted as she looked around twice, then shielded her eyes and looked around a third time.

"Very refreshing and very salty," Jason's responded.

Alethea did the same as Jason and joined him, once convinced they were alone. "You're right. Very refreshing, but very salty," she said as she floated near her husband. They enjoyed themselves for some time as they laughed and played in the water. Alethea warned about sunburn, then soon after they emerged from the water. The two visited the stream near where the asses were tied as they washed the salt from their bodies before dressing. Alethea went back to the shore, and brought back a small stone with salt encrustations, then placed it in her bag. Jason looked at her curiously.

"I've been picking up stones from our journey wherever we stop. I intend to give them a special place in our home," she said.

Jason smiled at his wife and embraced her. He spoke softly, "I never thought of that. The fact that you did makes me love you even more. We now have precious memories."

Jason and Alethea traveled north along the Dead Sea until it ended, then veered off toward the west. They sought trees for shade and firewood to camp overnight. They were traveling along the Jordan river, so there was no lack of water with plenty of trees and the valley floor made for easy travel. The dry landscape gave way to areas of green, once they left the Great Salt Sea behind. It was a welcome environment after spending so much time in arid regions.

The couple found a beautiful place to camp, so that it was tempting to stay there for a couple of days. There was something beginning to set in upon both, however; they were missing their friends.

"We have a decision to make," Jason said as they sat down for the evening meal. "We'll reach the Jabbok River, then we can follow it to the east. It should lead us to the bridge outside of Gerasa, after about two days, where we could visit Ammayu. Or, we could travel along the Jordan until we reach the Yarmuk River, which would get us back to Emmatha in less time," he said.

Alethea responded, "I don't necessarily want our trip to end quickly." The firelight was illuminating Alethea's face so that Jason lay back and admired his new wife as they nibbled. "I miss everyone at home, but I'm enjoying being alone with you. I like Ammayu, so I say we go back the way we came. Perhaps we'll get an opportunity to speak about Jesus again in Gerasa. We haven't encountered many people on this trip, except for wicked ones," she said while looking into Jason's eyes.

Jason smiled, as Alethea expressed feelings aligning with his own. He lay there and studied her for a moment; her long, dark, wavy hair was very clean following the salt bath and rinsing. He just had to reach out and run his hand through it. "It's settled then; we travel north tomorrow, then head east and back through Gerasa," he said.

Alethea smiled at Jason, while removing his hand from her hair to kiss it, then returned it to the place it had been. "I never thought it was possible to be this happy," she said as she lay back with Jason. The colors of the sunset began their full display across the sky....

Lukas struck out on his own as he tried to cope with his feelings. Deep down, he had to acknowledge the fact that he was not as confident as Jason, or as adaptable. He often felt awkward in most social situations, for he had never received any instruction on basic human interaction. Lukas felt comfortable with Jason, but Orpheus and Eustace made him feel uneducated and awkward, even though they loved him as a brother. Orpheus was spending a lot of time studying the scriptures in Jason and Alethea's absence. Eustace had been away frequently tending to his affairs. Lukas knew nothing about business and couldn't read. All the while, he was very concerned about Jason and his new wife; he couldn't stop worrying about them.

He walked aimlessly around Emmatha as he occasionally greeted strangers and attempted to tell them about Jesus, but with limited success. He thought about the possibility of soliciting a meaningful conversation with Melina but was unsure of himself. Lukas just didn't think she was as interested in him as he was of her. He walked along and imagined them sitting by the well in the courtyard the way Jason and Alethea had. It brought a smile to his face, but his loneliness endured. He just didn't have the courage to ask her to spend time with him. Evening approached, as the colors of the sunset illuminated the buildings and reminded him of Jason and the first evening of his deliverance. Lukas had the impulse to return to the caravansary for the evening meal but refrained. He was finding comfort in walking alone, while praying for God to intervene in his loneliness and awkwardness. He was having to do battle with familiar spirits that were tempting him to return to the hills and the tombs. The temptation was a comfort found in solitude. He had learned from Jason, however, and was successful in keeping his mind straight. Lukas silently rebuked the annoying spirits in the name of Jesus.

It was a rather slow evening at the caravansary for the evening meal; two drivers of a caravan, a scant number of people from the city, and Orpheus who was dining with Simeon. Most of the people had left, then Melina approached Orpheus.

"Have you seen Lukas?" she asked.

"No, since you mention it. I haven't seen him since early afternoon. I imagine he found something to occupy himself with; he said he wanted to go out and share his testimony with people, so perhaps he found some success," Orpheus speculated.

Simeon commented, "Earlier today, I saw him walking alone while on my way here. I shouted a greeting to him; I don't think he heard me, for he was pretty far away. It's probably like Orpheus said."

Melina looked toward the doors, then back at Orpheus saying, "He's never missed an evening meal before. I'm a little worried about him."

Orpheus glanced at Simeon with a grin, then looked at Melina and asked, "Any particular reason you're so worried about Lukas, Melina?"

"Oh, no, I just think it's odd that he's not here for the meal, that's all," Melina said quickly while trying unsuccessfully to make her concern seem casual.

Orpheus chuckled and said, "I know there's not much work for you here tonight. We could take a walk and see if we can find Lukas for you, if you like."

Melina quickly responded, "I'll get my garment."

"I speak to this spirit of a headache to go, in the name of Jesus!" Lukas prayed over the man with his hand upon his head. His wife seemed unimpressed until the man spoke:

"I feel better. Yes, the pain's gone! Thank you, Lukas! Thank you, Jesus! The pain's gone," he said as he looked at his wife.

"God has had compassion upon you this night; seek his ways! He is the one, true, living God, and Jesus is his Son," Lukas proclaimed with boldness.

He tried to engage the couple further, but they had to leave. He invited them to the fellowship and scripture reading at the caravansary. They said they would try to attend. They left Lukas with smiles, but he felt he just wasn't as good as Jason with street ministry. This encounter was the best of the evening, so he felt he had done all he could. He was growing tired and thought to himself that maybe it was time to head back to the caravansary. He decided to sit and rest a while before the long walk, as he had been walking for several hours. Lukas found a fairly comfortable spot: a patch of green grass at the corner of a row of buildings. He didn't intend to, but while resting he dozed off....

Lukas was about to get up when a stranger approached. He was wearing a long outer garment with his head covered. He stopped in front of Lukas for a moment, then asked if he could join him. Lukas was a bit suspicious at first, but then felt at ease for some unknown reason. He gestured to a space beside him and the stranger sat down.

"Taking a rest from a journey?" The mysterious stranger asked casually.

"No, not a journey. I've just been walking around wasting time," Lukas responded.

The stranger laid his head back against the wall and spoke, "You just healed a man in the name of Jesus, and offered a confused, misguided couple access to the word of God. You've been involved in spiritual warfare all evening and prevailed with great valor. I hardly call that *wasting time.*"

"How do you know these things?" Lukas asked as he looked over at the stranger but was unable to see his face.

The stranger responded, "I know a great many things, Lukas. You feel inferior to your companions because you have what you perceive to be shortcomings. You have a child-like faith; such things are counted as great in the Kingdom of God. You have a new heart; one that is only blessed in the service of others. You are surrounded by people who deeply love you, as there are three of them seeking you as we speak." The stranger arose and stood once again in front of Lukas.

"Who are you?" Lukas asked while straining to see the mysterious stranger's face.

The stranger spoke, "Who I am is not important; who you are is. There is one who is just now realizing how important you really are. You have potentials you are not aware of, yet." The stranger knelt in front of Lukas.

"Is Jason and Alethea alright?" Lukas asked as he could see a faint suggestion of the stranger's face; enough to see him smile.

"They will return to you, Lukas. Remember this: trust God no matter the circumstance," the stranger said.

"Who are you?" Lukas asked again.

"Trust God no matter the circumstance," the stranger repeated as he placed his hand upon Lukas's shoulder.

Something very strange happened. Lukas was suddenly very disoriented. The stranger in front of him seemed to change; different clothing, long white hair and beard: it was Orpheus!

"Lukas wake up! Lukas, are you alright?" Orpheus asked as he kept trying to wake Lukas, for he seemed to have been in a very deep sleep.

Lukas opened his eyes, then looked at Orpheus with raised eyebrows for a moment before he scrambled to get up. He could see that Orpheus was not alone, for standing behind him was Symeon, and to his delight Melina was there also. Symeon put his hand on Lukas's shoulder.

"Well, I helped you find him, so now I'm heading home. Seeing him sleeping made me feel likewise," Symeon said while patting Orpheus and Lukas on the back as well as bowing to Melina. "Have a good night," Symeon said as he smiled and slowly walked away into the darkness.

Melina stepped up and embraced Lukas and even kissed him on the cheek, then she stepped back. "You had us all worried! Why didn't you tell someone you were leaving like that?" she asked him a bit scornfully. Then she embraced him again.

Orpheus started laughing and said, "I think what she's trying to say is she's glad to see you, Lukas."

The three slowly walked back to the caravansary. Lukas told of his evening encounters with people, but refrained from discussing the dream, for now. Jason had shared some things with him he had experienced in dreams and visions, though he knew there were things he didn't want to talk about. He suspected he could have very well been visited by an angel of the Lord, but he was fearful that no one would believe him. He decided to share one thing:

"Jason and Alethea are going to be fine. They will return to us soon," Lukas proclaimed.

"How do you know this?" Melina asked.

"I just know, for I trust God no matter the circumstance," Lukas spoke boldly.

Melina smiled at Lukas as they walked back to the caravansary. Orpheus had a very healthy stride for his age, as he walked a bit ahead of Lukas and Melina. They walked a little behind him holding hands.

The evening was quickly approaching upon the Jabbok River valley. The setting sun creating its long shadows in the deepening auburn color upon the stone bridge. A slight gentle breeze from the west was the only movement in an otherwise quiet landscape. A soothing melody graced the scene, as two travelers with two asses crossed the bridge.

"We'll make it to Gerasa by nightfall. I told you we wouldn't need to camp tonight," Jason said as he led the animals across the bridge and looked back at Alethea. She smiled without pausing her pipe playing but changed to the melody she had played when the couple arrived in Gerasa many days ago. Jason smiled as he remembered the music at the beginning of their adventure. He was also thinking about the comfortable bed at Ammayu's caravansary.

Alethea continued playing for a bit, then jumped off of her animal to walk alongside her husband. She stated, "I'm looking forward to a good meal and a comfortable bed, since I've never camped this much before. I've enjoyed every moment, but the travel food and hard ground have made me appreciate the simple comforts of life."

"Well, at least we've had fresh fish traveling along this river. Lukas taught me to fish that way, now I've taught you," Jason said as he looked over at Alethea while peeking around her white head covering to see her face.

She looked at Jason and smiled saying, "I didn't learn; I was unable to catch a fish. It's amazing to me that you can throw a fish out of the water like that. I guess I don't have the patience you do."

"You just need more practice. I wasn't able to do it either at first. We'll practice in the Yarmuk River, for I thoroughly enjoy teaching you," Jason said as he peeked at Alethea once more.

Alethea thought about how he taught her, as he stood very close behind her with his hands on hers. She then asked, "Did Lukas teach you that way?"

"No, I observed him, then he explained it to me," Jason said without thinking.

Alethea then realized why Jason had spent so much time *teaching* her. She smiled, then abruptly gave Jason a playful punch in the arm. Jason started laughing, which emboldened Alethea even more. There was soft green grass alongside the road, so she jumped at Jason and knocked him over into the grass. She triumphed over her husband as she pinned him to the ground. Jason was very impressed with the unexpected strength of his wife as he shouted, "I submit!" The two collapsed laughing, then Jason noticed the asses were continuing without them. They both jumped up and ran to catch up with their belongings.

"Fortunate for you we had to chase the asses," Alethea warned but was unable to keep a straight face.

"Perhaps later we could continue the contest," Jason suggested while grinning as Alethea gave him another punch.

The sunset waned as nightfall approached. Jason and Alethea made their way down the cobblestone street toward the caravansary in Gerasa. They entered the courtyard, and it was obvious the establishment was busy. There were a lot of camels in the arched stalls that appeared to be of a large Egyptian caravan. Jason tied the asses to the well and gave them a drink. Faint music could be heard from within the community room; Stringed instruments, pipes, tambores, and other instruments could be heard, which Alethea recognized as Egyptian music. The couple walked up to the entry doors and knocked. One of Ammayu's housemaids answered in colorful Arabian dress as she smiled and gestured for them to enter. Jason allowed Alethea to enter first, then he walked in and uncovered his head. The Egyptian traders were in the midst of a feast. They seemed to be traveling with their own musicians, as well as dancers. One look from Alethea said a lot, as Jason refrained from looking upon their celebration. There was an exotic atmosphere to the room, which made the couple feel immersed in Arabian and Egyptian culture.

"Jason, Alethea, welcome!" A voice emerged from the noise of the full, busy community room. Ammayu came forth, while he greeted Jason and bowed deeply to Alethea. "How was your journey? You must tell me all about it!" he inquired, for he was excited as he gestured to the only empty table in the large room. The couple quickly reclined and exhaled deeply in appreciation of the soft pillows around the table. Then the refreshments came, which was even more of a treat. Jason intentionally sat with his back to the Egyptians, while focusing his attention upon Alethea. Ammayu, however, watched the Egyptians with a smile as he appreciated their commerce. He listened as the two told of their trip, but leaving out the encounter with the criminals, as well as the tomb; Jason didn't want to promote curiosity or grave robbing.

Ammayu spoke, "I have thought much about all you have told me, my friend. You have just about convinced me to become a follower of this *Jesus,* as I keep hearing stories about him. With you, I can see with my eyes what he has done." Ammayu thought for a moment, then continued, "I hear many stories here. These Egyptians brought a story with them as they traveled here from the City of Raqmu. Their caravan stopped at a village, which is about half-way between here and there to the south of Philadelphia. They speak of a group of thieves who turned themselves over to the elders of the village, after encountering a supernatural being. They claim he drew a flaming sword, then cut off one of their hands and sent them fleeing for their lives. They became very remorseful and wanted to change their ways. Did you see anything? It supposedly came from the area where you were traveling."

Jason and Alethea looked at each other with curious expressions, then Jason asked, "A flaming sword? No, we didn't see anything like that." Alethea looked at Jason with a little grin. "Perhaps it was an angel of the Lord who had compassion upon those men; when the truth is revealed it has devastating power over the forces of darkness. Sounds to me like the darkness was driven out of those men," Jason said as he leaned back while smiling and thinking to himself that his prayer was answered.

Jason and Alethea enjoyed the evening with Ammayu and conversed until late. A good meal, wine, and good fellowship left the couple exhausted once again. They slept deeply until early morning. Jason met with Ammayu at the bridge on the Jabbok River before they departed, for he had decided to make a commitment to God. He came with two of his friends, as well as one of his housemaids. Ammayu was the only one who spoke Greek, so he assisted by translating for the baptisms. Alethea baptized the housemaid; Jason the others. The couple left their new friends happy and changed forever.

Lukas found a quiet place on the south side of the caravansary. He felt like being alone after the evening meal for some deep introspection. He wasn't the same as before the dream; his faith had grown, as well as his self-confidence. Happiness prevailed in his spirit. He had a greater insight into his place in the fellowship, as well as a budding relationship with Melina. A new era in his life had begun and he longed to have a conversation with Jason. No one else could relate to the changes stirring within him. The spirit of fear that had been cast out upon his deliverance was quite different than the doubt in himself he had been living with. It was being replaced with a great sense of purpose and boldness. Darkness had fallen as Lukas was about to go back to the community room. A figure approached from around the corner: it was Melina.

"You're not going to disappear again are you, Lukas?" Melina asked while smiling at him.

"No, I just came out to think, and pray," Lukas responded as he arose to face Melina.

"I came out here because I care about you, but I've been hurt by men before; I need to go slow with this. Jason and Alethea were something special from God. I feel something special between us too, but right now I just want you to hold me," Melina said as she embraced Lukas. He held her tightly until they heard the sound of hooves upon the cobblestone street. The sound grew closer as they turned to see two figures. They were both leading asses and moving toward the caravansary: it was Jason and Alethea! They ran toward them as fast as they could and embraced them. The evening became a celebration.

Darkness was falling upon the Yarmuk River Valley. The landscape to the east of Gadara was rich in natural diversity of trees, plants, and wildlife. The flickering campfire upon a precipice above the river reflected on the two men's faces as they finished their meal of roasted fish. Jason covered his head and settled back with a very contented look upon his face. Lukas looked over at him and spoke:

"Reminds me of our first night together...on friendly terms," he said while grinning.

"Yeah, it's been a while now. A lot has happened," Jason said as he looked over at his friend and grinned as well. "This trip has been pretty uneventful; thank God for that," he added.

"I've been looking forward to this ever since you got back, for a lot has been happening with me. I was struggling with some things, but I'm working it out," Lukas said as he gazed into the fire.

"Everyone said you were worried about us. It's not like I went off to war or something," Jason said as he pulled a dagger out of his sash. He then started cleaning his fingernails.

Lukas said, "I learned an important lesson one night while out for a walk."

"What happened?" Jason asked.

"I learned to trust God no matter the circumstance," Lukas responded while staring at Jason with a very serious expression.

Jason dropped the dagger. He stared back at Lukas as a huge grin formed on his face and tears welled up in his eyes. He asked, "What was his name?"

"He didn't give his name. He told me who he was wasn't important; he said that who I am is important. I am Lukas of Gadara. I am a follower of Jesus, the Son of God. I am your friend. I may not be as smart as most people, but God has given me a new heart; a lion's heart! I have grown very fond of Melina, and I intend to pursue a righteous relationship with her. I want to be a blessing to others. That's who I am!" Lukas proclaimed with great boldness.

Jason was beside himself with joy as he stared at his friend with amazement. He said, "I don't know what to say, except that I know exactly how you feel. It's hard to put into words; it is enlightenment and confirmation of faith. We have been equipped and lack nothing. Our weapons are not of metal, but of the knowledge of who we are, and that God is with us. Power in the name of Jesus!"

Lukas extended his hand and Jason eagerly grasped it. "It's really something to have someone who can relate to the unbelievable. We have each other, for no one else could ever fully believe," Lukas said with great joy.

Jason spoke, "I shared with Alethea; I think she believes, although that's different. The word of God says we've become one flesh. I was glad she was able to experience what I found in that Rephaim tomb, that was one time I wish you had been there. Actually, there were several times I missed you, but most of the time I was glad to be alone with my Alethea." Jason looked into the fire as he smiled in reflection. "The one who spoke to me was, 'one who is concerned over the spirits of men.' I never saw his face clearly; he wore a long outer garment as you and I do," he said.

"That sounds right, for I only saw a suggestion of his face. I had fallen asleep against a building. He transformed into Orpheus; he had come looking for me with Symeon and Melina. That was the night I found out she kind of likes me. I don't know what to do, Jason; I feel like I'll do something wrong and scare her away," Lukas said as he obviously sought advice from his now more experienced friend.

Jason chuckled and then spoke, "As long as you don't invite the demons back and manifest in front of her, I think you're fine. I've seen how she looks at you; she's attracted to you as you are." Then Jason asked, "Remember what you just proclaimed?" He looked at Lukas for a moment with a smile and continued, "That is who you are, except I don't agree that you're not as smart as most people; you're different, like I am. In many ways I think you're smarter than most people. We'll get settled into the house, then I'll start teaching you to read. You know many can't read; it doesn't make you less intelligent."

Lukas smiled at Jason, then went back to gazing into the fire. "How many times have you had such a vision, Jason?" he asked.

"With the angel, twice. The first time it was a dream, like you had. I saw him at the wedding the second time," Jason said while staring into the fire.

"At the wedding? Where?" Lukas asked while looking over at Jason with a curious expression.

"He sat where I usually sit. I still couldn't see his face, but enough so that I could see him smile. He disappeared right after the ceremony, before the Glory of God came down," Jason said as he continued staring into the fire in deep reflection.

"I wonder if he'll come to my wedding," Lukas pondered after a moment of staring into the fire as well, which inspired Jason to chuckle. Then the two men started laughing. Deep conversation abounded way into the night, before the two close friends fell asleep next to their warm fire beneath a starry, moonlit, Autumn sky.

The day finally came, as the last details were completed at the new home of Jason and Alethea. Everything had been moved out of the caravansary except for a few items. The two asses that had served the couple well on their adventure were loaded with clothing and gifts from some well-wishers around Emmatha. Orpheus, Lukas, Jason, and Alethea entered the community room for a special mid-day meal before they officially took up residence at Jason's property. Eustace was waiting and was happy for his friends, for they had become family. It was a bittersweet day for Eustace, as he would have been happy if everyone lived at the caravansary indefinitely. Everyone understood, which inspired Eustace to be a regular visitor at the new house. Eustace said likewise, as he told Jason they were always welcome, and to consider the caravansary as a second home. Everyone was enjoying the gathering, then Eustace asked Jason to speak with him privately. Jason accompanied him into his residence, then Eustace poured them some wine and the two men reclined at his table.

Eustace began, "I've been meaning to speak to you about an issue I have, Jason, but I've not been able to bring myself to do it. I need you to pray for me, and possibly give me advice on how to overcome this enemy I face."

Jason knew Eustace. There was something secret about him, and it was about to be revealed; Jason had a sense as to what it was. "I'll do anything I can to help, Eustace," he said.

"It's my flesh; I haven't been able to give up submission to my flesh. I've tried, and I've failed," Eustace confessed.

"I've known. I don't know how exactly, but I've always known. I also know you have a genuine desire to overcome this. How bad is it?" Jason asked.

"I have two women I meet on a regular basis. They ridicule me for wanting to change, but I've been reading the scriptures and hearing the word. I'm convicted, but I get weak," Eustace said with a growing look of concern on his face.

"The first thing you need to realize is your flesh cannot win this battle, but the power of God can. You have a lustful spirit upon you causing this problem. In the name of Jesus, COME OUT OF HIM!" Jason commanded with authority.

Eustace seemed to have been taken by surprise, as he threw his head back and screamed in his deep voice. In no time a knock came upon the door. Jason got up and answered: it was Lydia and Alethea.

"We heard what sounded like Eustace scream; is everything alright?" Lydia asked.

"Everything's fine," Jason said quickly, then smiled and closed the door.

Alethea and Lydia looked at each other curiously, then shrugged and went back to the table.

Jason reclined once again across from Eustace, as he was weeping and recovering with his head down. "I should have had you do that the first day you were here," he said while sobbing, then looked up at Jason. "I need to tell you the whole story," he added.

"Go ahead," Jason responded.

"Lydia and I were lovers once," Eustace said. After pausing briefly and collecting himself he continued, "We were going to be married. She was unwilling to accept my infidelities, but we still love each other. I told her I would always take care of her, which led to the current situation. I think what God just did in my life may have changed everything. Thank you, my friend, thank you," Eustace said as he got up and embraced Jason.

Jason looked Eustace in the eyes with a very serious expression and said, "You must understand and know that they will try to come back. Lukas, Orpheus and I can all tell you how much we must resist every day; often many times a day. What I've learned is that God will never let you be tempted beyond your ability to escape it. God is with you, Eustace, don't ever forget that. Trust God no matter the circumstance."

Eustace's concern and emotion were replaced with a big smile and a look of confidence on his face. "We need to get back to the others, but I have to tell you that I'm not looking forward to the meal ending," Eustace said which inspired Jason to embrace him once more.

The time came to leave, and emotions ran high. Lukas and Melina were involved in a long conversation; Jason and Eustace, as well as Alethea and Lydia were involved also. It took some time, but they were finally off to their new home. Orpheus was the only one to be lighthearted and attempted to lift the spirits of the others. Everyone seemed to be in deep reflection as they made the trip to Gadara.

"Linus will be very disappointed if he sees you all show up with long faces. He's been working very hard to make everything ready for our arrival today," Orpheus said. He went around and smiled in each one's face until they would relent and return the smile.

"Maybe we should have put off our departure a few days," Jason said as he led his animal while walking next to Alethea.

"We'll have to go back in a couple of days for a visit, so we can see how they're doing," Alethea suggested.

"If you ever consider hiring a housemaid, I know a good one," Lukas said as he looked over at Alethea, which brought a smile to her face.

Orpheus spoke, "The Lord has ended our time at the caravansary. We will still be there for the scripture readings, as well as frequent visits. I really sense a door closing and another opening unto endless possibilities." The encouragement of Orpheus began to have the desired effect as the conversation picked up.

The family approached Gadara as a large group of Roman soldiers marched by them. Not an uncommon sight, for the Tenth Legion would often use this route to march and train. This time, however, Jason felt a bit of foreboding. None of the soldiers took notice of the group as they marched with eyes straight ahead. Alethea sensed Jason's anxiety and locked arms with him. He was relieved when they had passed.

"I suppose they would have spoken if they wanted me," Jason said while reassuring himself.

"I think the Roman Army has more important things to do than to come after you, Jason. We only do good in the community," Lukas said.

Jason took comfort in the encouragement coming his way. He resigned himself to the fact that the Romans would have already made their move, if they were going to have an issue with him.

The days passed into weeks and life was good at the home of Jason and Alethea. The house had transformed into a very comfortable refuge from the world. Alethea had filled it with color and style, and the love within its walls enriched the whole family. Jason and Alethea both constantly gave great thanksgiving and praise to God for blessing them.

One particular day everyone sat down for the evening meal. Jason, Lukas, and more recently Linus kept the house stocked with fish, which became the common meal of the house, as well as fresh bread. Pleasant conversation abounded, then a loud knock came upon the door. Jason got up to answer it. He opened the door, and all hell broke loose. Many Roman soldiers burst into the room with drawn swords. Two of the soldiers laid hands on Jason, then threw him outside where there were many more soldiers with full armor and shields. A Centurion who seemed to be the commander spoke in Greek but with a heavy accent:

"Jason of Gadara, you are hereby under arrest for numerous crimes spanning many years. Most recently, for breaking in and terrorizing the house of Andris. You are also being accused of poisoning and killing many members of the local Temple Guard. SEIZE HIM!" he shouted.

Jason attempted to speak but was being severely beaten by the soldiers.

"NO!" was the only word from Alethea, as she charged the soldiers. Lukas and Orpheus could barely contain her as she desperately tried to help Jason.

One soldier taunted them and said, "Let her go! We'll take care of her!"

"Get her out of here; they'll kill her!" Jason managed to shout as the beating resumed. Jason lay upon the ground. He looked up as the commander approached and was accompanied by another man with his head covered. Jason was forced to his feet; fetters and chains were quickly put on his wrists and ankles. The man with the commander uncovered his head: it was Andris.

Andris gloated, "I told you I would see you dead, beast! They're going to nail you to a cross, as well as your friends. I'm going to sit and watch you die slowly; I'm going to celebrate!"

Damon and his wife had arrived and went into the house to comfort Alethea. Soldiers went in, then came out with Lukas and Orpheus in chains also.

"She's in shock Jason; not talking or moving," Lukas managed to report to Jason before the pommel of a sword silenced him.

They beat poor old Orpheus as well for no apparent reason. There was a lot of laughter and ridicule as the soldiers made sport of the battered men. Alethea could hear everything, which deepened her trauma. Damon, Letha, and Linus tried to comfort Alethea, but she just stared into space.

All she could do was silently speak to God. "Your will be done," she prayed as the now bruised and bloody men were finally led away.

Letha sat with Alethea and held her as she stared at the half-eaten meal she had prepared. Suddenly, she began to cry uncontrollably as Letha held on to her tightly. Damon and Linus decided to walk outside for a moment.

"Those soldiers just took away three of the finest men I've ever met. They took me in like family," Linus said as he began to weep himself.

Damon spoke, "I've heard the stories of the *beast*. They will most likely execute them. I know it hurts, but I'm just being realistic; many times, I've seen people crucified for far less. I agree, they turned out to be fine men, but Rome has a long memory and a lust for blood." Damon paused while placing his hand upon Linus's shoulder and said, "I'll do whatever I can for you, and Alethea. I suggest you contact Eustace as soon as possible; he could, at least, find out exactly what the Roman's intentions are."

"Yes, Eustace is friends with one of their magistrates. I will leave right now to bring him the news. There is another horrific scene coming when I tell them," Linus said as he thought of Melina.

Damon said, "We'll stay here with Alethea; go and do what you have to do."

It had been a quiet, slow evening meal at the caravansary. Eustace sat alone while waiting for Lydia to complete her chores so they could sit and converse a bit. The entry door opened: it was Linus. Melina could see right away that something was wrong.

Linus cried out, "Jason, Lukas, and Orpheus have been arrested by the Romans. Alethea is not well. We need help...." Linus broke down and started weeping. Eustace ran up to him and got him to sit at the table.

"Bring him some wine!" Eustace shouted. Melina brought a goblet to Linus. "Tell me, how is Alethea? Did they harm her?" he asked.

Linus responded the best he could, "They didn't harm her physically; she tried to charge at them at first, then she went silent. Her inner suffering is great."

Melina sat beside Linus as she tried to comfort him with her arm around his shoulders. "What have they done to them?" she managed to ask as she wept.

Linus slowly looked over at her with tears in his eyes. "They severely beat them and put them in chains, then led them away," he said.

"Where is Alethea now?" Eustace asked while trying to maintain his composure.

Linus responded, "She's with Damon and Letha in the house. We were having a meal together...," he said but stopped, unable to speak. He then took a huge gulp of the wine sitting before him.

Eustace spoke, "You made it here, thank God." He then prayed, "I ask right now in the name of Jesus, that we all receive strength. Almighty God help us!" He raised his hands and looked to the heavens. He then looked at Linus and asked, "We must go, Linus, can you make it back?"

"Yes, of course. That is my home, and they are my family. I have nowhere else to go. You know one of the magistrates at the Roman camp; can you help them?" Linus asked Eustace with a measure of hope in his voice.

Eustace looked Linus in the eyes and said, "I don't know if I can, but you know I'm going to try!"

Eustace had a guest who was a close friend, and hastily asked him to watch over the caravansary in their absence. Immediately Eustace, Lydia, and Melina got themselves together and accompanied Linus back to Gadara....

Chapter Eight

Refiner's Fire

It was a clear late Autumn evening in Gadara. A nightmare was in the process of unfolding; one in which there was no awakening. Eustace sat with Linus at the table in the house he had helped restore. Not much could be done at night. The weeping coming from the upper bedchamber was like an open, bleeding wound. Damon and Letha had left. Linus was in a state of shock. All Eustace could do was rehearse in his mind what he would say in the morning. He could hear Lydia and Melina attempting to comfort Alethea, but to no avail; her mourning was deep and intense. Alethea was very intelligent and knew what was most likely going to happen. Melina wasn't doing much better but tried to stay strong for Alethea.

Eustace sat and pondered his friendship with Marcus. He was a Roman magistrate who had been assigned to the Tenth Legion Camp for several years. Eustace knew him to be a fair and reasonable man, but he was all Roman. Compassion was something to be reserved for the upper class; Jason and the others were not upper class. The Roman's viewed them as being just one step above slaves. He had spoken to him a few weeks ago regarding Jason. Marcus told him there was no proclamation issued for his arrest at that time, and that Jason would most likely be left alone if he behaved himself. Unfortunately, this was not the case. Andris had made false accusations, which prompted the arrest. From what Linus had described of the apprehension the Roman soldiers were full of bloodlust. Putting criminals to death was something they typically enjoyed and made sport of it. Eustace knew what he had to say, and it was very dangerous.

It had been a long, dark, depressing night. Eustace set off at first light for the Roman encampment, as he had discussed a plan with Lydia to return to the caravansary. She was very good at improvising and knew how to go about seeking temporary help. Eustace couldn't think about business right now; he trusted her completely. He walked in the dawn as the sun rose casting long shadows upon the landscape. It was still early morning as he approached the encampment, then came upon a spectacle that made him sick to his stomach. There were two crucified men along the road near the encampment. He spotted them and dropped to his knees, then prayed that it wasn't his friends. He got closer and could see that it was two thieves according to the signs on the crosses.

Eustace continued into the encampment, after seeing the horror he was there to oppose. He was stopped by sentries and felt nervous about identifying himself. He was relieved that he, too, wasn't arrested. Eustace declared he was there to see Marcus. One of the sentries gestured to a rather large mudbrick structure that served many functions. Most of the encampment was made up of tents; the large structure served as an administration building, as well as a holding place for prisoners. Eustace knew his friends were in there, if they were still alive. He knew where to go and entering the building, then Eustace came face to face with someone that chilled his blood. A Roman officer who seemed of very high rank was coming out with two Centurions flanking him. He had very ornate armor and a costly outer garment, which was green with embroidery. What struck Eustace the most, however, was his eyes. He glanced at Eustace briefly as they passed, which made his stomach feel the same as when he passed the crucified men on the way in. He detected evil in the officer's eyes.

Eustace went to the chamber of Marcus only to find he wasn't there. He found three soldiers in the central common area and asked them if they knew when Marcus would arrive.

"He'll be here when he gets here," was the response from one soldier as the others looked on, then they scrutinized Eustace. He was surprised the soldier spoke Greek; it was probably why he was stationed in the administrative building.

"Can I see the prisoners you brought in yesterday?" Eustace asked.

"NO!" was the quick response from the same soldier. "They get no visitors," he barked.

Eustace immediately felt foolish making a request from these men without Marcus. The soldiers were staring at him now, and he quickly wanted to disappear.

"I just came to visit my friend Marcus. I'll wait for him by his chamber," Eustace said as he walked away from the soldiers. He almost expected then to harass him; he felt like he was walking away from a hungry lion. He went back and sat upon a bench by the door of the chamber.

Marcus arrived after he had waited for some time. He looked at Eustace and nodded without smiling, for he knew why he was there. He gestured for Eustace to enter his chamber. The magistrate followed Eustace, then sighed slightly as he ran his fingers through his short brown hair and scratched his stubbly, shaved chin. He removed his dark red outer garment and settled behind his desk, then gestured for Eustace to take a seat in front of him.

Marcus started the conversation saying, "I know why you're here. I want to start out by telling you how fortunate you are to have escaped this, for the witness claimed you did not participate in the attack. I know you're trying to help these men, but you're wasting your time; we expect there to be a very short trial. My advice to you is to leave here and forget any association with this *Jason.* You could be caught up in all the accusations, if you persist, and hang with them."

Eustace was more frightened than ever, for he had just been warned not to do what he came to do. He stated, "Let me tell you the truth about what happened during this so-called *attack*: Jason went to the house of Andris to ask for his daughter's hand in marriage. Andris and his men tried to kill us, and we only defended ourselves. I have no idea what happened as far as this *poisoning*. Jason and the others were with me during that time, for it was the day before his wedding. I do know Andris was plotting to attack the wedding between Jason and Alethea, his daughter. I personally think it was God Almighty that wrought the tragic incident at the house of Andris."

Marcus asked, "Which God?" He paused, and attempted to warn Eustace with his expression, then continued with his response. "Let me tell you what the truth is. Truth is who has the most evidence and who prevails considering that evidence. The evidence against Jason is ten dead men, as well as a dead prostitute. Witnesses that claim swords were drawn; a sword wound on one of Andris's men, as well as a small, fresh scar on Andris's throat prove it. What do you offer as evidence, Eustace? Your word only? It won't stand. You are one voice against many. I've seen too many cases like this. I'm truly sorry, for I know you're attached to these men; forget about them," Marcus said with a look that suggested indifference.

Eustace swallowed, then stated, "You must condemn me, if you condemn Lukas and Orpheus. I had just as much involvement as they did."

"I was afraid you were going to say that," Marcus said as he arose, then walked over to the door and shouted for the guards.

Eustace was compelled to run, but Marcus raised his hand and shook his head. Two of the three soldiers he had encountered earlier arrived quickly. Eustace felt instantly defeated and thought this to be his last moment before he drew his sword and died.

Marcus spoke, "On my authority, release the prisoners named Lukas and Orpheus. Unchain them and bring them here."

The soldiers both looked at Marcus with curious expressions. One simply replied, "At once, magistrate," then they quickly departed.

"If I owed you any favor it has been paid in full," Marcus said while grinning. "Jason is the one who's wanted. Actaeon, the Praefecti in charge of this camp has wanted him for some time. He now has all the evidence against him he needs to justify what he has in store for him. I won't be going into any details, Eustace. If I speak against him, well, men have disappeared. There is absolutely nothing I can do. I hope our friendship survives this, for you are a good man," Marcus said as he put his hand on Eustace's shoulder.

Eustace had just been on a wild ride. Maybe these Romans are used to this kind of violent threat, but Eustace was sweating profusely even though the room was chilly. He just sat there and rubbed his brow, then managed to say, "Thank you, Marcus."

The deep, dark silence of the holding cell was punctuated by the heavy breathing and low moaning of the three men. They were laid out upon the filthy floor in heavy chains and were suffering not only from pain but the damp cold. They had been deprived of any clothing except their undergarments. The men were beaten during the arrest, then Jason, Lukas, and Orpheus were welcomed to the Tenth Legion Camp by being tied to posts and flogged. The soldiers took particular interest in Jason, as they mocked and ridiculed him because of his scars.

"Why didn't they finish us?" Lukas asked in a raspy voice, but not expecting an answer.

"They want to prolong our suffering," Orpheus said during a long exhale.

303

"Trust God no matter the circumstance," was the only thing Jason kept saying. "We must all pray for God to intervene on our behalf. Trust God no matter the circumstance," he repeated.

It seemed like they had been there for an eternity from their point of view. The only light in the large chamber was a very dim glow from the other end of a long corridor, where a couple of lamps burned for the guards stationed there. There were no windows, only plain mud-brick walls and a dirt floor. The air was very foul, musty, damp, and heavy with the smell of rot and death. The glow came through a barred opening in the heavy wood door of the chamber. There was no way to tell if it was night or day, as all three men had drifted in and out of consciousness.

Suddenly, sounds came from the door, then it opened. Two soldiers came into the chamber, and one carried a lamp. The light was a somewhat welcome sight regardless of the horror it represented. One of the soldiers released the chains of Orpheus and Lukas from a chain attached to the floor, then addressed them:

"Lukas, Orpheus, GET UP," the soldier commanded. The two men slowly and laboriously managed to get up on their feet. "You're coming with us, MOVE!" one of them shouted.

"I guess this is it. I'll pray for you, Jason…pray for us," Lukas said.

One of the soldiers smacked him across the head while saying, "Shut up."

Orpheus reached down to touch Jason's hand, and received a smack as well.

One of the soldiers said, "Forget about him; worry about yourself!" Both soldiers snickered a bit.

They departed, as the soldiers closed the door and returned the environment to the very dim, cold place of torment. Jason was alone now; alone with his fears and sorrow. He prayed for his friends and asked that any further suffering would be short-lived. He thought to himself: why didn't the soldiers take all of them? As bad as it was before, now that he was alone the experience was even more horrific. He thought about Alethea and prayed for her. The fear of what might be happening to her was the worst torment of all. The only comfort was to keep focusing on the assurance: trust God no matter the circumstance. Jason prayed as he drifted into blessed unconsciousness....

Eustace wasn't prepared for what he saw when the soldiers brought his friends. They were still chained at the wrists and ankles with blankets thrown over them. Both men had swollen faces and were bleeding, as the blood was soaking through the blankets. Eustace was horrified.

"When is the trial?" was the only question from Eustace.

"Three days. We've put it off so witnesses could be present," Marcus said very coldly. He then requested the soldiers remove the chains from Lukas and Orpheus. "I'm still preparing what to say about releasing these men, so I strongly recommend leaving with them quickly," he advised.

Eustace nodded to Marcus in agreement. He then said, "You know, I will be here to speak for Jason; he's not the criminal you think he is. Somehow, it will be proven."

I wish you well then my friend, if that's the case," Marcus responded while gesturing for the men to depart. He picked up a small scroll from his desk and handed it to Eustace. "Just in case any soldiers stop you on your way out, this is a release with my name on it," he said.

"Thank you, Marcus, you are my true friend," Eustace said as he locked arms with Lukas and Orpheus. Moving was slow, but before long they were out of the encampment. It was a very solemn moment as the three men passed the crucified thieves. Lukas and Orpheus were silent, but both looked up and acknowledged how close they came to be alongside them. All three men were thinking of Jason with heavy hearts.

Jason didn't know how long it had been since the guards took his friends. He sensed a presence and strained his eyes to see in the impossibly dim light. He sniffed the air, then saw what appeared to be a man sitting against the mud-brick wall to his right. The figure moved closer to him upon realizing he had been noticed. The mysterious figure seemed to be dressed in a long outer garment with his head covered.

"Who are you?" Jason asked with a very weak, raspy voice.

"I'd rather not tell you my name; names are dangerous, so I try not to use them," the mysterious man said very calmly. He spoke in a deep, echoing voice, "Take you, for example; you are Jason, but you're going to die for being Legion."

"Who are you?" Jason repeated. He noted this man knew a lot about him, although he was very disoriented.

The strange figure responded, "I'm one who's curious. Why do you put up with all of this misery? You know, you could bust out of here. You could pick these pathetic Romans apart on your way out. You know you could. I strongly recommend you try; do you realize how agonizing crucifixion is? They will behead you, if you're lucky, but it's not likely. And what of your dear Alethea? Word is from these proud military men that they're going to confiscate your property, and they will confiscate everything there. I understand they're already casting lots for her."

In his weakened state Jason summoned all of his strength, then jumped up and pounced on the mysterious man only to find he had vanished. The man, or whatever it was, then started chuckling and appeared against the wall where he was before. The cloaked figure then got up and walked just out of reach of Jason's chains.

The mysterious figure spoke, "Sooner or later, you're going to realize that you only have one choice, Gadarene. We want to come home. This God you serve is going to let you and everyone you love die horribly, then where will you be? Let us come home, Jason. You may not get another chance. It's the only way to save those you love."

"THE LORD REBUKE YOU IN THE NAME OF JESUS!" Jason managed to shout with a raspy voice, but bold authority. The figure instantly vanished. As bad as the environment was it was better now that he had thrown out the wicked entity that had come to tempt and torment him. The statement it had made about Alethea, however, left him with an open wound emotionally. He was racked with worry and went back to meditating on the assurance: trust God no matter the circumstance. He did this and prayed until he once again passed into merciful unconsciousness....

Linus and Melina sat out in front of the house, as Alethea had requested to be left alone to pray. They sat in silence, while praying themselves. Some time went by. Suddenly, Alethea emerged from the front door. She was wearing a black mourning garment, which obscured everything but the lower portion of her face. Linus and Melina longed for a comforting word for her, but none came forth. They got up and took turns embracing her.

Alethea spoke, "I want all of us to pray for the safe return of our loved ones. I'm tired of sobbing and feeling sorry; the evil of this world has come against us. 'Trust God no matter the circumstance,' that's what Jason would say if he were here. I don't understand this. I knew there was a chance of this when I married Jason. I'm convinced that God has something for him to do; it's not over. I choose to trust God." She knelt, and inspired Linus and

Melina to join her. Her voice was brimming with courage, which deeply impressed the others. They proceeded to pray in front of the house for some time. They were so involved in prayer, that no one noticed Eustace approach with Lukas clinging to him and Orpheus over his shoulder. Alethea was the first to notice as she heard the shuffling of feet.

"Behold, an answer to prayer," she said as she sprang up and ran to the three men followed closely by Melina and Linus. They were horrified by their condition. "Get them into the house!" Alethea shouted as Melina grabbed Lukas to lighten Eustace's burden. Linus gestured for Eustace to set Orpheus down and the two men helped him walk the rest of the way. Lukas and Orpheus were disoriented and weakened by the walk from the encampment. Melina and Eustace peeled the blanket off of Lukas, once inside. Melina started crying uncontrollably, then Linus and Alethea removed Orpheus's blanket as well. Alethea shouted to Linus, "Go get a physician!"

Jason awoke to the thick quiet of his torment. He had no idea how long he had been out; no idea what day it was. He simply existed, while wrapped in severe anguish over his love for Alethea, his friends, and not knowing what was happening to them. He found it a bit easier to move and managed to sit up. Jason drew his knees up, then bent forward to give himself a little warmth in the chilly, damp, hellish environment. He could hear skittering sounds occasionally and recognized the sound from his previous life: rats. He thought to himself that he would be hunting them, if they didn't come for him soon. Water was foremost on his mind at this point; he wouldn't have to worry about eating a rat if he didn't get water. He giggled to himself. All he could do was pray and asked God to strengthen him. Jason began to drift into despair, then asked God to let him die; thus, denying the filthy Romans their sport. He passed out once again....

Jason regained consciousness while still curled up. The pain had greatly diminished. He cracked open his eyes and realized the light in the room had increased a bit. He raised his head to see a figure sitting as he was right in front of him. He was startled, then tried to make out the face but it was obscured by a long outer garment covering his head. He was expecting it to be another attack.

The stranger spoke, "Do not be afraid, Jason." It was a familiar, calm voice that soothed his spirit.

Jason was suddenly filled with conflicting emotions. "Why did all of this happen? What could any of this accomplish?" he asked with great bewilderment.

"It is not your place to question it, Jason. I know you do not want to hear that. You must trust God no matter the circumstance; he is in control," the stranger said calmly.

"What must I do?" Jason asked with a measure of understanding, but quite emotional.

The stranger responded in a calm, comforting voice, "What you have been prepared to do. There is a great evil that you are going to have to face. Do not give in to the temptation of familiar spirits. You have been tempted, but it is a trap. If you give in to hatred and revenge it will destroy you. God will never leave you nor forsake you. Do not pray for death. Do not tempt the Lord your God, for he is with you...."

Somehow, Jason found his head down again. He lifted it to continue the conversation and was shocked to see a soldier in front of him with a lamp. He was unlocking the chain attaching him to the floor.

The soldier spoke in Greek, but with a heavy accent. "You're coming with us," he said as he grabbed Jason's arm and pulled him to his feet. He then noticed another soldier with him. both were very large men that he believed to be Centurions. The light from the lamps was almost too intense as they made their way down the corridor to the guard station. They continued through a maze of corridors until they reached a heavy wood door. One of the Centurions knocked upon the door, then a faint response could be heard from inside to enter. He opened the door to a very well-appointed chamber; Shields and banners depicting the wild boar, bull, and the Latin words *Legio X Fretensis*, or Tenth Legion of the Strait were displayed on the mud-brick walls. There was a very large window, and next to it there was a statue of the god Neptune standing alongside a banner depicting a ship. It was a large room with a desk, furniture, and a table with pillows. The room also contained an ornate throne; with a very impressive, large, muscular man sitting upon it. He wore no helmet but had very ornate armor with shoulder guards, gauntlets, shin guards, and an embroidered green outer garment. The man had a shaved face with very rugged features and well-groomed brown hair. He seemed to be an officer of high rank. He studied Jason for a moment, then spoke in Latin:

"Go and get this man a garment," he said to one of the Centurions who nodded and quickly left the room. "Take these chains off of him," the man said to the other, then the Centurion nodded and nervously unlocked the chains on Jason's wrists and ankles. He quickly picked them up when they fell to the floor. The other Centurion returned with a clean outer garment and handed it to Jason. He put it on and felt an instant warmth from the cool breeze coming through the open window. The man glanced at both Centurions, then said, "Leave us." The soldiers immediately departed and closed the door. He took a long look at Jason, then after a moment he spoke:

"I am Actaeon. I am the Praefecti in charge of this encampment and region," he proclaimed as he continued to sit upon his throne while studying Jason. "I've wanted to meet with you ever since I heard the tale of you becoming *civilized*," Actaeon said as he rose and walked over to the large open window, then scanned the activities within the camp. "Are you hungry?" he asked.

"I need water," Jason said in Latin, but with a raspy voice as he stood before the Roman officer.

"But of course," Actaeon said as he gestured to a side table across the room on Jason's right containing various vessels, as well as a bowl of fruit and some bread. "Help yourself," he added.

Jason slowly walked over to the table, then poured some water into an empty goblet and drank. He tore off a piece of bread and ate it as he walked back to his original place. Actaeon waved his hand beckoning Jason to walk over and join him. He stood beside Actaeon, as both men gazed out of the window. Outside there were various drills and practices taking place.

"What happened to Lukas and Orpheus; the men who were arrested with me?" Jason asked.

"They were released. Does that make you feel better?" Acteon responded. Jason sensed that he had a disagreement with it.

"Yes, it does. I thought they had been killed," Jason said with some relief.

"Do you remember me, beast?" Actaeon asked without breaking his sight of the outside activities.

"No, I don't. I'm truly sorry if I've caused you any harm or pain. Jesus, who is the Son of God, has delivered me from a lifetime of demonic possession. I'm a different man now," Jason said as he looked over at Actaeon. A stiff smile formed on the Roman's face. He slowly unbuckled his breastplate and removed it.

"Let me refresh your memory," Actaeon said as he opened his tunic to expose a row of diagonal scars across his torso. He quickly restored his armor and faced Jason, then said, "That happened when you ripped my armor off more than fifteen years ago. Many of my fellow soldiers were put to death for failing to arrest you. I and another were spared but beaten near death."

Jason then confessed, "Yes, I remember now. I deeply regret the pain and suffering you have endured; I pray for peace upon you in the name of Jesus."

Actaeon ignored the words of Jason. He continued, "I must give you some credit. My encounter with you made me somewhat of a zealot. My hatred for you drove me to advance through the ranks to be where I am today. I was given another chance; now, I'm extending to you another chance."

"What must I do?" Jason asked. He wanted to get to the bottom of what Actaeon was leading up to.

Actaeon replied, "You must renounce your allegiance to this *Jesus.* You must regain your former strength and power. I offer you discipline! You will no longer live in tombs, but here with me and given every desire. A short time of training, then I will start you out as Centurion. This cult you belong to is problematic for the future of the Empire. The only future you have with it is death; I'm planning to murder, burn, crush, crucify and behead all of you." Actaeon looked intently at Jason but spoke frankly as if describing an engineering project. "I want an answer, now!" he exclaimed while glaring at Jason.

Jason was about to throw up the bit of bread he had eaten. He decided to play along, for the moment; he sensed something very dark and familiar with Actaeon. "What of my wife and friends?" he asked in a mock negotiation.

Actaeon responded, "You won't care about them, once you've made the necessary changes. I'll let you keep the wife, but you must slay the rest to prove your obedience to me. That is my offer. I'll send you home to your wife right away, if you accept." Actaeon seemed encouraged, for he thought the negotiation was going well.

"What if I reject your offer?" Jason asked.

Actaeon answered quickly, "You have a trial coming up in two or three days and I can guarantee you will be crucified. We will confiscate your property, as well as anything upon it." Actaeon was making his point as he stared at Jason in quite a threatening manner.

Jason stood beside Actaeon and was sickened by the foul exchange. He responded, "I could ask you for some time to think about it, but that won't be necessary. You're coming against me with all of your hatred and filthy desires, as well as the power of the Roman Empire. I stand against you with the power of the Almighty God, as well as an anointing from my Lord Jesus, and the steadfastness to declare that I trust God no matter the circumstance."

"So be it," Actaeon said and was strangely calm as he walked over to the heavy wood door of his chamber. He opened it and called for the Centurions. He then turned to face Jason, but his countenance had changed; the features of his face had become contorted with evil and his eyes had darkened. His voice had changed as well, which was very deep and echoing as he spoke, "You just made a very poor choice, Legion. You have until the trial to change your mind. I will instruct my men to crucify you, and they know how to keep you alive for days."

"The Lord rebuke you," Jason said. Then with authority he shouted, "COME OUT OF HIM IN JESUS NAME!"

Actaeon recoiled a bit, then glared at Jason and shouted, "You have bowed down to God; I have rejected him! My Lord will exalt himself above the stars of God; he will set his throne above the

Most High! We will defeat the Son of God! You are fighting a losing battle!" His powerful demonic voice echoed from the walls.

The two Centurions arrived, then stood at attention in silence. Jason could sense their fear, for Actaeon was still exhibiting a demonic manifestation. He walked back to the window and gazed out for a moment, then looked back; his appearance was normal once again. He spoke calmly as before, "See that he is treated well. Give him a meal, then have my physician tend to his wounds. I'll be speaking with you again, *Jason.*" The Centurions led Jason away. They held his arms on either side as they moved through the corridors. Jason could feel them both trembling as they walked in silence.

Alethea was covered in her black garment as she sat at the table beside Orpheus. He was still very weak from the arrest and the beatings. Lukas had rebounded quickly and was out walking with Linus and Melina. Eustace was off searching for support and witnesses for Jason's trial tomorrow.

"I'm feeling better thanks to you. I think I'll be able to go tomorrow," Orpheus said as he looked over at Alethea. "Are you sure you want to go?" he asked.

"Of course, my place is to be there for Jason. I've prayed for a good outcome. I trust Eustace will gather enough evidence to bring him home," Alethea said as she stared into space while attempting to hide the emotions tormenting her spirit and her heart.

"It's going to be hard for me, so I can only imagine what you must be feeling," Orpheus said. He wanted only to comfort Alethea, but the situation was bleak. To try to minimize it was insulting to her. "I stand in agreement with you, that God is not finished with Jason; I'm looking forward to seeing him delivered from the Romans," Orpheus proclaimed.

Alethea smiled at the old man. "I believe it more than you know. I've had dreams about him coming home, for I trust God. This has happened for a reason. Perhaps, we may know when he is delivered, as you say. I can almost connect with his heart. I looked up at the moon last night, then I wondered if he could see it and if he was looking at it also. I feel dead without him. He will come home," she said.

Jason sat in the cell he was placed in after the meeting with Actaeon. He had a window and a small bed, which was very comfortable compared to the holding cell he was in before. No chains were needed as the door was very heavy with a barred opening, and the window was barred as well. He sat and thought about how much he missed Alethea and all his friends. He also thought about the exchange with Actaeon. He was able to control his countenance, like wearing a cloak to hide his true appearance. Why didn't the demons come out of him? The only thing he could reason out was that the man himself was so wicked and evil that he didn't allow the deliverance. He did see a reaction, but Jason longed for Jesus to explain why the spirits within Actaeon were so tenacious. He thought about the evil there which was to threaten the followers of Jesus. He cried out to God, for he felt so alone and helpless. "What can I do?" he asked in a session of prayer, but not receiving an answer. He was disappointed that he couldn't remember the dream of encouragement more accurately since he was arrested. He could remember, however, a demonic spirit harassing him. He looked out of the window, as he gazed at the bright Autumn moon. He wondered if Alethea was looking at it as well.

Andris had been drinking all day at an establishment where he was tolerated. He had already lost social status, but few people wanted to be associated with him after the tragic sickness and death that happened at his house. He was convinced that his testimony at the trial tomorrow would make everything right. The Roman's weren't interested in arresting the beast without his report, for there was not enough evidence. He bragged to anyone who would listen as to how he had brought the menace of the city to an end. Andris was persuaded that he was not only removing a threat but protecting their beliefs and lifestyle. He was confident that Zeus was with him. Finally, the proprietor of the establishment asked Andris to leave, for he was being a nuisance to the other patrons. He left, after a bit of a drunken argument.

Walking was very difficult for Andris, as well as seeing where he was going in the waning evening light. He wandered in the general direction of his house. A man driving an oxcart was coming up the street, but also unable to see well. He saw the drunken man staggering off of the walkway and into the street but was unable to stop. Andris fell beneath the oncoming oxcart and his head was caught between the heavy wooden wheel and the hard cobblestone street. The man finally stopped the oxcart, then ran back to see Andris as a few others had gathered as well. He was unrecognizable. The man wept and cried out that he couldn't stop. The witnesses told the driver it wasn't his fault; they had seen Andris walking and told him it was no surprise it had happened.

Jason waited in his cell as the morning crept by before the trial. It was cold, so he sat wrapped up in his garments and a blanket as he looked out of the window. He wondered if Alethea would be there. He hadn't been allowed visitors; other than responding to orders from the guards, and his bizarre encounter with the demonic Actaeon he had spoken to no one. He prayed as he waited, for it was all he could do. At last, four guards came to escort him to the trial. He was asked if he had reconsidered the proposal of Actaeon. He simply shook his head indicating no. He was glad this was obviously moving forward one way or another. The guards put chains upon Jason's wrists and ankles before exiting the cell. He walked through the maze of corridors, as he silently acknowledged God and proclaimed his continuing trust in him.

The guards led him out of the building, then he saw Actaeon approaching a very large tent accompanied by two Centurions and they were all upon impressive horses. Actaeon wore an ornate plumed helmet along with his very fine armor and green outer garment. Jason wore the brown outer garment he had been given, as well as a Roman tunic. He walked in obscurity, as he was wrapped up with his head covered; his hands were bound together in front with the chain hanging. It was obvious that the tent was where the trial was to take place. Jason was excited at the prospect of seeing Alethea, if even for a moment. Would he be allowed to speak with her? With any of his friends? Jason remained optimistic. He had done nothing wrong. He had never killed anyone but had only defended himself. If Jason was to be judged for his previous life as Legion, so be it; he would tell the truth.

They entered the tent, and many people were seated on both sides. There was a long table at the back side upon a raised platform. Huge banners of the Roman Tenth Legion hung behind the table, which depicted the wild boar and the bull with the Latin words *Legio X Fretensis.* He assumed the two men seated at the table were the magistrates, as they were dressed in white tunics with fine outer garments. Eustace had described his friend Marcus in a conversation once, so he assumed the younger man might be Marcus; the one seated in the center was a much older man. Jason scanned the crowds and spotted his family. He saw Eustace, Lukas, and Orpheus. Next to him was a figure he hardly recognized wearing black. When he looked at her, she uncovered her head: it was Alethea. She had tears streaming down her face and as much of a smile as she could manage. Then he noticed Lydia, Melina, Symeon, Theophanes, Damon, and Letha as well. He knew they had all been praying for him and felt a surge of joy for the first time since his arrest.

Jason smiled at everyone with an expression of confidence, but he was not allowed to speak. He was slowly led around before the crowd. No one really had much of a reaction, except for those he knew. There was a bench near the long table to the right and he was seated there with a soldier on either side, as well as two behind, standing. Actaeon made his way to the long table accompanied by his honor guard; the two Centurions that had attended to him in his chambers. There were also scribes to the left, so the event could be recorded. Actaeon removed his helmet and sat at the table with the two magistrates on his left, and his two Centurions standing behind him. One of them shouted for the crowd to be silent, then announced the proceedings were to be spoken in Greek.

The magistrate in the center spoke in a very business as usual way, "I understand there is a spokesman for the multiple witnesses regarding the old reports. Come forward now." Two men came forward. "This is your opportunity to face the accused. Do so, then make your statement," he said. The two men looked around with awkward expressions, then one spoke:

"You said it was our opportunity to face the accused, where is he?" one of them asked. The two men scanned around the tent, as well as looking at Jason.

"All of the witnesses present come forward," the magistrate requested. Many more came forward and looked around as well. Actaeon gestured to the guards to stand with Jason, so they uncovered his head and stood. The small crowd was still scanning the people and were looking more and more perplexed.

"Where is the beast? bring him out so we can identify him!" the spokesman shouted.

The two magistrates and Actaeon leaned together and discussed the proceedings for a few moments. Then Marcus, the magistrate to the right, announced that the witnesses were to return to their seats. Actaeon looked over and stared at Jason with hatred in his eyes. The crowd assembled began murmuring as the three at the table continued discussing the proceedings. Two soldiers entered the tent and approached the table, then one leaned forward and spoke with the magistrates. Actaeon suddenly grimaced, then returned his evil stare toward Jason. He desperately wanted to see Alethea once again, but he couldn't see them from his vantage point. It was obvious to him, and confirmed by the look on Actaeon's face, that the witnesses were unable to identify him as the beast. Jason couldn't help grinning a bit as he closed his eyes while praising God. He awaited the appearance of Andris, which was the reason he was arrested. He never showed up. Jason was wondering why.

"Are there any further witnesses regarding the accusations of Andris, or the attacks on his estate? Come forth now!" Marcus spoke loudly, but no one came forth. He continued, "I must announce at this time that Andris, the accuser for most of the charges against this man who calls himself Jason of Gadara, was found dead yesterday evening in an accident of his own making. Are there any more witnesses? Come forth now!"

Jason heard a commotion from the area where Alethea was sitting. He looked over and saw Orpheus lead Alethea out of the tent; she was sobbing. He was touched by the heart of Alethea, even at a distance. He silently prayed for God to comfort his wife and give her peace. Jason was sorrowed himself, for he had given Andris many opportunities to repent. He silently prayed for God to have mercy upon him. Then he realized that the accusations against him had fallen apart despite the ongoing discussion between the magistrates and Actaeon. A period of murmuring erupted unchecked, as the endless discussion at the table continued. Jason saw Orpheus and Alethea return, and at a distance he made eye contact with his wife. She looked very distressed, as she looked up toward heaven, then returned her tear-filled eyes toward Jason. Alethea was confident he would be released. Marcus stood, then the Centurion behind him called the crowd to order.

Marcus spoke, "These proceedings have failed to yield any evidence, or even accusations, except one. I will now ask the commander of this camp, Praefecti Actaeon, to speak. My fellow magistrate and I have moved to dismiss the case." He then gestured to Actaeon as he stood up.

Actaeon spoke, "I propose that justice was not served here. I was injured by this *beast* many years ago, and I am not afraid to identify him. He has performed many tricks to evade punishments for his crimes. I have considered the statement made by the magistrates, but I am not satisfied. My authority is absolute for this camp and region, so I proclaim this man be kept in our prison. I will submit to Rome that this man should be put to death; thus, ridding this region of the menace he represents. We shall send a courier to Rome immediately, and request a Praetor return with a judgment from Caesar himself. This is my decision, and it is final. I pronounce these proceedings to be over. Guards: take the prisoner back to his cell."

Jason attempted to speak. "May I have a few moments with my wife?" he asked.

"Silence! Take him away!" was the response from Actaeon.

The four soldiers that escorted Jason to the trial got him to his feet and led him out of the tent. He could see Alethea and his friends quickly make their way outside. The soldiers and Jason passed out of the tent as the group was waiting outside. One of the soldiers looked toward Actaeon as they left; he was still seated at the table.

The soldier leaned over to Jason and whispered, "Make it quick, for we're supposed to take you straight back." The soldiers stepped back from Jason.

He was immediately embraced by Alethea. She had begun sobbing again following Actaeon's proclamation. "Don't talk; just hold me!" she said. He was unable to return the embrace due to the chains. She held him, and he buried his face in her hair. All of Jason's friends rushed to lay a hand upon him with a word of encouragement. The moment passed all too quickly, as the soldiers grabbed Jason by the arms and led him away. The group departed, except for Eustace. He waited for Marcus to emerge, then requested a conversation. Marcus agreed, then the two men walked back to the mudbrick building and into Marcus's chamber.

Eustace spoke, "What just happened, Marcus? He should have been released! This is not justice. I knew there was a chance Jason could have been condemned, but your case against him fell apart! No one could identify him! Andris, thank God, was unable to testify. How is it that Actaeon can overrule the obvious lack of evidence?" Eustace was beside himself with emotion as he demanded answers of his friend.

Marcus put his hand upon Eustace's shoulder and said, "This isn't about justice, Eustace. It's about a personal vendetta between Actaeon and Jason. Actaeon has the force and authority of the Roman Empire behind him. No one has ever won an argument against him, for he keeps everything legal and bent toward the glory of Rome. He has high favor among the Senate; he has been decorated by Caesar himself. Actaeon has his own private army within the ranks of this encampment that do his bidding without question. I've seen people disappear that have opposed him, like I've told you before. No, you're absolutely correct, my friend; this is not justice, but it is a reality. I must tell you that I stand with it. Our empire is bringing order to the world. My feeling is there will be peace and prosperity as time goes by." Marcus knew his words were falling flat with Eustace.

"Peace and prosperity? Accomplished by injustice? Jason is the most peaceful man I have ever known!" Eustace shouted. He paused for a moment to calm himself, then asked, "What's going to happen now?"

Marcus responded, "For now, nothing. Jason will be kept in prison. Actaeon has appealed to Rome. Everything stops until a judgment is proclaimed." Marcus knew what Eustace was thinking and said, "His property will not be confiscated, until the proclamation is issued. Everything is suspended; it's highly irregular. Actaeon has a peculiar interest in Jason, and its one that I don't fully understand. I do know he made an offer to Jason that he rejected. He turned down a commission in the Roman Army because he would not agree to renounce the Hebrew God, and this wandering troublemaker known as *Jesus.*"

"That evil son of a...," Eustace started but was cut off by Marcus in a panic.

Marcus spoke with fear, "Watch what you say! The walls have ears! Look, Jason has been moved to a private cell, and I understand he has been ordered to receive fair treatment. Don't even ask, for Actaeon has specifically ordered him to have absolutely no visitors. I must tell you; eventually, Actaeon will have his way. My advice to you is to get used to life without him. I know you have an attachment to Jason, but either way he'll never come back to you the way he was. Either he will submit to Actaeon, or he will be crucified; I can see no other outcome. I will give you a word of warning: if he submits to Actaeon he will become your enemy; I've seen how he changes men." Marcus could see Eustace was unwilling to accept his advice.

Eustace wasted no time with a response asking, "I know you don't believe as I do, but how can you deny the fact that Andris died before he could give testimony? How can you deny the fact that no one could positively identify Jason as the beast?" Suddenly, Eustace smiled, which surprised Marcus. He put his hand upon Marcus's shoulder while asking, "You interested in a little wager, Marcus?"

Marcus looked at Eustace with a surprised expression which slowly turned into a grin. He said, "You know me, Eustace. A game of chance is my weakness."

Eustace pulled a small leather pouch from his bag, then removed a gold coin and placed it upon Marcus's desk. He said, "I see a pattern happening here. If things work out the way you say, then you keep the coin; if what you consider impossible happens, then I return, and you give me back my coin. Afterward we have a meal together and you listen with an open mind, as I explain a great many things to you. I submit to you that there is but one, true, living God, and Jesus is the Son of God. I believe that with all that I am. Before this is over you will believe it too."

Marcus smiled, then grabbed Eustace's hand and said, "Done! I feel as though I'm taking advantage of your misplaced trust, however. There's no risk at my end. I can't remember ever making money so easily. I'll keep my end of the bargain; if it works out the way you say, then I'll need some explanation."

"So be it. Take care, my friend," Eustace said as he waved and departed. He left Marcus with a smile on his face. He walked out of the encampment and silently bid farewell to Jason. He walked in confidence that he would see his friend again. It wasn't long ago that Jason helped him to walk in victory, and in a closer relationship with God. He had felt the power of God, as he himself was delivered from unclean spirits. Eustace was learning to walk in faith.

Jason sat in his cell. Hours became days, then days became weeks. His life in Roman imprisonment stretched his endurance in many ways. There came the regular visits from Actaeon and his Centurions. The coercion ranged from verbal threats to beating and various abuse. The physician would come and tend to any injury that would occur. The cycle of misery wasn't the only onslaught; the spiritual attacks were relentless. It would come in his sleep, and always attempting to get Jason to compromise or relent in even a small way. The increasingly predominant nemesis in his dreams seemed to be an empty garment with no face. He came to identify it as something of a spokesman for a multitude of demonic spirits. Jason remained steadfast, but the temptations were increasing. He would hold on to his memories; the trip with Alethea, camping with Lukas, fellowship with his friends, baptizing the hopeful, the last encounter with Alethea, all kept him alive.

Jason was beginning to change a bit, so gradual that he didn't notice, but Actaeon did. He was becoming more aggressive when the regular abuse would come. Restraints were becoming necessary when Actaeon would come with his men. The change was very slow, as Actaeon was nurturing it and pushing Jason a little farther each time. Finally, Jason realized he was losing ground; he began to fast and pray for increased spiritual strength. The temptation was almost more than he could bear. He began to dream about embracing the power to crush the Romans. Then, something happened that shook Jason to the core. He descended during one of the sessions with Actaeon and a Centurion. The soldier approached Jason to beat him, so he snapped the leather restraints and pounced, then struck the Centurion repeatedly in the face. He could hear a strange sound echoing off the walls of the cell, which sounded like cackling laughter; it was him. He jumped off of the unconscious bloody soldier, then sat upon his bed and buried his face in his hands. He suddenly felt a hand upon his shoulder.

"Don't you feel better, Legion? You don't need to suffer any longer. Speak the word, and I'll have this Centurion put to death. I'll even use your recommendation as to the method," Actaeon said with an evil gentleness.

Jason lifted his head and glared at Actaeon. Speaking in a very deep voice he said, "The Lord rebuke you!"

"Your words don't seem to have the same effect now, Legion. You may as well embrace your old ways, for it seems your God has abandoned you, and rightly so. Just look what you've done to my Centurion. You will be invincible!" Actaeon said as he assumed a victory.

"GET OUT!" Jason shouted as his unusually deep voice echoed.

Actaeon called the guards to remove the Centurion, then departed himself but promised to return the next day. Jason felt completely defeated. Prayer was the wellspring of his strength; he didn't feel worthy to pray. He cried out for God to take him. He couldn't see going any further. He suspected he would fully manifest the next time he was pushed to that point. Jesus had given him a new life; he had squandered it for the sake of anger and hatred. The despair was just too much, so he lay back upon his bed and passed out....

Jason sat back up after what seemed like a brief time and put his face in his hands once again. It was night, and the light in the cell was very dim. No visitors, nor good or beneficial dreams; the only interaction he had was either evil men or wicked entities that chipped away at his mind and spirit.

"Trust God no matter the circumstance," a voice spoke. Jason thought it was his imagination. He lifted his head to see a familiar figure sitting beside him obscured by his outer garment with his head covered. Jason smiled a little and acknowledged the stranger. It was the first positive interaction since his arrest; other than a brief, faded recollection of encouragement in the cold, damp, holding cell. He doubted it was real. "It was real," the stranger said, for he had perceived his thoughts.

"I've been pushed too far. I've failed," was all Jason had to say.

The stranger responded, "That is why I am here. You drifted into relying upon yourself. You are not strong enough, but God is. God has not abandoned you. You must cease listening to the lies from your adversary." He then turned toward Jason. "Alethea and all of your friends are walking in faith; where is yours?" the stranger asked with compassion but firmness.

"I've fallen into despair and weakness somewhere amid the beatings and threats. It's too late now, for wicked spirits have begun to infiltrate me," Jason said as he put his head back into his hands.

"Did you think it was too late the morning you ran to meet Jesus? Run to him again. God is faithful to forgive you and cleanse you from all unrighteousness," the stranger said.

Jason closed his eyes. He recalled that morning while at the feet of Jesus. He recalled his repentance; the baptism, the first time he saw Alethea, and being ministered to by Jesus himself. He once again repented of the depth to which he had fallen. Suddenly, a surge of strength began to flow through his spirit unlike anything he had experienced. An epiphany emerged within his mind. This battle was not his, but God's. All fear of continuing misery and the danger to his loved ones passed and was replaced by trust in God. Jason raised his head and spoke to the stranger:

"I'm alright! I'm back!" Jason said boldly with absolute confidence as well as his normal voice.

The stranger smiled and replied, "I know, but you needed a little help. Do not be too concerned with this adversary you face. Just pray for God's will to be done. Trust God, for he will never leave you nor forsake you. I can tell you no more."

"How is Alethea?" Jason had to ask.

"She waits for you. Her faith has been an inspiration to others. Remember, that sorrow only lasts for a night; joy comes in the morning," the stranger said with a comforting voice and placed his hand upon Jason's shoulder.

Jason smiled at the stranger as he faded from view. He then realized he was in a dream. He found himself on the beach, where he had been at the feet of Jesus. It was a memory, but he was experiencing it as if he was there. He cried out, then Jesus dropped in front of him and embraced him. The vision faded, but the feeling remained as he slept.

Jason awoke, and realized a bit of bread and water had been left for him. He ate and drank as his senses sharpened; he realized the struggle and its temptation was gone. He had just awakened from a restful night's sleep without any demonic attacks and found himself with a different point of view. He didn't have to fight this battle; God would fight for him. The only thing that mattered was that God's will be done from this moment on. There was no temptation in embracing defeat. Sure, a brief victory and revenge could be his, but it would be incredibly short-lived; he would lose everything. Jason realized how he had been manipulated by Actaeon and was absolutely disgusted. He had a new approach to deal with the demon-possessed Roman when he returned. Jason didn't have to wait long, as the door to his cell opened. Two Centurions entered, then Actaeon walked in and grinned.

"Greetings, Legion. I trust you slept well. Let us talk about *future plans,* shall we?" Actaeon asked. He seemed confident that Jason had given in to despair.

Jason looked Actaeon up and down. He was not impressed with his armor and fine clothing. He ignored the Centurions. Jason spoke, "Interesting that you mention future plans. Yesterday, you and your men reminded me of my past...fair enough. Today, I choose to remind you of your future: you have none. You know it to be true, if you look deep. God is giving you a chance to repent. What good is it if you gain the whole world, yet lose your soul?

God will bring your reign of terror to an end; then you will be judged, you will be condemned, and you will go to hell."

Actaeon became furious and shouted, "Centurion, beat this animal like the filthy beast he is!".

Jason sat motionless. The restraints were applied. The Centurion began to strike Jason's head and face, but he remained motionless and expressionless. Then he smiled and praised God in the midst of it. Jason glared at Actaeon as he smiled, for his steadfastness became more powerful by the blood running down his face. Finally, he spoke, "You're going to have to do better than this; I've given myself more pain scratching my behind!"

Actaeon was beside himself and shouted, "ENOUGH!" The Centurion ceased. Actaeon grabbed him and pushed him out of the door, then commanded the other to remove the restraints and get out as well. He then turned to Jason while in his full demonic manifestation. Actaeon spoke loudly with his deep, echoing voice reverberating from the walls, "Very well, Legion. The Praetor will bring a proclamation from Rome soon; I'm going to nail you to that cross myself!" Actaeon was completely enraged and his dark eyes and demeanor were on full display. He simply couldn't take Jason's smiling anymore as he flew out of the cell and slammed the door. Jason's laughter followed him out. He visited Jason no more.

Alethea was having more and more difficulty sleeping. Nightmares abounded in her troubled sleep; they were mostly of her deepest fears about Jason's confinement. Also, the death of her father had opened a doorway of condemnation from wicked spirits, and they constantly ate at her soul. She had expressed hatred toward Andris; evil spirits tried to convince her that it was her words that killed him. One night, after praying and struggling to fall asleep she had the worst nightmare of all....

Alethea found herself in a cave with Jason. It started out as a blessed dream, for they were together once again. The nightmare quickly shifted, as Jason began to slowly transform into the monster she had witnessed as a young girl. His deep voice and insane cackling laughter echoed off of the cave walls. There was no escape. There was a cloaked figure in the cave as well with no face, and it was accusing Alethea of murdering Andris. The condemnation, as well as the horror and shock of Jason turning to evil made her cry out for death within her spirit. Then she realized she couldn't speak or move. The beast and the faceless figure were mocking and speaking insults to her, as if trying to crush her spirit.

Alethea thought she was going to lose her mind, then the dim light within the cave grew a bit brighter. She was able to look up, and to her amazement she saw Jason standing with Jesus! They were off to the side, and a way off. Alethea reached out to them in her spirit but still couldn't move. She could, however, see that the beast was not Jason. It was a trick; an imposter. Suddenly, she felt a presence next to her. She moved her eyes and could see that it was Lukas standing beside her. He drew his sword, and it was as a flaming barrier against the evil before them. With a voice of boldness and authority he shouted, "IN THE NAME OF JESUS, BE GONE WITH YOU, FOUL UNCLEAN SPIRITS!" The dark cloaked one and the beast screamed, then ran down into the bowels of the earth. She was now able to move. She looked over and saw Jason standing with Jesus. They were smiling at her, then faded from view. She felt a hand upon her shoulder, then turned and beheld a smiling Lukas. He spoke with his usual friendly voice, "It's time to wake up now, Alethea. Wake up!"

"Wake up!" Lukas kept repeating as he pushed upon Alethea's shoulder. She slowly opened her eyes. Just then, Orpheus entered the chamber as well. Alethea began weeping and embraced Lukas.

"It was horrible!" Alethea cried out. "Jason became the beast again, but it wasn't him; I'm so confused!" she shouted and continued to cry.

Orpheus came over to the bed and put his hand upon her shoulder. He then spoke with compassion, "It was only a dream; nothing to be confused about. It's over now, thanks to Lukas."

Alethea looked at Lukas and said, "Yes, thanks to Lukas. You are very formidable in the face of evil, so don't ever doubt it!" Lukas smiled. She stopped weeping and smiled with the tears still streaming down her face. "Lukas, you've just become my true brother, and Orpheus my true father. I feel very safe within this chamber now. Jesus is with us always!" she proclaimed.

The three prayed for protection, for Jason, and praised God. Alethea declared afterward she was getting sleepy. Lukas and Orpheus embraced her and left the chamber to pray over the house. Alethea quickly drifted off into a peaceful sleep.

Eustace and Lydia unexpectantly showed up at the house of Jason and Alethea one morning and were very excited. Lukas answered the door.

Eustace announced, "We just received word: Jesus and his disciples are near Emmatha, and their ship is on the beach! The same as before! Many are flocking to see him and hear his teaching!"

Linus smiled and immediately left to share the news with Damon and Letha.

"Perhaps we can tell him of Jason and ask him to pray for him!" Alethea said as she smiled. It was good to see, for she hadn't smiled for some time.

Orpheus exclaimed, "What a welcome surprise! Let us go see him!"

"I agree, let us seek Jesus! He delivered Jason from the demons, so perhaps he can deliver him from the Romans!" Lukas shouted and was very excited.

Linus returned with Damon and Letha after a short time. They were as excited as everyone else. It was the first positive event for some time, and everyone was clinging to the joy that came with it. They gathered themselves and headed out to Emmatha. The family was joined on the way by crowds of people, and many of them had been baptized or ministered to by Jason, or the others. Melina Joined them when they reached the caravansary and walked with Lukas.

The road was packed with people as the group made their way toward the beach. They could see a great multitude upon the hillside once they arrived. Eustace was determined to speak with Jesus but getting to him seemed a daunting task. They could see at a distance that many were approaching him. There was a lot of talk about a man who had been deaf and couldn't speak: Jesus healed him! Many had come hastily; very few had brought provision. They learned that Jesus and his disciples had come three days prior and traveled around the Decapolis as they had gathered more and more people. It seemed they were here to get back on their ship and depart. This made Eustace even more determined to speak with him.

Jesus called his disciples unto him, and said unto them, "I have compassion on the multitude, because they have now been with me three days, and have nothing to eat: And if I send them away fasting to their own houses, they will faint by the way: for many of them came from far."

And his disciples answered him, "From whence can a man satisfy these people with bread here in the wilderness?"

Jesus asked them, "How many loaves have you?"

They said, "Seven."

And he commanded the people to sit down on the ground: and he took the seven loaves, and gave thanks, and brake, and gave to his disciples to set before them; and they did set them before the people. And they had a few small fishes: and he blessed, and commanded to set them also before them. So they did eat, and were filled: and they took up of the broken meat that was left seven baskets. They that had eaten were about four thousand.

The entire group tried to get through the crowd, but it just wasn't feasible. Eustace disappeared with Lukas. Orpheus had gone with them but returned and sat next to Alethea. He confided to her that he was experiencing pain associated with the beating that still re-occurred from time to time. Suddenly, baskets of food came around as they were being passed from one group of people to another: they were full of bread and fish! There seemed to be an endless supply, as everyone around them was eating. Alethea thought to herself, where was all this coming from? Then she looked out in the distance and could see Jesus standing and speaking to those near him. A smile came upon her face, then Alethea could see Eustace speaking with Jesus! Throngs of people were competing for his attention, but she, as well as the rest of the family could clearly see Eustace and Lukas being embraced by Jesus! Alethea was filled with enduring confidence from that moment on.

After some time, Eustace and Lukas returned. Eustace said, "I spoke with him. I told him of Jason, and he smiled; he said he would pray for him." Eustace then began to tear up, and said, "He forgave me."

Lukas was unusually quiet but smiling. He seemed content to stand with his arm around Melina. He just said, "Everything's going to work out. Trust God no matter the circumstance."

The family continued to sit for some time while listening to Jesus speak to the multitudes. By late afternoon, Jesus and his disciples boarded their little ship and departed. Many regretted not being able to get close to the Master, but Eustace and Lukas were exhausted from pushing their way through. Most everyone else was too old, tired, or emotionally drained to make the effort. Alethea found great peace in the knowledge of Jesus praying for Jason.

A few days passed. Alethea was finishing the evening meal and reflected upon all the changes that had taken place since Jason's arrest. Lukas and Melina had grown much closer, which delighted Alethea. He was at the caravansary for the evening, which had become more and more common. Linus was at the house of Damon and Letha sharing the evening meal with them. Eustace and Lydia had been there quite frequently, but as of late they were spending more time together alone. This also delighted Alethea. And, of course, they all got to see Jesus and his disciples, if only at a distance for most of them. It was just her and Orpheus this evening. He had a way of comforting her when nothing else would. Lately, however, her prayer life was yielding optimism and strength.

Alethea finished the simple meal for the two of them, then wondered where Orpheus had gone off to. She decided to go outside and look for him. Not so pleasant, as it was a cool evening and had started raining. She covered her head with her black garment, while walking around to the orchard. Alethea thought to herself that when the summer months return the plans will go forth. She paused and prayed for Jason, that he would return to see the work Linus had put into the garden, orchard, and vineyard; they had all contributed to the effort. Alethea looked at it as an act of faith. She longed for Jason; somehow, she knew he would be with her soon. She had been saying that for months but knew it was coming to an end. She walked around to the front of the house, as Orpheus was approaching.

"Weather took a little turn," he said as he walked up to his adopted daughter. She could see a smile amid his white hair and beard although his head was covered. "Spring will be coming soon," he added.

"Not soon enough for me," Alethea responded while taking Orpheus by the arm as they went into the house together. She was about to close the door, then noticed a group of Romans upon horses pass by at a distance. Alethea thought to herself that they must be on their way to the encampment. Orpheus looked for himself.

"Looks like someone of importance. I don't know, but that may be the Praetor we're waiting for," Orpheus said as he watched.

Upon further observation, Alethea agreed. "Yeah, looks like an important person surrounded by soldiers," she said. They kept watching until the Romans traveled out of sight. "Do you really think that's who they were?" she asked.

Orpheus responded, "No way to know for sure. We should be hearing about it soon if it was." Then he asked, "When is Eustace coming back?"

"I think he's coming tomorrow afternoon unless something comes up. That's what he told me," Alethea said.

"Eustace needs to visit his friend Marcus to find out," Orpheus said as he reclined at the table while deep in thought. "I wonder if those Romans tell Jason anything. We've never been able to communicate with him. He probably has no idea that Jesus and his disciples returned and were well received. I'm sure that would have given him a lot of confidence. I wonder how he's going to react to the fact that he missed seeing him?" he pondered.

"None of us was able to speak to him, except Eustace and Lukas," Alethea recalled. "Eustace told him of his imprisonment, and that he could not receive visitors. He asked him to pray for Jason. Eustace told me of his reaction, and since then I've been waiting for the day that he comes home," Alethea said as she set their meal down, then looked to Orpheus for a comment.

"Just a smile and a prayer from Jesus is more than monumental efforts from a man, for he is the Son of God. Perhaps tomorrow we'll know something," Orpheus said as he began eating.

The sun had returned the next day, but there was a chill in the air. A knock came upon the door: it was Eustace. Orpheus immediately told him what he and Alethea had seen the previous evening. Eustace looked at Orpheus with a smile of acknowledgment.

"You my friend are very observant. A courier came to me this morning and informed me to come to the encampment. I have no idea why the delay was so long, but a Praetor has arrived and will issue a proclamation this afternoon. I was just stopping to tell you all the news on the way," Eustace said. He seemed a bit nervous, then Orpheus was as well.

Orpheus said, "I'm surprised no one's here, for I know Alethea was expecting you. I think they're out walking. She's been doing that a lot; Lukas went with her, and I think Linus is helping Damon. Do you think it appropriate for me to come with you?" Orpheus asked, but he wasn't sure if he wanted to go to the Roman encampment. He did, however, want answers about his friend.

"I think Alethea was expecting me a bit later. I don't see a problem with you coming along. Get that little parchment that Marcus gave us when he released you and Lukas just in case," Eustace said. He waited a moment for Orpheus to gather himself, then they departed.

Both men were very anxious during the walk to the Tenth Legion Camp. Eustace and Orpheus took nothing for granted, for it was a miracle in itself that Jason had endured for as long as he had. The Romans were known for not keeping prisoners long; they didn't even keep a budget for it. They would either punish and release, or they would execute their prisoners.

Eustace spoke, "There's something between the Praefecti in charge of the camp, Actaeon, and Jason. Marcus spoke to me about Actaeon having a vendetta against him. That, however, should have hastened his demise instead of keeping him alive. I could almost sense it during the trial; those men have a past."

"Perhaps this *Actaeon* wanted to corrupt Jason and get him to turn back to evil so he could exploit him as a soldier," Orpheus speculated.

Eustace responded, "Actually, Marcus told me of just such a proposal; Jason rejected him. I didn't want to think or speak of it though. Jason must have been subject to torment and harassment unheard of by most people. I really hope that was not the case."

The two men approached the camp, and they were relieved that there were no crucifixions on display this time. They could see Actaeon flanked by two soldiers on horses parading around the camp at a distance. There were other activities as well; drills, marching, and sword practice in various places. The men identified themselves to the sentries, then walked silently towards the mud brick administrative building.

Alethea thought it strange that Orpheus was gone when her and Lukas returned from walking. He had spoken specifically that they were going to wait for Eustace together. She thought to herself that maybe he needed a little walk himself.

"Eustace may have come already, and Orpheus wanted to go with him," Lukas speculated.

"Perhaps you're right, Lukas; I'm tempted to go myself," Alethea said as she looked out of the window. The peace brought by walking was shattered by anxiety. She was a bit overwhelmed suddenly with the ambiguity of a decision made by wicked men. Lukas could see the anguish upon her face.

Lukas spoke, "If you want to go, Alethea, let us go; I'm not looking forward to waiting all day either. I certainly don't want to see you like this all day. We've waited for months now. I trust God, and I truly feel as though this will all be over soon. I know how much you want to see Jason, so do I."

Alethea looked at Lukas and said, "Let us go."

The two left quickly, for they knew that Eustace and Orpheus couldn't have left that long ago. Lukas did the best he could to encourage Alethea as they walked. Orpheus was the source of emotional support for her in Jason's absence, but Lukas saw his role as her protector. Lukas looked forward to telling Jason, after all this time, that he was always looking out for her. Alethea, on the other hand wanted to lighten the tension a bit.

"How are things going with Melina? You've been spending a lot of time at the caravansary," Alethea inquired of Lukas while glancing from beneath her black head covering and grinning at him.

"It's going slow but good. We've been watching Eustace and Lydia work on their relationship, and it seems to be flourishing. Another example of Jason helping people through the power of

God," Lukas said as he looked back at Alethea. He saw that his comment brought tears to her eyes. "I'm sorry," he added.

"No, it's alright. Don't be sorry for telling me how wonderful he is; it's just that nobody knows how much I miss him," Alethea said while sniffling.

"Let us see what we can do about getting him home. I suggest we pray the rest of the way," Lukas said, and they began to take turns praying as they walked.

Marcus had been expecting Eustace. He welcomed the two men into his chamber with as much cordiality as possible under the circumstances. He then offered Eustace and Orpheus a little wine and gestured for them to sit.

Marcus spoke, "I asked the Praetor about the proclamation. I'm not trying to dash your hope, but all he would tell me was that it was unusual due to the circumstance. I have experience with these cases, and unusual means that an example is to be made; typically, one that provides an entertaining spectacle for the glory of Rome." Marcus looked Eustace in the eye. "I must prepare you, for it may be gruesome," he said.

Eustace looked at Orpheus, as the old man swallowed hard and his imagination ran with him a bit. He looked back at Marcus and stated, "We're trusting God, so don't tell me he is to be condemned before he is. We're going to have to go back and explain whatever it is to his wife. Actaeon can accuse and condemn a man without any real evidence, but I tend to believe that God's justice will prevail."

"I hope you're right for your sakes, my friend. Come, for the time draws near," Marcus said as he got up joined by Eustace and Orpheus.

The men walked outside, and Eustace was very surprised to see Alethea and Lukas approach. Orpheus gasped a little as he looked at Eustace who was thinking the same. Eustace hurried over to meet Alethea followed by Orpheus. He tried to speak, but Alethea embraced him and spoke first:

"I know what you're going to say, but my place is here. We realized we missed you, so I had to come, and it was my idea. I'm prepared for whatever the outcome might be; I've been preparing for months now. If all I get is one moment with him, then so be it," she said with a very determined expression.

Eustace looked over at Marcus and said, "Go ahead. The four of us are going to pray to the one, true, living God before we go in."

Marcus responded, "Very well. I hope for the best outcome for you all."

Alethea led the prayer, "Father, in the name of Jesus I pray for your will to be done, that your love and awesome power would show mightily against the false pagan gods of the Roman people. Just as Jesus delivered him from demons; I pray now you would deliver him from this wicked Roman leader. We pray that the glory is yours, and not this evil empire. We praise you in the name of Jesus."

Alethea and the others finished praying, then the group slowly walked to the large tent where the trial had taken place. They saw the impressive Praefecti Actaeon arrive with escort upon horses, and waited as the men dismounted and went in. None of them wanted to get that close to him, for he smelled of evil. After a few moments they went in. There weren't as many as for the trial, and there was no sign of Jason yet. They found seating near the entrance of the tent, like before, so they could get a glimpse of Jason when the guards brought him in.

Jason was deep in prayer when the guards came to take him to the reading of the proclamation. He continued to pray as the two guards chained his hands and feet, which had become customary any time he left the cell. "Your kingdom come, your will be done," he kept repeating until the two led him out of the cell and were joined by two others outside. They walked through the corridors and out into the bright sunlight. Jason knew his long road of misery would come to an end soon. He wondered if Alethea was there. They entered the tent, then Jason heard his name spoken by the one he loved.

The soldiers had a slight bit of compassion and paused for a moment by Jason's wife and friends. Eye contact was made between Jason and Alethea, which filled them both with desperate warmth. He looked at his friends as well and smiled, then looked up and nodded. The moment passed, as Jason was led to a bench by the long table. The Praetor sat in the middle; with Actaeon on his right, and Marcus on his left. He appeared to be an older man, as he was weathered and wrinkled, but fit and tough. He had most likely lived through a long military career. He wore a simple Roman tunic but had an embroidered dark red outer garment. The Praetor was engrossed in a silent conversation with Actaeon as soon as he arrived; they leaned together and whispered privately. One of Actaeon's Centurions shouted for silence. The moment had come, as the Praetor stood and opened a scroll.

The Praetor spoke in Greek with a heavy accent, "I have come here today to deliver a decision from the Roman Senate, and the Court of Caesar himself. The unusual circumstances of this case called for a creative solution to honor Praefecti Actaeon. His testimony alone stands against the accused known as Jason of Gadara. Many accusations were dismissed, but Actaeon's accusations stand, so we owe him the respect of placing justice within his hands. First, however, there are three options to put this matter to rest. If Praefecti Actaeon concedes the accusation, then Jason of Gadara goes free." He looked over at Actaeon and gestured for him to stand.

Actaeon arose and spoke, "I alone have seen through the trickery of this menace; one who has caused disruption of trade, physical harm, damage, and terrorized countless individuals for many years. He has evaded several attempts by our military to arrest him for years as well. He has infiltrated this city to bring a strange God and corrupt our way of life. His violent behavior and deceptive ways are not conducive to the Roman Empire. I am honored to have justice placed in my hands, and I will execute that justice for the glory of Rome. I do not concede!"

Applause came from most of the attendants. Alethea and Jason's friends sat quietly and tried not to give in to despair until the entire proclamation was read. Actaeon sat down, and the Praetor arose again. The Centurion shouted for silence.

"Let the record state that Praefecti Actaeon does not concede," the Praetor announced.

The guards got up and pulled Jason to his feet, then turned him to face the Praetor.

The Praetor proceeded with the proclamation, "Jason of Gadara, you stand accused of various crimes as stated by the honorable Praefecti Actaeon. You are now to be given the option to concede to the accusations, which will result in a merciful death by beheading. If you do not concede, then we shall move to the third option. You are also given at this time an opportunity to make a statement." The Praetor gestured to Jason.

Eustace was very nervous as he spoke under his breath, "Don't say it. Don't admit to anything." Alethea and the others were in a state of shock and were staring at Jason as he was about to speak.

Jason spoke with surprising confidence and boldness, "Thank you, honorable Praetor, Praefecti Actaeon, Magistrate Marcus. I'm not going to dispute the accusations spoken of." There was an audible gasp from Jason's family. Jason glanced back, then smiled and continued, "I have been delivered from a lifetime of demonic possession by Jesus, who is the Son of God. My only purpose in life now is to teach his ways, as well as lead people to him and follow him. Jesus gave my life back to me. If the God who I now serve wishes to take that life, so be it. I do not stand against your empire; I stand against no one except devils. I have done nothing wrong. I have defended myself and stood for truth, which means I stand against false accusations. Legion is the one who is accused here; Legion is dead. I am Jason of Gadara, and I DO NOT CONCEDE!" Jason shouted with a voice of authority. He then sat down with a smile upon his face. There was minimal applause from here and there, but mostly from Alethea and the others.

The Praetor arose again to read the remainder of the proclamation. He said, "Let the record state that Jason of Gadara does not concede, which leads this proceeding to the final option. Since Praefecti Actaeon is the sole accuser and Jason of Gadara is the only accused; the wisdom of Rome has seen this dispute rendered down to a contest between two men. I shall remain to preside over the contest, which is to be held in seven days. The contest shall be hand to hand combat. It shall be held in the Great Amphitheater of Gadara. I encourage this camp, as well as the surrounding community to promote the event for the glory of Rome. The nature of the contest is that one or the other must concede, or battle to the death, whichever comes first. I understand the details of Jason's imprisonment, and it shall be in effect until the contest. However, Jason of Gadara shall be allowed visitors to help him prepare for the contest. Furthermore, if Praefecti Actaeon prevails, then Roman justice has truly been served, and Rome is glorified. If Jason of Gadara prevails, then Rome will graciously provide a proclamation of exoneration, as well as an honorary citizenship. Again, Rome is shown as merciful and glorified. These proceedings are now over; there shall be no disputing this proclamation, except for one or the other conceding. That concludes it." The Praetor quickly left the tent, as he was joined by his personal guard. A great deal of murmuring erupted.

Jason looked over at Actaeon, as he stared at him with an intimidating, wicked grin on his face. Jason then asked the guards to take him to his wife and friends, and they quickly led him over to the people he loved. They wouldn't take off the chains, so he put his arms around Alethea chains and all. The others surrounded him in a group embrace, and they were all praising God....

Chapter Nine

A Battle of Spirits

Jason awoke in his cell as the morning sun beamed in. The gentle breeze outside was fresh and clean: spring was coming. He lay there, and Jason acknowledged a new season in his life; one that would begin with a great battle. He was fighting his own battle within, for he was haunted by his temporary descent into darkness. It had been many days since the realization of his fall, and the subsequent visitation that brought him to his senses. Still, he couldn't come to the inner confidence he had prior to the psychological terror wrought by Actaeon. He felt as though it was not only to be a physical contest but a deeply spiritual one as well. Jason knew his strength only came from the Lord. He would fail if he fell into temptation during the battle, even if he prevailed; he would be compromised, and all would be lost. Being able to interact with his friends, especially Alethea, was nourishment to his soul.

He thought about all he had been told; the events and changes that had taken place during his imprisonment. What stood out most profoundly to him was that Jesus had returned to the region. He had been received with joy and a desire by many to follow his ways. Eustace, the one who had rejected him had spoken with him and asked for prayer, that alone filled Jason with enormous confidence. If only Jesus could have visited. Jason was very unsettled within himself that he was unable to see him. He made up his mind he would seek him at some point, if he was to survive this ordeal. Jason got up and retrieved his customary offering of bread and water from the guards. He was hoping his friends would come soon, for they had been bringing him real food. He thought to himself that there was one thing that had changed: he no longer craved bread. Yesterday, he requested roasted fish; Lukas said he would take care of it. Jason sat and nibbled on his bread, then thought about the coming contest the day after tomorrow. He drifted into silent prayer, while asking God to comfort him with peace and equip him. He also asked forgiveness once again and for a clear, sound mind.

Jason continued in prayer until he heard the unlocking of the door. He looked up and was delighted to see Alethea enter first. She immediately sat upon the bed beside him, then embraced and kissed him. Jason was happy to see she had agreed to stop wearing the black mourning garment; her pale green outer garment, white chiton, and white head covering were much more cheerful. She was followed by Eustace, Lukas, and Orpheus. He stood and they took turns embracing him. Lukas set a wrapped bundle upon the bed that Jason quickly opened. The aroma of roasted fresh fish filled the cell and brought a smile to Jason's face. He immediately started eating.

"Caught them for you this morning. Built a fire and roasted 'em right there. You can't get 'em any fresher than that," Lukas said as he smiled. He was pleased that he was able to bring such joy to his friend.

"I brought you something too, Jason," Orpheus proclaimed as he reached into his tunic and brought out a scroll. "Thought this would encourage you. I believe this was the segment of the Psalms you had requested," he said.

Jason quickly wiped his hands on his old Roman tunic and took the scroll from Orpheus. "Thank you, my friend, for I am truly blessed; Lukas brought food for the body, and you have brought food for the spirit," he said as he smiled at the old man. He looked over at Alethea. "You have brought food for my heart," he said as he kissed her.

"All I have to say is I love you," Alethea said as she sat close to her husband with her arm around him.

Eustace spoke, "Sorry Jason, I don't have anything for you this time. My focus right now is to bring you everything you need for this battle coming up. I've asked you before, but you haven't been very specific. Actaeon will have the strongest, finest armor and weaponry available to him; you must try to equal his equipment with your own. You do realize, that the Romans have no intention of letting you win. They're looking at this *contest* as a form of execution. The battle is set for the day after tomorrow. That's all everyone is talking about in Emmatha and Gadara. I'm asking you again, what do you want? Armor, weapons, anything; I will get it for you."

Jason responded while smiling with a great appreciation of his friend, "I'm sorry, Eustace, for I didn't intend to make light of your advice. I haven't answered you specifically because you probably won't agree with my choices. The contest is drawing near, so I intend to make my requests today." Jason looked around at each of his closest friends, then his wife. He said, "I will go barefoot; I want the old tunic that Simon gave to me on the beach the day I was delivered from the demons, as well the outer garment put around me by James. Also, the sash that I used to wear given to me by Simon that day. The weapons that I choose are to be the dagger that I took from the criminals that attacked Alethea and I on our trip, and my sword, as well as my leather belt and sheath." Jason trailed off while staring in recollection. "The sword that Legion took from Actaeon many years ago," he added.

The cell went quiet. Eustace was quickly filled with the impulse to argue but went silent after he started to speak. A curious emotion filled all of the friends of Jason. Alethea smiled and rested her head upon his chest. Eustace, Lukas, and Orpheus looked upon their friend with wonder. They had all suddenly realized they were in the presence of a very devoted, very brave man. A true warrior of God.

The morning came on the day of the contest. A large group approached the Great Amphitheater of Gadara amid the crowds that consisted of Jason's friends and family. Eustace, Lukas, and Orpheus led the group; followed by Alethea, Melina, and Lydia. Symeon, Theophanes, Linus, as well as Damon and Letha, followed behind them. Many others that had become acquainted with Jason or touched by his ministry followed also. They were all amazed at the spectacle; food vendors hawking their wares, commemorative baubles of different types being sold, jugglers, dancers, and all manner of attention seekers. All were using the event to promote themselves or make money. Eustace heard his name shouted from a distance. He looked around and spotted familiar faces; Aegeus, Calista, and Dimitri were there. The group made their way to find seating around them, for they had a good vantage point. They all met and shared warm greetings.

Aegeus spoke to Eustace, "We heard of this a few days ago. Of course, we had to come and show our support for Jason. We had heard about his trouble with the Romans, and we've been praying for him every day."

"Thank you, Aegeus, for I know you and your family mean a lot to Jason. He will be encouraged that you're here," Eustace said.

Calista embraced Alethea and requested she and the other women to sit around her. There were a lot of people there to support and encourage Jason; however, he had requested no one visit him this morning. He wanted to prepare with God in prayer.

Jason had awakened early. The cool misty morning was giving way to a clear spring day. He had his usual bread and water, then decided to start with the word of God. Jason wanted to focus upon a particular scripture that had special meaning to him, and the memory of his father. He opened the scroll to read what he had chosen:

"The Lord is my shepherd; I shall not want. He makes me to lie down in green pastures: he leads me beside still waters. He restores my soul: he leads me in the paths of righteousness for his name's sake. Yea, though I walk through the valley of the shadow of death, I will fear no evil: for God is with me; his rod and his staff they comfort me. He prepares a table before me in the presence of my enemies: he anoints my head with oil; my cup runs over. Surely goodness and mercy shall follow me all the days of my life: and I will dwell in the house of the Lord forever."

Jason meditated upon that scripture for some time, then prayed, "Father, in the name of Jesus I express my trust in you. It is well with my soul, whatever happens this day. I acknowledge that this is not my battle, but yours. I've repeatedly attempted to reach this man, Actaeon, with truth to bring repentance, but to no avail; I am forced into this contest. Lord, I have committed a great many sins, but I have never killed a man. I don't want to kill Actaeon. I cannot let him kill me unless it is your will. I pray that you would give me peace. I pray that you give me good, decisive judgment. You have already given me strength and speed. Lord, lead me not into temptation, but deliver me from this evil."

Jason heard the door unlock. Strange, for it seemed earlier than he was told. One of Actaeon's Centurions entered the room; one whose hands had brought Jason a lot of suffering. He took off his helmet to Jason's surprise and knelt in front of him. He spoke Greek well, but with a heavy accent.

He said, "Jason, my name is Neleus. I want to express how sorry I am to have caused you so much pain. I'm not sure what happened, but my eyes have been opened. I realize now that Praefecti Actaeon is pure evil. He seeks not the glory of Rome, but his own glory. He eventually wants to become Emperor. I fear the entire world would be plunged into darkness if that ever happened. Jason, I repent, for I have heard your words; I want to learn about this God that you serve, as well as Jesus. I'm not the only one, for others have spoken against Actaeon in secret. You must defeat him,

Jason! You must!" The Centurion was pleading with him. "Is there anything I can do for you? Is there anything I can get for you?" he asked.

Jason was shocked. He also took the confession of Neleus as a confirmation. It wasn't so much the Roman Empire he was coming up against, but the darkness of this world. He would have been released in a few days, if not for Actaeon. He was spiritually compromised and tortured all at the hands of Actaeon. This gave him a clear focus as he smiled at Neleus.

Jason spoke, "I have every intention of prevailing against Actaeon. I'm very happy for you; God himself has opened your eyes. I would consider it a joy to teach and minister to you." Jason put his hand upon the shoulder of Neleus and thought for a moment. "There is something you can get for me," he said. Jason looked up at the door that had imprisoned him for months. "I want one of the bars from that door. I also want one of those small leather shields I've seen your men practice with. Together with what I have I could make good use of them," he said.

Neleus smiled at Jason. He got up and called for the guards, then two showed up at the door. Neleus commanded, "I want one of these bars removed from this door at once." The guards looked at each other, then at the Centurion. Neleus responded, "That was an order. I'm going to leave for a few moments; when I return, if that bar is not in my hand, then you both may find yourselves doing stable duty with stripes on your backs: MOVE!" One of the soldiers quickly scurried off to obtain tools to perform the task. Neleus looked at Jason, then smiled and departed.

The time had finally come. The Great Amphitheater of Gadara was filled, as well as many gathered outside the venue. There had been a wide variety of events take place leading up to the main attraction; wrestling matches, dancers, and Rome's contribution: the execution of a murderer in public. The Romans didn't want a

350

large crowd to go to waste. A small group of soldiers marched out to the center of the stage. Then, two soldiers led a man in chains and tattered clothing to the center of the stage and forced him to his knees. The sound of the trumpets brought silence to the amphitheater. One of the soldiers produced a small scroll and read the charges against the man, which listed many petty crimes and murder. Many reacted with gasps while some cheered, as a large muscular soldier marched out onto the stage with a very large sword. He walked up to stand beside the condemned man, then looked up at the Praetor. The signal was given as the Praetor stood and raised his right hand with his thumb up, then nodded. The executioner took aim and with one swing of the huge sword it was over. Many looked away, and some gasped as the man was beheaded. The event brought out bloodlust for some as parts of the crowd cheered. The Praetor presiding over the event was surrounded by Roman aristocrats, and they were cheering the loudest.

Jason was led through the streets by four Roman soldiers and into the amphitheater. He walked along with his long outer garment covering his head. His hands were chained in front, and his ankle chain was dragging. He was amazed by the commercialized spectacle the event had become, but he wasn't really that surprised. The lower rows of seating had been kept clear and covered with dirt, as well as the stone stage floor. Some were cheering for Jason, but most were simply waiting for the main event. Some were calling out things like *lamb to the slaughter* and *two executions*. Many were laughing at Jason, as were the Praetor and his friends. Jason scanned the crowd and was delighted to see all his friends and family. He displayed a huge smile especially when he spotted Aegeus and Calista. Alethea kept smiling at him while pointing up. It started a trend, as others began doing it also.

Another soldier arrived carrying a cloth bundle, then set it down. One of the guards in front of Jason unlocked his chains, then removed them and walked away. The five soldiers assumed positions around the fighting area, while joining a few others to keep the crowds back. It was the first time Jason had been outside without chains for a long while. He wasted no time as he unrolled the bundle revealing the weapons he had chosen. He picked up his sword, for he hadn't held it since before his arrest. He flipped it over the back of his hand a few times, which brought a bit of cheering from the crowd. He felt the weight and the balance. Confident, he put on the belt and sheath, then tied the sash around his waist, and put the sword in its place. He picked up the dagger and tucked it into his sash. The heavy Iron bar and shield he picked up and held. Jason turned to where he supposed Actaeon would enter, then knelt and set the bar and shield upon the ground. He was as ready as possible, so he bowed his head and prayed.

It wasn't long before Jason heard thunderous applause and cheering, which was closely followed by trumpets proclaiming the arrival of Praefecti Actaeon. Jason would not be intimidated; he remained in prayer for the moment and thanked God for such a beautiful, clear, spring day. The Praetor had come down and stood by Actaeon to announce the event and lay out rules. Jason stood at attention, while still wearing his outer garment with his head covered. Actaeon was dressed for battle; he wore a gladiator's helmet with face shield, as well as his usual ornate armor, and a huge battle shield depicting the bull. He kept his sword in its place. A soldier brought to him the huge beheading sword recently used and bloody; Actaeon intended to use it on Jason. Everyone knew the Roman leader to be a master swordsman. He removed his luxurious green outer garment, then handed it to the soldier who had brought the sword. The trumpets blew again calling for silence.

The Praetor spoke, "To the great Roman Tenth Legion, friends and colleagues, people of Gadara and surrounding communities, welcome! This contest is between Jason of Gadara," he gestured to Jason, which brought scant applause and cheering with scattered laughter. He then gestured to Actaeon as he continued, "And Praefecti Actaeon, Commander of the Tenth Legion Camp." The applause and cheering were deafening. Jason looked over at his friends, as all were pointing up which made him smile. Silence was restored and the Praetor spoke again, "The rules of this contest are very simple: there aren't any. If one or the other concedes, then the fight is over. If one or the other dies, then the fight is over. The next sounding of the trumpets will signal the fight to begin. There shall be no breaks. There shall be no mercy. That is all I have to say, so let the contest begin!" The announcement raised the loudest reaction from the crowd yet. The Praetor returned to his seat. A short time passed, then the trumpets blew again, which set off a storm of unbridled bloodlust, cheering and shouting from the huge crowd.

Actaeon swung his large bloody sword a couple of times and slowly walked toward Jason. Jason threw off his outer garment and sniffed the air. He ignored the laughter from the crowd, as many were amused at the sight of his frayed tunic compared to Actaeon's armor. Jason was armed with his iron bar in his right hand and the small shield in the left, as he slowly walked toward Actaeon. Jason took him by surprise and jumped at his opponent, while blocking the huge sword with the iron bar. Jason got behind his shield, then brought the bar down on Actaeon's helmet which produced a loud bang. He then dropped down and rolled away, while barely evading a swipe from Actaeon's blade. Actaeon was a little dazed, so Jason got two more blows in from behind; another upon the helmet, and one across the left shoulder. He quickly backed up to survey the damage. Actaeon's helmet was badly dented, but not penetrated, yet. A great deal of murmuring replaced much of the cheering and laughter from the crowd. Jason was not expected to win, but he was very, very fast. Perhaps it wouldn't be a lamb to the slaughter after all.

Jason faced his opponent while moving slowly and circling him, as he waited for Actaeon to make the next move. The face of Actaeon was hidden behind the face shield of his gladiator's helmet with its wide metal brim and crest. He tapped his shield with his sword and advanced toward Jason. He decided to stop and allow Actaeon to attack, while looking for a vulnerability. Actaeon suddenly lunged at Jason. He swung his sword, which Jason blocked with his iron bar as a loud clang rang out. Jason was then hit hard with Actaeon's shield in the face and upper body; he was stunned and laid out on his back. Actaeon moved forward and started hacking at Jason as the crowd cheered wildly. Jason blocked the blows with his shield, while seeing the blade cut through with every blow and then slicing the back of his left hand. Jason quickly rolled away, as he barely avoided another swipe of Actaeon's sword. He retreated to quickly examine the cut on his hand: it wasn't too deep. Jason slid the bar into his sash and threw aside the now useless shield. He ripped a strip of cloth from his sash and wrapped his hand, as he walked circles to buy time.

Actaeon once again advanced toward Jason with a burst of speed. Jason met the blows of his sword with his iron bar, as he successfully blocked most of them. A couple of grazing swipes brought some superficial cuts to Jason's arms. The heavy iron bar was taking chunks out of Actaeon's blade with every hit. Jason thought quickly and waited for the right moment and the right blow. The crowd was screaming and cheering as it looked like Jason was soon to fall. Suddenly, Jason didn't just block the blow, but met the blade with a very hard swing of the bar, which produced a loud clang. The blade of Actaeon's sword broke. Actaeon thrust his shield at Jason again, but he had dropped and rolled away. The crowd went wild, but not because of the impressive Actaeon; Jason was demonstrating great speed, cunning, and resilience. Some in the crowd were beginning to chant his name. There was no more laughter; people were frantically making wagers upon the outcome. The Praetor was not pleased.

Jason had yet to draw his sword. Actaeon had retreated following the loss of his sword, then drew his short sword that was like Jason's. He faced Jason for a moment, then tapped his shield again signaling the fight to proceed. Jason decided to get to higher ground. He jumped upon the lower seats which were covered with dirt, so he could get a higher vantage point. Actaeon was coming at him quickly but was holding his shield low as he approached. Jason saw an opportunity as he reached for his dagger, for he knew he needed to inflict damage to even the odds. Jason pulled and threw the dagger with one fluid motion, which found it's mark between Actaeon's breastplate and left shoulder guard. Actaeon let out a deep, growling scream, then dropped his huge shield and immediately retreated. Loud cheers and applause blasted from the crowd. Jason felt comfortable enough to glance up at his friends, and Alethea. She was smiling, as were the others. They began to chant, JASON! JASON! JASON! It caught on, and before long many in the crowd were chanting his name as well.

The Praetor had said there were to be no breaks, but Jason had created one. Actaeon was surrounded by his Centurions, as well as his physician, and the Praetor himself. Jason sat down upon the lower seats. The Praetor was glaring at him, as was Actaeon. His helmet had been removed, and one of the Centurions was attempting to beat the dents out of it. They removed the left shoulder guard from Actaeon; loosened his breastplate, removed the dagger, and wrapped the wound. He was attempting to raise his left arm with great difficulty. Actaeon's Centurions were scrambling to put the armor back on. Jason got up and walked over to them with his iron bar tucked in his sash. He stopped a short distance from the men and spoke:

"Do you wish to concede, Actaeon?" Jason asked. "I would much rather both of us leave here alive. You're injured. The grievance you have against Legion is pointless! It's not worth it! You gain nothing if you kill me! Legion is dead!" he shouted with a futile attempt to reason with Actaeon.

Actaeon listened while displaying his dark eyes filled with hate. He then responded in Latin with a deep echoing voice, "What do you mean I gain nothing, Legion? I want to see your bleeding corpse laid out in this amphitheater; I call that something! I can still fight well enough to cut your heart out and feed it to you!"

Jason walked away and was disappointed that the man at the base of the demonic possession was not reasonable. He sat once again in the same spot and looked up at Alethea. She smiled, and even at a distance he could make out her lips speak, "I love you." He did the same in return and smiled at many who were watching him. Suddenly, the crowd cheered loudly. Jason looked over to see Actaeon approach him. His helmet was back on, but he was missing his left shoulder guard, as well as his shield. Jason stood up and surveyed his opponent. Actaeon was still heavily armored but appeared to be armed only with his short sword. Jason drew his sword and iron bar. He smiled at Actaeon and threw the bar aside. Actaeon's left arm was injured at the shoulder and useless. Jason had no armor. It was down to one sword against the other. The odds were even.

Actaeon let out a battle cry and quickly advanced. Jason descended to the level stage of the amphitheater. The two men met and unleashed the most furious sword fighting most had ever seen, even though many in attendance were battle-hard Romans. More slight wounds were beginning to appear upon the exposed flesh of both men. Jason, however, appeared more wounded, as he had received a glancing blow across his right shoulder. The swordfight went on for some time; howls, shouting, and much cheering erupted from the vast crowd. Many were chanting Jason's name, which seemed to make Actaeon more furious as the battle progressed. Jason felt him losing accuracy because of his anger and hatred. Jason was feeling none of these things; he had committed his life to God's hands before the battle had begun. Suddenly Jason swung hard, which knocked Actaeon's sword aside long enough to open a vulnerability. Jason could have jabbed at his throat and ended the fight; instead, he threw himself at his opponent, which knocked him onto his back and stunned him. Actaeon still had his sword in his hand, but Jason was quicker; he held the point of his sword at the throat of his opponent. Jason had just won the battle, except for the final thrust. The crowd was extremely wild with many chanting his name, as a growing chorus arose: "Kill him! Kill him!"

Jason pleaded with Actaeon and shouted, "CONCEDE! I don't want to kill you, CONCEDE!"

"I'll see you in hell before I concede!" was the response from Actaeon.

Jason pressed harder, which drew blood from Actaeon's throat. Unexpectantly, Jason jumped off of Actaeon, then raised his sword and walked over to face the Praetor. Loud chanting and cheering from the crowd indicated the victory, but there was a lot of booing as well. Some people just wanted to see death. Jason put his sword in its place. His intentions were to appeal to the Praetor and spare the life of Actaeon, but this was not their way. Suddenly, there was a change in the energy of the crowd, as they were cheering and shouting Jason's name, but he distinguished one voice say, "Behind you!"

From Jason's point of view time slowed way down. It was a strange sensation he had never experienced before. He knew that Actaeon was charging at him from behind. Jason was faced with either killing him or himself being killed. Jason had a purpose. The prominent prayer from his heart before this battle was that God's will be done. Was this God's will? He thought of his friends. He thought about Alethea, and the life they could have together. He thought about Alethea wearing that black mourning garment. Jason thought about all the lives he had touched. Then, he thought about the Centurion who had confided in him. He remembered what Neleus had told him about Actaeon, and the fear in the eyes of his so-called *honor guard*. He remembered the trial, and how Andris died a drunkard's death before he could bear false witness against him. Actaeon was about to commit murder after being shown mercy. Was this God's will? Jason was convinced that it was.

Time returned to normal from Jason's perspective. He spun around to see Actaeon charging at him with his sword in the air ready to strike. Jason drew his sword lightning fast and threw it with a great force. It penetrated Actaeon's face shield all the way to the handle with a loud smack, dead center. Actaeon stopped in his tracks, as his raised sword fell to the ground. Somehow, he stood for a moment, then fell forward like a dead tree. The blade of Jason's sword extended out of the back of Actaeon's helmet covered in blood. The crowd was roaring, but Jason calmly walked over to the body of Actaeon. He was remorseful. He bowed his head as he asked God to give him peace and forgive him for what he had done. The cheering and applause were deafening. People were beginning to descend to Jason, as he reached down and picked up the sword of Actaeon. It was identical to his own, except it had a very finely crafted dark wood handle with a gold inlay spiral and gold pommel. He slipped it into his sheath when Alethea, as well as all his friends and many others rushed up and crowded around him. Jason embraced Alethea and was oblivious to everything else.

Jason's friends waited as he held his wife for a long moment. Joy filled the air as Jason interacted with all of his close friends. Lukas had picked up his outer garment, then dusted it off and placed it around him. All at once the trumpets sounded again, which brought silence among the crowd. The Praetor approached with a delegation of aristocrats and soldiers. Alethea and the growing crowd of Jason's friends moved to stand behind him. Jason turned to face the Praetor who had a solemn look upon his face and carried two scrolls under his left arm. The Praetor stopped in front of Jason and extended his hand, which Jason grabbed. A cheer arose from the huge crowd, then the trumpets sounded once again calling for silence.

The Praetor proclaimed, "Jason of Gadara, I officially pronounce you to be the victor of this contest. I now present you with this proclamation of exoneration. All charges and claims against you are officially dropped by my authority as a representative of the Roman Empire. You are now to be considered a free man." He then extended one of the scrolls to Jason, and he accepted it. The trumpets sounded again, which was followed by a bit of cheering. The Praetor waited a moment until the silence was restored and said, "I furthermore bestow upon you this document, which makes you an honorary citizen of Rome with all the rights and privileges thereof." He handed Jason the second scroll, then grabbed Jason's hand once again. He stepped close and spoke to Jason privately, "Good luck to you, young man, for you've earned it." He smiled at Jason, then turned and walked away. The remainder of the delegation also shook Jason's hand before departing. Many Centurions lined up as well. Neleus approached Jason and embraced him.

Jason said, "I will come to minister to you if that would be appropriate."

Neleus replied, "No, Jason, I will come to you. I don't think you want to return to the encampment. I will come to you, and out of uniform, if we could set up a time. There are others who wish to join me. We have witnessed the awesome power of your God, and there are those who wish to learn his ways."

Jason smiled and said, "Of course, I'd be delighted. You know where to find me. By the way, I left something in my cell: a scroll." Then he asked, "Could you bring it to me when you come?" The Centurion nodded, then smiled in return and departed.

Many who had come to support and pray for Jason crowded around after the Roman delegation had departed, as they waited for an opportunity to interact with him. The love being shown by those who had been touched by Jason was immediately healing to his spirit, for he had been in a very dark place.

Eustace was standing with Lydia and embracing the joy around them when he was approached by an old friend. Marcus put his hand upon Eustace's shoulder, then he turned and noticed tears upon the Roman's face. Marcus smiled, then held up a gold coin. He placed it in Eustace's hand.

"I assume you're buying the meal, now that you have you're gold back," Marcus said with a grin amid his tears. Eustace embraced him.

Lukas and Orpheus approached, for they longed to interact with their friend.

"Do you think it may, finally, get a little easier, Jason?" Lukas asked with a huge grin.

Jason smiled and embraced him, then looked him in the eye. "You're my special friend. I know that you protected Alethea in my absence; I shall be eternally grateful to you. We shall take a little trip together soon, just you and me," Jason said as he embraced him again, then turned to Orpheus.

Jason looked the old man in the eye and said, "You have proven yourself worthy, and I consider you a father; not just to Alethea and me, but the entire fellowship. I know how important you have become to Alethea. I was tormented in prison with worry, but I knew you were holding things together, and that held me together. I may not have made it without you. I shall be eternally grateful to you as well." Jason embraced Orpheus.

Jason then saw Eustace, as he was engaged in a conversation with Lydia and Marcus. He had to interrupt. Jason looked at the big man, then embraced him and said, "Thank you, for everything." He embraced Lydia and Marcus as well.

Eustace proclaimed a spontaneous plan to all who came to support Jason, "I want everyone to gather at the caravansary tonight, for there shall be a great celebration!"

Jason was then approached by Aegeus, Calista, and Dimitri. Aegeus spoke, "I can't begin to tell you how happy we are for you, Jason. Argus wanted to come, but Calista wouldn't allow it. We heard of your arrest and imprisonment, so we've all been praying for you. We heard of this contest, then rushed to get here. God is awesome!" They all took turns embracing Jason.

"I hope you all will be at the caravansary tonight," Jason said. "Will Argus be there?" he asked.

Calista replied, "Yes, he will. He's staying with my sister who lives on the west side of the city. I think he's mad at me for not allowing him to come. Seeing what we witnessed here today; I'm glad he wasn't here. There will be enough real-life violence and horror for him to witness when he's older. I want you to know, somehow, I knew you would prevail. I could see the confidence in you today; I think you knew it too."

Jason responded, "I trusted in God, and I chose to ignore the circumstances." He suddenly became aware of an opportunity. "Excuse me," he said as he rushed off.

Everyone watched Jason with curiosity as he made his way up to the Roman delegation. He spoke with them for a few moments, then descended back down to the stage. Actaeon's body had been carried away and people were returning to their seats. Jason stood at the center of the stage; the Roman soldiers were ushering the remainder of the people off. A few moments went by, then the trumpets blew once again. Centurion Neleus made the announcement:

"People of Gadara, Jason wishes to address you!" he shouted. The Centurion turned to Jason as he placed his fist over his heart and bowed slightly, then smiled and departed. Jason stood alone upon the stage surrounded by thousands. He had recalled a daydream he had some time ago. The crowd fell silent.

Jason began to speak with boldness, "Fellow Gadarenes and people of Emmatha, Tenth Legion, and honored guests from Rome, I thank you for this opportunity to speak. I am Jason of Gadara. I was a lost soul, as I lived in tombs and walked in darkness. Thousands of wicked entities inhabited me for most of my life. Jesus of Nazareth, who is the Son of God, cast the demonic spirits from me and restored me in every way. The one, true, living God has had mercy and compassion upon me, as he will have mercy and compassion upon all who truly repent, then turn away from their sins, and seek him with their heart. Many of you remember the beast, or Legion, as he had terrorized this region for years. I am not that creature. I am a follower of Jesus. He is the way, the truth, and the life. He asked me specifically to tell all of you in this city of the mercy God has shown upon me. That is my life's quest. That is why I'm speaking to you today. I am nothing without God. I was delivered from the demons, and today I was delivered from death. I know many of you worship other gods. I speak the truth. Consider my words. God is calling out to you. I am but a messenger. I will dwell in this city. I have been exonerated from all past accusations. I wish to live in peace with all of you. God loves every single one of you, and so do I. Peace be unto all of you, in the name of Jesus, and by the grace of God. Thank you for hearing me, that is all I have to say."

Jason left the stage. The vast crowd was strangely quiet at first. Applause slowly began to erupt, then became deafening in a short time as well as cheers and the return of Jason's name being chanted. He sat down among his friends next to Alethea, as the applause continued. Jason just sat quietly and shed tears of joy.

Jason and all of his friends only remained a brief time, then departed before the crowd began to thin out. Jason wanted to see his home, as well as clean up and prepare for the festivities at the caravansary. Many of the group went straight there. Jason, Alethea, as well as the others who lived there went to the house of Jason and Alethea. Jason was pleasantly shocked at how beautiful it had become, thanks to Linus. The garden around the house, as well as the orchard and vineyard had exploded with healthy vibrancy. Not even Jason's memories of the place as a child compared to what it looked like now. Jason looked around silently with a huge smile upon his face.

Finally, Linus had to ask, "Well, what do you think?"

Jason looked at him and embraced him. Then he said, "I think you have exceeded not just in proving your worth, but you've blessed this property as if it were your own. You'll never know how much this means to me, after living in the nightmare of that Roman prison. You have a place in my home, my family, and my heart for the rest of your days. Thank you, Linus!'"

Jason walked into the house, then immediately walked over to a little niche in the wall of the main room. He picked up a couple of the stones that had been lovingly placed there. Alethea walked up beside him, as he leaned over and kissed her. "These memories were very important to me; I used them to get through some very hard times. I thank you, wife, for showing me the importance of such things," he said as he teared up.

"I spent a lot of time holding them," Alethea said while recollecting. She picked up one that she had collected from one of their campsites and said, "I slept with this one many times. You may think it was silly, but I don't; they got me through some hard times too."

Jason enjoyed a long-awaited deep interaction with his wife, but then realized he was dripping blood on the floor. A moment of reality that expressed itself as an obvious need of medical attention. Alethea ushered her husband into the back storage room. There, she lovingly cleaned and dressed his wounds, then helped him wash. Lukas came in with fresh clean clothing for his friend. Jason dressed and emerged from the back room feeling like a new man.

He embraced his wife again, then walked over to his table and collapsed into the pillows. He asked, "I'm a bit hungry; do we have any dates, or olives, or something ready to eat, and maybe a little wine?"

Alethea replied, "Sure, Jason. Letha baked some bread yesterday and brought it over. We can certainly put a small meal together for you; I'm a little hungry myself."

Jason quickly responded, "No bread! I'm sorry, but everything else sounds wonderful. Please, no bread or plain water. I want wine, and something other than bread." Jason lay back, then closed his eyes and rubbed his forehead. He then started chuckling. Everyone started laughing after that as they all joined him at the table while reclining upon the pillows. At long last their prayers had been answered. Jason was home.

Late afternoon turned to evening as the group set off for the caravansary. The beautiful spring day gave way to the amber tones, which illuminated the buildings and the landscape. Alethea, Orpheus, Lukas, as well as the others all walked along with light spirits and full of conversation, except for Jason. Having taken the life of Actaeon was troubling to his spirit. The calmness following the aftermath of the battle revealed remorse within his heart he hoped he would never have to face. Actaeon's opportunity for redemption had passed at Jason's hand. He had never killed anyone, even though he had been possessed by demons. He walked and contemplated these things, then Alethea tried to help.

"Are you alright, Jason? Anything you want to talk about?" Alethea asked her husband showing concern. She continued to look at him as she interlocked her arm with his.

"No, I'm alright. I was just thinking about what a blessing it is to be wearing decent clothing for a change," Jason replied with a superficial smile for his wife. He realized his pain was showing and continued, "I'm really looking forward to a good meal as well."

Alethea knew Jason; all was not well. She also knew he had endured much at the hands of the Romans. Things would take time, so she didn't press. "I suspect Lydia and Melina are going all out for this meal. I don't know what they're preparing exactly, but I know them. Prepare to be blessed," Alethea said while smiling at Jason.

"I'm prepared!" Lukas commented as he walked up alongside Jason. "I was fasting and praying, but now I'm ready to eat!" he proclaimed.

They arrived at the caravansary, and there was more activity than usual. All the stables were full, and many were walking around the courtyard. Jason uncovered his head to look around, then some shouted greetings and rushed up to him. They expressed congratulations for his regained freedom and victory. Jason smiled, but deep inside he felt no victory. He felt damaged by his fall, and what he had to do to survive. Word of their arrival had reached inside the community room, as Jason heard a young voice shout his name. He looked toward the entrance and saw Argus running to him. Jason smiled and stretched his arms out to embrace the young man.

Argus shouted, "Uncle Jason! I knew you would be alright! Everyone was so worried about you, and so was I, but I knew you would be alright! You have to tell me all about the battle!" Argus continued holding onto Jason for some time, then he looked and saw Aegeus and Calista standing in the entrance smiling.

"Let us go inside, young Argus. You can sit next to me at the table," Jason said as he really wanted to recline. The day's events had drained him. He thought about what Argus had said; he did not want to talk about the battle.

Once inside, Jason was overwhelmed by well-wishers expressing joy and wanting to embrace him. It was a true blessing, but the massive interaction was trying Jason's endurance a bit. He just kept smiling and expressing his love the best he could. Alethea became aware of Jason's trouble and tried to expedite his seating at the table. Jason saw Alethea acting upon her intuition, and it blessed him. At last, he was comfortably seated at his old favorite table with all of his close friends. Jason lay back upon the pillows, then breathed deep and exhaled.

"Is everything alright, Jason?" Aegeus asked as he sat across from him. "You look tired," he said. The old man also had intuition, and concern for his friend.

"Everything's fine, Aegeus," Jason said as he looked into his eyes. "Too soon to talk about it," he added. Aegeus nodded with a look of wisdom. Calista and Dimitri were on either side of Aegeus and they all engaged in friendly small talk for a few moments, which relaxed Jason.

Eustace arrived at the table and took the only spot available. He said, "Sorry, I had to finish some business out in the courtyard before the meal." He smiled at Jason and asked, "How's our guest of honor this evening?"

Jason attempted a bit of humor saying, "Very tired, and not very honorable, but very hungry!" Jason did achieve a bit of laughter from around the table and it was medicine to his soul.

Alethea pulled her double aulos from her bag and Jason was delighted. "I haven't played since Jason was arrested," she said as she raised the instrument to her lips. She began to play one of his favorite melodies. Jason wept, as everyone reached out to touch him as she played. Lydia and Melina had begun bringing the meal out, but Jason was entranced. It was as if God himself told Alethea exactly what he needed; the music was the most beautiful thing he had ever heard. Alethea finished, then leaned over and kissed her husband. Another wonderful surprise was given to Jason by his friend, Lukas. He reached into his tunic, then pulled out a small scroll and opened it. He began to read from the book of Isaiah:

"So shall they fear the name of the Lord from the west, and his glory from the rising of the sun. When the enemy shall come in like a flood, the Spirit of the Lord shall lift up a standard against him. And the Redeemer shall come to Zion, and unto them, that turn from transgression in Jacob, says the Lord."

Lukas struggled with a couple of words, though he did an excellent job of delivering the important scripture. Jason sat with a huge smile upon his face.

Alethea spoke, "Orpheus and I taught him while you were in prison."

"Yeah, I really wanted to tell you, but I decided to show you instead," Lukas said as he was obviously very pleased with himself and his accomplishment. "You never got around to teaching me, but I'm still learning. Alethea and Orpheus said you could help when you were delivered from the Romans," he added.

"I'm very proud of you, Lukas! Of course, I can't wait to help you. I regret not getting started sooner, but I didn't see the arrest coming. We won't make that mistake again," Jason said as he got up and embraced Lukas.

Before long, Jason was quite preoccupied with eating. The roasted lamb, as well as many delicious side dishes were served, and he never thought food could taste so good. He was feeling much better, as much of the fatigue from the day had passed. Jason was, however, caught off guard by young Argus. He was aggressively asking questions about the battle during the conversations. Jason's pain came to the surface.

He responded angrily, "There is no honor in killing, only mercy! Why are you so preoccupied with death? I'm sorry, but I don't want to discuss the details of two men hacking each other to pieces! I'm sorry…I'm sorry." Jason touched Argus upon the shoulder, then got up and fled to the courtyard.

Argus was shocked and was whimpering a little. Calista got up and went around to him, as well as Aegeus. Alethea followed Jason into the courtyard. They sat by the well and had a conversation.

"I saw it coming. I thought you were relaxing, but I think it's clear to see that you're having trouble," Alethea said as she embraced Jason. "What can I do to help?" she asked.

"I don't know. I can't believe I responded to Argus that way. I haven't told anyone, but some terrible things happened to me at the hands of Actaeon. I'm not what everyone thinks I am," Jason said while trying to maintain his composure.

Alethea looked Jason in the eyes and said, "I know. You've been through more than most people can imagine. You're going to have to trust God to get you through this."

Jason let loose and shouted, "You don't understand! Actaeon and his personal guard pushed me! He sat back ridiculing and mocking me while his men beat and tortured me! I fell, Alethea, I fell! I embraced the evil once again, then broke my bonds and attacked my tormentor! Now, I've killed a man! All I ever wanted to do is share the truth; the awesome truth of Jesus. What have I become, Alethea?" Jason began sobbing.

"You are Jason of Gadara," Alethea spoke with eye contact upon her husband. "You have been through a terrible ordeal. You are not that beast Jesus delivered you from. If you were; I'd know it. I expressed hatred for my father, then he died. I'm well acquainted with the struggle, Jason, for we're not strong enough without God," she said. Jason took note of what Alethea had said and raised his eyebrows. She continued, "Yes, wicked spirits tried to take me apart over that. I sought God. Listen to me, Jason, God has forgiven me; God has forgiven you."

Alethea's confession calmed Jason tremendously. He realized he had repeated a mistake and said, "I've drifted into relying upon myself. That was something a very dear friend of mine spoke to me amid my torment. You're right, we're not strong enough without God. I'm just a man...a very stupid one sometimes."

Jason and Alethea became aware of a presence as they looked up and saw Argus and Dimitri approaching. Jason got up and ran over to Argus, then embraced him tightly.

"I'm sorry, Uncle Jason. My brother and my parents told me you were hurting inside, but I didn't know. I would never do anything to hurt you. I feel terrible," Argus said as he started whimpering again.

Jason spoke with compassion, "My dear young friend, I forgive you, and, God forgives you. You didn't know; how could you? I'm going to make you a promise: when you're older and some time has passed, then I will tell you all about that battle. God has delivered me from the hands of the Romans, that's all you need to know for now. Violence and death are an all too real part of the world we live in. Pay attention to the beautiful and noble things, but not violence and destruction. That is the way of God."

"Thank you, Jason," Dimitri said as he placed his hand upon Jason's shoulder. He continued, "I'm encouraged every time I hear you speak."

Jason smiled as he released Argus and then embraced Dimitri. After a moment he said, "Let us go back inside."

The four returned to the table and reclined. Jason had a long, somewhat private conversation with Argus, which ended with play wrestling and giggling in the pillows. It brought joy to everyone, and no one brought up anything about the day's events again.

"So, Aegeus, you've traveled back, what are your plans now?" Jason asked as he continued eating.

"We're going to stay home for a while. We were hoping to have a meal at our house with you and Alethea, as well as the entire fellowship. We would like to share our experiences, for we have heard Jesus speak upon many occasions." Aegeus said while looking over at Calista with a smile.

Calista spoke, "I think it would be good for you, Jason. We have grown in faith and knowledge; we might be able to help with some of your struggles."

"Thank you," Jason responded. "I have been blessed with many good friends. I haven't spoken of it, but I plan to seek Jesus myself; I'm going to spend time at home first. Somehow, I know I need to inquire of the Lord myself. I'll know when the time is right," he said.

The evening was a great blessing for Jason, even though there was some discomfort. It all passed, however, once everyone became aware of the pain that he struggled with. Jason wanted to engage with all of his friends in conversation. A very special moment came for Jason when Eustace described, in detail, his interaction with Jesus. Eustace was already emotional when he told of Jesus forgiving him over the incident at the beach. Lukas moved close at the telling, for he was there also.

Eustace was smiling with tears in his eyes, which was a rarity for him. Lukas was smiling, for there was a confidence he had been carrying ever since. Eustace said, "He smiled when I asked him to pray for you. It was at that moment I knew you would be delivered. I still worried, however, when you refused armor. Please forgive me."

Jason himself was overcome with emotion. He teared up a little, but mostly he felt joy. He looked Eustace in the eye and spoke, "There's nothing to forgive, Eustace. You responded with a reasonable concern. We're only flesh and we are subject to the weaknesses of the flesh, that's why we need to look to God in all things. Yes, I could have benefitted from the use of armor, but I chose to disregard it. The best armor in the world wouldn't have saved me without God. I was in danger of losing everything, even if I prevailed, if God had not been with me."

Eustace's story ignited an even greater desire within Jason and the others to follow Jesus. Jason's desire was for the entire family to travel and do what Aegeus and his family had done. Aegeus and Calista expressed encouragement, and a desire to join them as well.

However, everyone agreed that this was a season for rest and family. As Jason had said, when the time was right.

Alethea became excited about the prospect of another trip. A journey to meet with Jesus would be extraordinary. "I would love to travel after everything that has happened, but right now is too soon. You need time to enjoy the home God has blessed you with," she said to Jason. "And the wife," she added with a giggle. The entire group erupted in laughter.

Eustace had resumed his usual demeanor and asked, "Do you all think it's time to unveil the surprise?" Everyone at the table shouted in agreement, even though some were unaware of just what the surprise was. Eustace smiled and gestured for Alethea and Jason to get up and come with him. He led them through the back door leading upstairs. Jason and Alethea followed Eustace up the familiar stairway to Jason's old room. He opened the door and they both gasped. The room was decorated with flowers and the lamps had been lit. It was exactly as it had been on their wedding night. Jason and Alethea embraced and kissed. "I'll be leaving you two alone now, goodnight," Eustace said as he closed the door.

"We love you, Eustace," he heard Alethea say through the door as he walked away. It put a smile upon his face.

A couple of weeks passed as Jason settled into the life he had before the arrest. There was no hiding the fact that he had changed. Much of the boldness and fire he had spoken with in the past was subdued. He was increasingly spending time alone, except for an occasional overnight fishing trip with Lukas. They set out with Orpheus and Linus one particular afternoon. Jason was seeking help from his friends, but he didn't know how to ask. He had sought answers through prayer but always came to the same conclusion: he had fallen and now lived in fear that it could happen again. The men had chosen a campsite with a clear view of the western sky to view the sunset. This had become important to

Jason, for his cell window had faced south. He could take in some of the colors, but viewing the actual sunset was impossible. Now, he cherished it more than ever. The clear sky was scarce of clouds, however, but there was a line of fluffy clouds in the distance to the west that became ablaze with crimson and orange as the sun descended. The wide-open view of it from the Yarmuk river valley was picturesque and brought with it much needed joy to Jason's heart. The sunset waned as the four men settled in around the fire to eat their catch.

"We're happy to have you two along with us this time," Lukas said as he ate. "It doesn't get much better than this," he added.

"Yes, but there is some advantage to a comfortable bed, Lukas," Orpheus commented as he finished the fish he had been eating. "These old bones are familiar with the hard ground, though. It's worth it to be out here with my friends," he said as he settled back against a tree. The flickering fire reflected off the old man's white hair and beard, as his aged face suggested serenity and wisdom.

Linus spoke, "There's something special about sleeping outside when you choose to, but not because you have to. I appreciate you asking me to come with you this time, Jason. This fish is delicious out here, for it does somehow taste better. I heard you two talk about it. I didn't believe it, but it's true!"

"What it is, Linus, is that we can all relate to having to sleep outside," Orpheus stated. "I can remember many nights going to sleep hungry. God has richly blessed all of us through Jason here," he said while gesturing to Jason, then continued, "We must never forget from where we came," Orpheus said as he looked at Jason and repeated, "We must never forget. Yes, the fish was quite tasty."

"If you're handing out advice, Orpheus, I'm listening," Jason responded. His eyes reflected the flicker of the fire as he looked over at Orpheus

Orpheus smiled and spoke, "I was just saying that we were all taken from a very dark, horrendous place. Maybe not in Linus's case, but he was rescued from poverty and a lack of purpose."

Linus responded to the comment of Orpheus, "A lack of purpose, yes; I was not compromised like you, but with a lack of purpose I could have been. I've done some things I'm not proud of. Without Jason inviting me into this family I could have easily fallen. I've developed a good understanding of such things from my friendship with all of you. The rejection I felt from society because of my poverty was unbearable at times. I was often tempted to run off into the wilderness, as Jason and Lukas did. I had no family to help, so I raised myself. When Lukas shared the knowledge of Jesus with me, for the first time I felt to be a part of something bigger than myself. The knowledge of God has given me a dimension of my life I never thought possible."

Orpheus stated, "See, Jason, how far this man has come, and he wasn't possessed by demons as we were. How much farther has the Lord brought you? We all have weaknesses. You must keep in mind where you came from. The Romans pushed you beyond what any of us can understand; you fell a little, but you didn't remain there."

Jason sat quietly listening to his friends, then spoke, "What does that have to do with the unknown?" he asked. "They still torment me in my sleep. My first day of freedom I spoke harshly to a young man who means the world to me. In a way, I did remain there. I just don't have the confidence I did before. My worst fear was losing control during the battle; now, my worst fear is losing control in any circumstance," Jason confessed to his friends.

"Jason, what have we learned?" Lukas asked. He spoke boldly, "Trust God no matter the circumstance!" Then he touched Jason's shoulder and shouted, "In the name of Jesus, I speak to these harassing spirits: COME OUT OF HIM!"

Jason recoiled a bit, then closed his eyes. He sat quietly as his friends watched, then opened his eyes and smiled. "Thank you, Lukas; I do feel calmer. Something was there that I failed to identify. Keep praying for me please; all of you," he said.

Orpheus said, "We have been for some time, and yes we will. You must get it through your head that the Roman imprisonment is over. We want you to come home, Jason. Sometimes it appears that you choose to return to that cell, but God does not want you to dwell there. You have a wife and friends, as well as a good portion of Emmatha and Gadara who love you. We all want you to come home, Jason…all of you!"

Jason smiled. "It's funny you put it that way. That's what the wicked spirits always say, that they want to come home," Jason responded with a slight chuckle.

"I'm so sorry, my friend. I had no idea that would relate to your nightmares. I'm sorry," Orpheus said as he was slightly embarrassed.

Jason responded with a smile for his friend and stated, "That's quite alright, Orpheus. I'm not that fragile. I just laughed because it was a coincidence. I am still Jason of Gadara. I love Jesus. I'm devoted to the ways of God. It's just that I have more scars on the inside now to match the ones on the outside." He stared into the fire for a moment, then went on, "God could heal all of it. Have I ever told you that I've dreamed of such? I've had several dreams that my skin was as blemish free as yours. The disappointment was unbearable the first time. Why would God show me that?" Jason asked as he sought his friend's opinions.

"Perhaps you were in a spiritual form," Orpheus theorized. "Or, perhaps, something from the future. Maybe it was a vision of your form after the resurrection at the end of time," he speculated.

Jason asked, "So, you think it may be the result of a future event, Orpheus? I've held out hope that it was, so why did Jesus not heal me when he cast out the demons?" He then realized the conversation was awakening a desire to seek Jesus and to inquire of him. "I have so many questions I would ask him. Honestly, I think my scars are a permanent reminder of my life as Legion; part of my testimony to myself and others. They help demonstrate the power of God to transform a life," he said.

Orpheus commented, "Your scars are, I believe, a powerful part of your testimony, Jason. They have helped you reach people from what I've witnessed."

Lukas said, "I agree, Jason, for I've witnessed the same thing. Your scars don't identify you as Legion but show proof that you were Legion. You are a walking example of the power of God to restore through Jesus and that resonates with people."

Jason replied, "Then, of course, it is a small burden and I should see it as an advantage, that I understand. But there is a part of me that longs to be as other men. God has blessed me with a woman that appears to be blind to the scars. To inquire of Jesus would, perhaps, answer questions that I have deep inside. I have such a desire to seek him, for answers only he could provide." Jason stared into the fire, the flickering light reflecting upon his face.

"Perhaps you should. We will come with you when you go to seek Jesus" Orpheus said.

"When do we go?" Lukas asked as he was excited at the prospect of a trip with all of his friends.

"I want to come with you, but this summer the vineyard and orchard are going to produce; I can't walk away from that," Linus said as he threw some wood on the fire.

Jason responded, "I'm not ready for a long trip just now. I'm with you, Linus; you all have worked so hard on my property. I want to be a part of it as well. I've been thinking about it quite a bit; early next spring is when I'm thinking to go."

"Alright, it's settled then," Lukas said. "I'm looking forward to what's going to be our greatest adventure. Meanwhile, there's lots of fish to catch and work to be done. We're all with you, Jason!" Lukas announced with boldness as he extended his hand. The men all joined in with a four-way clasping of hands which symbolized the strength of their fellowship around the roaring campfire.

The prayer of Lukas did cast something away from Jason. He fell into the most peaceful sleep he had since his release, and it was devoid of bad dreams.

The summer months passed as Jason slowly recovered from the months of hell he had endured. It had been just about a year since his deliverance. Jason and Alethea both were looking forward to a quiet evening, as everyone had decided to go to the caravansary for the evening meal. The men had been discussing the coming harvest. Jason was a little impatient and wanted to make wine. Linus wanted to wait for just the right time. Lukas was more impatient than Jason, so they were constantly inspecting the vines. Orpheus was the most patient of all and was content with the knowledge that there would be wine, eventually. Inspecting the vineyard gave Jason and Alethea an excuse for a pleasant evening walk and time for conversation.

"What do you think? Are they ready?" Jason asked as an attempt to bring another opinion in agreement with Lukas and himself.

"When Linus says it's time, Jason," Alethea said as she looked up at him with a smile. "It won't be too much longer I think," she added.

Jason picked a grape and ate it. "They taste ready to me," he said with a grin.

"Remember what Linus said, 'You can make good wine, or great wine if you harvest at just the right time.' It's not like we don't have wine," Alethea said while playfully addressing Jason's impatience.

Jason spoke in agreement, "Yeah, I do want it to be great wine, but it's something I'm looking forward to; our wine. The winepress is ready, and we've purchased enough jars to become wine merchants. Look at how thick they are, for we've truly been blessed. Thank you, Lord!"

"You seem so happy lately, my husband," Alethea said while displaying a huge, beautiful smile for Jason.

He leaned over and kissed her, then responded, "Yeah, I told you before about when Lukas and I went out fishing with Orpheus and Linus. Lukas prayed for me and cast out a spirit; I've felt better ever since. Through the power of Jesus, he was able to cast something out of me that I couldn't identify; something from my experience with the Romans. I still have the burdens, but the Lord is giving me the strength to carry on. I may be struggling with impatience about grapes, but I know, somehow, I'll be even stronger in faith as time passes. I'm very optimistic about seeking Jesus in a few months."

Alethea said, "I'm looking forward to traveling again; it won't be the same as when we were alone, but more like a family trip." Then she asked, "Could we take a little trip together soon, just you and me?"

"Of course! Sounds like an excellent idea. It had crossed my mind, but we've been pretty busy all summer," Jason responded. "Where would you like to go?" he asked.

Alethea replied, "I don't care. I just want to travel with you. We could go back to Gerasa to see how Ammayu and his family are doing, for we haven't seen them since their baptism. I like the idea of revisiting our first trip, for two or three days." Alethea looked up at Jason and awaited a response.

Jason smiled and said, "Very well, Alethea, we'll leave tomorrow. I want to be here for the harvest; I expect Linus to give the word any day now."

"Don't worry, we'll be back in plenty of time for you to pick your grapes. We can take our time on this trip. Perhaps you could try teaching me to fish again," Alethea said with a grin as she examined a cluster of grapes. She picked one and ate it as she looked at Jason, then he started to chuckle. The two embraced and slowly began walking back to the house.

Jason walked with great joy. He glanced back at Alethea as she sat sideways upon her animal while playing her aulos. Her pale blue travel clothing and white head covering made her look exceptionally beautiful to Jason. It was almost like living a memory, as if the horror of the Roman imprisonment was only a bad dream. Many wonderful events had also been healing to Jason's spirit. The visits of Neleus and his companions were a great blessing. He welcomed the opportunity to minister to the Centurions, as he shared the truth with his former tormentors as a Roman citizen. Teaching them the concept of loving your enemies and praying for them shattered their reality. Some of the liveliest debates of all Jason's endeavors of ministry was with the Romans. Neleus came alone the first time to bring Jason the scroll he had left behind. The next time he brought one companion, and more recently he came with three others.

Jason walked along and reviewed some of the street ministry he had performed within Gadara as well. The battle with Actaeon had given Jason some notoriety, which he always had to distance from the message. He taught that violence should be avoided at all costs, except when needed for self-preservation or defending the innocent. Lukas and Orpheus had become more involved with the ministry since Jason's release as well. All of them were becoming beloved within the city by their fellow Gadarenes, even if some weren't ready to accept all of their teachings. Many who had encountered Jesus themselves were attracted to Jason and the others due to the close connection. The teaching was becoming a movement, and the movement was confronting the Pagan Temples within Gadara and Emmatha. Jason and his friends were becoming formidable debaters in whatever public forums presented themselves. The truth of the teachings of Jesus, which was bolstered by their increasing knowledge of the word of God was a great challenge to the traditions and folklore. Many whom they debated became converts. Jason had regained his sense of worth, and stronger than before. His ministry was going well.

"I'm getting hungry," Alethea said as she stopped playing and broke Jason's thoughts. It was a pleasant distraction.

Jason looked around and saw a small meadow off to the right, which was surrounded by forest. A few boulders lay about the clearing; it appeared to be the perfect place to stop. Jason led the animals toward it and spoke, "Yeah, me too. We'll stop here for a while."

Jason walked up to Alethea, as she was putting her pipe away and preparing to slide off her animal. Jason scooped her up in his arms before she could, then whirled her around and kissed her. He set her down, then they decided to camp there and set about their usual routine. Jason set up their tent and built a fire; Alethea dug through the supplies to put a meal together. Jason figured they were about halfway to Gerasa. Tomorrow they would arrive early, so they could have more time to visit Ammayu. The evening was rather uneventful, as the couple finished their evening meal and settled back against one of the large rocks near the fire. They were at a high vantage point and the sunset was beautiful. Beams of subdued sunlight filtered through the trees, bathing the site with warm auburn tones. The crackling fire, as well as the closeness and the sense of lightheartedness made the evening seem like a pleasant dream.

"I feel like we've been completely restored, Jason. I'm happy like before, but more at peace. It's as if we were tested and overcame," Alethea said as she gazed into the fire with the flames reflecting a sparkle in her eyes. "I feel as though nothing can hurt us anymore," she added.

Jason responded, "Be careful with that, Alethea. Things have been going very well, but as long as we live in this world we'll have to deal with evil. For now, God has blessed us. I feel as you do, but I take nothing for granted. I've been wondering lately what the next challenge may look like."

"You haven't been waking up lately. I take it the dreams have subsided?" Alethea asked.

Jason replied, "Yeah, through a lot of prayers. I still have them, but not as severe as they were when I was first released; I've been sleeping well. The biggest problem now is that anything awakens me. No noise or movement ever escape me; it was one of the traits developed within Legion. It has returned, since my fall in the Roman prison. I don't want to carry around anything from my past, but it's not necessarily an evil trait. I've learned to live with it already." Jason looked into the fire as he revealed his innermost struggles with his wife the best he could.

Alethea responded, "Well, at least no one will be able to sneak up on us. I'm glad you shared that with me, for I had no idea." She snuggled closer to Jason, "I want to make you as relaxed and comfortable as possible," she said.

"You always do, dear Alethea," Jason said as he leaned over and kissed her.

Later that night, the two were sleeping in their tent as a very slight commotion occurred at the campsite. The thief crept in very quietly up to the packs to silently pilfer their goods. The pale moonlight and the glow of the dying fire illuminated the shabby figure only slightly as he examined the money sack he had withdrawn from Alethea's pack, as well as some food. He arose and turned to silently slip away, as he was satisfied with his acquisition. The thief was pleased with himself, for he thought he had slipped in unnoticed and proud of how quiet his movements had become. He was completely shocked to see the figure of a man standing directly in front of him leaning against a stone. The thief drew a dagger from his sash hoping to intimidate the man for his escape. Jason drew his sword and flipped it over the back of his hand. The thief dropped his dagger and began to plead for his life:

"I'll leave all that I took," he said as a couple of small bundles hit the ground. "Just let me go. I have a family and we're all very hungry. Please let me go," he begged with a shaky voice.

Jason was silent. He gestured for the thief to go over by the dwindling fire with his sword, then gestured for him to sit. Jason threw some wood on the fire, which illuminated the two men. He looked at the intruder up and down; he was a young man with very shabby, dirty clothing and a dingy banded head covering. "If you're going to lie you should become better at it. You have no family, for your appearance clearly states that you live outside, and away from civilized men. No woman would allow you to develop the level of filth that you demonstrate," Jason stated calmly. "If you're doing this because it's all you know, then why don't you just say so?" he asked.

"It's not all I know, but it's what I've become. I was an actor. I began stealing because I couldn't make enough money to survive. Now, it's all I do. That's the truth; I've never told anyone this," the man responded as he nervously looked around. "Who are you?" the thief asked as he was astounded that he had opened up to a man who could be ready to kill him.

"I am Jason of Gadara. I am one of a fellowship who follows Jesus of Nazareth. Fear not, for I have no intention of harming you; I want to help you," Jason said as he sat by the fire across from the thief. "What is your name?" he asked.

The man replied, "I am Rasmus." He was wide-eyed asking, "You're Jason of Gadara?" The trembling thief began to sweat and breathe erratically. "I pulled a dagger on you!" he exclaimed.

"I have no intention of harming you, as I said. A man's life is worth much more than a sack of coins and some food," Jason calmly stated with a smile upon his face. "Are you hungry?" Jason asked as he glanced down at the small bundles and the dagger he had picked up following the short-lived challenge.

"I'm very hungry. I haven't eaten for three days," Rasmus responded.

Jason picked up the bundle of food Rasmus had stolen and tossed it to him. He said, "Eat this, and there's more if you're still hungry when you finish."

Rasmus tore open the bundle and began to devour the dried fish and bread contained therein. Jason just smiled and sat back watching the hungry man eat. He then opened the sack of coins he had retrieved from Rasmus. He pulled out a couple of the more valuable coins, then closed the sack and tossed it to the thief as well. Rasmus stopped eating and stared at Jason in disbelief.

"You're giving me this? Why?" Rasmus asked as his voice was full of confusion.

Jason replied, "I'm showing you compassion. All I ask in return is that you listen to me and be honest." Jason gave Rasmus a serious look. "Tell me, beyond this world, what do you believe?" he asked.

"I believed in the gods of the stories told to me by my parents when I was younger but concluded that none of it is true. I've heard of this *Jesus* you say you follow, but I've yet to see anything to convince me. Yeah, heard a lot of stories, but I guess you could say I don't believe in anything. I believe I control my own destiny," Rasmus said as he finished the scraps of the food he had taken.

"You seem to have heard of me. Have you heard the whole story?" Jason asked.

Rasmus responded, "I've heard you were imprisoned by the Romans, and you fought a battle with one of their leaders to win your freedom. There is a legend that you were once the beast and lived in tombs. I find all that hard to believe. I've heard of the beast, like some kind of wild animal. I believe I saw it once at a distance."

Jason spoke, "I was possessed by thousands of wicked spirits for most of my life. I was much like you when it all started. My faith has grown from knowledge acquired from these spirits, as well as things Jesus has revealed to me. Jesus delivered me, and these wicked entities immediately recognized him as the Son of God, so did I. It's hard to explain, but the one, true, living God has had mercy and compassion upon me. I have had compassion upon you. It was no mistake that you were led here tonight; God loves you, and so do I. You are not possessed by demons, but you have been influenced by them. You must reject your current life and learn the ways of God and the teachings of Jesus. Otherwise, you too could end up as I did." Jason finished, then awaited a response.

"You were the beast?" he asked. "I saw it once; I find that hard to believe. You look nothing like that," Rasmus declared.

Jason pulled back his sleeves and raised his garments to expose his legs saying, "This is what Legion, the *beast*, did to himself. I now must carry these scars, but Jesus healed me and restored me in every way possible; not only that, but I have a wife and a family of friends, as well as a house and a vineyard. Seek the

Almighty God and follow his ways; he will fulfill the desires of your heart!"

"I saw those scars even at a distance...I thought they were stripes, like on a tiger. You really are...were the beast. You look normal now," Rasmus said as he was astonished. Faced with a truth he didn't want to accept, he asked, "Jesus changed you? How did he do it?"

Jason responded, "Jesus is the Son of God. He cast every single demonic spirit within me into a vast herd of swine that was feeding nearby. I can remember negotiating with him, for the spirits within were very fearful of being cast into the abyss. At that moment I became the man I am now. I repented of all my sins and God had compassion upon me. The swine ran into the Sea of Galilee and drowned. Jesus and his disciples ministered to me, then gave me clothing and money to start my new life. I wanted to go with them, but Jesus wanted me to stay in my own region and give testimony to all that had happened. That's what I've been doing ever since; I've now shared the testimony with you. You are living a life in rebellion against God. Turn away from your sin and God will forgive you and restore you as he did for me. It's up to you, what you do with the knowledge you've just obtained...it is the truth." Jason went silent and awaited a response.

Rasmus looked at Jason intently while he was speaking, then stared into the fire for some time in silence. Finally, he spoke, "I believe you." Then he asked, "What must I do now?"

Jason replied with eagerness, "First of all, you need to learn to pray. God hears you, so just speak to him. Approach him like a loving father, for he is the father of us all. He loves you more than you can understand. You must learn of God's word, for it is a lamp unto your feet in the darkness. God's commandments are not burdensome. Don't put any other gods before him, because they are all false. Don't worship idols. Don't commit adultery, or kill, or STEAL, or bear false witness. Don't covet that which belongs to your neighbor. Honor the Sabbath day and keep it holy. Honor your mother and your father. Never take the name of the Lord in vain. Stay away from anything to do with witchcraft, or calling upon the dead, or anything perverse. He is the one, true, living God and knows what is best for his children. Everyone has struggles making certain changes, but God will have mercy upon you; he is an ever-present help in times of trouble." Jason completed his teaching, then gave Rasmus a chance to speak.

"I feel like I've already gone too far, for I'm known far and wide. I live in the wilderness because I'm wanted everywhere. I was arrested by the Romans, but escaped," Rasmus said remorsefully as he contemplated the chance of redemption.

Jason responded, "You may have to face the consequences of your actions...I did. God delivered me, but I can't guarantee you will escape the wrath of men. All I can tell you is eternity with God is never ending; this life is very short in comparison." Jason watched his new friend across the fire. He bowed his head, and Jason could see that Rasmus was praying; he smiled, then bowed his head and joined him.

Dawn had broken, as the early morning yellow warmth embraced the two men. There was a slight stirring within the tent nearby, as Alethea poked her head out. She was very surprised to see they had a guest with the campfire roaring. She emerged a moment later from the tent fully dressed, then offered a brief but friendly greeting and scurried off.

"My wife," Jason mentioned to Rasmus as they watched her for a moment, then returned to the quiet conversation. Jason said, "I was praying for you to receive the wisdom I know you're seeking." He asked, "I'm curious, what were you praying?"

Rasmus responded, "I prayed to have an experience as you've had; not exactly like yours, but basically I was praying to meet Jesus sometime before I die. I want to seek him." He then asked, "Where might he be found?"

Jason said, "He travels around the Galilee, Samaria, and Judea with his disciples as he teaches and performs miracles. In a few months my friends and I are going to seek him ourselves. He has no one place where he resides; I remember him telling me: '*Foxes have dens and birds of the sky have nests, but the Son of Man has nowhere to lay his head.*' His kingdom is not of this world."

Rasmus stood up. "I wish to depart before your wife returns. I will never forget the friendship we forged together here. I don't know how hard it will be for me to change, but I'll keep praying. I'm going to seek Jesus; it sounds like it will be an incredible journey," he said.

Jason stood as well and embraced Rasmus. "I have something for you before you go," Jason said as he walked over to his pack. he pulled out an extra outer garment and handed it to Rasmus. He said, "Here, the one you're wearing looks like it will fall apart soon."

Rasmus responded, "You said last night that God loves me and so do you. I want you to know that I love you as well." Rasmus embraced Jason, then turned and started to walk away.

"Wait!" Jason shouted before he got too far. He reached into his sash and pulled out the dagger Rasmus had pulled on him. He flipped it around, then handed him the weapon handle first.

Rasmus smiled, then received the dagger and put it in its place. He looked up and said, "Goodbye, my friend."

"Go with God, Rasmus. I'll be praying for you!" Jason said as he raised his hand in a farewell gesture.

Rasmus disappeared down the road, then Alethea returned and asked, "Where's the man who was here? Just someone stopping by from the road?"

Jason responded, "He was a thief who snuck into our camp last night. Quite a ministering opportunity. I feel as though I've helped save him from himself, and the enemy who seeks to devour us all. He was introduced to the Almighty God last night. Salvation for him; healing for me. It was a good night; except I didn't get much sleep." Jason looked into Alethea's eyes and smiled saying, "I love you and by the way, good morning."

Alethea took a moment to process all that Jason had told her, then smiled broadly. She said, "Good morning to you too, my husband. And a good morning it is, for I'm married to Jason of Gadara, and he's always about God's business. You should go rest in the tent, then I'll cook you a delicious meal…and by the way, I love you too."

Jason embraced Alethea and kissed her. He then said, "I'm looking forward to the remainder of our trip, for I feel as though it will truly be blessed. And the grapes will be ready for harvest when we return home. I just know it!"

Jason crawled into the tent and immediately fell into a very peaceful sleep.

Chapter Ten

A Harvest of Souls

The intense summer sun beat down upon the road as the travelers made their way through the familiar landscape of the Decapolis. It was mid-afternoon when Jason and Alethea came within sight of the City of Gerasa; a perfectly clear day, and it was quite warm. A small caravan had left the city and passed the couple heading north toward Gadara. Jason didn't recognize any of the traders, so they stopped for a moment to offer a friendly gesture as they passed by. The couple continued on and encountered two men in ragged clothing sitting outside of the city seeking alms. They drew near to the men; then could see why they were isolated. Jason noticed right away the men bore the marks of leapers. Most were afraid to get close to people with such an affliction, for there were concerns about contracting the dreaded disease themselves. Alethea grimaced a bit and sighed as they approached. She felt compassion but wanted to keep her distance. Jason was not afraid but realized he had given most of their extra money to Rasmus, the thief. Alethea hopped off of her animal to hold both of them so Jason could make contact. He took a sack with him containing the remainder of their travel food, since they were at their destination.

"Be careful, Jason," Alethea said as she placed her hand upon his shoulder. "Don't touch them," she added.

Jason responded by turning and giving Alethea a quick kiss on the cheek. He said, "I'm as careful as God wants me to be. Fear not, Alethea, for God's word will not return void, nor will his compassion be met with evil. I sense God wants to show mercy upon them."

Jason walked toward the men. They were covered, except for their exposed limbs. They both had bandages over what he assumed were great sores upon their flesh. One had the lower portion of his face bandaged; he could see they were both heavily afflicted with the disease. Jason saw the one with his face exposed smile from beneath his head covering as he approached.

The man called out, "Bless you sir, but please don't come any closer. We are all that remains of a colony living at the edge of the Eastern Desert. There is no cure for this disease. We appreciate your help, but please keep your distance."

Jason stopped at a respectable proximity from the men and set the sack of food upon the ground. "I have no money to offer you, but there's a couple of days' worth of food here," Jason said as he gestured to the sack. He continued, "I would also like to pray for you in the name of Jesus, the Son of God."

The man responded, "We've heard of Jesus; we attempted to seek him when we heard he was in the region. There were three of us then. It is difficult for us to travel, and we kept arriving where he had been but missed him. Our brother may have been saved, if only we had found him."

"So, you believe that Jesus is the Son of God? Where did you receive this teaching?" he asked with great interest.

The man answered, "We were seeking alms outside of Gadara a few months ago. There, we sat at a distance and heard two men speaking to a group of people. They were telling them about Jesus and how the power of his name had delivered them from demonic possession. A man who was delivered by Jesus himself had delivered them in his name. They said that Jesus had cast his demons into a vast herd of swine. We believed these men: one was an old, white-haired man with a white beard; the other was a younger man. Orpheus and Lukas were their names, if I remember correctly. They spoke of their friend, but said he was being held by the Romans. They said his name was Jason. We were being ridiculed by many, so we had to flee the area. The three of us prayed that we might find them again, or this *Jason* they spoke of. I believe that if this man were to pray for us, we could be healed. We've heard of Jesus healing some like us...I'm afraid we're running out of time."

Jason looked upon the humble men as he realized that he had been led into a great opportunity. "What are your names?" he asked with a huge smile, which was almost inappropriate for the circumstance.

"I am known as Lander, and this is Belen," he said gesturing to his companion. "He cannot speak, since the disease has cursed his mouth and tongue. I want to thank you for your kindness, for you're the only one so far today. A caravan passed us a short time ago, but none would look upon us," he said. "You are a very kind man, what is your name?" Lander asked.

"Be of good cheer, for today God has chosen to have mercy upon you. I am Jason of Gadara," he proclaimed. "Do you both truly believe that God can heal you of your affliction?" he asked.

Both men were shocked with no response. Jason didn't wait for a response. He quickly stepped up and knelt, while laying his hands upon the men as they bowed their heads.

"Jason, NO!" Alethea's alarmed voice rang out from where she was waiting and watching.

Jason was focused upon the Lord, while realizing Alethea's concern but following something much more prevalent within his spirit. He was being obedient and disregarding his own personal well-being. He prayed silently at first, then shouted with boldness as he continued, "I speak to the spirits behind this affliction: IN THE NAME OF JESUS, COME OUT OF THEM!" He closed his eyes and continued praying, as he could hear Alethea in the distance sighing and weeping a little. Suddenly, Jason felt a hand touch his shoulder. He looked up and could see it was Lander; he was wide-eyed and gasping. Both men watched as the sores upon Lander's arm dissolved leaving behind unblemished flesh. Then Belen uncovered his head and tore away the bandages that had concealed his face. In just a moment both men were completely healed! The men examined themselves; they were shocked and filled with joy. All three men arose as Alethea slowly approached. Lander and Belen were overcome with excitement as they jumped up and down, then embraced Jason. Alethea stood just behind Jason as a look of amazement turned into a wide smile. Jason turned and put his arm around her.

"This is my wife, Alethea," Jason said as he turned back to the excited men. "This is Lander and Belen; friends I've just met," he said to Alethea.

Alethea slowly reached out her hand to the men as they greeted her with bows. She smiled at the men, then looked up at Jason. It was obvious she was a bit embarrassed. Jason took a couple of steps back with her to address her discomfort.

He said, "It's alright, dear Alethea, for your faith has been stretched a bit; the normal reaction was fear." Jason consoled his wife, then continued, "You should know by now that I, however, am abnormal. I choose to believe the Almighty God can do anything. I sensed it was his will; there was no doubt."

Alethea looked deep into her husband's eyes and said, "Thank you, my beloved Jason, for opening my eyes even further. Forgive me, for I'll never doubt your judgment again."

"Please, don't say that. We would have harvested the grapes already if it were up to me, and ending up with inferior wine," Jason quipped. He raised an eyebrow at his wife, which made her giggle.

The four sat together for a small meal. They found relief from the intense sun and warm summer day beneath a grove of olive trees. Sharing the food Jason had brought out was like a feast for Lander and Belen.

"It's been some time since I've spoken," Belen said as he nibbled on a piece of bread. "I never thought I would again. Now that I can; all I want to say is I love God, I love Jesus, and I love you two," he said while smiling at Jason and Alethea. Then he looked over at Lander. "I guess I love him too," he said as a bit of laughter seasoned the conversation.

Lander looked at Jason and spoke, "What must we do now? We shall be eternally grateful for the blessing we've received. We could come with you. Our bodies are evidence of the truth you speak, and we can share our testimony!"

Jason responded, "Your testimony stands by itself, as mine does. I spent most of my life possessed by demons. These scars I bear are my testimony; I was the notorious beast. Jesus delivered me upon the shore of the Sea of Galilee, and I wanted to go with him. More than anything else; I wanted to go with him." Jason paused as he re-lived the memory. "He forbade me; told me to go throughout the city, and to all who I knew, then proclaim that God has had mercy upon me. I realize now that he has set me upon a mission, but at the time I was devastated. What I did here was speak in the name of Jesus. Anyone who has faith that Jesus is the Son of God and has no doubt in their heart can ask of God the father. He will respond, if what you ask is aligned with his will. You've both been given a special gift, like me. You cannot deny that God himself has delivered you from a slow death. Now, seek God with all your heart. Follow his ways and seek out the teachings of Jesus. Let your light shine into the darkness of ignorance. Challenge false gods and superstition with the truth. If you wish to thank God, then do these things," he said. Jason took a bite of dried fish, then awaited a response.

The two men looked at each other for a moment, then Belen responded, "We will do as you say. I know I was near death; the least I can do is to spend the life God has given back to me doing such things."

"I agree. We will do as you say, Jason of Gadara," Lander said as he reached out his hand to Jason. Belen also clasped their hands when he took it. Jason smiled, while silently acknowledging the sign practiced by the fellowship.

Alethea noticed it herself. She smiled at Jason, then reached into her bag and pulled out her pipe, as well as a small pouch. "This was extra money I had tucked away for the unforeseen; I think you two are a good investment," she said as she tossed the pouch to Belen. Alethea smiled, then began playing a beautiful melody.

The small group enjoyed the remainder of the afternoon. Eventually they parted ways. Lander and Belen were going to walk into the center of the City of Gerasa, unashamed. They wanted to purchase new clothing and share their testimony. The two men departed with a promise to visit Gadara; Jason assured them they would be welcome in his home. Jason and Alethea continued on to the caravansary at the southern edge of the city. Alethea mimicked the previous time they had passed that way, as she played the same melody. Jason was amused, while glancing back at his wife with a grin. The couple approached the courtyard of the establishment of Ammayu. Activity at the caravansary seemed slow, for only one stable was occupied by four camels and no one was around. Alethea slipped off her animal to hold the asses while Jason knocked upon the door.

An Arabian woman opened one of the large double doors, then greeted Jason with a smile. He didn't recognize her. He bowed and spoke a greeting, in Greek, hoping she understood.

"Welcome, we have rooms ready, eh, will serving meal, eh, soon," she said.

Jason realized she spoke Greek, but not very well. "We've come to visit Ammayu. Is he here?" Jason asked slowly and clearly, then awaited a response.

She responded, "No. Ammayu and his family, eh, just left the morning. Went Raqmu for, eh, business. They be back in days."

Jason was disappointed. He spoke to the woman slowly, "My wife and I will stay. We have two asses that need to be cared for. We will stay overnight." He smiled at the woman, then walked back to Alethea as she waited with the animals.

Jason reported, "Ammayu isn't here. It appears he's gone to Raqmu on a business trip. I suppose they have some stable help, but I saw no one. Let us tie up the asses in one of the stables and give them some feed."

Alethea exhibited a look of disappointment as well. They led the animals to the side of the courtyard where the stables were located. A tall Arabian man emerged from one of the side doors across from the stables and was wearing all white with a white turban. He smiled at the couple and offered to take the animals. They both nodded in a friendly gesture, then walked up to the large double doors and entered. The community room was empty, so they chose a table and reclined together. They were disappointed, but the comfort was welcome after almost two days of travel.

"Perhaps this trip wasn't the destination, but the trip itself," Alethea speculated as they relaxed. They smiled as wine, bread and a bowl of dates were brought out to them by another Arabian woman neither of them recognized. Alethea commented on her clothing, while appreciating the colors and style of the traditional garments they wore. The woman just smiled and disappeared. Alethea assumed she couldn't understand.

"It appears that Ammayu has family or friends keeping his establishment going in his absence," Jason assumed as he took a drink, then grabbed a couple of dates. "The woman I was speaking to first speaks Greek. Ammayu and his family most likely left after the caravan we saw departed. He obviously takes advantage of slow periods to conduct business, like Eustace. Looks like we came all this way to have a quiet meal with an overnight stay," he said.

"Well, I can certainly think of worse things to travel to," Alethea said as she leaned over and kissed Jason on the cheek. "As I said, this trip wasn't the destination. God has used you in remarkable ways. Makes me wonder what may be in store for us on the way back to Gadara," she added.

"Hopefully, an uneventful and safe journey," Jason said in response. "I strive to be ready, if God wants to use us again. Perhaps we can take a walk after the meal and see what the City of Gerasa has to offer us," he said.

Alethea nodded in agreement, then popped a date into her mouth and lay her head upon Jason's chest. Jason looked around and was impressed with the decor within Ammayu's community room. He had thought about suggesting such ideas to Eustace; the painted murals depicting travel with landscapes and camels were interesting. Just then, the man they had met outside came in and gestured for the couple to follow him.

He led them outside to one of the rooms opposite the stables. They looked inside, and saw two large, very comfortable looking beds. Also, there was a table with pillows, and all their belongings had been placed neatly along the wall just inside the door. Upon the walls was plaster with two different tones of color, and two lamps set within niches. There was also a window facing the courtyard. Jason and Alethea were very pleased with their room and smiled at the stableman. Jason was so pleased that he reached into his pouch and handed the man a denari. The man smiled broadly, then bowed several times and spoke something in a very friendly way that Jason couldn't fully understand. The Nabataeans spoke Aramaic in a way that he had trouble with, and Alethea spoke Greek only. Jason understood enough to know the man was extremely happy and blessed. He just smiled and touched the man's shoulder. The man smiled again, then bowed and departed.

The evening meal was a new experience for the couple: Roasted fish, which was delicious due to an interesting seasoning. That was common enough, but there were many other items brought to the couple they were unfamiliar with. They smiled and tried everything; some were very good, some were a little strange, but they would smile and show all the respect and courtesy they could. The young woman returned that spoke Greek, so Jason seized the opportunity to open a conversation. It started with average small talk for some time, then Jason showed a personal interest.

"What is your name?" he asked as he wanted to know if Ammayu had shared the truth of Jesus with her.

"I am Nahal. I know of you, Jason and Alethea. Ammayu, eh, spoken of you much time," she said. Nahal began to smile as she looked at the couple. "I like both you," she added while smiling.

Jason looked at Alethea with a smile, then continued to communicate with Nahal, "Ammayu is a good man. We met him through a friend of ours whose name is Eustace." Then he asked, "What has Ammayu told you about us?"

"He told us, eh, you are from Jesus. He say you brought, eh, good words from Jesus," Nahal said as she continued to smile, then arranged some pillows and sat with them. Jason and Alethea were delighted. She continued, "We are family with Ammayu, eh, he put us in river to walk with Jesus. Son of God is real; not like stone faces. Many Nabataeans reject Jesus. Some, eh, accept truth. He there now, in Raqmu, talk to many Nabataeans with Jesus and, eh, eh, commerce."

Jason began to tear up as Alethea put her arm around him. "Has Ammayu spoken about my testimony?" Jason asked as the question brought a slightly more serious expression upon Nahal's face.

Nahal responded, "Yes. He told about you were, eh, illness from many bad, eh, spirit. The story of, eh, *beast* we knew. Ammayu told us Jesus took Jason from beast. Now, Jason walk with Jesus."

Jason acknowledged he had planted a vine and he was seeing it grow before his eyes. He said, "I want you to know how happy we are to be here and to meet you. We love you, as well as all of your family. You have richly blessed us. Be sure to tell that to Ammayu, and that we will return someday soon."

Nahal arose and said, "I get back to working. Ammayu will, eh, sad he's not in here. We love you, eh, big."

Jason and Alethea wouldn't let her leave without embracing her. Alethea spoke to her since Jason had been doing most of the communicating. She spoke very slow, "I want to thank you for a wonderful evening, Nahal. We will return someday. I would like very much to spend some time with you and learn more about your fascinating culture."

Nahal smiled saying, "I will look, eh, forward. You are, eh, beautiful, good in with Jason." She touched both upon the shoulder and quickly departed through one of the back doors.

Jason and Alethea exchanged smiles and decided to take a walk around Gerasa. They freshened up a bit in their room, then the couple left the courtyard and walked east. A short distance up the cobblestone street they came to the south gate with its high arch allowing passage into the city. The light of the setting sun cast a warm glow upon the stone buildings as they made their way into the heart of the urban complex. It was a beautiful scene, as the columns and edifices took on the color pallet inspired by the evening sky. The couple walked northwest, and immediately became aware of a pagan ritual taking place at one of the temples.

Jason decided to pray as they walked past, while asking God to open their eyes. Alethea was displaying increasing anxiety as they approached.

"I've learned there isn't much to be gained attempting to minister to people when something like this is in progress. It's like throwing our precious gift before a wild animal," Jason said as he glanced over at a few scantily clad worshippers who were obviously full of wine.

Alethea was silent and looked down as they walked. Jason suddenly realized she was faced with her nightmare; the worshippers were paying tribute to Dionysus. He knew how she had been traumatized as a young girl by such activity. Jason put his arm around his wife as they hurried past, still praying against the deceptive spirits and false gods. They were leading people astray and causing them to indulge in playful wickedness; direct rebellion before the one, true God. Alethea appreciated Jason's intuition, as he knew of her pain without her having to say a word. She smiled and patted Jason's shoulder as they departed the close proximity of the spectacle. They continued on and encountered people in passing with friendly gestures, but not really engaging anyone. Alethea was now at ease, as the walk had become quite enjoyable. They approached a plaza and lingered there a bit.

They were approached by a couple who asked if he was Jason of Gadara. Jason smiled and bowed slightly. They were excited to meet Jason and his wife, for they had been at the event of the contest in Gadara. Jason found the encounter refreshing, for the couple was talking about his statement at the end and not the battle. Jason was further delighted by the fact they had both made the decision to seek Jesus, and the one, true God. It was a pleasant conversation, then the couple from Gerasa started to walk away. Jason told them of Ammayu's caravansary and said they could find fellowship there. They warmly thanked him and Alethea, then departed.

"That was very pleasant," Alethea commented as they walked.

"Yeah, makes me feel like some good came from that nightmare," Jason responded as he looked at Alethea and gave her a peck on the cheek, which made her smile.

Darkness was descending upon the City of Gerasa. Jason and Alethea decided to turn back and return to the caravansary. They turned around, rather abruptly, and noticed two dark figures had been following them. They stopped when the couple turned around; Jason immediately sensed wickedness and sniffed the air. The mysterious figures were at a respectable distance, but Jason spoke with boldness in words loud enough for them to hear:

"The Lord rebuke you in the name of Jesus!" he proclaimed and witnessed an immediate response.

They both appeared to be older women; one of them let out an ear-splitting scream and fled, then quickly disappeared between the buildings. The other stood motionless for a moment, then slowly began to approach. She drew closer and raised a withered, crooked finger from beneath a dark, tattered, filthy garment. She pointed directly at Jason.

"Perhaps you should let me handle this one," Alethea said with a boldness that took Jason by surprise.

He looked at his wife with a grin and gestured to the woman with his hand. "There is more than meets the eye with this one; she's a witch," Jason said as he braced himself spiritually. The darkly cloaked figure came close and stopped while continuing to point her finger at Jason. Only the lower portion of her face was visible, as well as unkept wiry gray hair and withered, bony fingers.

She began a very unpleasant rant, "Mighty man of God! You come through here challenging the great ones. Mighty man of God! Only a shadow of the One who has come to save mankind. We will destroy him, and we will destroy you! We control the hearts of men. Your own people will turn on you and will turn on him! We do not want you here, so go back to where you came from! Where you say? The tombs! go back to the tombs! You are Legion! They will come back; they will set you straight!" The old woman looked upon Alethea. "What do you have here? Very pretty. They will come back, and they will destroy her too!" she shouted, then began cackling with insane laughter.

Alethea had heard more than enough and with authority shouted, "IN THE NAME OF JESUS, COME OUT OF HER!"

Alethea covered her ears having heard the scream from the other; Jason wished he had. The witch let out a scream that, most likely, woke the whole city. The old woman suddenly collapsed down upon her knees and put her face into her withered hands. She began sobbing uncontrollably. Alethea was hesitant at first, but her empathy soon took over and she knelt beside the woman attempting to comfort her. Jason knelt also and prayed. He felt weakened by the incident. They were all but oblivious to a small crowd gathered, as they had been drawn by the very loud scream. No one was being attacked, so they slowly began to dissipate. Jason remained in prayer, as Alethea held the sobbing old woman which went on for several moments.

Finally, the woman lifted her head and spoke while still sobbing, "I repent; I have been the most vile, corrupt, indecent person to ever walk the earth. I want to die. Please, just let me die! How can anyone come back from where I've been? Let me die!"

Jason broke from his prayers, as he had prayed for all three of them. He moved closer and joined Alethea while putting his hand upon the woman's back. He spoke in gentle words, "The Lord God has had compassion upon you this evening; you are free."

"You are a kind man," the old woman said. "Who are you?" she asked.

"A kindred spirit," Jason responded as he smiled at the woman. She returned the smile, but it seemed very awkward to her. "I am Jason of Gadara, and this is my wife, Alethea," he said. The old woman smiled, then looked around as if extremely disoriented. Her countenance had changed, and her appearance softened to a normal looking older woman. She looked at Jason with a questioning expression but said nothing.

"What is your name?" Alethea asked, which directed the woman's attention toward her. She looked at Alethea for a moment with an almost dazed expression.

"I am Cassandra," she said and nodded as if answering a question to herself. "Yes, my name is Cassandra," she repeated as she looked back at Jason with a curious expression.

"Are you from Gerasa?" Jason asked as he tried to help Cassandra get her bearings. She began to weep.

"I don't remember!" she exclaimed as she began sobbing again. Jason and Alethea attempted to comfort her. "I cannot remember anything except evil. I don't remember a time before; I must have always been evil!" she cried. Cassandra hid her face in her hands again while crying profusely.

"It doesn't matter," Jason proclaimed. He spoke to Cassandra with boldness, "You have been delivered from the wicked entities that had enslaved you for a long time. You are a child of the Most High God! He has had mercy and compassion upon you. Listen to me, for I was as you were!" Jason pulled up his sleeves. "Look at this! I bear the marks of demonic spirits forcing me to conduct bloodletting in exchange for supernatural power. Now, I am a disciple of Jesus, the Son of God! He delivered me from a lifetime of demonic possession himself. He set me upon a mission: to share my testimony and carry his words of truth forward into this wicked world. God led you to us, and by the authority of Jesus you have been given a new life, for he is the way, the truth, and the life! The one true God is just and faithful to forgive you of your sins and cleanse you from all unrighteousness. The only thing that matters now is that you are sitting here with us and your future is bright," he proclaimed.

Cassandra stopped weeping and lifted her head while wiping the tears from her eyes with her dirty, shabby outer garment. "I don't know anyone except you two," she said as she looked at Alethea, then at Jason. "I scarcely remember the other witches I was associated with. I don't know where I'm from; I cannot remember any family, and I don't know where to go, or what to do," she spoke with a voice full of fear and confusion. She then looked at Jason somewhat panic-stricken and asked, "What must I do now?"

Alethea asked Jason to step away for a moment to speak privately. They both patted Cassandra on the back, and she responded with a beautiful smile for both of them. The couple stepped off the curb and out into the cobblestone street.

Alethea asked, "What are we going to do with her, Jason? She has nowhere to go."

"I'm concerned as well," Jason responded. "I suspect she would be confronted by the other witches, then they will attempt to turn her back to evil, or possibly kill her," he said. Jason thought for a moment, then placed his hand upon Alethea's shoulder and said, "Let us pray together."

Jason led the prayer, "Father, in the name of Jesus we come to you for guidance. We ask that you place within our hearts and minds that which is your perfect will." Jason finished the simple prayer as a warm feeling filled them both. They opened their eyes, then looked at each other and smiled. The couple looked over at Cassandra as she was looking around with a serious expression like a lost child. Jason and Alethea walked back to her and he offered his hand to help her to her feet.

Jason spoke with compassion, "Cassandra, we want you to come with us if you want to. We have a home in Gadara; we're here visiting, but we're leaving tomorrow. There is a whole family of people there who will except you; not for what you were, but what God has made you to be." Jason and Alethea took turns embracing her as she eagerly accepted their offer of love. The three set off through the now dark city streets, and back to the establishment of Ammayu.

They arrived at the caravansary; the dim moonlight, flaming urns, and torches illuminated the quiet courtyard. Cassandra looked at Alethea, then Jason with an expression of wonder. She smiled as she looked around at the impressive stone building. Jason walked over to the well in the center of the courtyard and drew water, then took a drink with his hand. He gestured to the women who drank also.

"Doesn't appear to be any activity inside," Jason remarked. He looked at Alethea and said, "I'm very tired, if you two want to go into the community room, go ahead. I'm going to rest, for I feel really drained," he said. Jason was feeling more than drained; he just didn't feel well. He refrained from sharing it and thought a good night's sleep would set him right.

Alethea looked at Cassandra, then responded, "I think we'll join you. We've had a very long day, and Cassandra here needs some quiet, peaceful rest. If you're really tired, Jason, we could sit quietly at the table and talk while you go to sleep. We have a full day of travel ahead of us tomorrow." Alethea walked up close to Jason, then kissed him upon the cheek. "I just want you to know that I love you, eh, big," she said with a slight giggle.

Jason smiled at his wife and said, "I love you big too." He then gestured to the room as the three walked over and entered. The wall lamps had been lit and they were pleasantly surprised that a large basket filled with bread and other food items had been placed upon their table. "We won't have to purchase food for the return trip, since we have all of this," Jason commented.

"I'm so hungry!" Cassandra exclaimed as she eyed the basket.

"Perhaps we should purchase some food, Jason," Alethea said as she gestured to the basket, then looked at Cassandra with a smile. The old woman began to eat ferociously while making pleasant moaning sounds as she went. "When's the last time you've eaten?" Alethea asked.

Cassandra answered, after a moment of chewing, "I don't remember." She immediately went back to eating.

Alethea sat beside her and put her hand upon her shoulder. She looked at Jason and smiled, then picked out a piece of fruit to nibble on herself.

Jason was smiling broadly despite the way he felt. He announced, "I'm going to lay down. Goodnight you two."

"Goodnight, my love," Alethea responded while smiling at her husband with just a hint of concern.

Cassandra expedited her chewing, then swallowed and said, "Goodnight, Jason of Gadara!" She smiled and proclaimed, "I love you too, and I love Jesus!"

Jason smiled and sat upon the bed. He removed his outer garment and everything he was carrying, then the sandals. He lay back, and Jason was almost out before he settled in and got comfortable. The peaceful sleep was cut short. He was in for a busy night....

Jason found himself in a vast cave, as he sat against the wall. The entrance of the cave was some distance off, and the light barely made it to where he was sitting. It was very quiet. He looked himself over and appeared to be fully dressed. He had his sword, as well as his sack, and his waterskin. He couldn't remember what he had been doing before this moment, or how he got there. Jason had been through this many times, as he realized it was a very vivid dream. He established within his mind that Alethea was safe, then proclaimed the name of Jesus. There was a harassing wicked spirit which had inspired the dream, this is what he felt before he went to sleep. He had been in this place before, for it was part of the underworld; a place where darkness dwells. Jason could have escaped the realm, but he wanted to know what they had to say. He was confident; the weapons of his warfare were mighty, through God, to stand against such things. He sat and waited, but he didn't have to wait long.

A figure approached from the depths of the cave. It was shrouded in an outer garment similar to his own and covered from head to foot. The familiar figure drew near as Jason looked to see its face; the spirit had no face, only black darkness. Suddenly, a side table appeared with two burning urns on either side of it. The table was set with a delicious spread of bread and fresh fruit, as well as two goblets.

"Strange way to intimidate me," Jason said as he arose and walked over to the table. He picked up one of the goblets and sniffed it.

The figure chuckled and spoke with a deep echoing voice, "I assure you that it's very good wine, Gadarene. Who says enemies cannot treat each other with respect and dignity? Please, help yourself. Everything you see here is the best the world has to offer, I assure you. I'm here to have a conversation with you."

Jason took a sip of the wine, then looked at the goblet and raised his eyebrows. He looked at the mysterious figure and said, "Your right, this is the best wine I've ever tasted. The trouble is, I'd rather have a conversation with a worm." He then smiled at his adversary.

The spirit, or whatever it was laughed and then spoke, "Come now, Gadarene, I'm here to reason with you. We've suffered devastating losses because of you, and this Son of God that you cling to. By speaking his name, you and that wife of yours sent many into the dry places today. And for what? An old woman. What are you going to do with her, Gadarene? Add her to your collection of misfits? She'll be tempted, then she'll turn on you, as they all will when the destruction begins."

Jason was increasingly sickened by the wicked but extremely polite host of this nightmare. "Why don't you cut all of this ridiculous charade and say what you came to say. In the name of Jesus speak straight to me!" he said with authority.

The spirit recoiled, then responded with a harsher tone, "Use that name once more, and I will vanish. I offer you knowledge of what is to come." It then asked, "You ponder these things relentlessly; don't you want to know?"

"What makes you think I can trust the likes of you?" Jason asked as he took another sip of wine while staring into the darkness of the cloaked figure. "I have every reason to believe you will deceive me. By the way, nice coat," he said.

"Yes, I know you no longer frighten easily. Very well. What if I told you that even as we speak the Nazarene has told his disciples that he would offer himself up to be put to death, and they don't believe him!" the spirit said as it moved closer to Jason.

"The Son of God cannot die; I have been with him, and I know who he is," Jason said with absolute confidence. "That's like saying the sun will not rise tomorrow," he added.

The spirit spoke, "Oh, the sun will rise tomorrow, and the Son of God will be put to death, as well as all of his disciples. The seeds of his destruction have already been planted. Let me tell you something else. You think killing Actaeon was a great victory? There is one coming that makes him pale in comparison. All the pathetic followers of *Him* will be tracked down and killed. The Romans are a bit indifferent now, but the followers of the Nazarene will become their hated enemies. I think you get the picture; you and all you love will become enemies of the state, even after they've honored you with citizenship." The spirit asked, "Do you still want to pursue your current path?" It paused and backed off while awaiting a response. It took a sip of wine as it lifted the cup with invisible hands, then poured it into the darkness. Jason thought it strange, like speaking to an empty garment. This was, after all, a dream.

"The only seeds I see being planted here are your dramatic attempts at discouragement," Jason said as he stood straight after leaning on the table. He walked quite close to the spirit as he stared into the darkness and said, "I simply don't believe you." He took another sip of wine but continued staring into an empty head covering. "Who are you, anyway?" he asked with a curious expression.

The figure responded, "We've met before, remember? Names are not important. You will contemplate these things as the days go by. You will search your deepest self. You will know it to be true!" The spirit backed off as if fearing an offensive move from Jason.

Jason smiled and said, "Don't worry. Do you think I would attack an empty garment? The weapons of our warfare are much mightier than this sword. In the name of Jesus...."

Jason awoke startled as the dream abruptly ended. He was in the bed exactly as he had laid back the night before and felt much better despite the dream. Alethea was sound asleep next to him with her arm across his chest. The sunlight beamed in through the window as he heard activity in the courtyard. He assumed it was the small caravan preparing to depart. He didn't want to disturb Alethea, or Cassandra in the bed next to them. It was early morning, so Jason decided to pray right where he was. He was a bit troubled by the dream; it must have been his imagination, but he could still taste the wine. Jason prayed for his family and friends, as well as the city they were in, then he inquired of the Lord.

Jason spoke in prayer, "What was the meaning of the deceptive prophecy from the dark spirit? I ask that you give me peace. I pray for clear understanding. I know these things are lies, for who could possibly stand against the Son of God? Adversity, yes, as I've been tried by adversity. I see your words of truth going forth. I see the works of your hands upon people's lives. I have stood against the spirit of discouragement before and have again. I know the only way Jesus could die is if it was your will. I go forth this day, and I pray for strength. I pray for Jesus and his disciples to continue in strength. I ask that you unite us once again in the coming months. I trust in you, and you only. I give you praise, honor, glory...."

Jason was distracted by Alethea awakening, as she patted his chest where her hand had rested. She had yet to open her eyes but began to smile as he looked down at her. Suddenly, he realized he had to get up, as he indicated so with a little kiss upon her forehead and moving her arm aside. He returned and found Alethea sitting on the edge of the bed, while looking at the pile of blankets on the other bed. Beneath was Cassandra as she slept soundly, only visible by a mass of dirty gray hair poking out. Alethea stepped out as well, then returned and revealed a plan to Jason.

Alethea said, "As the disciples of Jesus helped you, now I must help her. We must take her to the bridge over the Jabbok river. There, you can watch over us as I spend some private time with her. She is in desperate need of washing and new clothes."

"Yeah," Jason acknowledged as the smell in the room made the need obvious. "The first thing, however, is baptism," Jason said as he looked at the motionless old woman beneath the blankets.

"I agree," Alethea said as she looked up at Jason. "I hate to wake her; she's sleeping so soundly," she said as she looked upon the pile of covers. "You did too; you didn't seem to move all night. Good dreams?" she asked.

Jason wasn't going to share the dream, but responded, "Uh, yeah, good dreams. It was interesting." He wasn't trying to be deceptive toward Alethea, but he didn't want to share anything that could descend into discouragement. He changed the subject and said, "Maybe you should awaken her. Don't forget, we have a long day's travel ahead of us."

Alethea agreed. Jason left to settle up with Nahal. He spoke to her in Aramaic at first; they managed to understand each other, but Nahal was a bit amused at Jason's speaking. He spent a few moments with her sharing a brief, friendly conversation and a promise to return someday. He came back to find Alethea and Cassandra had already loaded the asses so that both women could ride. Jason smiled as he approached, then greeted Cassandra with a warm embrace. He thought to himself they should burn her clothing when Alethea was finished with her. He assisted the women in mounting the animals, then led them out through the courtyard.

They headed out through the southern edge of Gerasa, and down the main road to the south toward the Jabbok river valley. The short trip to the bridge was accompanied by a sweet melody. It was obvious Alethea was full of joy, as it came out through her music. Cassandra was absolutely delighted with Alethea's pipe music; she was moving her hands as she listened. The couple had donned their favorite travel clothing. Alethea wore a white chiton with a pastel light blue outer garment and white head covering. Jason had removed his outer garment soon after starting out and traveled in his off-white tunic with a banded white head covering. They were quite a contrast to Cassandra, still wearing the tattered, dark, shabby cloak she wore when they met. Alethea didn't want to give her anything until she had washed. They arrived at the bridge, then tied the animals and headed down the path upon the escarpment to the water's edge.

Jason entered the water first, then turned and gestured for Cassandra to follow. "It's alright," Alethea said as she comforted the old woman, for she was hesitant to enter the water; it reminded Jason of his experience. "It's alright; I'll be right beside you," Alethea reassured her, but Cassandra was still hesitant.

"But...I'm afraid of water," she said as she looked at Alethea, then Jason. There was fear in her eyes; Jason expected as much.

"In the name of Jesus, I speak to this harassing spirit: leave her!" Jason spoke calmly but with authority. The result was immediate. Cassandra entered the water as she smiled at Jason while clinging tightly to Alethea's arm.

"I'm not afraid anymore!" Cassandra said with a huge smile as she ran her hand through the water.

"They didn't want you to come in here," Jason responded, then gestured for the two women to come closer. Alethea brought her into position beside Jason.

Jason looked upon her with a serious expression and asked, "Do you accept Jesus as Lord? Do you repent of your sins, and agree to follow the ways of God for the rest of your days?"

"Yes, I repent wholeheartedly, and I accept Jesus as my Lord! I agree to learn and follow the ways of God for the rest of my life, as well as commit to helping others do the same. I have experienced the power of God and his mercy; I want a new life with my new family!" Cassandra proclaimed boldly with strong emotion as she began tearing up.

Jason and Alethea were tearing up as well, for Jason had never heard such a heart-warming confession. He spoke with boldness, "In the name of Jesus, I baptize you for the remission of sins!" He then proceeded to place his hand upon her back and submerged her. Cassandra emerged with a huge smile upon her face, but that wasn't all; her face, hands, and forearms appeared to be different.

She actually looked younger! She looked nothing like the wrinkled, withered old witch that had confronted them the night before. She now had the appearance of a beautiful older woman, but in desperate need of a bath.

"I'll leave you two now," Jason said as he waded back to the riverbank. He looked back and asked, "Do you have everything you need, Alethea?"

"Yeah, I brought my clothing sack, and it has everything I need. We just need some private time. Take a walk, but don't go too far." Alethea responded with a smile, then turned to size up the work before her.

Jason smiled and departed, then he walked back up the escarpment to check on the asses. He looked to see if the women were visible from the road; they weren't. Alethea had a very good sense about such things. He pet Alethea's animal on the neck. He pet his also, and it didn't try to bite him! At long last, it appeared Jason and his travel animal were at peace with each other! He thought to himself that the blessings of God abound! It was going to be a great day! Cassandra had been riding upon him, so perhaps the ass liked her, as he thought to himself.

Jason decided not to take a walk, but to rest. He changed his clothing, then hung his wet garment over the side of the bridge. He had not moved all night while sleeping, but it was far from being a restful night's sleep. He chose a spot at the edge of the bridge to sit and rested his back against the short wall that lined both sides. Jason entered into prayer, and thanked God for another beautiful day. He began contemplating the dream once again, and quickly passed it off as harassment; an attempt at discouragement. Why wouldn't they? Many were coming to Jesus; his ministry was going well. Had Jesus made the statement to his disciples the spirit spoke of? The only way to know for sure would be to ask him. Jason desperately wanted to see Jesus once again, so many things he wanted to discuss with him. He wanted to reject the dream altogether, but it was there in the back of his mind. He was determined not to let a dream prompted by wicked spirits influence him.

Jason thought about home and his friends. Had they begun the harvest yet? He wondered if they would make it back to Gadara by evening. Most likely not, since the women seemed to be taking a long time at the river. Just as well, for arriving tomorrow would make for easier travel, and safer. Traveling in the dark of night had its share of dangers. He prayed for the harvest, that God would bless all their hard work. It was then that Jason realized he was already taking part in a harvest of sorts. A harvest of souls. He thought of Rasmus, Lander, Belen, and now, Cassandra; all in a day's time. He thought about the fellowship. They had lost count long ago as to how many had come to Jesus through them. Jason was hit with a blessing, as intense emotion. He had found grapes that were ready for the harvest. He had brought them to God, and the knowledge of Jesus. He began praising God with fervent delight.

Jason sat for some time, then found himself fighting the urge to doze off. He was there to watch, not sleep. How long would it be? He checked his clothing, which dried quickly in the intense sun. Jason abandoned any hope of reaching Gadara by evening. He decided to check on the women, then heard them coming up the escarpment as they were talking and giggling. He arose to await the women's return. They emerged around the corner of the bridge, and Jason was thoroughly shocked in a very nice way.

Cassandra approached Jason and extended her hand while smiling broadly. Jason took it gently and kissed it, then bowed. She stood before him a very beautiful older woman. Her silvery gray hair was still a bit wet but was silky and slightly wavy. The features of her face were soft and graceful: classic Greek. Jason thought to himself she could easily pass for Alethea's mother. She wore one of Alethea's white head coverings, as well as one of her white chitons with a pale green outer garment. Cassandra was very pleased with Jason's reaction: he was speechless. He couldn't help remembering his own transformation. With a huge smile he embraced her, and then Alethea.

Cassandra looked over at Alethea. "I take it he approves!" she said with excited happiness.

Alethea commented, "Of course he does. All I did was help you reveal your true appearance. The beauty that God has placed within you is now visible for all the world to see. It was always there; the evil that overcame you, as well as those ugly, dark garments kept it hidden."

"I never want to wear dark clothing ever again!" Cassandra said as she looked down at herself, then spun around to watch the garments flow. "I feel new, like a blossoming flower," she said with joy.

Jason finally spoke, "That's because you are new. The old things have passed away and behold: all things are new. Acknowledge God in all your ways, and he will fulfill the desires of your heart. Engrave upon your heart that God has forgiven you. The wicked spirits that roam this world will try to deceive you; stand against it in the name of Jesus! I can help you, Cassandra, for I've been down the road you have just set out upon. This is the first day of your new life; a new day! You will meet others who understand as well. We've all been touched by the Master's hand."

The early morning sun quickly began to warm the air. It promised to be another warm, clear, late summer day. Lukas and Linus were the first ones out of the house, then followed by Orpheus.

"Do you think Jason will be disappointed he wasn't here for the harvest?" Linus asked his friends as he stretched and prepared for another day's work.

"We discussed that yesterday," Lukas responded. "He knew it might come to pass while he and Alethea were gone. You explained to him over and over about harvesting at the right time. He'll understand, but he might be a little disappointed. They could return today or tomorrow, and there will be plenty of work to do when they come home," he said.

"I don't know how useful I'll be today. The pain in my hands is giving me trouble from yesterday," Orpheus proclaimed.

Indeed, about half of all the grapes were picked, for the men had worked feverishly all day yesterday. Melina was going to bring more help, as she had promised Lukas. Damon and Letha were going to help as well. The harvest already gathered sat in baskets by the winepress ready to be crushed. Lukas walked over and placed his hand upon the shoulder of Orpheus.

"No need to worry, Orpheus my friend," Lukas said as he smiled at the old man. "You don't have to use your hands today; I think you, as well as Damon and Letha can begin crushing. We'll get what we have into the press, then you can start while we get back to picking," he said. Orpheus smiled as he looked toward the house of Damon, for he could see the elderly couple approaching. Lukas also looked over and smiled saying, "Behold, your help arrives."

The men immediately began to dump the many baskets of grapes into the winepress. Lukas called them to begin the day with prayer as Damon and Letha arrived.

Lukas prayed, "Father, in the name of Jesus I pray you would bless this day. We thank you for the abundance of this harvest, for the vines that have burst with more grapes than I've ever seen! We pray you would send more helpers, and that you would keep us all safe from injury. We pray that you would have mercy upon Orpheus and comfort his pain. Lord, I've prayed that you would bless Jason and Alethea's trip, and father we ask that you return them to us quickly and safely. In the name of Jesus, we give you praise, honor, and glory. Thank you, Lord."

They gathered the empty baskets, then Linus and Lukas headed out to the vineyard. Orpheus sat and removed his sandals while looking at Damon and his wife. "I suppose we get to use our feet today. I don't know about you, but I don't think I could pick even one grape; overdid it yesterday," he said.

"I want you to know that we're very honored to stomp grapes with you, good friend," Letha said to Orpheus affectionately.

"Yeah, nothing like taking a walk in one place," Damon said as he and his wife sat to remove their sandals as well. They also tied their garments in the appropriate fashion to keep them out of the crushed grapes.

Orpheus led the way, as he raked the huge mass of grapes to spread them out evenly. He then quickly scanned the vat and channels for any unwanted debris that may have fallen in. Satisfied, the three stepped in and began their stationary journey.

"It's actually a great pleasure to help," Damon said as he moved his feet. "We decided not to grow grapes this year: our orchard is enough work; we need Linus to help us with that. Our trees were very generous this year, as are yours. That will be the next thing," he said.

"Linus truly has a gift from God; everything he touches grows and produces," Letha proclaimed.

"Last year we had grapes that he helped us with, but not nearly as much as here," Damon recalled. "It was some of the best wine I've ever tasted. Didn't last long, for everybody wanted it. We couldn't pass the offers; local establishments were paying more than the top price for a jar. We kept getting visitors looking for more when it was gone. If this wine is as good as ours was, then

Jason will be very popular with the wine merchants. You're going to have quite a bit," he said.

Orpheus was getting excited and said, "No one appreciates good wine as much as me. If what you're saying is true it will be very profitable; I can't wait to taste it!"

The elder trio was busy crushing and conversing, so they didn't notice the Master of the House approach. Jason had stood silently and watched for a moment.

"What's this about great profits?" Jason asked with a huge smile.

The three were a little startled, then immediately joyful by the unexpected arrival of Jason and Alethea. "Jason!" Orpheus exclaimed as he turned to see Jason standing there along with Alethea and....

"Let me introduce you to the newest member of the family," Jason said while putting his hand upon Cassandra's shoulder. "This is Cassandra," he said, then gestured to the three in the winepress. "This is Orpheus, a very dear friend and sort of a father to us all. And the lovely couple with him is Damon and Letha, our neighbors. I see I'm late for the harvest," Jason said as he looked out to the vineyard and observed Lukas and Linus hard at work.

Orpheus jumped out of the winepress onto a small pile of old clothing they had placed there to clean the feet. He had given friendly smiles to Jason and Alethea but was looking intently at Cassandra. Orpheus embraced Jason and Alethea, then stepped up to Cassandra. He very respectfully took her hand and kissed it. He knew his appearance was a bit off. He bowed, then made eye contact with her. It was a long moment. Cassandra then embraced Orpheus. Jason looked over at Alethea as she was grinning. He looked at Damon and his wife, and they were also enjoying the moment. Suddenly, shouting from the vineyard distracted everyone.

"Jason! Alethea!" they shouted. Lukas and Linus were running back to the house, and both were laden with baskets of grapes. The two men ran up to Jason, then dropped their baskets and took turns embracing him and then Alethea. Lukas took notice of Cassandra, as she stood there with a curious expression.

"Who's this?" Lukas asked as he looked her up and down, then looked at Jason while grinning.

Jason responded, "This is Cassandra. She has come to us by the grace of God and has joined our family. Cassandra, this is Lukas, my dear friend and brother." He then stepped over to Linus and said, "this is Linus, and he is also my brother as well as the one responsible for this bountiful harvest you see before you."

Both men took her hand, then bowed and were very impressed by such a beautiful older woman. Cassandra was obviously excited to meet the people Jason and Alethea had been telling her about. It was becoming apparent to Jason, however, that she was dealing with a bit of anxiety. He looked over at Alethea and made a suggestion:

"Why don't you take Cassandra and show her through the house while I unload the asses and care for them. I want to get settled in as quickly as possible so we can help with the harvest and crushing," he said.

"I think that is an excellent idea," Alethea said as she pecked Jason upon the cheek, then walked over and placed her arm around Cassandra. It was apparent she had made the same observation as Jason. The two women waved and disappeared around the side of the house. Jason watched them walk away with a smile upon his face.

"Where did you find her, Jason?" Orpheus asked. "She looks like an angel!" he added as he watched the two women walk away.

Lukas grinned while looking over at Orpheus, "Maybe she's your angel, Orpheus!" he said, then started chuckling.

It was apparent to all that old Orpheus was quite taken by the unexpected blessing of a new member of the family; especially one closer to his age. Orpheus just stood there for a moment while smiling. Meanwhile, Damon and Letha had kept crushing, and beckoned him back. Orpheus suddenly broke out of his daydream and chuckled, then shook his head and re-entered the winepress. Lukas dumped the baskets they had brought, as Linus collected the empty baskets and started back toward the vineyard. Lukas walked toward Jason to speak for a moment.

"Melina said she would bring all the help she could find; she was here yesterday with Eustace. Today, the plan is to complete the picking and get everything crushed and into the vat. Linus says the quicker the better," Lukas said as he prepared to follow Linus to get back to picking.

"I'll be out there with you as soon as I get things put away and settled," Jason said as he looked in the direction the women walked. "She was delivered by God the same as us. Alethea spoke the words in the name of Jesus! I'll tell you, Lukas, two days ago she was one of the most wicked, vile, shriveled up witches I had ever seen. Cassandra belongs here. Orpheus asked me where I found her, actually, God brought her right to us. I feel she is going to be a great blessing to our fellowship," he said.

"I'm with you, Jason my friend," Lukas said as he started walking away. He quickly turned and embraced Jason once more. "I want you to know I prayed for your safe return this morning. God is awesome!" he declared.

"Yes, he is!" Jason said as he waved at his friend. He then walked over to the winepress and took a deep breath. He said, "I almost want to jump in there with you; by the end of the day I probably will."

Orpheus spoke, "Thank you, Jason. Thank you for just being who you are."

Jason responded, "Thank God, Orpheus my friend. I just try to do what he tells me." He smiled and then disappeared around the side of the house.

Cassandra's head was spinning as the two women descended the wooden stairway from the upper bedchambers. Alethea had shown her the guest chamber that was to be hers. She was quite emotional, and very impressed with the simple but well-appointed room. It was like a dream manifesting before her eyes. She kept commenting on how beautiful everything was. Alethea's influence permeated the entire house, as her sense of color and style made the well-built but simple stone house very warm and comfortable. It surpassed Cassandra's expectations. Alethea poured out two goblets of the standard water mixed with a little wine, then gestured to the large table and the two reclined.

Alethea spoke, "I feel guilty for relaxing with all the hard work going on outside. We were sitting upon those animals all day yesterday and this morning, so we'll take a little rest. Don't think you have to help, for nothing's going to be required of you. We all contribute according to our gifts, so take your time." Alethea then took a sip from her goblet.

"Oh, but I want to help any way I can," Cassandra proclaimed as she took a sip also while looking at the goblet and smiling. "This is very good," she commented.

"This is the daily wine. We're hoping for the harvest to produce exceptional wine. Jason has been looking forward to this for months, since his release from the Roman prison. God has blessed us here, and I think he will bless you also," Alethea said as she smiled at Cassandra.

"Tell me about Orpheus, Alethea. He seems very interesting," Cassandra inquired as she gazed out of the window.

Alethea smiled broadly and spoke, "He is very interesting. He was delivered, as we told you from demonic possession by the authority of Jesus. Actually, I witnessed it, before I met Jason. I saw him cast the demons out of Orpheus; he invoked the name of Jesus right in the middle of the marketplace in Emmatha. It was the beginning of his *reputation*. I think it was that day that I fell in love with him."

Cassandra listened to Alethea with a smile and a look of wonder. She asked, "That's a wonderful story, but what can you tell me about Orpheus now? He seems very kind, and a little mysterious."

Alethea laughed and said, "I think you just described him pretty well! Orpheus has become my adopted father. I love him almost as much as I love Jason. I couldn't have survived him being in prison without Orpheus, for he saved my life many times," Alethea trailed off while recalling memories. She continued, "He's very intelligent and well-traveled, as well as devoted to prayer and reading the word of God. He deals with an inner sadness; regrets from losing his family when evil took over his life. Yes, I've gotten to know Orpheus very well." Alethea smiled at Cassandra and said, "I sense you want to get to know him too."

Cassandra responded, "Let's just say I want God's will to be done. Jason said he will fulfill the desires of my heart; I see the potential of two hearts being made whole...we'll see." Cassandra continued looking out of the window, then was distracted by Jason entering the house.

Jason dropped down at the table next to Alethea and spoke, "I'm going to change my clothes and head out to the vineyard. I see you're getting Cassandra settled in." He looked over at her. "What do you think?" he asked as he smiled at Cassandra.

"I can't begin to describe my happiness, Jason. You really do walk with Jesus," Cassandra said. She looked at Alethea and asked, "Do you have some old clothing for me, so I can help?" She added, "I want to step on the grapes! It looks like fun!"

Alethea responded, "Yes, of course, we'll go out shortly; I'm going to work in the vineyard." She looked over at Jason and asked, "Would you like a goblet?"

He responded by grabbing Alethea's goblet and stealing a little saying, "No, just stopped to rest for a moment and go to work. Couldn't pass the opportunity to speak with two beautiful women in my house." Jason kissed Alethea upon the cheek, then got up and headed up the stairway.

Cassandra smiled as she sipped her wine, then said, "I'm really looking forward to stepping on the grapes." She looked at Alethea and asked, "What if he asks me about my past?"

Alethea responded, "Just tell him you would rather talk about the future." She then placed her hand upon Cassandra's shoulder and smiled.

Orpheus, Damon, and Letha warmly welcomed the new addition to the grape crushing effort. Cassandra's bubbly personality began to shine. She not only warmed the heart of old Orpheus but became fast friends with Damon and Letha as well. She had said it looked like fun, and she was thoroughly enjoying herself. The new wine was flowing through the channels, and the vat was getting deeper and deeper. Cassandra looked up at the house as some noise attracted her attention. Four people were approaching around the side of the house. Cassandra felt a bit of anxiety once again but felt reassured with Orpheus next to her.

"Welcome!" Orpheus shouted as he noticed his friends approaching. He proceeded to make the introductions, "Cassandra, meet Eustace: he owns the caravansary in Emmatha. Next to him is Melina: she works at the caravansary and is betrothed to Lukas. Behind them are Symeon and Theophanes. They are all beloved friends and members of the family." He then proudly gestured to Cassandra and said, "This is Cassandra. God led her to Jason and Alethea while upon their journey. She's come to join our family and brighten our lives!"

The newly arrived group were all smiles as they approached Cassandra. Eustace took her hand and kissed it, then bowed deeply. Melina took her hand and gave her a warm greeting. Symeon and Theophanes also kissed her hand and bowed. Cassandra was a little overwhelmed and almost burst into tears. She had never been treated with so much respect. No one showed up in fine clothing and there were no pretenses. Cassandra suddenly felt silly for feeling anxiety, for she truly felt as though she was among family; a completely new experience for her. A bit of small talk ensued, then the four new arrivals headed into the vineyard. Cassandra could see the warm greetings at a distance.

She looked over at Orpheus and asked, "Was your deliverance as beautiful as mine?"

Orpheus looked upon Cassandra with a warm smile. "Yes, and it keeps getting better," he responded as he gazed deeply into her eyes. A relationship was born as the two embraced while knee-deep in mashed grapes. Damon and Letha sat upon the rim of the crushing vat as Damon put his arm around his wife.

Letha whispered into her husband's ear, "I've never seen anything so beautiful in my whole life. If love is to be an ingredient, this wine will be legendary."

The morning passed into early afternoon, as another group came around the side of the house to offer help. Damon looked over and acknowledged the arrival shouting, "Aegeus!" Cassandra looked up to see an older couple with two handsome young men. She decided to introduce herself.

"My name is Cassandra. I've heard of you! All of you! You're the one who witnessed Jason's deliverance! And you are Calista, Dimitri, and Argus. Jason told me all about you! I traveled here with him and Alethea from Gerasa," Cassandra said as she demonstrated her friendly personality.

Aegeus leaned his staff against the house and walked over, then took her hand and bowed, as did the rest of the family. Dimitri traded his staff for baskets, then he and Argus left quickly to work in the vineyard. Aegeus and Calista remained as they removed their sandals to join the other elderly to work on the crushing. Six people were now crushing in the large winepress, and the new wine was flowing more than ever. Jason, Lukas, Linus, and Eustace then brought more heavily laden baskets and dumped them into the winepress.

"The vines just keep giving! We'll finish the picking today, but it's a miracle!" Jason proclaimed.

"God has blessed your vineyard, Jason! Happy to be here to help!" Aegeus said as Jason walked up to the winepress to embrace him and his wife. The other men offered a warm welcome as well.

Cassandra had a broad smile upon her face that wouldn't fade. She had never imagined such a warm, loving group of family and friends. Overcome with emotion, Cassandra spoke, "It just occurred to me that the real miracle here are all of you," she said as she began to tear up. "I've never imagined anything so beautiful. You have welcomed me into your family. You're demonstrating the kingdom of God right here on earth!" she said as she began to weep. Orpheus embraced her, then the others in the winepress reached out and touched her while smiling.

Jason quickly evaluated the situation and said, "Orpheus, I think you and Cassandra should take a break; take her for a walk and show her around." He looked at Cassandra as she smiled with tears in her eyes and said, "I don't want you to think we brought you here to work, for we have more than enough help. I know this is all new to you; go, enjoy the remainder of the afternoon with Orpheus, for he will take good care of you." He looked at Orpheus and said, "Don't be gone too long. We're having a celebration this evening!"

Orpheus and Cassandra left the winepress and stepped onto the mound of old rags to wipe their feet. Jason also told Damon and Letha not to work too hard, and that they should take some time off as well. He turned to Aegeus, then pointed his finger and said, "You two are the new arrivals; you must work hard!" Everyone erupted in laughter. Cassandra was delighted to see Jason's sense of humor in action. Orpheus and Cassandra washed their feet, then went into the house to change clothes. Damon and Letha walked home for a while. Jason went into the house, then returned with two goblets, as well as a wineskin. He set the goblets upon the edge of the winepress and filled them, then nodded to his friends with a smile. He and the others then returned to the vineyard with their empty baskets.

Orpheus had chosen his best tunic and outer garment. He could tell Cassandra approved, for he had been a little embarrassed to meet this woman dressed in rags. Cassandra emerged with the garments Alethea had given her. The elderly couple walked out to the main road around the city. Greetings from acquaintances and smiles from just about everyone they encountered filled Cassandra's heart with joy; she was accepted. She was growing increasingly fond of this man and intrigued; she liked his long white hair and beard, his gentle demeanor, his wit, and charm. He was so important to her already that she opened up with the truth.

Cassandra spoke, "You must know something about me, Orpheus: I have no past. I can't remember a previous life, except for witchcraft. I can't remember being a child or having a family. You are full of interesting stories; I have no stories. I choose to forget what I do remember. I'm afraid I will be incredibly boring to you. Jason has helped me to accept that I have been forgiven; actually, we found much we have in common while traveling. He helped me understand a great many things. God delivered me from those wicked spirits, then I was disoriented and asked Jason who he was. He told me he was a kindred spirit. He really is, and I feel we are as well. I want you to know, however, that I understand if you want to keep your distance from me."

Orpheus stopped and turned to Cassandra. He put both hands upon her shoulders, then kissed her. He looked deeply into her eyes and spoke, "I have prayed a long time for you to come into my life, Cassandra. I thought my life with a woman was over. You have no idea how blessed you are to have no memory, for mine has almost destroyed me many times. You have received a precious gift from God. Bad memories are a curse; I have more than enough for both of us. Good memories are a blessing; we're making some right now. God has truly made you a new creation. I think the Lord has much more interest in your present, as well as your future, than your past. God's word says not to covet anything that belongs to your neighbor, but I can't help but envy you. I'm so glad you shared that with me. My descent was gradual. The evil overtook me through strong drink; I became a liar and a cheat, then lost my family and began to wander aimlessly. I was engulfed by incredible darkness until Jason acted upon me in the name of Jesus. God has had compassion and mercy upon me, as he has upon you. Years upon years of darkness. Now, I say the same; I understand if you want to keep your distance from me."

Cassandra jumped at Orpheus as she embraced him tightly and kissed him. Then they smiled at each other and walked. They reached a spot Orpheus had in mind, then sat beneath a tree while taking in an exceptional view of the Sea of Galilee and the City of Gadara.

Jason was amazed. The collection vat of the winepress, which had been carved out to exceed a huge harvest was almost filled to overflowing. Everyone wanted at least a brief go at crushing, and at times there were many in the crushing vat. There was more dancing in the vat than actual crushing, as the grape mash had yielded nearly all of its goodness. The mood to celebrate was as abundant as the new wine. The amber, yellowish tones of the early evening sun added to the relaxing atmosphere of the beautiful garden behind Jason and Alethea's house. Lydia had arrived, while leaving the evening meal at the caravansary in the hands of temporary help. She was the last of the guests to show up and Eustace was delighted. He had a very successful business and Lydia had been a big part of it. It was getting to the point, however, that they didn't like being apart. Eustace announced that soon they were to be married.

The celebration was full of joy, and it seemed romance was the theme. Lukas and Melina also announced a desire to be married, as they had worked out their differences. Now, it appeared that Orpheus and Cassandra had a new relationship. Love was in the air at the house of Jason and Alethea. The evening meal was ready, but there were so many that the main room in the house would have felt crowded. The meal was set up at the table inside, but everyone brought their food out to the garden to eat. It was a great time of fellowship; a perfect evening for Cassandra to see her new family at their best. Jason began the evening with a prayer, while giving enormous thanksgiving and praise unto God, and their Lord Jesus. Many others rose to offer praise to God. No one in attendance had any doubt that God was a very big part of the happy event.

Aegeus said, "Jason, Alethea, we have something for you."

Jason and Alethea arose and walked up to Aegeus as Calista joined him. It was obvious they had planned a special moment. Young Argus ran up to Alethea and grabbed her hand to help escort her to see his parents. He spoke proudly, "We have a surprise for you, Uncle Jason!" The couple both smiled broadly at their young friend, then approached Aegeus and Calista with anticipation. He unwrapped the package and handed each of them one of the two small objects. Jason looked at it, then smiled and chuckled a bit. Alethea examined hers closely, then smiled at Calista.

Aegeus smiled and spoke loudly, "We had two stamps made up for the clay seals of the wine jars; I have a friend who makes signets of high quality. They read, 'From the House of Jason and Alethea,' written in Greek, Hebrew, and Latin."

Jason was very excited and began laughing. "I carved one out of wood with a crude mark on it. Well, I'm going to burn that one in the fire. These are absolutely beautiful, Aegeus!" he exclaimed as he embraced Aegeus and Calista. He passed them around so everyone could appreciate the exquisite detail and beauty of the pieces. He couldn't resist giving Argus some well-solicited attention, as he roughed up his hair and launched a play assault upon the giggling young man.

The unanimous desire to celebrate reached a pinnacle, as everyone began dancing and laughing. Alethea brought out her aulos, and Melina produced a tambor, while following whatever Alethea played. Melina had also brought small cymbals, which were eagerly played by Lukas. As the evening wore on, however, the festivities quieted down to a mellow time of fellowship. Most had worked hard; Jason and Alethea had just returned and immediately went to work, while Eustace and the others had worked for two days at the labor-intensive harvest. Linus was exhausted as he had put forth more effort than anyone, but he had an unmistakable expression of satisfaction as he rested. Jason built a fire once twilight descended and everyone found a comfortable place. There came a time of conversing and the telling of stories.

Damon arose and spoke, "I just want to say, and I speak for my wife as well, that we are honored and delighted to have Jason and Alethea, and indeed all of you, as our neighbors. We feel like part of your family. It all started with Jason and his amazing experience with Jesus. We've seen how God impacts the lives of those who love him. We are much richer for knowing all of you good people. You've made a decrepit old abandoned house the most vibrant, beautiful place in the community. Thank you, all of you." He sat back down amid applause and smiles.

Jason stood up and spoke, "Thank you, Damon, and we consider you both members of this family. I want to thank everyone here, and I want to officially welcome Cassandra, our newest member." Everyone looked over at her while smiling and applauding. Jason continued, "She is yet another walking testimony of the goodness and mercy of God. This entire house is filled with that which was lost, but we've been touched by the Master's hand. The Lord Jesus has touched all of us, and God is blessing us. Praise, honor and Glory to God!" Jason looked around smiling as applause and cheering erupted.

Jason went on to tell the tale of Lander and Belen, as well as describing the healing. Orpheus and Lukas were touched that their street ministry had impacted the men, but they had not seen them. They expressed sorrow when they heard the men had been ridiculed by others, for they didn't know. Also, Jason told of the thief who he had an opportunity to minister to. Everyone was amazed at the fruitfulness of their journey.

Alethea moved close to her husband and said, "The man we went to visit wasn't there, but we met Nahal. We were blessed that the truth of Jesus had reached them. I feel that our trip wasn't the destination, but the trip itself."

Jason said, "I found grapes that were ready for harvest: a harvest of souls!" That brought laughter from everyone who was familiar with his impatience.

The time came for Theophanes to get up and tell a story. His appearance had changed, for he had let his hair grow a bit and now wore simple clothing. Eustace and Symeon got up as well. It had been planned to share the story at the right time.

429

Eustace spoke first, "I just want to verify what Theophanes is going to share, as myself and Symeon were present when we heard it. A trader, as well as a believer shared it with us; one who I know to be truthful and reliable."

Symeon said, "I not only wish to verify, but I want to add that my spirit bears witness to the truth. I also heard this from another source, which was a reliable one."

Theophanes began to tell the story as they had heard it....

This happened in the town of Bethany, which is about fifteen furlongs from Jerusalem. A man named Lazarus lived there with his two sisters, Mary and Martha. They are personal friends of Jesus. Lazarus became ill; his sisters sent word to Jesus, so he might come and heal him. Jesus delayed his arrival in Bethany, and the man died. Jesus arrived, but the family was grieving intensely. They even blamed Jesus and said that his friend would have lived if he had come sooner. The Lord Jesus grieved also, as he loved Lazarus. Jesus then said something that shocked them. He said he was glad he delayed his arrival for their sakes, so they might believe. He spoke to Martha and said that her brother would rise again. She thought he was referring to the resurrection at the last day. Jesus then spoke some amazing words:

"I am the resurrection, and the life: he that believes in me, though he were dead, yet shall he live: And whosoever lives and believes in me shall never die."

He asked Martha and the others if they believed his words. They expressed their faith the best they could but were grieving heavily, as was Jesus. He followed them to the tomb where Lazarus had been laid. Jesus then told them to remove the stone laid against the tomb, but he had been dead four days. The family protested, for they feared the smell of death would fill the air. Eventually, they complied, for Jesus spoke to them:

"Said I not unto you, that, if you would believe, you would see the glory of God?"

Jesus then raised his hands to heaven while thanking God for hearing his prayers, so that the people might believe. Then he extended his hand before the open tomb and spoke:

"Lazarus, come forth."

The family and many witnesses observed Lazarus come forth from the tomb, as he was bound in grave clothes, but very much alive! Jesus spoke to the shocked people:

"Loose him, and let him go."

"Many came to believe in Jesus as the Son of God that day. That is the story, as it was told to us. The Jewish Trader who brought the story to us was not an eyewitness but heard it himself from one who was. The three of us believe him. We pass the story on to this fellowship, so that we might encourage one another and believe."

The gathering became solemn, as everyone quietly discussed the impact of the story from Theophanes amongst themselves. The fleshly joy that had been prevalent earlier was replaced with spiritual joy.

The story had particular importance to Jason. He thought of the dream he had the night before last, as well as the discouragement and doubt the wicked spirit attempted to sell. Jesus is the Son of God; the power of God had raised a man from the dead! He looked over at his beloved wife and shared a meaningful glance....

Chapter Eleven

Riches More Precious Than Gold

The sun rose above a crisp, clear, Autumn morning in the City of Gadara. The amber warm light gradually illuminated the buildings and trees, while casting long shadows upon the cobblestone streets and stone features of the urban landscape. Beyond the city was a more rural, peaceful community. The southern outskirts, which consisted of mostly houses and small farms were beginning to show signs of activity. The day was starting out slowly at the house of Jason and Alethea. Jason quietly slipped back into bed in the early morning, while trying not to awaken his wife. He liked to begin his day praying and having private thoughts next to Alethea. Jason was focused on giving thanks to God for all he had this particular morning. He never lost sight of where he came from and loved Jesus with all his heart. He was mulling over questions he would ask him when Alethea awoke. They followed their routine, as Alethea got up but quickly returned to have a quiet conversation with Jason. The last few weeks had been filled with activity, so much so that the couple greatly appreciated this time alone. The harvest celebration had kicked off many joyous occasions; starting with the wedding of Eustace and Lydia, then Lukas and Melina, and a few days ago Orpheus and Cassandra were married.

The need for space had necessitated Linus to temporarily move to the house of Damon and Letha, as plans were underway for him to build his own house upon Jason and Alethea's property. Alethea was looking to the future with great anticipation, for she longed to see children added to their large family. Jason brought up his obsessive desire to taste the wine, for he and Lukas were both impatient as with the harvest. They were outnumbered, however, as everyone else was content to wait until Linus determined the process was complete. Jason lay in bed looking out of the window, while envisioning the massive array of huge jars behind the house. Alethea was amused.

"Any day now, Jason," she said playfully as she leaned over and kissed him on the cheek.

Jason responded, "That's what you said last week; how long does it take?"

Alethea giggled and said, "Sometimes you're like a little boy who's impatient to go out and play on a rainy day. Of course, it's one of the things I love about you."

"Linus is supposed to come over this morning to test it, and I'm going to be right there with him. I just want to see the blessings come from all of our hard work, that's all," Jason said as he got up and looked out at the jars. They had, indeed, put a lot of effort into the processing and straining of the wine. The jars had been covered with cloth and filled the garden with a variety of fragrances at first. In the last few weeks, however, the odors had diminished; Linus said it was normal, and that the wine needed to age a bit. Jason was worried and wondered, "What if something went wrong?"

Alethea laughed out loud this time and said, "Oh, come back to bed. It's too early for Linus to come. Remember what Jesus teaches, that all the worry in the world will not add one cubit to one's stature. Trust God no matter the circumstance, remember?"

Jason broke from his obsessive staring out of the window and looked toward his wife with a huge smile. He then slipped back into bed. "I love you big," he said.

"I love you, eh, big too," Alethea responded with a giggle as she reached out to embrace him.

Lukas awoke and decided to slip out and pray in the garden. He kissed his sleeping Melina, then quietly left the room and emerged into the clear, cool morning. He woke up with an incredible urge to thank God for his enormous blessings. Lukas was also thinking that today might be the day the wine is ready; he was surprised Jason wasn't out in the garden. He knew they had plans to meet with Linus, and perhaps the waiting would soon be over. Lukas gave thanksgiving to God and prayed for the wine to surpass their expectations. He looked up, and his solitude was pleasantly broken as he was joined by his elder friend.

"Good morning, Lukas!" Orpheus proclaimed as he entered the garden and sat beside him. "Out here keeping the wine company, I see. Linus said about four weeks from when the odors ceased, so I think today might be the day," he said with a smile.

"I hope it is. I'm alright with waiting, but I'm afraid Jason is beside himself wanting to taste it," Lukas commented as he looked toward the jars.

Orpheus began laughing, so much that he had to calm himself down to keep from waking the entire house. "Jason's not the one out here looming over the jars, Lukas. We're all anxious to taste the wine; be patient, for I think it's almost ready," Orpheus said while still chuckling.

Orpheus seemed to be constantly full of joy since his wedding. Lukas was very happy himself. They spent some time in the garden, as they praised God and conversed about their experiences as newly married men. They were both pleased they had more in common than ever before. The time passed quickly, then the smell of food attained the attention of both men. They entered through the back of the house and found Melina preparing a meal of eggs and vegetables in olive oil.

"You can see, Orpheus, that I chose well. Her experience at the caravansary is blessing me already; maybe too much!" Lukas said as he grabbed his stomach while chuckling. "I think I'm getting larger," he added.

Melina responded, "Yes, you chose well my husband, and as your devoted wife I must advise my husband: you eat like a horse!"

Lukas looked at Orpheus with an expression of mock bewilderment on his face, then smiled and began laughing as he walked over to kiss Melina.

Orpheus let loose with a booming laugh. This time it did wake the entire house, as well as the aroma of the morning meal. First Cassandra came out and greeted everyone, then walked over to Orpheus and embraced him. Jason and Alethea came down the stairway next, as they waved and smiled.

"What's so funny, Orpheus?" Jason asked as he walked over to the side window and looked out toward Damon and Letha's house.

"Just watching these two at it again," Orpheus responded. "Melina was commenting about Lukas's eating habits. I'm sorry, Lukas, but I agree with her," he said while chuckling.

"So, I like to eat!" Lukas shot back at Orpheus. "You eat like a bird," he said which caused Orpheus to open his mouth in a joking shocked expression.

"Alright, let us enjoy our meal without the judgment," Alethea stated as she assisted Melina to take the meal to the table. "I just hope there's enough here for everyone with Lukas around," she added as she looked at Lukas sideways with a grin.

Everyone laughed, for it was true. Lukas ate more than anyone else despite his slight build. He just shrugged his shoulders and reclined at the table, then grabbed a piece of bread. The three couples had already developed a strong family relationship and enjoyed spending time together; especially meals. Jason spoke a prayer of thanks, then the morning conversation revolved around the wine and the remainder of the orchard fruit. The family had harvested the figs, dates, and olives they needed, as well as about half of the apples and pomegranates. There was still plenty on the trees.

"I would like to put out a sign and invite gleaners into the orchard; we have enough store with some to spare, even for Lukas here," Jason said as he solicited a remark from Lukas.

Lukas just looked up briefly from his bowl as everyone chuckled, then went back to eating. Melina smiled at him and rubbed his back a little.

This meant the harvest for the family was officially over. God had blessed the family with abundance. Linus and Lukas had taken some of the fruit to the marketplace, but everyone agreed to let gleaners take the remainder.

"Do you think today is the day, Jason?" Orpheus asked as he hoped to get an amusing reaction; he wasn't disappointed.

"I've given up hoping, Orpheus. All I hear is soon, soon," Jason said as he displayed his impatience. "Why does it take so long to make wine?" he asked as he looked around the table. He wanted to taste the wine.

"It takes what it takes, Jason," Cassandra responded with her gentle voice. "I know how you feel, though. I want it to be ready too," she said as she smiled at Jason.

"See, Jason? We all want the wine to be ready. There's no reason to be angry at it," Alethea said as she touched Jason's face while pushing his hair aside a bit. He looked at her and smiled just as a quick knock came upon the front door.

Linus entered and looked around at everyone. "Greetings," he said while smiling.

"Linus! Are you hungry? Better get some before Lukas finishes it," Jason remarked as he looked over at Lukas with a grin.

"Alright, alright!" Lukas responded. "There's plenty, Linus," he said while gesturing to the cooking pot in the back of the house.

Linus smiled and got himself a bowl, then joined the others at the table. He spoke very calmly while tearing off a piece of bread, "I think today is the day, for I've already taken a look. I say we go out and taste the wine as soon as we finish the meal." Jason and Lukas got very excited; Linus enjoyed the reaction while amused that it was so predictable.

It was a beautiful clear morning in the garden, as the morning had warmed quite a bit since earlier. Jason spoke a simple prayer, and asked God to bless the wine. Everyone gathered around Linus and Jason as they removed one of the cloth covers from the nearest huge jar. Melina handed them a serving pitcher and ladle she had brought from the house. Jason held the pitcher as Linus drew out a ladle and sniffed it. He smiled and poured it into the pitcher, then another until the pitcher was full. Orpheus and Cassandra had slipped away, then returned with seven goblets and distributed them. It had been decided that Linus would be the first to taste. He poured a bit into his goblet, then sniffed it again. He took a small sip and noticed everyone was watching him intently. His eyebrows went up as he swished the wine in his mouth, then a huge smile as he swallowed. Jason immediately poured his own sample. Linus spoke only one word:

"Success!" he said. Linus actually teared up as he took another sip.

Jason sniffed it as Linus had, then took a sip. The first thing was an extraordinary refreshing sweep of the mouth, then an explosion of flavor. Not too sweet or tart, nor was it bitter, but it was a perfect balance. The only thing Jason had to compare it to was the high-quality wine he had experienced in his dream. The wicked spirit had touted it as the best the world had to offer. In Jason's determination it paled in comparison to this. He grabbed the pitcher to fill Alethea's goblet, and she had a similar response. It seemed to raise the eyebrows with a smile was the automatic reaction.

"We've really got something here, Jason!" Orpheus commented with a serious expression as he took another sip. "I've never tasted anything like this!" he added.

"If heaven has a taste, this is it!" Lukas said with a big smile.

"I can't believe that I helped make this!" was Cassandra's reaction. "Those mashed grapes turned into this? Incredible!" she said.

"I think Eustace will taste this and offer you a business proposition," Melina commented. "I think you can name your price with this!" she said with a huge grin.

Alethea immediately began to pray as she thanked God for this extraordinary blessing. "Father, in the name of Jesus, we thank you and praise you! We pray this wine to be a blessing, and all who taste it would come to know you. We thank you for bringing this family together who produced it, and we thank you for creating it. Thank you, Lord!" she prayed with emotion as her voice was cracking a little.

"I'm going to get Damon and Letha," Linus said as he departed the Garden.

Jason understood Linus's enthusiasm, for he wanted everyone to taste the wine. He exclaimed, "I want Eustace to taste this, so I say we all make a trip to the caravansary!" Jason was beyond excited. "I'll get the asses ready; Orpheus, Lukas, fill four of those shipping jars and seal them. Let's go bless Eustace, Lydia, and whoever's there!" Jason said enthusiastically, then disappeared around the side of the house.

Orpheus and the ladies weren't as excited and chose for the moment to sip wine and enjoy the beautiful morning in the garden. Lukas brought out four teardrop shaped shipping jars with slender necks and handles, then went back to his wine. Linus returned with Damon and Letha. They tasted the wine, as they had brought their own goblets. Their reaction was similar to the rest.

"This wine tastes as though God himself has touched it!" Damon proclaimed as he took another sip. Letha just smiled as she nodded in agreement with her husband.

Jason returned from the house fully dressed and ready to travel. Seeing everyone relaxing with their goblets gave him pause as he sat next to Alethea and re-acquired his goblet. "Yeah, let's enjoy the morning; I got pretty excited, but there's no hurry," he said as he raised his goblet.

Eustace and Lydia sat at a table going over the list after the morning meal. They had made an inventory of supplies, and today was the day to go shopping. There was a large caravan there staying until tomorrow, so some things had to be acquired before the evening meal; among them: wine.

"I know I let the stores of wine go low, but I was expecting Jason to bring a sample by now," Eustace said as he looked over the list, then at Lydia. "I want to give him my business, if it's good enough. We're going to have to purchase some today, though I want to hold back on a big order," he said.

Lydia responded, "I agree, Eustace. Linus said it would be any day the last time I spoke with him. He seems to know what he's doing, but we must keep the quality up for our reputation. I love them as much as you do, but we can only use so much if the wine is of inferior quality." Lydia was speaking realistically, for there was a lot of good quality wine and most people knew the difference.

"I have confidence that the wine from Jason and Alethea is going to be something special; wait and see," Eustace said as he leaned over and gave Lydia a little peck on the cheek. She smiled and placed her hand upon his.

The owners of the caravansary didn't have to wait long, as a knock came upon the front doors. Lydia got up to answer just as the door opened. She was surprised to see Lukas standing there beside Melina with a jar in his arms. Lydia welcomed them and smiled while stepping aside to allow them entry. They were followed by Jason, Alethea, and Linus, and both men were carrying jars. Then Orpheus and Cassandra entered, as Orpheus carried the fourth jar. Eustace got up and shouted a warm greeting to his extended family. The jars were set side by side upon the table next to the list that Eustace and Lydia had been mulling over.

"We'll be needing goblets for everyone!" Jason exclaimed with excitement. Eustace, Lydia, and Melina left the room through the back-left door, then quickly returned with nine goblets and a serving pitcher.

They were asking Melina about the wine, but she would only say, "See for yourself."

Lukas quickly broke the fresh clay seal on one of the jars. He and Jason filled the pitcher from the heavy shipping jar, then leaned it against the others. Jason began to fill the goblets and said, "I hope this is good enough, Eustace. All I can say is we did the best we could." Jason was doing the best he could to keep a straight face. He had asked everyone to play along, as he attempted to portray a slight disappointment. Orpheus and Cassandra were smiling broadly, which threatened Jason's unusual humor and playful deception.

Eustace and Lydia took their goblets and tasted together as they faced each other. The three couples and Linus watched intently as they awaited their reactions. Chuckling and giggling slowly erupted as Eustace and Lydia simultaneously raised their eyebrows. Eustace grew a huge smile after swallowing and looked at his goblet, then at Jason and Linus. Lydia's mouth dropped open as she looked at her goblet, then took another sip.

Amid chuckling Jason asked, "Well, do you think the wine is good enough for the caravansary, Eustace?"

"I think this wine is good enough for the courts of kings, Jason!" Eustace proclaimed as he took another sip. He then walked over and put his hands upon Jason and Linus's shoulders as he stood between them with a smile. Looking at both he said, "Jason, you'll be one of the richest men in Gadara if you can do this again next season!"

Jason immediately thought about the upcoming trip in the spring. He would have to think about that as time went by. There was a huge amount of wine to deal with for now. "Linus, could we reproduce the same wine again?" he asked Linus as Eustace looked on.

"Ahh, I think so. I used good judgment, and we prayed a lot," Linus said as he looked away for a moment in deep thought. "Honestly, I think God had more to do with this than we did. Do I think we could do it again? Yes, if it is the will of God, then we certainly could do it again!" he said while smiling. He enjoyed the encouraged expressions coming from Jason and Eustace.

"Eustace, we have a lot of wine right now; I want you to be the distributor. No reason you shouldn't have an opportunity to make some money from the wine as well. You know everyone, and you know about trade and commerce in Emmatha and Gadara better than anyone," Jason said to a delighted Eustace. "What do you say?" he asked.

Eustace embraced Jason and Linus eagerly. "I think we're in business, my friends!" he said. The big man gave each member of the family a firm clasp of the hands. "We're not just going to turn a profit, this wine will turn into gold, you watch!" he exclaimed with great excitement.

Jason spoke, "These four jars are a gift, Eustace. You need some to share with others. We'll move most of it to your storehouse as soon as we can manage it. I trust you with my life, Eustace; I can certainly trust you with my wine."

Eustace looked at Jason seriously for a moment, then broke into a huge smile and said, "You'll never know how special you've become to me, Jason. Don't worry about moving the wine; I'll get my men on it right away. We'll use your oxcart together with mine, that way we can transport it in no time." Jason reached out his hand and Eustace clasped it.

The deal was settled. Jason was confident of Eustace's business abilities. He knew he would get the best possible price for the wine, and it would be a big boost to his caravansary. Truly a superior business deal between good friends, as everyone was happy. A celebration ensued as the afternoon visit led up to the evening meal. Jason thought about sending word to Aegeus but decided to visit his house next. A couple more shipping jars needed to be filled for him anyway. He wanted to bless him almost as much as Eustace, while surprising him with the exceptional wine. Jason also wanted to speak with him about the trip in the spring, for they had discussed traveling together. For now, the visit to the caravansary was, as always, a chance to relive some fond memories. It wasn't long before Alethea asked Jason to walk out to the courtyard with her. She wanted to sit by the well with her husband, where they first got to know each other. They both recounted their whirlwind romance, which was punctuated by drama and tragedy. So much had happened in a little more than a year, and it all seemed like a long time ago.

"I remember how I felt when you asked me to marry you. It was an answer to prayer," Alethea said as she stared off while recalling the memory. "It surprised me so much...I never dreamed you would ask me so soon," she added.

"Yeah, I didn't know any better," Jason said while looking off with a blank stare. He held a straight face for a moment, then his playful grin crept up as Alethea looked over at him. She punched him in the shoulder when he glanced at her. "Ouch!" Jason exclaimed as he rubbed his shoulder. "That hurt! Keep in mind how strong you are!" he jokingly complained.

Alethea giggled and said, "Sorry Jason, I guess I didn't know any better." She then smiled as though very pleased with herself.

"Seriously, Alethea, I would have waited longer, but at the time I had very little understanding of social graces. I was a demoniac, after all," Jason responded with a sly grin.

"Thank God for that!" Alethea shot back with a playful grin of her own. She continued, "Not that you were a demoniac, but that you were brutally honest about what you wanted; it got us together, and without the courtship games. I love the way it worked out, and I love you, eh, big."

Jason chuckled, then leaned over and kissed Alethea as he responded, "I love you big too. I hope we get a chance to see Nahal again, but I hope her Greek doesn't improve; I found her attempt to speak it adorable. Perhaps we could make another trip to visit Ammayu before we go to seek Jesus in the spring."

"Perhaps," Alethea said with reservation. She paused, then said, "I'm not wanting to travel in bad weather. Perhaps we should go afterward."

Jason's demeanor got serious as he looked at his wife. He said, "We're likely to have some big decisions to make, Alethea. I haven't shared this with anyone, now I'm sharing it with you. We stand to have an incredible life here if that's what we choose." He then asked, "What if I told you that we may have to lay it all down to follow Jesus?"

Alethea immediately understood the gravity of what Jason was saying. She had also contemplated the same thing deep within her heart. She surprised Jason with a prepared answer and proclaimed, "I go where my husband goes; I would quickly lay it all down and follow Jesus to the ends of the earth. I belong to you, Jason, and we both belong to Jesus. I'll never forget, while you were in that Roman prison: I saw him. Just that somehow gave me all the strength I needed to carry on. Jesus is a hope that transcends the things of this world. We will travel with many when we go. I don't want to be one you have to worry about; I'm yours, and I always will be." She sealed her statement by touching Jason's face, then looked into his eyes and passionately kissed him. They were interrupted by Orpheus as he cleared his throat.

Orpheus and Cassandra had approached but stopped at a distance. They were both smiling. "Do you mind if we join you, or do you want me to ask Eustace to make a room ready?" Orpheus asked as he and his new wife chuckled. Jason and Alethea smiled back and waved them over.

"I was just saying how wonderful it would be if I had a youth to remember," Cassandra mused as she sat down on the stonework around the well. "Of course, this one makes me feel young," she commented as she glanced over at Orpheus with a playful grin. She was learning from Jason.

"You know, there are two ways to take that, dear Cassandra," Orpheus replied. He sat next to Cassandra as she began laughing. "I can still keep up with the best of them!" he stated

"Of course, you can!" Cassandra responded while putting her arms around Orpheus and kissing him even more passionately than Jason and Alethea. Then she proclaimed, "I have no complaints!"

Jason and Alethea were both charmed and amused by the elder couple. They all sat by the well conversing until Jason saw Symeon and Theophanes approach. They often came to the caravansary for the evening meal. Jason jumped up and greeted them, as he was anxious for a chance to have more friends taste his wine.

Linus had disappeared with Eustace into his residence. Lukas was in the back room, as he eagerly helped Melina and Lydia prepare the meal. The work was almost done, so Lukas and Melina decided to take a little walk. They didn't go far and settled down at a spot overlooking the Sea of Galilee.

"Have you thought about it much?" Lukas asked his new wife as she sat next to him beneath an olive tree.

"Thought about what?" Melina asked as she was bit puzzled by his vague question.

"The trip coming up. I'm sorry, for I think about it all the time. Just wondering what you think about it," Lukas responded a bit awkwardly. He was still working on communication skills.

Melina smiled and said, "It's alright, my husband. I know what you were trying to say. To be honest I'm a little anxious about it; I've never traveled much. My desire to follow Jesus is strong, however, and I have full confidence in you."

"I have a feeling it could change all of our lives, Melina. Does that frighten you?" Lukas asked as he looked over at his wife.

"Yes, I suspect it will. I'm not afraid, as long as I'm with you, Lukas," she said as she leaned over and kissed him on the cheek. "My place is with you. I never would have married you if I didn't feel that way. We will seek Jesus together," she said while looking into his eyes.

"I feel much better, for I sensed you were afraid," Lukas said as he looked into Melina's eyes as well. "We have a good life here, but there may be something better if we had to give it up. I remember sitting in this very spot, while trying to get up the courage to talk to you. It changed my life when I finally did. Jesus is the Son of God. I feel that seeking him could only lead to something wonderful," Lukas said as he trailed off while gazing at the sea.

"I want you to know how blessed I am to be your wife, and to know you, Lukas. I know we have spats occasionally, but I know your heart; I know you would never betray me. I'm glad you brought this up, and I think we're both more confident about it. Seeking the Son of God can only lead to something wonderful, like you said. It's the unknown, but we'll face it together. Besides, you might not be so obsessed with food if we're traveling," Melina said with a grin.

Lukas grinned as well and said, "I hope the evening meal will be served soon." They both laughed.

The couple just sat and looked out at the beautiful view for a while. They realized that the evening meal was approaching, so they got up and headed back to the caravansary.

"So, it's settled then?" Eustace asked Linus as they reclined at the table while sipping wine and conversing.

Linus looked troubled as Eustace awaited a response. They had stepped into Eustace's residence to have a private conversation, but he felt guilty as if hiding the truth from his friends. Linus took another sip of wine, then said, "We're both members of this family. I know Jason will be disappointed if we don't go on this trip to seek Jesus, for I've spoken at length with him on the subject; he wants all of us to go. I've never considered not going on the trip throughout the process; however, I never thought we would come up with wine like this. Jason's thoughts are that we might be gone for some time. You're absolutely right, of course, from a business standpoint. The best way we can serve Jason is to look after his interests and his home."

"I know how you feel, Linus," Eustace said while doing the best he could to encourage him. He continued, "I want to go, and I know you do too. I've thought about it over and over, but there's no way I can leave for an indefinite period of time. I'll lose my standing in the community and possibly my business. And you're the one who's skill produced this wine, so you know that it's as good as gold; it could make Jason rich beyond his wildest dreams! I've had this conversation with you, and there's no one who could repeat the process but you; there are too many variables. If that wine cannot be repeated, what we'll have is a flash in the pan. Yes, we stand to make a lot of money, but it will come to an end." Eustace looked off while deep in thought, then continued, "I want to grow old with Jason, as well as all of you. I'm thinking of his future; it's not like we're conspiring against him."

"No, of course not," Linus quickly replied. "I could never repay what Jason has done for me. I can start by looking after his home, and start the next batch of wine," he said. Linus was feeling better about the arrangement. "I want to announce our plans tonight. I don't want to keep anything from any of my family," he added.

Eustace responded, "Understood." He nodded and stood up, then offered Linus a hand as the two men walked out into the community room. Neither man, however, looked very happy. They found all their friends seated at the regular table, as Symeon and Theophanes were paying particular attention to their wine.

"Hey, you two don't look very happy, this is supposed to be a celebration!" Jason exclaimed with a big smile as the two men approached and joined them.

"We have something to say, Jason my friend. We were discussing the upcoming trip. Eustace and I aren't going," Linus said with a remorseful expression as he looked Jason in the eye.

"We need to stay behind, Jason. I need to look after our business. Linus is going forth with the continuing wine production, as well as looking after your estate. We're not happy about it, but feel it's necessary," Eustace said with regret in his voice.

Everyone went silent. Jason looked at both men, then cast his eyes down at the table while deep in thought. Alethea put her hand upon his shoulder. He smiled after an uncomfortable moment.

Jason responded, "I saw it coming. I want you both to know I'm disappointed, but I understand. I know you're acting out of love, and I appreciate it. I guess it's selfish of me to expect everyone to make such sacrifices." Jason then looked at Symeon as he somehow knew what was coming next.

"You're very perceptive my friend," Symeon said with a compassionate voice. "I'm sure you've noticed that the scripture readings have become very popular. Many have come to depend upon it. Theophanes and I have discussed it; we've been the ones to put it all together and we just can't walk away from that," he said with a voice that suggested faithfulness and commitment.

Theophanes spoke, "We truly wish we were going with you, Jason. The decision we've made is based on love also, for those who believe, and for those who are yet to believe."

Jason looked at the two scholars and smiled. He said, "Again, I'm not that surprised, for I agree with you. My mission here is to share the truth of Jesus throughout the city, and beyond. You two are helping to fulfill that mission even in my absence. I'm not forgetting how much I saw the scripture reading grow while I was in prison. I expect to see it grow even more by the time we return." Jason looked around the table. "Anyone else?" he asked.

Lukas spoke up quickly, "We're with you, Jason. Melina and I have already discussed it; just as long as we bring plenty of food!" he said as he looked over at Melina with a smirk. Everyone laughed.

"Yes, he needs me to be there," Melina added as she looked at Lukas with raised eyebrows and a grin.

Orpheus spoke while still chuckling, "Of course we're with you. I had a taste of life without you around, so I don't want to go there again; Cassandra's kind of fond of you too."

Cassandra said, "Yeah, Orpheus and I kind of look at all of you as our children. You need us along to keep you out of trouble!" Cassandra's contribution not only raised more laughter but lightened the mood of everyone.

The friends of Jason should have known better than to suspect he would react with anger or sadness. He had become used to battling demons, and those were the realms they operated in. He expressed sorrow and the fact he would miss them greatly. He brought up that Aegeus and his family left to follow Jesus and his disciples, then returned after a few months. Now, they were all going to join together and return to follow him once again. Jason kept reiterating that they would return, God willing; he just didn't know exactly when.

There was nothing like walking along while leading the asses and listening to Alethea play her aulos. Jason looked up and wondered if they should have waited for another day, for the sky looked increasingly threatening. He glanced back with a smile as he checked on his precious cargo: one animal held his beloved wife; the other carrying two shipping jars of the phenomenal wine. They were traveling to the house of Aegeus and Calista un-announced, so the others stayed home to avoid filling their friend's house with guests unexpectedly. Besides, both other couples had expressed a desire to spend time alone. Orpheus and Cassandra had plans to go to the marketplace in Emmatha and then spend the night at the caravansary; Lukas and Melina were going to spend time at home.

Jason just wanted to see the look upon Aegeus's face when he tasted the wine. His anticipation grew as they approached the impressive stone house. The arched entry and wall around the estate framed the Greek architecture of the porch; complete with four columns with capitols and carved cornices around the roof. Alethea loved the house, as Calista's taste and style were similar to her own. The two women went on for hours talking about it the last time they visited; they had become close friends. Jason knocked at the double door entry. They had no servants, although Calista could afford them; she preferred her sons to hold responsibilities of the household. They were not around this time, so Calista opened the door and smiled.

"Jason! Alethea! What a pleasant surprise!" She exclaimed as she stepped out and embraced both of them. She said, "Dimitri and Argus are out fishing, and I don't expect them back until tomorrow. They'll be disappointed they missed you." She looked up, then commented, "I hope they stay dry, since it looks like rain. They did take a tent; they took a camel with all sorts of things. Come in!" she said while gesturing in through the door.

"I have a couple of heavy things to bring in. Is Aegeus around?" Jason asked just as Aegeus appeared in the entry room.

He smiled and embraced Jason and Alethea, then looked out at the animals that were tied up by the wall. Jason gestured to the animals as Alethea went in with Calista. "Ahh, wine jars!" Aegeus said while still smiling. "Did it turn out any good?" he asked.

"I'll let you be the judge, Aegeus. We did the best we could; I think it's acceptable," Jason said. He fought to keep a straight face, once again. The two men untied the heavy shipping jars and carried them inside.

The men passed through the entry room and into the main room, as Calista and Alethea had already reclined at the table. Calista and her first husband spared no expense in decorating their home. There were large murals upon two walls: lush landscapes with animals and Greek figures were depicted, which gave the large room great depth. The beautiful mosaic tile floors also had interesting patterns and images. Wooden side tables bore several small sculpted art pieces. Alethea's favorite thing in their home was the exquisite, finely crafted pillows around the table that were made from colorful, intricate silk fabrics from the far east. The walls had lamps which had been lit, as well as fire urns around the room which Aegeus would usually light when entertaining guests. There were four empty goblets waiting. Alethea played along with Jason, as she had told Calista they could try the wine, but they may want to bring out some of their own as well. The stage was set. Jason opened one of the jars with his dagger after displaying the stamped seal with enthusiasm.

"At least the Jars appear to be top quality," Jason said jokingly. Aegeus helped him fill a pitcher from the jar, then rested it against the other. He filled the goblets and gestured to them. "Hope you're not too disappointed," Jason said with a blank expression. Alethea had to cover her mouth, which threatened to blow the surprise.

"What's wrong, dear?" Calista asked Alethea as she looked at her with mild concern.

"Nothing," Alethea said quickly while desperately trying to keep from breaking out with a severe case of the giggles. "Just taste the wine, please," she insisted.

Calista looked at Alethea with a curious expression which made things worse. Jason was proud of his wife and her earnest attempt, for she was barely smiling now. Aegeus and Calista picked up their goblets and looked at each other while smiling. Aegeus tasted first. Jason and Alethea couldn't hold out any longer; they both started laughing as Aegeus's eyes went wide, then raised his eyebrows and swallowed with a huge smile. Calista saw his reaction, then quickly tasted with a similar reaction. They were all laughing now.

"Well, what do you think? Do you think people will pay for this?" Jason asked.

"I think you can name your price for this, Jason!" Aegeus exclaimed. "How did you do it?" he asked.

"Well, Linus made the decisions, but we all worked and loved on it, as well as prayed over it. The finishing touch was God blessing it," Jason said, then put his hand upon Aegeus's shoulder. "Both of you helped, for you had your feet in it!" he exclaimed while chuckling. The laughter refreshed as the two couples reclined around the table.

"The two jars we brought are a gift. Eustace is going to handle the distribution, if you want more after that," Jason remarked as he looked at the teardrop-shaped shipping jars.

Calista responded, "Thank you, Jason! That's quite a bit of wine for us, and it will probably last until we leave for our trip."

Aegeus thought for a moment and said, "You've got a lot of wine; I think you and Eustace are going to make a lot of money on this. Do you think you can reproduce it? You'll be rich if you can."

Jason began revealing the plan and said, "Linus thinks he can. He's not going with us, nor is Eustace. They both want to continue the wine business in our absence, so Linus is going to stay in our house. I'm a bit sorrowful about them not going, but it makes sense. Eustace would stand to lose a great deal; much more than me."

Alethea said, "Symeon and Theophanes are staying around as well so they can keep the scripture reading going at the caravansary. Again, we agree as many are coming. Theophanes put it best, 'for those who believe and those who are yet to believe.' I think his transformation was almost as dramatic as Jason's." She looked at Jason, then smiled and said, "Almost." Jason laughed.

Aegeus was thinking and asked, "So that's six of you and the four of us. Do you think there will be any others, Jason?"

"Somehow, I think we should consider the possibility of two or three others to join us. That's ten of us that are committed, for now," Jason said as he pondered the matter. "There's always the possibility for someone to join us on the way," he added.

Aegeus stated, "I think we have enough camels to outfit our journey nicely. As you know, that's what I've been doing; acquiring and selling camels is not as hard on these old bones as herding. You, my friend, sort of putting an end to my herding vocation," he said as he looked at Jason with a serious expression. Everyone laughed, as did Aegeus after a moment. Aegeus couldn't help it, for there was a little trauma associated with the ordeal of the swine.

Jason responded, "I feel the same way about wicked spirits as you, Aegeus. I lived with them for twenty-five years. Tragic what happened to your swine, but I wouldn't be here if not for Jesus doing what he did; I'd still be living in that tomb. I have a lot of things I wish to discuss with him. Perhaps you could ask him why he chose to cast the demons into the swine." Jason spoke with only slight seriousness. The wives watched the exchange with grins as both men had a similar sense of humor.

"Actually, I was going to, Jason," Aegeus responded. "However, it's amazing how one's priorities change when one finds himself in his presence," he said, obviously speaking from experience as he stared into space and paused a bit. "It was a horrendous experience, but it no longer has any importance to me, for it's in the past," he declared. Old Aegeus thought for a moment, then said, "All I can say is, if he casts out demons near us...we should, perhaps, hide the camels."

Everyone erupted in roaring laughter as Jason patted Aegeus on the shoulder. The two couples enjoyed a meal and good fellowship. Jason and Alethea decided to spend the night, as the rain began to descend upon Gadara.

Plans were made for the immediate future, as everyone settled into a routine. The house of Jason and Alethea was full of joy and peace. One night, however, that peace was shattered. Cassandra began to toss and turn in her sleep late one night. She had been sleeping very well, but not dreaming very much. Orpheus had told her it was probably because of her lack of memory. She suddenly found herself in a very vivid dream....

Cassandra was standing on the side of a street in Gerasa. She knew of her new life, and her love for Orpheus as well as the others; however, it was as if she was transported back to where she had been before the deliverance. She looked down at herself and was wearing the same clothing she had worn that day. She was very confused, for she didn't understand that it was a dream. It seemed to be late at night and it was very dark, only faint light from the moon and stars made a very dim visibility possible. There was no movement anywhere as the streets seemed deserted. She began to hear noises: chattering voices from her past. She had avoided such memories, but now found herself in the midst of them. Cassandra was very afraid.

She began to see shadowy specters in her side vision, which avoided direct visual contact. They moved around buildings, behind columns, and even on the rooftops. Then she saw shadowy figures down the street coming toward her: witches she once associated with. Cassandra was panicked and attempted to run, only to find she couldn't move. She tried to scream, but nothing came from her mouth. She thought to pray and spoke the words in her mind. The figures continued to approach. Suddenly, there was a flaming fire right in front of her. A figure in a long outer garment stood before her, but on the other side of the flames. She could feel the presence of the witches standing behind her. Cassandra was frozen with fear as she was completely vulnerable and unable to speak; she was feeling a temptation to fall into the flames. The figure before her had no face, only darkness. She kept thinking prayers, while invoking the name of Jesus in her mind as best she could. Her spirit was in wild turmoil. Suddenly, Cassandra heard the voice of Orpheus loud and clear: "THE LORD REBUKE YOU! BE GONE IN THE NAME OF JESUS!" She was able to look to her right, and Orpheus was standing beside her. He stepped in front of her and stood between her and the flames, then reached out and put his hands upon her shoulders....

"Cassandra, wake up!" Orpheus called out to his wife. She had been thrashing about in the bed, and the covers had been thrown in the floor. She opened her eyes to see Orpheus just as she had seen him in the dream with his hands upon her shoulders.

"Orpheus!" she cried and embraced her husband while sobbing. They held each other for a long moment until a knock came upon their chamber door. Orpheus opened the door to find everyone there.

"Can we come in?" Jason asked in a very compassionate voice. Orpheus stepped aside and allowed entry to the family who had come to help.

Cassandra wiped the tears and sweat from her face, then smiled the best she could. She said, "I don't know what happened. I guess I had one of those nightmares I've heard you all speak of."

Orpheus and Jason sat on either side of her. Orpheus spoke, "That was like one Jason had soon after his deliverance. I was hoping you would be spared, for you told me you didn't dream very much."

Jason spoke, "Yeah, my first one was frightening." He asked, "You couldn't move or speak, could you?" He looked at Cassandra with a reassuring smile.

"How did you know that Jason? Is that what happened to you?" she asked with amazement.

Jason spoke, "Remember when I told you I would be able to help? That time has come. I hoped you would be spared this, like Orpheus. All of us get harassed from time to time." He paused for a moment while looking at her with compassion. "I wasn't there, but it was along the lines of getting you to go back to your old ways, was it not?" he asked.

"It didn't get that far, but I felt a very strong temptation to fall into a fire that burned before me. I know now that it represented the evil I was delivered from," Cassandra said while trying to keep from crying again.

"And the terror would be just beginning," Orpheus said as he was aware of the ways of familiar spirits. "They seek to destroy you," he added with an expression of great concern.

Lukas said, "Orpheus is right, Cassandra. Don't ever give in; just speak the name of Jesus and it all stops. Eventually, so do most of the dreams."

"Did you pray for protection before you went to sleep?" Jason asked.

Suddenly, Cassandra felt very foolish. She confessed, "I was very tired. I prayed for all of you, that's how I start. I fell asleep before I could. I remember you telling me how it keeps things like this from happening."

"Always remember: your adversary roams about and seeks who he may devour. They were awaiting an opportunity," Orpheus said.

Jason spoke, "We'll pray for you right now, but you must always pray for spiritual protection before you sleep. We will always be here for you in times of trouble. If it happens again speak the name of Jesus, as Lukas said. The forces of darkness, or the empty garment, or whatever it is cannot withstand the authority of that name. It is enough, even though you can barely speak." He then smiled and embraced Cassandra.

Jason, Lukas, and Orpheus then left the chamber to pray over the house, which gave Alethea and Melina an opportunity to minister to Cassandra with great compassion. They were well aware of the trauma associated with such things. The men returned, and the entire family laid hands upon Cassandra. They prayed for greater strength against the harassing spirits for her, as well as restoration. Dawn was showing its faint light, but everyone was exhausted. The family returned to bed, and Cassandra fell back to sleep in the arms of Orpheus, for he had rescued her. She slept very peacefully with a smile upon her face.

And so, time went by. The weather during the winter months was mild, but there was an unusual amount of rain as well as a couple of snowfalls. Linus was excited and believed that God was watering the earth in preparation for the next grape harvest. Jason and Lukas decided to go on a camping and fishing trip despite the weather. There was a special friendship there; a comradery that only two former demoniacs could develop. Old Orpheus was part of it too, but as of late his devotion to Cassandra, as well as his increasing age made him quite fond of hearth and home. He would go with Jason and Lukas occasionally in fair weather.

A dry period had set in upon the region, so the two loaded the asses with extra clothing and a tent, as well as other things. Jason had a plan that was a little out of the ordinary. Lukas smiled as the two men made a brief side trip through the eastern outskirts of Gadara. They arrived at the house of Aegeus and Calista for a short visit, and to invite Dimitri and Argus. The young men were excited, and quickly loaded their camel for the trip. They headed northeast and passed through the Yarmuk River Valley to one of their well-established camps. This one featured a nearby cave in case the weather turned foul. It would provide shelter in an extreme circumstance, but neither Jason nor Lukas was fond of caves; they represented bad memories. They both preferred the light of day and the light of the moon and stars at night. Dimitri and Argus couldn't wait to explore it and disappeared not long after arriving. Jason and Lukas set up their camp as it appeared that the night would be clear and chilly. Lots of firewood was gathered, then the two men relaxed a bit.

Dimitri started a small tinder fire and lit the torch he had brought, then the two young men entered the cave. Dimitri gave Argus his staff to carry, since he had the torch. The entrance was rather small and obscure but opened up large once inside. They went further and further, as the darkness seemed to envelop them despite the flaming torch. Both were quiet as the entrance slowly became more distant, which was unusual for young Argus. They proceeded on, as Dimitri lead with the torch. Suddenly, Argus grabbed his arm.

"Let us get out of here, Dimitri," Argus said with a very serious voice, which was also unusual for him. "It's not good that we're in here." He added.

Dimitri wanted to continue and said, "I thought you were excited about exploring. It goes a lot farther."

A mysterious noise came from deep within the cave. Dimitri passed the torch to illuminate Argus's face, for he could tell the young man was frightened. "Yeah, there could be a beast in here," Dimitri said which brought even more fear upon the face of Argus. He grinned and said, "Come on, we'll head back to the camp."

Argus stated, "Uncle Jason and Lukas might be worried about us, or I would go farther." Dimitri chuckled.

"Fishing with a net seems lazy to me," Lukas commented as he reclined against a tree while folding his hands behind his head. "I may just go in and fish the simple way tomorrow," he said.

Jason responded, "There's no denying the efficiency of nets. We came to get away, but also because our fish stores run low; I want to take home lots of fish."

"You've got a point," Lukas relinquished. "It's more fun to grab 'em though," he said as he looked over at Jason and smiled.

Jason smiled and nodded as he set about pulling out his fire kit and started a fire. They had set out late, and the evening was quickly approaching. Lukas began sorting through their food bag and set out their usual efficiency meal of dried fish and bread. He also pulled out a bag of dates and a premixed wineskin.

Dimitri and Argus came walking up from the path to the cave, as Argus ran the rest of the way. Dimitri looked up and smiled at his brother.

Argus spoke, "See, we weren't gone that long. You're right, Uncle Jason, that cave is kind of scary. I wouldn't want to sleep in there!"

"You would if it started to snow," Dimitri said as he snuck up and tugged on Argus's hair. It was enough for him to look back at his brother with an annoyed expression.

Lukas said, "I agree with Argus. I'd rather deal with the snow than that eerie cave, or better yet I would just go home." He then nodded with a serious expression.

Dimitri and Argus started laughing. Jason smiled and thought to himself that young Argus was actually demonstrating an awareness of the spiritual realms. He too had sensed a prevailing darkness within that cave. He had prayed against it and nothing ever manifested, but the feeling endured. It was as he and Lukas had determined before, that the cave was best left alone, except in an extreme case. Jason smiled at his young friend and recalled the prayer he had spoken over him.

Jason said, "Sorry we didn't have time to catch some fish before dark, so I hope you brought enough for your evening meal. We have plenty, if not."

"Yeah, we brought plenty to eat," Dimitri said. "Argus and I have been going out often, after listening to you two talk about it. Thank you for inviting us this time," he added.

Jason said, "I remember that you were out when we brought our wine to your house. You two have discovered why we go out. It's good to get away, but don't go too far. Lukas and I can both tell you about the attraction of solitude. Make sure you go with God, if you're going to be alone for a time."

Lukas joined in, "I've had to struggle with familiar spirits, for they tried to entice me to return to the wilderness early on. I've cast them out since then through the authority of Jesus. Don't get too far away from those who love and support you. When darkness attacks it does so when you're vulnerable."

Dimitri and Argus looked at each other with wide eyes. Jason and Lukas started laughing as they realized they had gone a little too far into the realms of recovered demoniacs. Lukas got up and patted both young men upon the shoulders while still snickering.

"Let us eat!" Lukas announced which quickly shifted the focus of the evening.

The men ate their meal with a lot of good fellowship around the warm fire. They reclined by the fire as darkness began to descend and enjoyed the colorful light of the setting sun. The stars began to pop out and there was a three-quarter moon, which promised a clear, chilly but dry night.

"What are the stars, Uncle Jason?" Argus asked as he gazed up at the night sky with a look of wonder.

"They're all part of God's creation, young Argus," Jason replied.

"I think they're angels watching over us," was Dimitri's opinion.

"They're beautiful, whatever they are," Lukas commented as he looked up.

Jason looked over at Dimitri with a curious expression, then smiled. He looked up at the beautiful night sky and reflected as he said, "Different time of the year, but this is exactly the way the sky looked the first night of my deliverance." He looked back at Lukas, then gazed into the fire. "I've come a long way since then, so have you," he said.

Lukas gazed into the fire also, then spoke, "Do you think people will remember us when we're gone, Jason? We've given our testimony to many people far and wide. We've taught and demonstrated how the power of Jesus can transform lives; how he has powerful authority over the devils that infiltrate this world, and how speaking his name, in faith, gives power to the weak." Lukas pondered what he had said, then asked, "Your mission has been a great success, but will our story survive time after we're gone, or will we be forgotten?" He then went silent as the firelight flickered in his eyes.

Jason looked at his friend. He was amazed by, in some ways, how strikingly similar they were. He had deeply contemplated the same thing. He spoke, "Yeah, I understand what you're saying. The scriptures survive, only by the efforts of many scribes and scholars preserving them. False myths and legends survive because Nephilim freaks and their descendants ended up being portrayed as gods and heroes carved in stone. Will we be remembered? Of course, I think Jesus will be remembered despite the Pharisee's desire to erase his presence from history; I'm confident the stories of Jesus will survive. He cannot die. Perhaps we'll be mentioned in those stories."

"He cannot die? How do you know this?" Lukas asked with great curiosity. Argus and Dimitri were also listening intently.

Jason responded, "I can only speak of what I know to be true. Jesus is the Son of God. He is the manifestation of God as a man. Men die, but the Son of God is immortal. He appears as flesh, but he is much more than any man. The only logical conclusion is that he cannot die, for it would be in opposition to his nature."

Lukas and the others sat staring at Jason. Then Lukas said, "My spirit is bearing witness to what you're saying, for I was in his presence briefly; he even embraced me. You're right, of course. I never really thought about it but you're right. He cannot die. I believe it as much as you do."

Argus and Dimitri looked at each other, then Dimitri said, "My spirit bears witness as well; I believe it too."

Argus just stared into the fire with a serious look of contemplation upon his face.

Jason smiled and got up, then walked over to the large bag he had brought and returned to the fireside with a long bundle. Everyone looked at it with curiosity. "I have something for you, young Argus," he said as he untied the cords holding it together.

"What is it?" Argus asked with increasing curiosity.

"Neleus the Centurion brought me this the first time he visited. I want you to have it," Jason said as he slowly unwrapped the bundle to reveal a sword. A Roman sword. "This is the sword that Legion took from Actaeon many years ago. It is the sword I carried as I began my new life. I cut Lukas's hair with it after his deliverance," he said as he looked at Lukas, and everyone chuckled. "Also, it is the sword that God used to delivered me from the Romans and death. Neleus cleaned and sharpened it, as well as fitted it into a new Roman scabbard. You're younger than me; perhaps, you'll be around longer than me. I want our story to survive. I feel strongly about you having this. When you are old, and I am gone; share the story often. Show them the sword if they don't believe. It's not proof of anything but kept in the right hands it will outlast all of us. Pass it down to your children; tell them the stories, then tell them to tell their children the stories. I fear that devils will attempt to destroy such, and true faith will diminish," Jason spoke emotionally. He then handed the sword to Argus.

Argus reached out and carefully received Jason's gift with great honor. "It will be as you say, Uncle Jason. I will do everything I can to see that the story of Jason: *The Gadarene Demoniac,* and his family will endure many generations," he said.

Dimitri spoke, "I'm going to keep it for you, for now, until you're a little older. We've already discussed it with mother. This is a big responsibility, Argus." He looked at Jason and nodded, then smiled at his younger brother.

Lukas stood up before Argus and extended his hand while grinning at the boy. Young Argus clasped his hand, then Jason and Dimitri joined in. It was the symbol of the fellowship backlit by the roaring fire. The special event passed, and they all relaxed. Argus sat close to his Uncle Jason and shared a blanket. Everyone then listened intently as Jason told, in detail, of his experience in the Great Amphitheater of Gadara....

Orpheus and Cassandra had started a routine to have a meal at a quiet eating establishment once a week. The place wasn't elaborately decorated, and there was no dancing or music, but the food was excellent. They grew fond of the place because they could have private conversations with no interruptions. The food would be brought, and payment would be made without much interaction. They loved eating at the caravansary, but it was more like having a meal with family; lots of interaction and conversation. The newlywed elder couple liked to share their innermost feelings and deep faith. The two settled in and began to eat, as they counted their blessings, and their concerns:

"We're going to be leaving the region soon, Cassandra, excited?" Orpheus asked as he took a bite and looked into her eyes which were flickering by the light of the lamp upon their table. "We've been talking about it a lot, but you're silent when it comes up; are you afraid?" he asked.

"No, not afraid. Unsure about the unknown, perhaps. I've had similar feelings when Jason and Alethea brought me here from Gerasa. That turned out pretty wonderful," Cassandra said as she smiled, then leaned over and kissed Orpheus upon the cheek. "I don't want to lose what I have," she added.

"Well, you'd have a hard time losing me," Orpheus said, and further responded by kissing her upon the forehead. "I don't think you'll have to worry about losing your new family either. Everyone loves you, Cassandra; especially this one," he said as he chuckled a bit.

Cassandra smiled and went back to eating for a few moments. Then she looked at Orpheus and said, "There aren't too many who can relate to how I feel. I was hoping by now that at least a few memories would return. That's why all of this is so important to me, Orpheus, for it's all I know. I avoid the only memories I have. I surely wasn't born a witch...or was I?" She trailed off staring into space.

"Had any bad dreams lately?" Orpheus asked his wife with compassion.

"Well, yes and no," Cassandra said with a slight grin. "They don't last very long. I mentioned it to Jason not long ago and he just smiled," she added.

Orpheus smiled as well and said, "I think Lukas, Jason, and I can relate to you more than you know. I've said before that you should count it a blessing. Of course, I can't relate to not having memories...I wish I could."

"Would it help to talk about your family that you lost?" Cassandra asked as she suspected she was treading upon sensitive ground, but Orpheus smiled.

"I have peace with it now, sweet Cassandra...you helped me with that," he said as he reached over and took her by the hand. "I had a wife, a son, and a daughter. The children were grown by the time I fell apart. I traveled a lot, so when I was home everything I did mattered a lot. They came in through my mouth, as I became quite fond of strong drink. Demons have a way of cloaking their work, since one becomes unaware of how disastrous behavior affects others. I was never physically abusive to my family, what I did was worse; I began to lie to cover things up, lie to manipulate people, finally, to lie for the sake of lying. I had many good friends, and I lost them. My wife and children were going to leave, so I left. I got a proclamation of divorcement from my wife and my children disowned me."

Orpheus became emotional but refrained from weeping. He continued, "I traveled, as dark entities began to take over my thoughts. I became a depository of foul spirits that roam this earth before I knew it. Jason helped me understand their nature, for they are disembodied spirits of them that lived in the old world, before the flood. They were the Nephilim: abominations that should have never been. Such hybrid creatures were the result of fallen angels breeding with human women. They are the unforgiven; cursed by God and wander the earth as evil spirits. Jesus has come to set mankind free of such. Through Jesus, we have the power and authority to stand in the face of hell itself. He is the only way. His virtue, through Jason, healed me as of a dreaded disease. Still, I am but a remnant of what I once was. I was a very successful trader; I've seen a good portion of this world. They destroyed it all, and I cooperated. Many are all too eager to cooperate, for they offer that which is pleasing to the flesh. That's my story…sorry you married me?"

Cassandra responded with emotion, "No, no, not at all, my husband. Who am I to judge you, but a former witch. The only memories I have is of witchcraft. I know how they can manipulate, like you; I just have a different point of reference. You had a family, a life, and a childhood before the darkness fell; all I have is the last few months, but I understand what you've told me, nonetheless. I realize that my life has become exceptionally blessed. It's all much more than I think either of us deserves. Naturally, I'm apprehensive about losing anything. You must understand that I'm longing to meet Jesus. He is the source of the blessing we share; he is the source of life itself." She trailed off for a moment, then said, "This conversation has helped me get my priorities in order. No, I'm not afraid, nor doubtful with you by my side." She again paused for a moment, then asked a question that troubled her, "Does the guilt and shame ever diminish, Orpheus?"

Orpheus responded, "In my case, no, not completely. It's pain that you learn to live with through the grace of God. Repentance is the weapon we use to combat it. You must always remember that you have been forgiven. We hold on to the hope that someday God will erase all of the pain. God has brought you to me, as well as friends that understand. You need never suffer your pain alone."

"Thank you, Orpheus, for you've given me a great deal of comfort. I love you," Cassandra said as she looked into her husband's eyes.

Orpheus responded softly, "I love you too, dear Cassandra. I want you to know that whatever is left of my life...you make me complete." The elderly couple smiled at each other while holding hands at their favorite little spot. The server had taken note of the love exhibited by the elderly pair as she smiled in the distance but was unnoticed by Orpheus and Cassandra. She pondered asking them about the secret of their happiness before they left....

"Well, we've done this before," Aegeus said as he stood leaning upon his staff beside Calista. They took a long look at their house as they had before, so long that Dimitri and Argus became a bit impatient. The cool but clear sunny morning promised the fair weather of early spring. The two young men were ready to start the journey, as they had eaten a good morning meal and prepared early. They had so many camels that they were going to walk to the house of Jason and Alethea, for it was easier to manage so many on foot. Calista's sister and her husband had moved in to keep up the estate in their absence. They waved from the large porch as the family slowly made their way through the arched gateway and out onto the cobblestone street. Aegeus and Calista led the train of camels, as Dimitri and Argus helped manage them from the sides.

"It's a bit hard to leave, but it feels good to get back to traveling," Aegeus said as he looked over at Calista. "It was good to be home for a while, but I've been longing to return to following Jesus," he confessed.

"Yes, it was good to be here for Jason," Calista responded. "We saw the hand of God move that day. I know Jason has been desiring to see Jesus more than anyone, since his release. I'd love to hear the conversations they may have when we catch up with him," she said and quickly glanced over at Argus as he had snuck up beside her. He smiled at his mother, after she thwarted his attempt to startle her.

"We're going to meet with Uncle Jason! I'm going to ride beside him!" Argus boasted as he drifted back again.

"Watch what you're doing!" Dimitri scolded Argus as one of the camels on his side wandered a bit too far into the street. "Narrow street! Keep them in line!" he shouted.

"Oh, there's no one coming; most people are still in bed," Argus replied to fend off his brother's instruction. He quickly brought the camel in line, however.

"Bet you can't wait to see your Uncle Jason. It's been a while," Dimitri said as he looked over and smiled at his younger brother between the camels.

"Yeah! I'm going to ride beside him! We're going to see Jesus!" Argus exclaimed and threw his hands up to the sky. It put a huge smile upon Dimitri's face as he shook his head. He bowed to the joy and silliness of Argus and thought to himself how much he loved his younger brother.

They proceeded west through the early morning quiet streets of Gadara. The post-dawn glow was reflected upon the buildings and cobblestone streets, which was a very pleasant beginning to their journey. Aegeus and his family drew near to Jason and Alethea's property, as they could see that many were out of the house. They arrived at the arched entry gate, and Argus immediately ran through followed by Calista. Aegeus and Dimitri remained to secure the camels.

"Uncle Jason!" Argus shouted as he ran up to Jason and embraced him. "Can I ride beside you?" he asked boldly as he was called down by his mother. Calista just smiled though, while engaged in joyfully greeting their extended family.

"Of course you can, Argus!" Jason responded to his young friend. "You have much more experience with camels than I; perhaps you can help me manage mine," Jason said as he engaged in a little rough play with the young man. It was true that Jason didn't have a lot of experience with camels, nor did Lukas. They were a little intimidated by the large beasts. Orpheus had spent his life around camels and had convinced Cassandra how sturdy and practical they were. Alethea and Melina were of an open mind as they had a little experience. Jason and Lukas exchanged glances of concern as Aegeus and Dimitri entered the property walking with their staffs.

"Good morning all!" Aegeus shouted as he and Dimitri went about greeting and embracing. "There's fourteen camels, and they're all here," he stated as he scanned the load of bags, packs, and other items set out to be loaded. "Is this all you have?" Aegeus asked as he looked at Jason and Lukas.

"Yeah, I believe so. It seems like a lot to me, but we all followed your advice on what to bring since you have the experience," Jason said as they began to pick up a load.

Aegeus responded, "No, not at all, Jason. We chose well the number of camels. Four are to carry the cargo, but we only have one loaded and a few things upon another. You and the others seem to be traveling even lighter than us."

"I added in some of my own experience, Aegeus. Alethea and I are accustomed to traveling with asses. Even if we're to be gone for a very long period we've done well with what we bring. More clothing, but the same equipment," Jason said.

Lukas made his contribution. "You have to remember, Aegeus, I used to travel with nothing but the clothes upon my back; Jason with even less," he said with a serious expression which achieved a good belly laugh from Aegeus and Dimitri. Jason laughed too, although a bit embarrassed. Lukas grinned, while pleased with himself having delivered a friendly jab to his best friend. Also, a good laugh from anyone close enough to hear.

"What's this about traveling light, Jason?" Orpheus asked as he and Cassandra came walking around the side of the house from the back garden. "You've told me of those days, but I don't think your hair is long enough now," he said while holding a straight face perfectly. Cassandra, however, started giggling.

"I really don't want to see Jason travel quite that light anymore, Lukas," Alethea said as her, Calista, and Melina strolled up to the men. This time everyone started laughing, as well as Jason, although he was blushing. Alethea walked up and kissed Jason upon the cheek. "Good morning, my husband," she said with a grin.

"Good morning everyone," Jason announced. "I was just thinking that we probably need an extra camel; not only to carry enough food for Lukas, but all the jokes everyone seems to be overburdened with this morning," he stated. He looked over at Aegeus after looking around at the family. "What do you think, Aegeus?" he asked.

"I don't think I have that many camels, Jason," Aegeus said with a straight face, then started chuckling as everyone laughed once again.

Everyone sat for a brief morning meal before setting off, as they joked that they were to leave a significant mess for Linus to clean up. He responded by saying he would try to clean up before they returned; he couldn't keep a straight face, but achieved a good laugh, nonetheless. There was pure joy and excitement among the family as they prepared to embark upon their long-awaited journey.

471

The camels were loaded, and it came time to look at the property one last time. Jason and Alethea embraced while looking at the garden around the house they had all contributed to. Orpheus and Cassandra also embraced and looked around before mounting their camels. Aegeus and Calista mounted their animals as well, but the rest were going to walk to the caravansary along with Linus. He was going to share in the big meal and departure celebration, then return to take up residence. Damon and Letha were coming along as well but had yet to arrive. Linus was going to collect them, then the elderly couple appeared as they walked slowly through the meadow separating the two properties.

Damon asked if they could ride, for he was a bit stiff and sore this morning. Dimitri and Argus assisted them in mounting two of the camels. Jason walked up to Damon, before his camel arose, and laid a hand upon him praying for his pain to be eased in the name of Jesus. Damon then reported feeling better and smiled as the caravan began to move away to the east. They passed the large bathhouse, then headed north up the main road to Emmatha and the caravansary. It was to be a bittersweet day; painful goodbyes and the prospect of leaving for an indefinite period. It was already very dry for that time of year, as everyone who was walking stayed way behind due to the dust stirred up by the camels. Everyone wanted to keep their clothing clean for the day's events. The morning wore on, as the familiar sight of the cobblestone turnout and the large structure of the caravansary came into view. Jason, Lukas, Alethea, Melina, and Linus were walking together.

"It's a strange feeling," Jason commented as he gazed at the establishment of his good friend Eustace. "We lived there and constantly observed caravans come and go. We spoke with them and traded stories. Now, we're one of those caravans," he mused.

"Do you suppose we could travel a different way; perhaps through Gerasa to stop at the caravansary of Ammayu?" Alethea asked as she recalled fond memories of their trip many months ago.

Lukas quickly interjected, "We're following a plan to reach Jerusalem by a certain time. Aegeus recommended we travel west, then follow the Jordan River south."

"It's the same direction, Lukas," Melina added in favor of Alethea's suggestion. "I think it merits discussion. Alethea told me all about the exotic caravansary in Gerasa, and I'd like to see it myself," she said. Melina persuaded Lukas very effectively, as she put her hand on his shoulder and kissed him upon the cheek. He responded with a huge smile.

Jason said, "We'll discuss it this evening with Aegeus and Calista, for they've been doing this for some time. It's important that we reach Jerusalem at a particular time. We know that Jesus will, most likely, travel to Jerusalem for the Jewish celebration of what they call *Passover*. If we miss him it may take some time to find him; I've heard he and his disciples move around quite a bit."

They entered the expansive courtyard of the caravansary. Jason saw that it wasn't very busy, only one stall was in use. They were quickly approached by two men who were Eustace's stable help; they were obviously expected. Aegeus dismounted his animal as he patted one of the men on the back, then offered a hand for Calista to dismount her camel. Aegeus was confident in the camels receiving expert care during the overnight stay. Dimitri and Argus quickly assisted with Damon and Letha dismounting, as they coaxed the camels to kneel. Orpheus helped Cassandra, for he was an old hand at it. Everyone was assembled, then they approached the double door entry.

Both doors flung open. Eustace and Lydia were smiling and extending their arms to embrace their family. It was an immediate warm, loving event in and of itself. Symeon and Theophanes were also inside and became involved in friendly greetings and gestures. There were two new housemaids that were smiling and friendly, while wearing cheerful, colorful garments and white head coverings. Lydia had retired to join Eustace in managing the business. Melina had, of course, quit work for the journey. Eustace assured her that she could return at a later date; perhaps, as he insinuated, as a coordinator of sorts, as Lydia had been. Fresh bread, as well as wine and other dishes to nibble on were brought out. Everyone reclined around the two front tables and engaged in usual small talk. Eustace called everyone to prayer.

Everyone bowed their heads. Eustace stood up and began to pray, "Heavenly Father, we here in Emmatha and Gadara who have come to know Jason and his family will miss them terribly. I ask that you comfort our hearts. I pray for Jason, Alethea, Lukas, Melina, Orpheus, Cassandra, Aegeus, Calista, Dimitri, and last but not least, Argus. I pray you would protect them and that your will would be done upon their journey. I pray there would be a fulfillment of the mission, and that someday soon they would return safely to us. I pray you would preserve the love that has been established here within these very walls. I pray that all of us be made stronger by this separation, so we can better serve you. Father, you have already blessed us; I pray for it to continue for many years to come. I pray that you would bless this time of fellowship, as well as the food you have provided, and the wine which you have already blessed. Thank you, Lord."

Jason stood up and prayed, "Father, I too pray for protection for Eustace, Lydia, Symeon, Theophanes, Linus, Damon, and Letha, as well as all the others we leave behind as we go to seek Jesus. I pray you would prosper our business. I pray your word continues to be spoken in this house and that it goes forth throughout the city and the region. Father, there is so much I'm grateful for, but I want to thank you for my deliverance from evil. I thank you for the wonderful family and friends you have brought together. I too pray the love that you have established continues for many years and even beyond this life. I thank you for this time of fellowship and love. I pray that you would also mend our hearts when we depart. For your glory, in the name of Jesus."

Jason once again reclined at the table, and everyone was smiling. A pleasant but solemn moment passed, for the seriousness of the matters at hand was apparent. This gave way to quiet conversations, as deeply felt emotions were shared.

Symeon expressed a desire to read a text he had received from a scribe in the Galilee. It was a parable from Jesus himself, and was copied while in his presence. He said, "I've been in correspondence with the scribe for some time. He translated it into Greek, then sent it to me. I feel that, given the occasion, what better reading than the actual teaching of our Lord Jesus, the Son of God." Symeon then pulled a scroll out of his tunic.

Everyone responded with great enthusiasm. Some shifted positions for a good view of the scholar as he took a sip of wine and began to read:

"A certain man had two sons: And the younger of them said to his father, Father, give me the portion of goods that fall to me. And he divided unto them his living. And not many days after the younger son gathered all together, and took his journey into a far country, and there wasted his substance with riotous living. And when he had spent all, there arose a mighty famine in that land; and he began to be in want. And he went and joined himself to a citizen of that country, and he sent him into his fields to feed swine. And he would long have filled his belly with the husks that the swine did eat: and no man gave unto him. And when he came to himself, he said, how many hired servants of my fathers have bread enough and to spare, and I perish with hunger! I will arise and go to my father, and will say unto him, Father, I have sinned against heaven, and before you, and am no more worthy to be called your son: make me as one of your hired servants. And he arose, and came to his father. But when he was yet a great way off, his father saw him, and had compassion, and ran, and fell on his neck, and kissed him. And the son said unto him, Father, I have sinned

against heaven, and in your sight, and am no more worthy to be called your son. But the father said to his servants, Bring forth the best robe, and put it on him; and put a ring on his hand, and shoes on his feet: And bring out the fatted calf, and kill it; and let us eat, and be merry: For this my son was dead, and is alive again; he was lost, and is found. And they began to be merry. Now his elder son was in the field: and as he came and drew near to the house, he heard music and dancing. And he called out one of the servants, and asked what these things meant. And he said unto him, your brother is come, and your father has killed the fatted calf, because he has received him safe and sound. And he was angry, and would not go in: therefore came his father out, and intreated him. And he answering said to his father, Lo, these many years do I serve you, neither transgressed I at any time your commandment: and yet you never gave me a kid, that I might make merry with my friends: But as soon as this your son was come, which has devoured his living with harlots, you have killed for him the fatted calf. And he said unto him, Son, you are ever with me, and all I have is yours. It was appropriate that we should make merry, and be glad: for this your brother was dead, and is alive again; he was lost, and is found."

Symeon simply smiled and rolled up the scroll, then returned to his spot at the table and reclined. Everyone sat in silence for a moment while contemplating the parable. All were very emotional; the story had a special meaning to the former demoniacs. Cassandra began openly weeping while Orpheus comforted her with tears in his eyes as well. Jason and Lukas stared into space as they teared up. Alethea rubbed Jason's back and smiled at him. Melina pushed Lukas's hair out of his face and kissed him upon the cheek. Even Theophanes let loose weeping. Aegeus and his family were moved, as Argus ran up and hugged his mother. It was a beautiful moment, and one that revealed to all why the journey to find and follow Jesus was so important.

Eustace approached Jason after the emotion had passed and asked him to come into his residence. Jason smiled and arose from the table, then followed Eustace through the side door.

"I have something here for you, Jason," Eustace said as he opened a cabinet and took out a wooden box. He opened it, then lifted out a leather pouch and set it upon the table with a thud sound. "This is your profits so far of the wine sales. I didn't know if you wanted to take it on your journey or not," he said.

Jason opened the heavy pouch and beheld a massive amount of gold coins. He then looked up at a smiling Eustace who was pleased with what he had done for his friend. Jason smiled and said, "I want you to keep it here, Eustace. We have plenty of money for the journey. I could take this, but it could be attractive to thieves and robbers if they knew we had so much gold. I'll trust you with it, for I know you'll keep it safe, if that's alright with you. I'm very impressed, my friend. Linus may have needs in our absence; give him of this if he requires it. I would appreciate it if you keep a watchful eye upon Damon and Letha as well, for they're getting very old and have become cherished among this family."

"It is such an honor to know you, Jason my friend. You are the most unselfish, trustworthy, honorable man I have ever known. I wish I was going with you. Lydia is going to miss all of you as well. Promise me you will come back to us," Eustace said as he struggled to hold back the emotions.

"You are my special friend, Eustace, for it all began with you. You saw something in me and welcomed me into your life. I may have failed if not for you...I'll never forget that. Yes, we will return if the Lord wills it, that I can promise you," Jason said with his voice cracking a bit.

The two men arose from the table and embraced, then Eustace put the gold back into its place. They entered back into the community room and returned to their places at the table. The mood of the group had lightened quite a bit, as there seemed to be a determination to subdue sorrowful emotions. Jason leaned over and told Alethea of the gold they had acquired. She smiled. Jason went on to tell her that now they were to seek riches more precious than gold; riches that transcend the things of this world. She smiled even wider, then leaned over and kissed him.

Aegeus moved over to have a conversation with Jason. Lukas, Alethea, and Melina joined in. Of course, young Argus was a part of it as well; he was constantly by Jason's side. They were to discuss the journey and the plan as it was so far.

"I understand there is a desire to pass through Gerasa, as opposed to following the Jordan River south. Is that correct?" Aegeus asked as he had already been briefed by Jason on the change in plans.

"I want to go to Gerasa!" Argus proclaimed, for he knew that Alethea and Melina wanted to pass that way.

Aegeus smiled at his son and said, "I know you do, but we must decide the correct way. You've been taught that you don't always get what you want, Argus."

Alethea spoke, "We wanted to visit Ammayu at the caravansary in Gerasa. We missed him when Jason and I went there a few months ago. It's not critical that we go that way, but it is the same direction. Melina here would like to see it."

"Yes, I've heard a lot about the establishment of Ammayu. I would like to go that way, if it were possible," Melina said.

"I wouldn't mind seeing Ammayu myself, Aegeus. I don't want it to interfere with our reason for this journey, however," Jason said as he looked over at Argus with a grin.

"I haven't seen Gerasa for a long time," Orpheus said as he contributed to the opinions. "How do you feel about it, Cassandra?" he asked with concern, for it was where she came from.

"The few memories I have were within the city. The caravansary is well outside the city walls. I think I would enjoy it; I'm confident enough that I'm not afraid to confront something, if necessary," she stated. Cassandra felt good about what she had said. She looked at Orpheus and he smiled, then kissed her upon the cheek.

Aegeus just smiled and said, "I think it's settled. We leave for Gerasa in the morning. The only difference is, as Jason and Alethea can verify, that it will require a certain amount of desert travel. Following the Jordan would be easier in many ways, but popular opinion wins. I'm all for it, if everyone is willing to accept the added difficulty."

Eustace spoke, "Send my regards to Ammayu. Tell him that I, as well as my new wife will visit him later in the summer. Tell him we'll go fishing."

"I have only one thing to say," Lukas said as he leaned closer to the table and getting everyone's attention as he had not yet spoken. "When is the meal coming?" he asked with a serious expression.

For the first time since they had arrived everyone broke out in laughter. It lightened the mood to the point that a few patted Lukas on the back. He just looked around at everyone with a curious expression upon his face, which made it even more humorous. It was like old times, as everyone felt more comfortable. Lukas smiled as he suspected he had done a good thing. Melina just shook her head and kissed him. The evening was thoroughly enjoyed by all.

The morning came, and it was time to depart. Everyone assembled in the courtyard after the morning meal. Symeon and Theophanes had said their goodbyes the night before and returned home. Damon and Letha had spent the night, as they opted for another camel ride back to Gadara. Every member of the family had a difficult time saying goodbye to Eustace and Lydia. There was the reassurance that they would return someday, hopefully soon. They left the caravansary of Eustace and Lydia as many caravans do; rested, well fed, and cared for. The difference was the tears. The short trip to the east side of Gadara brought the group near the large bathhouse, where they said their final goodbyes to Linus, Damon, and Letha. They had decided to walk the rest of the way home, so Aegeus's caravan could proceed south. They paused a bit and watched their three loved ones disappear between the buildings along the cobblestone street. The warm glow of the morning sun and the cool, crisp breeze promised a good day of travel. Everyone mounted their camels this time. They headed south but went a bit slow at first as everyone got the feel of the animals. Jason coaxed his camel into line with the help of a friend. They were off to Gerasa led by Aegeus and Calista. They were followed by Jason as young Argus rode by his side....

Chapter Twelve

A Caravan of Hope

The morning coolness had passed into a warm, clear, spring afternoon in the Decapolis. The caravan passed through the increasingly rocky terrain with patches of wooded groves. Most had adapted well to the camels, except one.

"He knows you're afraid of him, Lukas, relax," Dimitri said as he rode beside his friend. He had continuously kept his camel in line following the disaster of Lukas dismounting, then trying to mount his animal without leaning back as it rose. Lukas had fallen onto the neck of the camel, then onto the ground which startled the beast. He had lost a bit of confidence about camel travel.

"How is it that this beast knows what I'm thinking? That's ridiculous!" Lukas responded as he continued to struggle to keep his camel in line. He also refused to cross his legs in front, as Dimitri had suggested. The movements of the camel seemed awkward to him, and he was afraid of falling off.

"They do, Lukas," Dimitri said as he desperately tried to convince his friend. "Take my word for it. Your attitude while riding the camel is everything. Just allow your body to sway with him and you won't fall off," he advised.

"What do you mean? I've already fallen off! I don't see how everyone's riding these crazy beasts. Maybe I should walk," Lukas said as he was continuing to lose confidence.

"You'll slow the rest of us down if you walk," Dimitri reasoned with Lukas. He thought for a moment. "Remember when you told me about walking in the spirit? Well, Lukas, ride in the spirit! Pray for God to give you peace. Think of it as sharing the truth with your camel," Dimitri said. He had a special way of communicating with Lukas, that's why they were such good friends.

Lukas understood, as he immediately brought his favorite saying into the situation: trust God no matter the circumstance. He began to put together all the instruction from Dimitri. He then prayed, and asked God to give him peace. Lukas opened his eyes expecting to be off the road again, but he was right in line with no help from Dimitri. Suddenly, he found himself moving with the camel, and not against it. He crossed his legs in front of the saddle and it felt comfortable. Somehow, he now felt as though he was born to ride camels! A huge smile came upon him, as he cocked his head from side to side in an expression of happiness. His camel looked back at him with a sideways glance.

"Now you're getting it!" Dimitri shouted at Lukas with joy. Joy for his friend, and joy that he didn't have to manage two beasts any longer. "Just remember all I've told you, Lukas. You look like you've been doing this for years!" he shouted with a smile.

The time came to stop for a meal soon after that. There was a sudden chatter of sounds, as everyone brought their camels to a stop. Aegeus had taught everyone to signal to the camels with a sound, so they would lay down. It translated into something like *deek deek*. Some came up with their own sounds, whatever worked. Jason requested they stop in the same place he and Alethea had stopped once on their journey. He knew how Alethea liked to reminisce; it was a good halfway point as well. Lukas dismounted his camel like a seasoned rider. He was so happy about his accomplishment that he wanted to look the camel in the eye and thank him. Dimitri didn't have time to warn him, as his camel spit a huge amount of white, foamy saliva right in Lukas's face and hair.

"I was going to warn you not to do that," Dimitri said while desperately attempting to keep from laughing. Lukas slowly looked over at him, then reached up and cleared his eyes with his fingers. He didn't look very happy anymore. Melina and Alethea walked up.

"If that's a new look for you, Lukas, I don't approve," Melina joked which spawned a huge round of laughter from all three.

Jason walked up while chuckling and offered his waterskin to Lukas, then handed him a piece of cloth he was carrying. Lukas poured water over his head as he looked around at the increasing group of friends around him.

"Let him see you coming, but don't get close to his face, Lukas; approaching from an angle is best," Aegeus instructed the best he could amid laughing.

Finally, Lukas began to laugh as well. "We stopped for a meal, so let's get to it!" he said. It appeared his stomach overcame his embarrassment. He was still rubbing the cloth on his head saying, "Oh well, it gave me an excuse to wash my hair."

Jason, Aegeus, and Dimitri removed a few items from one of the pack camels, then carried them over to the level grassy spot surrounded with mostly oak trees. Everyone contributed to spreading two large covers upon the ground and preparing a quick meal. The jabs at Lukas continued, from Jason:

"You should do very well now, Lukas. No one else knows their camel so intimately," Jason said with a straight face, which inspired chuckles from some. "It was just the camel's way of saying it loves you," he added.

This time it was Lukas's turn. "What was that disturbance I saw this morning when you approached your camel in Gadara, Jason?" Lukas inquired as he took a bite of bread.

"Oh, uh, you saw that?" Jason asked. He wasn't grinning anymore. He didn't think anyone had noticed. Lukas had watched him closely, however, to get encouragement. "Uh, the camel bit me," Jason admitted.

"Where did the camel bite you, Jason?" Lukas questioned his friend after quickly swallowing. Everyone looked at Jason.

"Uh, I'd rather not say. It's enough that we all know more about camels now," Jason said while trying to dismiss the issue.

"Well, when I saw it, I was terrified; now that I look back on it, I think it was hilarious!" Lukas said as he unsuccessfully attempted a straight face.

Everyone started laughing all over again. It was a refreshing meal and good fellowship, but the time came to pack up and continue to Gerasa. Jason walked up to Alethea to have a moment before they mounted the camels.

"Anything you need me to take a look at Jason?" Alethea asked with a sly grin.

"No, let us just say I'll be reminded of it while riding for the next couple of days. I really miss your pipe music, my wife," Jason said while trying to change the subject as he gave her a kiss. "I understand why you're not playing, but I miss it," he said.

"Perhaps by the time we reach Gerasa I'll be confident enough to ride hands-free, if someone leads my camel; I'm not quite there yet," Alethea said as she looked into Jason's eyes. "Camels are faster than asses, but not as easy to ride. I did play after the meal," she said with a smile.

"Yes, it was beautiful, but I would rather you not play at all if it's in any way dangerous. Play for us when we've stopped, or this evening if you like," Jason said as he smiled at his wife, then put his hand upon her shoulder.

"I love how much you appreciate my music, Jason. I wish I didn't need both hands to play," she said as she kissed him. They then turned and mounted their camels.

"How are you faring, my dear? Orpheus asked as he assisted Cassandra in mounting her camel. "I'm a little stiff and sore, but not as bad as I feared," he added.

Cassandra responded, "Not bad, not bad at all. You did a very good job of teaching me. I think we're both of the fortunate ones; I wouldn't recommend this for poor Damon. I miss them already, but they couldn't endure this kind of travel."

"We'll see them again, Cassandra, and probably sooner than you expect," Orpheus said. He kissed her, then turned to mount his camel.

Lukas was the first to be mounted and ready. "Come on, let's go to Gerasa!" he shouted as he looked back at Melina with a smile.

A bit of chuckling passed through the caravan as they continued south upon the road to Gerasa. Lukas's enthusiasm was an inspiration to all. They met a large caravan headed north to Gadara before long. Aegeus, as well as Jason recognized the trader leading. The well-traveled, bearded man with a banded head covering was one who Jason had met long ago. He shared his testimony with many merchants when he lived at the caravansary. The trader was very excited to hear they were going to Jerusalem to seek Jesus. They shared a brief friendly exchange, then the two caravans passed and went their way. Jason wondered to himself how far his testimony had traveled with that man.

The rest of the trip was rather uneventful until Jason encountered another remnant of his past. Aegeus and Calista were the first to spot two camels headed north toward them. They waved which made Jason take notice and he waved also, while trying to make out details as they approached. Soon Jason smiled as he recognized the two men, even though their heads were covered: it was Lander and Belen! He and Alethea were full of joy, as they recalled the encounter during their last trip to Gerasa. What a pleasant surprise it was. Everyone stopped and dismounted as Jason and Alethea ran up to embrace the two men, then they introduced them to the rest of the family.

Lander proclaimed, "We were on our way to Gadara to visit you, Jason. I can't believe we encountered you here; it must be God!"

Belen said, "I never expected to see you this soon, Jason!" He asked, "Where are you going?"

"We're on our way to Jerusalem!" Jason exclaimed with a huge smile and excitement. "We hope to meet with Jesus and his disciples, for they should be there to celebrate the Jewish Passover; we plan to follow him for a time. Your welcome to join us if you both want to," he offered.

Lander and Belen looked at each other. Belen spoke, "Well, we were prepared for a day's journey, and everything we have is upon these two camels; we were thinking of staying in Gadara."

Lander said, "Yes, we were curious about the scripture readings you spoke of and the work you do there. We decided we wanted to join you, so we could get involved. Belen and I have been sharing our testimony in Gerasa; some believe, but many reject the Son of God. You're going to seek him, that's wonderful! Yes, I want to join you!"

Belen spoke in agreement, "I as well, Jason, if it's alright with the rest of your group." He looked around at the faces and most were smiling.

Jason looked around and explained, "Remember? We told you of them the night of the harvest. We met these two just outside of Gerasa as they were seeking alms; they were afflicted with leprosy.

I prayed for them in the name of Jesus and God had mercy upon them! They stand before you now, as a living testimony of the compassion and power to heal from God!" Jason looked at Aegeus and Orpheus as they had been observing the two men.

"You have no signs of the disease?" Aegeus asked. He was being cautious.

Belen responded, "None whatsoever! We even went to see a physician shortly after the healing. He found no trace of the sickness; the Lord cleansed us!"

Lander looked at Orpheus, for they saw him and Aegeus as the elders of the family. "We don't want any strife. We understand if you don't want us to join you," he said.

Orpheus just smiled and said, "If Jason wants you to join us and you say you've been cleansed by God, then I'm more than happy to have you both with us."

Aegeus added, "I agree, they look like two healthy young men to me. We're traveling for an indefinite period of time. Your welcome to join us, if you desire." He then smiled at the men saying, "We're headed to the caravansary just south of Gerasa. I recommend we make haste to arrive there before evening."

The caravan then made its way south toward Gerasa, now sixteen camels. The outline of buildings became visible in the distance after a short time. The dust stirred up by the camels seemed to be increasing the further south they went. The weather must have been even dryer here than in Gadara, as some thought. Everyone began to take out a covering to wrap their faces due to the increasing dust. Aegeus had proven his valuable experience, for he had insisted everyone had such protection at the ready. He had demonstrated the appropriate way to wear it: sort of a loose turban that wrapped around the face and covered all but the eyes. They approached the city as Jason and Alethea rode ahead, for they knew the exact location of the establishment of Ammayu; Aegeus and his family had never been there. The dusty road changed to cobblestone, then everybody relaxed and loosened their face coverings a bit. Alethea asked Jason to lead her camel.

"Are you sure?" Jason asked while showing concern for his wife.

"Yeah, I feel pretty confident now; I feel like I would have to try to fall off. I can grab with one hand if I need to," Alethea assured her husband. She reached behind to her bag and pulled out her aulos. Jason received the reins of her camel, then she smiled at him and started to play.

Alethea's music was enjoyed by all as the caravan completed the final leg of the day's journey. Jason realized how much faster the camels were, for it was still late afternoon. The city wall, as well as the visible rooftops, stone walls and columns beyond assumed the yellow glow of the waning sun. Jason thought to himself that he was almost disappointed as the caravan entered the courtyard of the caravansary. Alethea's pipe music ceased, then he instantly realized how sore and hungry he was. Another good meal before they headed out into the expanse of the high desert; as well as a chance to see an old friend. Everyone began to dismount, as signaled by a chatter of coaxing sounds. Two Arabian men approached to see to the camels. One immediately started drawing water from the well, while the other went up to Jason and Alethea, for he had recognized them.

"Welcome, friends!" he said. Jason knew he didn't speak Greek, but his practiced greeting warmed the heart. Jason smiled and embraced him, then offered a greeting in Aramaic. Suddenly, they heard a shout:

"Jason! Alethea!" a familiar voice echoed off the walls around the courtyard. Ammayu exited the entry of his community room and ran toward his friends. Jason and Alethea ran toward him as well, then he warmly embraced them both. "I was so sad that I missed you when you came. Please, gather your things and come in quickly! Come in and relax! Get out of the sun!" Ammayu spoke with excitement and friendly gestures.

Jason glanced back at the rest of the family. They were smiling at the tall Nabataean dressed in white with his enthusiastic joy. "I have brought most of my family, Ammayu. Many I've told you about and I've told them about you," he said.

"Excellent! We will have a great meal this night and a celebration! I am so happy to see you, my friend! Many Nabataeans have heard of Jesus and accepted him as Lord because of you. I will tell you all about it. Come! Come inside and enjoy! Your friends are my friends, and everyone is most welcome. I want to meet everyone but come inside!" Ammayu said as he gestured to the double door entry.

By this time everyone had what they were going to take in with them. Jason and his fellow travelers followed Ammayu into his community room. It was just as Jason and Alethea had remembered it; the murals depicting desert travel and caravans, the copper ornaments, the aroma of frankincense and the Arabian decor with rich colors and fabrics were stunning to the senses. Jason was delighted, as he immediately noticed that the depictions of the Nabataean gods were missing. The square faces that had been carved here and there had all been destroyed. He didn't make mention of it, but he smiled at the evidence of Ammayu's devotion to the one true God.

"Alethea and I met Nahal when we were here last time and she was very good to us. Is she here?" Jason asked.

Ammayu smiled and responded, "No, she is at home, but it is not far from here. I could send one of my men to ask her to come if you wish."

"Yes, that would be wonderful. We would like to have fellowship with her, for we've grown fond of her since then," Jason said and then began to make all the introductions. Everything was very warm and cordial until Jason introduced Cassandra to Ammayu. His reaction brought back an old memory to Jason: his introduction of Orpheus to Eustace.

"She is a witch, Jason," Ammayu said as he looked upon her with disdain. Cassandra froze, then tears welled up. Orpheus stood beside her, and was just about to speak up; Jason spoke instead:

"Ammayu! Are you forgetting that I am a former demoniac? Are you forgetting the restorative authority of Jesus, the Son of God? The Lord God has had mercy and compassion upon her the same as me. The Lord led us to her, and we spoke the words he gave us to speak. She has been delivered in the name of Jesus! She is a beloved member of my family!" Jason shouted.

Suddenly, Cassandra fled the community room into the courtyard, and was closely followed by Orpheus. On the way out he shouted, "We'll sleep outside with the camels!"

Ammayu was stunned as he realized he had made a terrible mistake. He said, "You are right, my friend. I was familiar with the witch named Cassandra. She was incredibly wicked; I'm sorry for my reaction, for I didn't have time to reason it out. Come with me, and we will go out to speak with her and Orpheus." The two left the community room in silence as all the guests were shocked at Ammayu's display of undue judgment.

Ammayu and Jason found the elderly couple sitting by the well in each other's arms. Cassandra was weeping uncontrollably as Orpheus attempted to calm her. The men approached, then she looked up at them and cried even harder.

"Just go away and leave us!" Orpheus said angrily. "She doesn't need any more judgment, Ammayu!" he shouted.

Ammayu knelt down and prayed aloud, "Heavenly Father, in the name of Jesus I cry out for forgiveness. I have hurt this beautiful child of yours because of my stupidity. Please restore the peace and love you have bestowed upon this gathering." Ammayu then began to weep bitterly.

Cassandra stopped weeping. She lifted her head and looked upon Ammayu with compassion. She immediately broke away from Orpheus and knelt beside Ammayu while placing her arm around his shoulders. She said, "Don't cry, Ammayu. Everything's fine; I forgive you."

Ammayu raised up and embraced Cassandra tightly saying, "I am so sorry, Cassandra. I am a stupid man! You shall always be welcome in my house. I am sorry, for I reacted with fear...I am sorry!" He continued to weep as Cassandra consoled him.

Jason and Orpheus had stood by watching a beautiful moment. Jason smiled, then looked at Orpheus and said, "Behold, the love of God."

Orpheus walked over to his wife and Ammayu, then placed his hand upon Ammayu's shoulder. He looked up at Orpheus as the old man simply said, "A momentary lapse in judgment is something we're all guilty of, Ammayu. I forgive you as well."

Ammayu stood up and embraced Orpheus. "Thank you, my friend...I do not feel I deserve your forgiveness, but I gladly accept it. Thank you," Ammayu said as he smiled at Orpheus. The tall Nabataean looked him in the eye with a sincere expression. "Thank you," he repeated.

The four went back inside, where everyone had reclined around two tables in front, the same way they would usually sit back at Eustace's place. Everyone looked solemn as they observed Ammayu with a very humble expression.

Ammayu immediately spoke, "I made a terrible mistake here today, for I have insulted my friend and his family. I am deeply sorry for the trouble and pain that I have caused all of you, but especially Cassandra. They have forgiven me, though I do not deserve it. I deeply love all of you, but I reacted with fear; I thought she was taking advantage of you. Cassandra just demonstrated to me that she has become a very loving and compassionate soul, and all of you are a very unique family. Every one of you has been touched by the Master's hand. I stand humbled by the compassion and grace of Cassandra and I am honored that she still sits in my house. I ask all of you to forgive my ignorance."

Everyone stood, then approached Ammayu and took turns embracing him. It was determined that the incident was an understandable error in judgment, although hurtful. Ammayu had known Cassandra as an evil witch; his gut reaction was that she had infiltrated Jason's family. He had forgotten briefly one of Jason's primary attributes of his ministry: to seek out those under the influence of demons and set them free in the name of Jesus. A bit of conversation, then everyone was once again smiling and enjoying fellowship in Ammayu's beautiful and exotic caravansary. He and Jason spoke privately for a bit, as Ammayu wanted to hear about Jason's experience with the Romans. A special blessing for Jason and Alethea came when Nahal arrived and sat with them for a visit.

Nahal smiled upon entering and embraced Jason and Alethea. She said, "Ammayu worker came, told you were here. I very, eh, joy! Eh, eh, took care you. Missed when you two be gone."

Jason and Alethea smiled at each other. Alethea said, "The love you showed us was remembered, Nahal. You found a special place in our hearts. We wanted to see you again."

"I hope see you again, eh, al, eh, also. We got big wine from Eustace, from you, big wine!" she said while smiling broadly.

Jason responded, "So, you like our wine. The whole family you see here contributed to making that wine. We believe it was blessed by God. Very special wine!"

Nahal responded, "Yes, special big wine. You bring Jesus to Gerasa again? Ammayu, eh, bring Jesus every place. We, eh, address, eh, adore…love Jesus!"

Jason and Alethea looked at each other again smiling, and silently grateful that her Greek hadn't improved. They both found her broken Greek and her pure loving heart precious. Alethea spoke, "We're on our way to see Jesus in Jerusalem. We're going to follow him and listen to his teaching."

"I, eh, happy that one. I has happy time, I here marry in days, eh, seven days!" Nahal said with a huge smile.

"Congratulations!" Alethea proclaimed as both of them patted her shoulder.

Ammayu joined them. He said, "She is among my favorite cousins. We are holding her wedding here in a few days, as she told you. She is very faithful and helpful in the family businesses. I am so pleased that you have struck up a friendship, for she is a special woman."

Jason said, "You should come visit us in Gadara, and bring Nahal and her husband with you. They shall be welcome in our house. By the way, Eustace sends his regards. He said he, as well as his new wife will come to visit you later this summer. He said you two could go fishing."

"Excellent!" Ammayu said with excitement. "He told me of a future visit when he came to promote your wine, but he was not sure when. I am looking forward to meeting his new wife. That wine has improved my business; are you going to continue production?" he asked.

Jason and Ammayu settled into a conversation as Alethea and Nahal became involved in their own. The other women joined them as well.

Jason said, "Actually, yes. My good friend Linus was the talent behind it, but we all contributed. He and Eustace are continuing its production in our absence. We're going to follow Jesus, but we're not sure how long that will be, like I said before. We've chosen a similar route that Alethea and I took to Mount Nebo, but heading southwest this time, for we plan to cross the Jordan and on to Jerusalem." Jason asked, "It seems very dry this year, so can you tell us about travel there?" He then shouted for Aegeus and Orpheus to join them. Lukas and Melina had gone for a walk. Lander and Belen joined to listen as well.

Ammayu responded, "I would recommend following the Jabbok River Valley instead of going down into the desert. Going southwest you would avoid the Eastern Desert, and there is the City of Gedor, which is about a day's travel from here. However, there have been dust storms coming out of the vast Eastern Desert. They have been blowing to the northwest following the low-lying regions. If I were going to Jerusalem I would stay in the hills as much as possible. There have been many caravans report of severe winds and torturous dust and grit during these storms." Ammayu paused while staring into space as the men listened intently. "Some have gone missing. A trader out of Raqmu, and a very good friend has not been heard from for some time. Perhaps he lies buried out there; somewhere in the desert. These storms can be very dangerous, my friends," he said with a serious expression.

Jason shared his knowledge, "Alethea and I traveled the Jabbok River route Ammayu spoke of. It will be slow going, since we're traveling with camels. Our asses made it alright, but it's much rougher terrain than descending into the lowlands. I remember hills to the west, that's where I suppose Gedor is located." He then asked, "Would these hills afford shelter from the dust storms, Ammayu?"

Ammayu responded, "Not completely. There are valleys there that could be vulnerable to the dust if a storm comes upon you. If you can see it coming at a distance, then you can head to high ground. It looks like you have decisions to make. I will be praying for all of you, my friends."

Aegeus said, "The next thing we encounter is the Jabbok River. I say we pray about it tonight and make the decision when we reach it tomorrow."

Orpheus spoke, "There is a bridge there. It will take a short time, in my opinion, to get through the danger of the dust storms. We could be beyond those hills in a day or two."

"Yes, and it's only a small chance one would hit in that time," Belen said. "Ammayu lost a friend to these storms; they're nothing to gamble with. We lived near the Eastern Desert for some time, so we know that these dust storms can be frightening. We will go along with whatever decision is made," he said while looking over at Lander who nodded in agreement.

Everyone enjoyed the evening meal and the music that Ammayu brought in to entertain his guests. The Nabataean culture was an enriching experience, as well as the exotic meal and Jason and Alethea's wine, which all made for a very satisfying evening.

The caravan got an early start the following morning, as Ammayu and his people prepared a morning meal and brought out the camels. They had all been brushed, fed, and well-watered. Jason and Aegeus met with Ammayu to thank him and settle up. Ammayu just smiled and put his hands up.

He stated, "Your money is no good here, my friends. I could not take your money after the unfortunate misunderstanding yesterday. Consider it a gift and a blessing as I send you back upon your journey. I send my love of Jesus with you. Tell him of all the Nabataeans who love him when you see him!" Ammayu was insistent and refused to take their money.

Cassandra walked up to Ammayu and embraced him. She then said, "You are my special friend, Ammayu; more so than if you had not made an error. You would not have had an opportunity to show what kind of a man you are by correcting it. Go with God, my friend." Ammayu teared up a little and smiled at her.

Everyone stood and waited to embrace Ammayu, as they all left him with smiles and love. Before long, everyone was mounted up and headed out of the courtyard while giving a final wave to their new Nabataean friend. The caravan headed south to the bridge over the Jabbok River. It was another beautiful spring morning as there wasn't a cloud in the sky. Not quite as cool, for the intense sun was quickly warming the dry air. Many had donned their protective headwear but wore it loosely around the neck. It was difficult to imagine the severe dust storms discussed the night before. Cassandra was reminiscing about taking the same journey months earlier; a journey that transformed her life. She asked Orpheus to accompany her down to the river where she was baptized when they arrived. He smiled and nodded with understanding, for he had shown her the place where he was baptized in the Yarmuk River, as well as several hundred others. The trip to the bridge went swiftly and without incident as the group was much more comfortable now with the camels.

Lukas was now riding as if he did it for a living. He wore a new outer garment he had purchased; it had stripes, which was similar to ones he had seen Jewish men wear. The other men were dressed like caravan traders: banded head coverings with head and face protection and light-colored garments. The women were dressed for travel as well: head coverings with the protective head wrap around the neck. Lander and Belen had come prepared also, as they had experience from living near the Eastern Desert. They arrived at the stone bridge, and everyone dismounted in an open area off the road. The men gathered to discuss which route to take. Lukas said he would go any way they decided; he wanted to go down to the river with Cassandra and Orpheus; Melina and Alethea joined them as well. The others strolled across the bridge to have a conversation on the other side. Aegeus walked close with Calista while taking full advantage of the time off their camels. Jason was by his side and Argus was close to his Uncle Jason.

"Well, what do you think, Jason?" Aegeus asked as he looked as far as he could beyond the bridge. "I think we could get through without any fear of storms on a day like this. I'm concerned about the river route and the camels," he said.

Jason responded, "I agree, as I've been there, and some may have difficulty. The path is sometimes narrow, and at the very least much slower. I would recommend it if we were traveling with asses. I say we descend to the lowlands, as Alethea and I did. Due south, then southwest to keep near the hills. I'll leave it up to you as to whether or not you want to visit Gedor."

Aegeus looked around at the faces of Dimitri, Lander, and Belen. Argus was preoccupied with looking over the edge of the bridge, while dropping small pebbles into the water. He smiled and looked up at Aegeus as the old man smiled back at him. "Any comments or suggestions?" he asked the men.

Dimitri spoke, "I think Ammayu might have been speaking through fear, for he had lost a friend to one of these dust storms. I say we go with the easier route."

"Lander and I have never traveled this way," Belen added to the conversation while looking over at Lander. "We'll follow whatever you men decide," he said. Lander nodded as he looked at Aegeus, then Jason.

"I just want to go to Jerusalem to see Jesus!" Argus contributed, which brought a chuckle from the others.

"I guess that settles it. We take the quickest possible route to Jerusalem to see Jesus." Aegeus said with a smile toward Argus. The young man smiled back and acted a bit silly which inspired

Jason to launch a friendly little attack against him. They all chuckled as young Argus wrestled with his Uncle Jason.

Cassandra became a bit emotional visiting the spot where Alethea had helped her transform into the woman she is now, and where she had made her commitment to God as well. Lukas had the impulse to strip down to his undergarment and catch some fresh fish but refrained due to the women present. Melina had warned him of such.

"No, when we go back up to the bridge everyone will want to go," Melina reasoned with Lukas. "We have plenty of food," she added.

Lukas responded, "Not fresh fish! It wouldn't take long. I'll catch one for everybody; you can stay and watch."

Melina just shook her head and smiled at her sometimes-juvenile husband. "If we get back up to the bridge and Aegeus, Jason, and the others want you to spend the morning fishing, then I'll join you in doing so," she said.

They spent a pleasant time at the river, then the group headed back up the steep path to the road above. Sure enough, Lukas expressed his desire to catch some fish. Aegeus looked at him curiously. Jason just smiled, for he would have been more surprised if Lukas hadn't brought it up.

Aegeus looked at Lukas as if he had challenged him to a wager. "How long would it take you?" he asked as he was little surprised that he was entertaining the idea. Most of the women had a similar expression.

"Not long, if I help him," Jason spoke up to the delight of Lukas.

Before long, Jason, Lukas, Alethea, Melina, and Argus headed back down the escarpment. No one could see the activity, but they heard a lot of splashing and laughing. Alethea and Melina returned to the road with many fish corded together, and much sooner than most were expecting.

"Lukas said someone may be really hungry, so they caught fourteen," Melina said while displaying the impressive bunch of fish.

"They apologize for how long it took. They kept their tunics on, now they're changing," Alethea said. Lukas popped up from the escarpment soon after, as well as Jason with Argus close behind giggling. The wet haired men walked over to the pack camels, then rung out and spread their wet clothing over two of the mounded loads of supply packs. Melina and Alethea placed the still twitching fish in sacks and hung them on the pack camels as well.

"The clothing will be dry by the time we stop for the mid-day meal," Lukas said as he noticed everybody was smiling at him and Jason.

"The fish should still be nice and fresh by the time we stop. I guess Lukas did have a good idea," Melina said as she looked over and smiled at her husband.

Aegeus just shook his head with a smile upon his face. "You men amaze me!" he said as he walked over and patted Lukas on the back. "Well, let us mount up!" he shouted.

The morning passed into the afternoon as the caravan descended into the lowlands. The arid plain, which was filled with dry grass and sparse clusters of trees was easy going for the camels. The ground was a little rocky with a lot of sand and dust, which inspired everyone to don their face coverings. There was only a slight breeze blowing, so the dust stirred up by the camels tended to rise, as it made its way into the eyes and coated the throat. The caravan began to veer over toward the hills to the west and high ground in case of a dust storm. Once there the decision was made to stop for a mid-day meal; the fresh fish was on everyone's mind.

Jason pointed out a large cluster of mostly olive trees and bushes, as he and Alethea had learned it was an indication of a possible stream coming out of the hills. The region was not without resources, although dry. The caravan arrived at the spot, and Jason was correct; there was a small brook winding its way through a peaceful spot which provided shade, as well as a large level area for the camels. Dimitri quickly dismounted and began gathering firewood. Jason and Lukas joined him, as well as selecting sticks to roast many fish. Dimitri then set about starting a fire, as everyone else brought items from the camels. Covers were spread out, and before long the smell of roasted fish was whetting the traveler's appetites. Everyone enjoyed the anticipated meal, as well as a welcome break from the camels. Some expressed a desire to camp there, but the goal was to reach the City of Gedor by evening.

Aegeus responded to the idea of camping, "I know this is a pretty spot with plenty of water, but we haven't traveled that far today. I want to reach Gedor by nightfall, then we still have a day's travel or more to reach the Jordan. There we'll come to a bridge and a road that crosses the Jordan and will lead us right to Jerusalem."

Jason spoke, "We couldn't travel the main trade route around that lies to the east, that's what Ammayu warned us about for fear of dust storms. The way we've chosen is shorter, but now that we're traveling in the hills it will probably be slower. We must stay with the plan we've calculated if we're going to arrive in Jerusalem by the Passover. I want to follow Jesus, but we'll spend a lot of time searching if we miss them. That's why we have no idea how long this journey will be."

"A bit slower, but there is a good system of roads and trails around the City of Gedor," Orpheus advised as he had extensive knowledge of the region.

"Yes, we've spent a lot of time searching," Calista said while recollecting. "Jesus and his disciples move around a lot. It's easy to find ones' self being just a day or an afternoon behind them. Take for example your deliverance, Jason. We've heard that Jesus finished speaking to a multitude, then he and his disciples abruptly left in their boat to sail across the Sea of Galilee; the same when they returned to the Decapolis." she said.

"I'm glad they did," Alethea said as she smiled at Jason. "I think Jesus knew Jason was there waiting for him," she added.

Lukas said, "Yeah, then Jason came for me; and Orpheus, and Theophanes, and...."

"And he woke me out of my slumber!" Aegeus said as he completed Lukas's statement. "He transformed every life sitting here. Lander and Belen were healed; Jason, Lukas, Orpheus, and Cassandra were delivered, I was awakened to faith, and families have been brought together. Everything Jesus touches is healed and saved, that's why we're going to follow him," he said with a joyous smile.

After conversing, everyone was enthusiastic to get to Gedor by nightfall. Everything was quickly packed up as the caravan was once again headed into the hills to the southwest and left the Decapolis region for Perea. Beyond that they were to cross the Jordan River, and then enter the region of Judea, and Jerusalem.

It was early afternoon on a clear, spring day, as Jesus with his disciples and many following came near to Jerusalem. They arrived at the villages of Bethphage and Bethany, which was near the mount of Olives. Judas and a couple of the other disciples went to secure lodging for the duration of their stay. Jesus called Simon, who he had given the name Peter, as well as Andrew; he had a special mission for them.

Jesus said unto them, *"Go into the village over against you, and straightway you shall find an ass tied, and a colt with her: loose them, and bring them unto me. And if any man say ought unto you, you shall say, The Lord has need of them; and straightway he will send them."*

The brothers went into the village of Bethany. Peter noticed an ass with a young colt tied alongside after walking a little way. They were tied near the door of a corner mudbrick house where two streets met. Peter felt very strange untying the animals, but he was speechless when the door opened.

"Why are you loosening my animals?" the man asked as he looked at Peter with a curious expression.

Peter responded, as he trusted his faith and shunned embarrassment, *"The Lord has need of them,"* he said in a very matter of fact way.

The man just looked at him for a moment, then said, "The Lord has need of my ass and colt? Uh, alright, but try to bring them back when the Lord is finished with them."

The stunned men smiled at the man, then headed out of the village with the ass and colt. They brought them to Jesus, then Peter and Andrew removed their outer garments and lay them upon the colt as they gestured for Jesus to mount it. He did so, then all the disciples began shouting praises to God and shouting of the miracles they had witnessed. They all threw their outer garments upon the path of Jesus, as did many others who gathered very quickly.

And the multitudes that went before, and that followed, cried, saying, "Hosanna to the son of David: Blessed is he that comes in the name of the Lord; Hosanna in the highest." Many who were there for the Passover immediately gathered palm branches, while waving them and shouting with joy at the arrival of Jesus in Jerusalem. There was a small group of Pharisees in the crowd that were not so joyful. One of them approached Jesus directly and spoke:

"*Master, rebuke your disciples!*" the Pharisee demanded with a clear look of disdain upon his face.

Jesus responded, "*I tell you that, if these should hold their peace, the stones would immediately cry out.*" He then looked away while smiling at the multitude that had gathered as he rode by. *Thus, the prophecies of Daniel and Zechariah were fulfilled.*

They passed deeper into the city, then Jesus dismounted the colt. He walked around with his disciples, as he looked upon the City of Jerusalem with an expression of a heavy burden. He looked upon the temple, then found a place in a small garden and began to weep. The disciples were suddenly solemn as they beheld their Master speak:

"*If you had known, even you, at least in this your day, the things which belong unto your peace! But now they are hid from your eyes. For the days shall come upon you, that your enemies shall cast a trench about you, and compass you round, and keep you in on every side, and shall lay you even with the ground, and your children within you; and they shall not leave in you one stone upon another; because you knew not the time of your visitation.*"

Jesus wept for some time. Evening approached, and Peter suggested they leave for the night to have a meal. And so, they left the city and returned to Bethany.

Evening approached, as Aegeus sighted the City of Gedor. The caravan moved close to the city and they found a perfect place to camp right away: a huge grassy level area surrounded by trees with a stream nearby. Everyone was anxious to get off the camels, so they dismounted and immediately went to work establishing a camp. With so many helping hands; tents were up, a fire was going, and the camels had been watered and cared for in a short time. The evening meal was enjoyed by all, then everyone sat in a circle around the fire and beheld the sunset. The cloudless sky was lacking in color, but the glow of the setting sun played upon the rocks and trees, as well as the faces of the family and friends. There was talk of assembling a group to visit the city, but after relaxing most seemed content to simply lounge around the fire. Everyone was quiet at first, then Jason broke the silence.

He said, "I want to share something I've been feeling all day. I'm asking all of you to pray tonight, for I feel we're all about to be challenged in some way. I can't explain it, but it's a very strong feeling." Jason sat and stared into the fire as he spoke.

Alethea sat next to him and asked, "Was it a dream?" She looked over at him as he returned the glance.

"No. I haven't had any of *those dreams* for some time," Jason said and then smiled at her. "Lately, I only dream of you, my wife," he said as he leaned over and kissed her, which made her smile.

Aegeus asked, "Do you feel something will happen while we're traveling, Jason?"

"No, I don't know what it is. I'm just asking everyone to pray tonight. We've had a very successful journey so far, but we must not take that for granted, that I can tell you," Jason said as he looked at his friend across the fire.

Orpheus said, "We should listen to Jason's intuition. I had something like that once and I didn't share it...right before we were arrested by the Romans."

Lukas speculated, "I also have felt something, but I thought it was because of Ammayu warning us about the dust storms. Maybe that's it, Jason."

Aegeus spoke, "We'll cross the Jordan tomorrow, then I don't think we'll have to worry about dust storms. I'm hoping to reach Jericho by tomorrow evening."

Jason spoke quickly, "We don't want to camp very close to it, that is a place of evil. You don't want to know of the unspeakable wickedness that took place there. No good can come from there."

Cassandra added, "Jason's right. I'm not sure how I know, but I know he's right. There are still bad spirits associated with that city…I don't want to sleep there," she said.

"That's good enough for me," Calista said as she added her opinion. "Jason speaks from his spirit, and so does Cassandra; I've gotten to know her. They have an intuition that we cannot understand," she advised.

Belen said, "I just want you all to know that Lander and I have absolute confidence in this journey, and the motives behind it. I think it was God that brought us together, for we've discussed it. I feel that whatever comes of this journey we're sharing with you was meant to be."

Lander said, "I agree, we spoke about it last night. We feel that we're following the Lord by partaking in this journey with you. We want a chance to thank Jesus for all he has done in our lives."

Dimitri spoke, "I too feel strongly as though this journey was meant to be. I came to faith by what I witnessed. My feeling is that we're all going to witness much more."

"We'll face it together, whatever it is. Right, Uncle Jason?" Argus asked with a boldness that made Jason smile. He roughed up the young man's hair as he sat next to him.

Melina snuggled up to Lukas and said, "I'm longing to meet Jesus, but we both knew this journey might change our lives. We'll face it together, as Argus said."

Aegeus stated, "Well, I say we all get a good night's sleep. Tomorrow, we'll get much closer to Jerusalem. If we get an early start, and nothing comes up to delay us we should be there by the day after tomorrow; most likely by afternoon."

Jason spoke, "Pray tonight for God's protection. For us, as well as for Jesus and his disciples. I can't forget the trouble we've had with the Pharisees and how opposed they are to Jesus. That might have something to do with my feelings. He threatens their authority among the Jews; perhaps we do as well." Jason then went silent as he gazed into the fire.

Silence once again fell upon the group as they relaxed around the fire. Most were deep in thought or prayer as the firelight flickered a warm glow upon their faces. The quiet night, good fellowship and deep conversation left everyone tired and at peace. They all slept well, for all in their own way were learning to trust God.

The morning came, as Jesus and his disciples left Bethany and headed for the City of Jerusalem. On the way, Jesus saw a fig tree and approached it, for he was hungry. The tree seemed healthy and full of leaves, but there were no figs, for their time was not yet.

Jesus spoke to the tree, *"Let no fruit grow on you henceforward forever."* He then walked away as some of the disciples heard what he had said.

They continued into the city and approached the Great Temple of Jerusalem. Jesus and his disciples entered the outer courts, as the disciples were very impressed by the grandeur of the architecture; Jesus was not impressed. He became enraged, as he viewed the money changers, as well as those selling sacrificial animals. The disciples were shocked, as Jesus began turning over tables and cages. He drew a cord from his waist and chased many of those involved in the commerce of the temple out of the courts.

Jesus shouted loudly, *"It is written, my house shall be called the house of prayer; but you have made it a den of thieves!"*

Jesus began to openly teach in the temple after the incident had passed. The scribes and Pharisees watched, while knowing that many saw him as a prophet: a man of God. The blind and the lame came to him and he healed them. Many children were crying and praising Jesus in the temple, as they said, *"Hosanna to the son of David."* The Pharisees were very displeased.

They said unto him, "Do you hear what these say?"

Jesus said unto them, "Yea; have you never read, out of the mouth of babes and sucklings you have perfected praise?"

The Pharisees couldn't lay hands upon him, for fear of rebellion from the people. They pondered how they might trap him by his own words. One approached Jesus and asked him questions.

The Pharisee asked, *"By what authority do you these things? And who gave you this authority?"* He waited for a response with a smirk on his face as the others watched.

Jesus responded with his own question, *"I will also ask you one thing, and answer me: the baptism of John, was it from heaven, or of men?"*

The spokesman of the Pharisees went back among the others to discuss the discourse, and said, *"If we say, from heaven; he will say unto us, why did you not believe him? But if we say, of men; we fear the people; for they all hold John as a prophet."* They looked nervously at Jesus as he smiled at them. The spokesman returned to confront Jesus.

"We cannot tell," the Pharisee sheepishly responded while avoiding direct eye contact with Jesus.

Jesus responded with a smile, *"Neither do I tell you by what authority I do these things."*

The Pharisees discussed among themselves how they might trap him with his words. They sought to be able to deliver Jesus unto the power and authority of the governor.

The spokesman returned and asked, *"Master, we know that you are true, and teach the way of God in truth, neither do you care for any man: for you regard not the person of men. Tell us therefore, what do you think? Is it lawful to give tribute unto Caesar, or not?"*

Jesus perceived their wickedness, and said, "Why tempt me, you hypocrites? Show me the tribute money." They brought to him a penny. And he said unto them, "Whose is this image and superscription?"

They said unto him, "Caesar's"

Jesus said, "Render therefore unto Caesar the things which are Caesar's; and unto God the things that are God's."

Jesus went on teaching in the temple throughout the day. All were astonished by his doctrine, for he taught with authority. The scribes and Pharisees watched but didn't interfere. Even the Sadducees had been silenced by him. They didn't ask him any more questions; instead they plotted how they might destroy him. Jesus and his disciples left the city and returned to Bethany when the evening came.

Jason was the first to awaken. After reviving the fire, he began to awaken everyone else. The group worked to break down the camp and have a morning meal before departing. Suddenly, a noise was heard from beyond the trees. Immediately, the camp was infiltrated by Roman soldiers on horseback. Some jumped off and began looking through the packs and tents around the campsite. Many were shocked, for they had memories of the arrest of Jason, Orpheus, and Lukas. Fear began to take hold, then Jason shouted in Latin:

"Why do you come into our camp? Who is the commander here?" he asked with boldness. He recognized the insignias of the Tenth Legion: *Legio X Fretensis.* A Centurion came forward and dismounted near Jason, then spoke to him in Latin:

"I am commanding these men. We're patrolling the area looking for thieves," the Centurion proclaimed. "Who are you?" he asked as he stood before Jason with an imposing stance.

"I am Jason of Gadara, and these are my family and friends. We're traveling to Jerusalem for the Passover," Jason responded to the Centurion; respectful but with no fear.

The Centurion immediately put his fist over his heart and bowed his head. He shouted a lengthy command which brought all the activity of the others to a sudden stop. He then spoke to Jason, "I know of you, for your story has reached us from our eastern camp. I'm sorry if we have bothered you and your family, Jason. There have been rampant crimes being committed against travelers such as yourself. Many are traveling to Jerusalem this time of year. We caught two thieves yesterday. Have you had any trouble on your journey?"

Jason responded, "No, we just want to get an early start. I would appreciate it if you would leave us, so we can pack up and continue on our journey."

The Centurion shouted more commands in Latin, and all of the soldiers mounted their horses. The Centurion saluted Jason once again, then smiled at him and mounted his horse. The soldiers disappeared in a cloud of dust, as quickly as they had appeared.

Alethea ran up to Jason and embraced him, as he was quickly surrounded by the others.

Aegeus put his hand upon Jason's shoulder and said, "Thank God for your reputation, my friend."

Everyone set about packing up quickly as Melina and Alethea made up a morning meal. Everyone sat around the smoldering fire, then Lukas spoke:

"Do you think the Romans were what you were thinking about last night, Jason?" Lukas asked as he took a bite of bread.

Jason quickly responded, "No, that was a mere chance encounter; we have nothing to fear from the Romans, for now."

Orpheus said, "I prayed last night; I agree, something is going to challenge us. That was not a challenge…but it was a terrible way to wake up."

Everyone chuckled as they slowly got up and prepared to mount the camels once more. Before long, the caravan was moving again. They traveled out of the hills of Perea and down toward the Jordan River Valley and Judea beyond.

Jesus and his disciples once again approached Jerusalem in the morning. They passed the fig tree Jesus had encountered the previous morning, and all grew silent. The fig tree had not only withered but appeared as long dead. They entered the city and made their way to the temple. Jesus was welcomed by the people but met with disdain by the scribes and Pharisees.

Then spoke Jesus to the multitudes, and to his disciples, "The scribes and Pharisees sit in Moses' seat: All therefore whatsoever they bid you observe and do, but do not do after their works; for they say, and do not. For they bind heavy burdens and grievous to be borne and lay them on men's shoulders, but they themselves will not move them with one of their fingers. But all their works they do for to be seen of men. They make broad their phylacteries and enlarge the borders of their garments. They love the uppermost rooms at feasts, and the chief seats in the synagogues, and greetings in the markets. They love to be called of men, Rabbi, Rabbi. But be not called Rabbi: for one is your Master, even Christ; and all of you are brethren. And call no man your father upon the earth: for one is your Father, which is in heaven...."

Jesus went on for some time with a very scathing rebuke toward the scribes and Pharisees, for he continuously referred to them as hypocrites and blind guides. Afterward, Jesus retreated to the outer courts to pray. His disciples approached him, and heard him speak:

"O Jerusalem, Jerusalem, you that killed the prophets, and stoned them that were sent to you. How often would I have gathered your children together, even as a hen gathers her chickens under her wings, and you would not! Behold, your house is left to you desolate. For I say unto you, you shall not see me henceforth, till you shall say, blessed is he that comes in the name of the Lord."

Peter, with a few of the disciples approached their Master. They attempted to uplift him a bit, so they started a conversation about the temple's architecture. Jesus looked up as they stood and marveled at the impressive stone structure.

Jesus said unto them, "See all these things? Verily I say unto you, there shall not be left here one stone upon another that shall not be thrown down."

The disciples, as well as their Master then left the temple and walked up onto the mount of Olives. It seemed to have been a long day already. *And as he sat upon the mount of Olives, the disciples came unto him privately, saying, "Tell us, when shall these things be? And what shall be the sign of your coming, and of the end of the world?"*

Jesus answered and said unto them, "Take heed that no man deceive you. For many shall come in my name, saying, I am Christ; and shall deceive many. And you shall hear of wars and rumors of wars: see that you are not troubled: for all these things must come to pass, but the end is not yet. For nation shall rise against nation, and kingdom against kingdom: and there shall be famines and pestilences, and earthquakes in diverse places. All these are the beginning of sorrows. Then shall they deliver you up to be afflicted and shall kill you: and you shall be hated of all the nations for my name's sake. And then many shall be offended, and shall betray one another, and shall hate one another. And many false prophets shall rise and deceive many. And because iniquity shall abound, the love of many shall wax cold. But he that shall endure to the end, the same shall be saved. And the gospel of the kingdom shall be preached in all the world for a witness unto all nations; and then shall the end come."

Jesus continued to teach in detail about the signs of his coming, as well as prophecies of the future laced with instruction in righteousness. There were concepts which many found difficult to comprehend. Many found it impossible to accept Jesus saying he would lay down his life for many and then take it up again. Peter had been sharply rebuked by the Lord for failing to accept it. No one was quite prepared for what was to come. Jesus knew, but little did the disciples know that this very evening plans were being laid against him.

They assembled together the chief priests, and the scribes, and the elders of the people, unto the palace of the high priest, who was called Caiaphas. They consulted that they might take Jesus by subtilty and kill him. But they said, "Not on the feast day, lest there be an uproar among the people."

Jesus and his disciples left Jerusalem to return to Bethany. As they walked, Jesus spoke:

"You know that after two days is the feast of the Passover, and the Son of man is betrayed to be crucified," he said as they walked. Everyone remained silent.

Now when Jesus was in Bethany, in the house of Simon the leper, there came unto him a woman having an alabaster box of very precious ointment, and poured it on his head, as he sat at meat. But when the disciples saw it, they had indignation, saying, "To what purpose is this waste? For this ointment might have been sold for much, and given to the poor."

When Jesus understood it, he said unto them, "Why do you trouble the woman? For she has wrought a good work upon me. For you shall have the poor always with you; but me you have not always. For in that she has poured this ointment on my body, she did it for my burial. Verily I say unto you, wheresoever this gospel shall be preached in the whole world, there shall also this, that this woman has done, be told for a memorial of her."

Later that night, *one of the twelve, Judas Iscariot, went unto the chief priests.*

He said unto them, "What will you give me, and I will deliver him unto you?" And they covenanted with him for thirty pieces of silver.

And from that time, he sought to betray him.

The caravan had made excellent progress throughout the day despite the way it began. The late afternoon sun cast a warm glow upon the hills on either side as they passed into Judea. Jason, Aegeus, and Orpheus had calculated the last time they stopped that they would be in Jerusalem tomorrow. The caravan was traveling upon the western side of the Jordan River Valley but had yet to rise in elevation. The plan was to reach the hills ahead and camp. Jason had been leading Alethea's camel so she could play her pipe, then suddenly Lukas rode up beside him with a look of alarm upon his face. Jason looked over at his friend.

"What is it, Lukas?" he asked as he saw Lukas look behind to the east.

"I just happened to look back, so I could see how far we had come. I don't think those are clouds," Lukas said while pointing to the east. Melina, Cassandra, and Orpheus rode up and stopped. Alethea looked back and gasped.

Jason shouted, "Aegeus, everyone stop!" The caravan came to a stop, and everyone looked back.

There, upon the eastern horizon was a dark mass which seemed to be getting larger. It appeared to be moving out of the southeast and approaching fast: it was a massive dust storm. They looked around quickly, and the closest hills were to the southwest, which appeared rocky and full of canyons. Aegeus pointed to them.

"Either we make it to those hills, or we attempt to shelter where we are," Aegeus said with some urgency.

"I don't want to be entombed here. Let us see how fast we can make it to those hills!" Jason shouted.

And so, the race against the dust storm was on. The hills looked rough. Jason, as well as others were praying for there to be a passage into the rocky hills. They appeared to overlook the Dead Sea. Many were shouting expressions of encouragement: "Were almost there! Trust God no matter the circumstance!" They reached the first rocky hills and cliffs, but the storm was almost upon them, as the wind was picking up. Many prayers went up. Suddenly, a canyon appeared before them, which seemed to transcend deep into the hills. The caravan traveled into the canyon, then it hit. Visibility went to almost nothing. Aegeus and Jason began shouting to bring the camels close together as the choking, blinding dust overwhelmed the caravan. They were not able to see, but detected they were climbing a bit in elevation.

Jason prayed aloud, as he shouted so all could hear, "Father, in the name of Jesus, deliver us from this filth!"

They pressed on. Nothing seemed to change for a while as they slowly moved into the rocky, craggy, landscape. The wind began to die down and the visibility began to improve. The caravan made it around a bend in the canyon, then the air became clear. Only wisps of dust remained, which were swirling about as they looked back at the bend. Everyone was there, as well as all of the pack animals. Some dismounted quickly, while others began praising God while still mounted. Everyone still wore their head protection, now colored like the rocks, as well as the rest of their clothing.

"Well, we can proceed ahead to see if we can find water. We won't be buried in here; at least I don't think so," Aegeus said as he looked around.

"It will be getting dark soon in this canyon," Jason said as he also looked around. "Can you imagine if it got dark while we were still in that dust?" he asked.

Lukas spoke, "That's how people are lost, Jason my friend; we are never lost, for we walk with God." Melina walked up to him, then smiled and embraced him.

Alethea and Calista walked up to the group and embraced their men while covered in dust. Orpheus and Cassandra stood facing each other, as they held hands and prayed. Lander and Belen knelt. Argus came running up and made a proclamation:

"I wasn't afraid, for I trusted God. I heard you, Uncle Jason, as you shouted in the dust storm. God knew we would be alright.

Trust God no matter the circumstance! This is all for a reason; God wanted us to stop here!" he shouted.

All of the dusty travelers smiled as they watched young Argus dance around. They gathered their senses, then dusted themselves off a bit and thanked God once again. Everyone mounted up and proceeded deeper into the rocky landscape. The caravan didn't make it very far before darkness descended early in the deep canyon. They decided to make camp among the rocks and rely on their water reserves. Wood for a fire appeared to be scarce, so Jason broke out two torches he carried to search for brush and anything that would burn. Anyone who had lamps brought them out as the darkness increased. Aegeus and Dimitri took a torch; Jason and Lukas took the other as the men went farther into the canyon to search for firewood and water. Alethea and Melina set about putting together an evening meal the best they could.

Peter was troubled as he attempted to fall asleep. His feelings of foreboding overtook his need of rest as he contemplated the future Jesus had spoken of. The world would pass into a season of severe wickedness; perilous times would come. Jesus had said, *'For as the lightning comes out of the east, and shines even unto the west; so shall also the coming of the Son of man be.'* It would be a period of great deception, and there would be no mistaking it. *'As the days of Noah were, so shall also the coming of the Son of man be,'* Jesus had said. Peter thought of the frightening days of Noah. *'And they knew not until the flood came and took them all away,'* he had said. When would these things be? The disciple of Jesus wrestled with all he had heard way into the night. Peter finally fell asleep, then had awful dreams about the tribulation Jesus had spoken of. He ended up sleeping much later into the morning than usual, then arose and joined the other disciples for the morning meal. Jesus came in after praying alone through the quiet morning.

Now the first day of the feast of unleavened bread the disciples came to Jesus, saying unto him, "Where will we prepare for you to eat the Passover?"

And he said, "Go into the city to such a man, and say unto him, The Master says, my time is at hand; I will keep the Passover at your house with my disciples."

And the disciples did as Jesus had appointed them; and they made ready the Passover. Now when evening had come, he sat down with the twelve.

And as they ate, he said, "Verily I say unto you, that one of you shall betray me."

And they were exceeding sorrowful, and began every one of them to say unto him, "Lord, is it I?"

And he answered and said, "He that dips his hand with me in the dish, the same shall betray me. The Son of man goes as it is written of him: but woe unto that man by whom the Son of man is betrayed! It had been good for that man if he had never been born."

Then Judas, which betrayed him, answered and said, "Master, is it I?"

He said unto him, "you have said."

And as they were eating, Jesus took bread, and blessed it, and broke it, and gave it to the disciples, and said, "Take, eat; this is my body." And then he took the cup, and gave thanks, and gave it to them, saying, "Drink all of it: For this is my blood of the new testament, which is shed for many for the remission of sins. But I say unto you, I will not drink henceforth of this fruit of the vine, until that day when I drink it new with you in my Father's Kingdom."

517

And when they had sung a hymn, they went out into the mount of Olives.

Then Jesus said unto them, "All of you shall be offended because of me this night: For it is written, I will smite the shepherd, and the sheep of the flock shall be scattered abroad. But after I have risen, I will go before you into Galilee."

Peter answered and said unto him, "Though all men shall be offended because of you, I will never be offended."

Jesus said unto him, "Verily I say unto you, that this night, before the cock crow, you shall deny me three times."

Peter said unto him, "Though I should die with you, yet I will not deny you." Likewise, also said all the disciples.

Jesus said unto them, "When I sent you without purse, and script, and shoes, lacked ye any thing?"

They said, "Nothing."

Then he said unto them, "But now, he that has a purse, let him take it, and likewise his script: and he that has no sword, let him sell his garment, and buy one. For I say unto you, that this that is written must yet be accomplished in me, and he was reckoned among the transgressors: for the things concerning me have an end."

And they said, "Lord, behold, here are two swords."

Jesus said unto them, "It is enough."

Then came Jesus with them unto a place called Gethsemane, and he said unto his disciples, "Sit here, while I go and pray yonder." And he took with him Peter and the two sons of Zebedee, and began to be sorrowful and very heavy. Then he said unto them, "My soul is exceeding sorrowful, even unto death: tarry here, and watch with me." And he went a little farther, and fell on his face, and prayed, saying, "O my Father, if it be possible, let this cup pass from me: nevertheless, not as I will, but as you will." And he came unto the disciples, and found them asleep, and said unto Peter, "What, could you not watch with me one hour? Watch and pray, that you enter not into temptation: the spirit indeed is willing, but the flesh is weak." He went away again the second time, and prayed, saying, "O my Father, if this cup may not pass away from me, except I drink it, your will be done." And he came and found them asleep again: for their eyes were heavy. And he left them, and went away again, and prayed a third time, saying the same words. Then he came to his disciples, and said to them, "Sleep on now, and take your rest: behold, the hour is at hand, and the Son of man is betrayed into the hands of sinners. Rise, let us be going: behold, he is at hand that has betrayed me."

And while he yet spoke, lo, Judas, one of the twelve, came, and with him a great multitude with swords and staves, from the chief priests and elders of the people. Now he that betrayed him gave them a sign, saying, "Whomsoever I shall kiss, that same is he: hold him fast." And forthwith he came to Jesus, and said, "Hail master;" and kissed him.

Jesus said unto him, "Friend, wherefore have you come?"

Then they came, and laid hands on Jesus, and took him. And behold, one of them which were with Jesus stretched out his hand, and drew his sword, and struck a servant of the high priest's, and cut off his ear.

Then Jesus said unto him, "Put up again your sword into his place: for all they that take the sword shall perish with the sword. Do you not think that I could pray to my Father, and he shall presently give me twelve legions of angels? But how then shall the scriptures be fulfilled, that it must be?" In that same hour, Jesus said to the multitudes, "Are you come out as against a thief with swords and staves to take me? I sat daily with you teaching in the temple, and you laid no hold on me." But all this was done, that the scriptures might be fulfilled.

Then all the disciples forsook him and fled.

Jason awoke to find Aegeus and Orpheus sitting by the fire, so he went out to join them. It was early morning, although the sunlight had yet to bring any significant light into the deep canyon. The men were discussing the trip and re-calculating the expected arrival in Jerusalem. They didn't know if the dust storm was still raging or not. The scant firewood they were able to obtain from dead brush had all but run out. The need for water made itself evident as well, after watering the camels. They were about to walk back through the canyon to see if the dust storm had ceased, when a man approached leading an ass loaded with a pack and was coming from within the rocky hills. The three men watched as the man uncovered his head and moved closer. He was an elder man; with long gray hair and beard, wearing a traditional Jewish outer garment and walking with a staff. He appeared a little ragged but had a very friendly expression as he drew closer.

"Shalom!" he shouted in a gravelly voice; he looked even older than Orpheus.

Jason stood up, then the other two followed. "Greetings. Who are you?" Jason asked in a friendly way, in Greek.

"I am Ehud. You're Greek; I speak Greek very well. I saw the smoke from your fire, so I came to see if you need any help," the old man said while smiling.

Jason responded, "I am Jason of Gadara, and this is Aegeus and Orpheus, also of Gadara. We were traveling to Jerusalem but ended up here due to the dust storm."

Ehud spoke, "Ahh yes, I've heard of you. You have been touched by the Master's hand. You shall be most welcome among my people."

"Do you know if the storm has passed?" Aegeus asked as they approached the man and his animal.

"Yes, it has," Ehud responded. "We live up high upon these rocky hills. You're not the first to take refuge in these canyons. I am of the Essenes: we are a Jewish sect committed to preserving the word of God," he proclaimed.

Jason gestured to the fire and they sat. Jason smiled at the old man and was curious about what he had said. "Sounds like you have a blessed vocation. I too, as well as many others in our city have begun to study the Hebrew scriptures. There is a growing hunger among my people for the truth. I believe my wife and I saw your settlement once, while atop Mount Nebo," he said.

The old man spoke, "Ah, yes, I believe you can see it from up there. You're traveling to Jerusalem? We are all from there originally. We fled Jerusalem long ago, for we disagreed with the Pharisees and the Sadducees. We have separated ourselves so that we might follow God our way."

Jason said, "Yes, I can understand why you have separated yourselves. We have encountered the Pharisee's many times."

"We're going to Jerusalem to seek Jesus," Orpheus said.

Ehud smiled and spoke, "He is the Son of God. He speaks the truth and opposes the Pharisees. There was another holy one named John; I've heard he was killed, so sad. He lived with us for a time when he was young."

"Is there any water nearby?" Aegeus asked. "We were trying to get to Jerusalem for the Passover to meet Jesus while he's there.

We need to get back to our journey as soon as possible so we don't miss him. I think we're about a day behind now," he said.

Ehud replied, "Yes, at least. There is water straight ahead in this canyon; you would have found it had you continued in. There's a spring that pours out of the rocks and flows for a bit along the canyon floor until it disappears into the ground again. It's not too far from here." Ehud looked around. Others were awakening and were curious about the unexpected guest.

Jason and Lukas, as well as Argus, then took three camels with all of the waterskins and headed out further to obtain the water Ehud had spoken of. Everyone else woke up and introduced themselves, then began preparing a morning meal. All of the travelers enjoyed a friendly visit with Ehud as they ate, then began packing up for another long day of travel. Jason ended up having an extended conversation with the old man privately as everyone prepared to depart. Jason was torn, as he had a great desire to meet with Jesus but wanting more time to engage a very wise and knowledgeable man. He assured Ehud that he would return someday. Everyone said goodbye to their new friend as they mounted their camels and headed out of the canyon. The caravan emerged from the deep rocky gorge into another clear spring morning. The only remnant of the dust storm was a lot of dust upon the ground, which was stirred up readily by the camel's broad feet. Everyone secured their head protection as they proceeded west toward Jerusalem.

It was very early the next morning in the courtyard of the extravagant palace of the High Priest Caiaphas. Peter kept his head covered as he moved about trying to keep himself warm by the fires for the servants. They were all out in the courtyard due to the disturbance of the interrogation and beating of Jesus. Peter knew what was going on, but he didn't know what to do. Despite trying to conceal himself the servants knew he didn't belong. *A woman came unto him, saying, "You were also with Jesus of Galilee." But he denied it, saying, "I know not what you're saying." And when he went out to the porch, another maid saw him, and said unto them that were there, "This fellow was also with Jesus of Nazareth." And again, he denied with an oath, "I do not know the man." And after a while they that stood by came to him, and said to Peter, "Surely you are one of them; for your speech betrays you." Then he began to curse and swear, saying, "I know not the man!" And immediately the cock crew. And Peter remembered the word of Jesus, which said unto him, 'Before the cock crow, you will deny me three times.' And he went out, and wept bitterly.*

When the morning had come, all of the chief priests and elders of the people took counsel against Jesus to put him to death: And when they had bound him, they led him away and delivered him to Pontius Pilate the governor.

Then Judas, which had betrayed him, when he saw that he was condemned, repented himself, and brought again the thirty pieces of silver to the chief priests and elders, saying, "I have sinned in that I have betrayed the innocent blood." And they said "What is that to us? You see to that." And he cast down the pieces of silver in the temple, and departed, and went and hanged himself.

And the chief priests took the silver pieces, and said, "It is not lawful for us to put them into the treasury, because it is the price of blood." And they took counsel, and bought with them the potter's field, to bury strangers in. Wherefore that field was called, 'The field of blood,' unto this day.

Jesus refused to speak in his own defense. The scripture had to be fulfilled. The ultimate sacrifice had to be made, for the sake of all mankind.

Almost two more days of travel, and the caravan was, at last, within sight of Jerusalem. The great walls and gleaming temple could be seen at a distance, for they reflected the warm glow of the afternoon sun. The caravan had joined in with many who were traveling to the city, as they approached from the northeast. It was early afternoon, but a strange darkness fell; an un-natural coolness set in, which stopped them for some time. They had endured the dust storm, but now the premature darkness spawned foreboding among the travelers. Jason thought about the premonition he had of an upcoming challenge...what was it? Was it a challenge to their faith? A physical challenge or danger? All in the caravan were quietly waiting and hoping the darkness would soon pass. It seemed to go on for a long time. The daylight finally began to return, and everyone was relieved, but still somewhat fearful. No one understood the meaning of the event but took it as a sign from God.

Then, as if the darkness had not been terrifying enough a violent earthquake began to shake, which caused rocks to tumble and dust to stir up around them. Fissures opened here and there. Aegeus, Jason, and the others held onto the camels to keep them from panicking and running off. A couple of the pack animals did run off. This went on for several long moments, then finally subsided. Alethea ran up to Jason with a terrified expression upon her face and embraced him. The same played out among the others. Everyone was silent as they looked around. No one had a response as they looked at each other.

"I don't know what just happened, but we came to seek Jesus," Jason spoke in a loud voice while trying to overcome the fear. "He would have an answer, if he's still here. Come, let us complete our journey!" he shouted.

They were still collecting themselves from the wild event, then everyone agreed and mounted their camels once again. Lander and Belen volunteered to chase down the two camels that had run away. Aegeus nodded and said they would wait for them at the Damascus gate, then quickly explained where it was. He had mentioned that he was familiar with services for the camels near there. The two rode off to the south, for the camels had run in that direction.

The caravan proceeded southwest toward the City of Jerusalem. The imposing walls and the gleaming temple were quite a sight to behold. The caravan neared the city, and Aegeus chose to veer to the south at a crossroad to approach the north side of the city walls. They followed the road outside of the walls; everyone was excited. Cassandra had never seen Jesus and mentioned many times throughout the journey how she longed to look upon his face. Jason was very excited, for he had not seen him since his deliverance other than in dreams. They were all hoping Jesus was still in the city, or nearby. They were now traveling along the northern wall, as the caravan followed the road to the Damascus gate. There appeared to be a large rocky escarpment ahead by the road.

Aegeus and Calista veered off the road, then the caravan suddenly stopped. Jason, Alethea, Lukas, and Melina rode up alongside them. Aegeus had seen it first; he wanted to prepare everyone for the ghastly sight ahead. The Romans had crucified three men right alongside the road at the base of the escarpment. Aegeus, Jason, and the others spoke for a moment, then Jason rode back to warn the remainder of the caravan. He recommended the women cover their faces. He especially warned Argus to look away as they passed. Everyone was prepared, so they proceeded slowly. Once the caravan arrived at the site everyone looked away, except one. Jason looked up and was immediately overwhelmed. The other men sensed his reaction and looked as well. Jason quickly dismounted, then staggered up to the edge of the road.

"Aegeus...get the women out of here!" he shouted with a cracking voice, for he was unable to contain his emotion. Lukas and Orpheus were instantly by his side.

Everyone looked despite their efforts. A large number of travelers upon the road walked by with indifference, as some gawked, then continued about their business. There were a few Roman soldiers standing guard over the men, as well as a handful of people mourning at the foot of the crosses. Jason staggered across the road and was bumping into people as if he was drunken. Everyone in the caravan was weeping uncontrollably. Jason looked up and saw signs sitting in niches of the rocky escarpment. There were three; written in Aramaic, Greek, and Latin: *Jesus of Nazareth, King of the Jews*. He looked up at Jesus, as he hung upon the cross. He appeared to be dead; he had been beaten almost beyond recognition. Jason noticed a huge crack running down the escarpment right through the base of the cross. The crack was typical of those that appeared during the earthquake.

To the right of Jesus was someone Jason recognized also. It was the thief he had ministered to many months before, Rasmus. He was still barely alive. He opened his eyes, then smiled at Jason before he passed out. Jason was horrified, as two of the soldiers came up to the men, and one carried an iron bar. They broke the legs of Rasmus, then the other man. They came to Jesus, but the soldiers determined he was already dead. Instead of breaking his legs a soldier pierced the side of Jesus with a spear to make sure he was dead. The Romans wanted to hasten their demise; he overheard them say they were to remove the bodies before sundown. Jason again looked upon Jesus. He was in a state of shock. He saw the open wound upon his side as blood and fluid ran out, then down the cross and into the crack in the rock. He saw the demonstrated cruelty of the Romans, as they had forced some kind of thorny band upon Jesus's head.

Jason couldn't endure anymore and collapsed. He came around some time later. Orpheus and Lukas were there, and they had poured a bit of water upon his face. He looked up at his friends; their solemn, tear-streaked faces trying to understand. Jason had regained consciousness, and one thing became apparent in his mind: this was not possible. There was something here more than meets the eye.

"Maybe we should just go home, Jason," Orpheus said gently to Jason as he lifted his head and put some cloth beneath it.

Lukas was still sobbing and shouted, "I don't know what to believe anymore!" He asked, "What do we do now, Jason?"

Jason rose up. It appeared the others had ridden away to escape the horrific scene. He looked at his two closest friends and said, "You don't understand. He cannot die...it's impossible. I know who he is, and you two should as well." He then asked, "Where are the others?"

"Aegeus took them all to the Damascus Gate," Orpheus replied. "They're going to wait there, for us, as well as Lander and Belen," he said as he struggled to refrain from weeping.

"I have something within my spirit ever since I awoke, and it is to wait!" Jason exclaimed as he scrambled to his feet. "I'm staying right here!" he shouted with great determination.

The light was quickly diminishing as evening approached. The Romans were beginning the process of taking the now dead men down from the crosses. There appeared to be two men showing an interest in the body of Jesus; they wore costly garments and their servants were present. The body of Jesus was laid in a traditional burial shroud, then wrapped and taken away. Jason, Lukas, and Orpheus followed at a distance. They observed the servants carry the body into a garden area, where there were rock-cut tombs. One of the tombs was lit with men around it, as they seemed to be expediting the burial. Jason and his friends watched as the body of Jesus was placed in the tomb. The servants rolled the huge, round stone over the entrance, then drove a large iron pin into the rock to lock the stone in place.

Jason looked at his friends and said, "Let us assemble once again with the others, then I'm going to return...."

Epilogue

Alethea continuously looked to the west, while praying for Jason and the other men to return. The sun was setting. In Alethea's clouded mind she hoped Jason would return to share it with her. The thought would only bring more uncontrollable weeping. She sat with the other three women on a cover near the resting camels. Aegeus sat a little way off with his sons. Everyone was in a state of shock. Alethea thought of how this had been her and Jason's favorite time of the day. Everything seemed to have changed. She fought to avoid the memory of Jesus and the other two men hanging on the crosses, which brought gut-wrenching agony. Jesus had become the foundation of all their lives. She felt lost as if the dust storm had enveloped them, or the earthquake had swallowed them. Melina suddenly embraced her, and she responded in kind as she desperately needed someone to hold on to. No one spoke, for there were no words to speak. All seemed hopeless. Calista and Cassandra were holding each other as well while sobbing. Aegeus walked over to the women after grabbing a waterskin from one of the camels.

"Would anyone like some water?" he asked as he desperately tried to bring a small level of comfort to the women.

Cassandra asked Aegeus, "Could you go and get Orpheus and the other men? They've been gone for a long time, and I'm worried about them...how long will they be gone?" She was disoriented, then broke down in heavy weeping. Aegeus knelt and patted her back as Calista continued embracing her.

Argus and Dimitri walked over. Argus had been crying, but now both young men were expressionless and quiet. Argus sat by his mother, then began crying again as Calista turned and embraced him.

Aegeus looked at Cassandra. "I'll take Dimitri with me, then we'll see if we can find Jason and the others," he said with a need to do something other than wait.

"Let me come too," Cassandra said as she arose. She needed to do something as well, and in her mind this level of desperation called for action.

Aegeus nodded in agreement as he embraced Cassandra, then knelt to Calista and Argus. He said, "We're going to take a walk. Keep an eye out for Lander and Belen, for it will be dark soon." Calista nodded while holding young Argus as they both wept.

He looked upon Alethea and Melina asking, "Do either of you want to go with us?" Alethea was sobbing upon Melina's shoulder. Melina shook her head, then bowed and began weeping again also.

Aegeus, Dimitri, and Cassandra slowly walked away from the plaza outside of the Damascus gate and toward the escarpment by the road. It was twilight, but Aegeus could see that the crosses had been taken down; he gave thanks to God. They reached the road, then Aegeus looked around and stopped for a moment. He could see three figures approaching: it was Jason, Lukas, and Orpheus. Cassandra saw them too and took off running. Aegeus stood beside Dimitri and gave thanks to God once again.

"What do we do now, Aegeus?" Dimitri asked.

"I suppose we go home. We came to follow Jesus...but they've killed him. What's left?" Aegeus replied as he watched Cassandra embrace the men in the distance with tears streaming down his face. He then said, "I think there is something left: we have each other."

They waited until the four walked up, then Aegeus and Dimitri embraced their friends. Jason and the others looked solemn but were not weeping.

Aegeus asked, "How are you feeling, my friend?" He placed his hand upon Jason's shoulder.

Jason responded, "Like there's a sword in my stomach twisting, but I'm filled with curiosity. Now I know what the challenge to us was. This is why I asked everyone to pray. This isn't over, Aegeus. We saw where they laid him. The three of us are going to return to watch...he cannot die."

Aegeus was shocked. His friend Jason was speaking irrationally. Aegeus had never known him to be so, since his deliverance. He just patted his back and realized Jason was heavily traumatized. He spoke gently, "Whatever you say, Jason; your wife is longing for you. Let us return to them."

Jason nodded while looking at Aegeus and knowing he didn't share the faith he was walking in. He said nothing more as they walked back toward the city gate to join the others.

Darkness had fallen. Aegeus, Jason, and the others approached the camels as they could see a glow where the women were. A benevolent stranger from within the city had brought out a lamp and placed it by them. There was still no sign of Lander and Belen, or the missing camels. Unfortunately, one of those camels had most of their food supplies, but no one felt like eating. Alethea and Melina jumped up and ran to Jason and Lukas. They just stood holding each other for some time.

"Perhaps we should go looking for Lander, Belen, and the camels," Dimitri said to Aegeus as he was looking toward the road.

Aegeus responded sharply, "Follow that through, Dimitri. You want to do something, but what then? Jason and Lukas come looking for us? Then Orpheus comes looking for them? Leaving the women alone? We wait here until Lander and Belen return." Dimitri said no more, as Aegeus seemed very irritated; an unwelcome symptom of grief. Aegeus took a moment to collect himself. "I'm sorry Dimitri; just sit and wait," he said calmly. Dimitri patted his back as the two sat together.

Lander and Belen arrived after some time. Belen led the way carrying a lamp, and they had recovered both camels. Aegeus and Dimitri quickly assisted, as they hobbled the camels and brought them to rest.

"We found one right away, but the other took some time," Belen said as he dismounted.

Aegeus told them what had happened. They expressed disbelief at first, then both began to weep and sat down near Jason and Alethea. Jason told them it wasn't over, but neither of the men understood what he was trying to say.

Aegeus looked over the wayward camels and everything seemed intact. "We should find a place for the night, for it's getting late," he said as he looked toward the city walls and the gate.

"I don't want to sleep in this city, Aegeus," Jason proclaimed as he followed Aegeus's glance toward the walls of Jerusalem. Many had the same sentiment as it turned out.

Orpheus spoke, "Let us go find a place to camp, Aegeus. We don't have to go far, as long as it's away from here. I know of a place just to the north where there is water, if my memory serves me correctly, and it's not far."

Jason pulled out two torches, then Lukas produced one from his pack as well. The idea helped everyone, for the activity gave them something to do. They had waited a long time in emotional agony. Before long they were mounted, and the caravan started back down the road from where they came. Orpheus and Cassandra led the way with one of the torches as they left the road and headed north. It was a dark night, and difficult to see at a distance. The grief-stricken group traveled a little way, then Orpheus shouted, "Straight ahead!"

They arrived at a grove of trees next to a large, grassy meadow which was faintly visible in the light of the torches. The caravan stopped, then everyone attempted to dismount in the dim flaming light. The moon was now rising which added a bit of visibility. Dimitri immediately knelt with his fire kit and started a small fire. The camp was set up quickly, as everyone seemed to be finding comfort in staying busy. The large meadow had plenty of room for six tents, as well as a good-sized area to bed down the camels; it was a good campsite. A small brook just within the trees provided the camels with plenty of water. Some dried fish and bread were brought out, but no one was interested in eating. The activity died down, and everyone was quiet.

Orpheus broke the silence and said, "I've camped here many times over the years. Been a long time. Near enough to the city to walk, but it's not in the city. I'm glad no one decided to build a house here; it would be a good place for one."

Cassandra smiled at her husband, then kissed his cheek. "Keep talking, that's what we need," she said.

"I'm sorry...I don't have a lot to say," Orpheus responded with a poor attempt to smile.

Jason was hesitant to say anything. No one knew, but he was burning within his heart to return to the tomb where Jesus lay. He gazed into the fire, then looked upon the flickering glow reflected from the faces of his friends and family. He didn't want any of them to think he had lost his mind. They probably would, if they knew what he was thinking. He held his peace while thinking of ways to gather information. "I think we should try to find some of his disciples, so we might find out what happened," he said. "Aegeus, you know the city. Could you go in tomorrow and see what you can learn about what happened?" he asked. "Lukas, Orpheus and I are going out tomorrow as well to ask around," he said while being intentionally vague about his own plans.

"Yes, of course. We'll go as a family. We enjoyed ourselves the last time we were in Jerusalem; not so much this time. Yes, we'll go and see what we can find out," Aegeus said as he gave Jason a half smile. He had Calista on one side and Argus on the other snuggling up to him.

Lukas and Melina sat a little way off from the fire as they were having a private conversation with Dimitri. Lander and Belen were the quietest of the group and scarcely said anything since they received the news.

Lander spoke while staring into the fire, "I think Belen and I are going back to Gerasa tomorrow. We want to come to Gadara sometime soon after things have settled down. We hope to visit you all in happier times."

"Yeah, Lander's right," Belen added. "Too much sorrow. We're just an extra burden upon you at this point, but we're glad we were of some assistance to you in the confusion of the earthquake. This is just too much for us; we just want to go home," he said.

"I understand," Jason said as he stood and walked over to Lander and Belen. They embraced, then Jason looked over at Alethea. "I'm exhausted; I blacked out for a bit back there and it took a lot out of me. I think I'm going into the tent to pray until I can fall asleep," he said.

"I'll join you," Alethea said as she got up to accompany her husband. She lit a small lamp from the fire, then the two offered warm gestures to the others and disappeared into their tent.

Jason sat instead of laying down, once inside. Alethea sat also while looking at her husband, then she began to weep again. Jason touched her face and smiled. "I need to talk with you. There are many here who don't understand," he said while almost whispering.

Alethea looked at him curiously and responded in a whispering voice, "What is there to talk about Jason? There's no one to follow...we should go home."

"Please, dear Alethea, for you must listen to me and believe," Jason said as he looked into Alethea's eyes, "Jesus is not dead; at least not permanently. He cannot die. I've been thinking about it all; there's something going on here and it's something extraordinary. Do you remember the report we heard from Theophanes? How Jesus raised Lazarus from the dead after he had been in the tomb for four days?" Alethea nodded with tears in her eyes. Jason continued, "He was demonstrating something; he waited until there was no question that Lazarus was, in fact, dead. He had begun to decompose. He lives just to the east of here; anyway, no man has the authority to take the life of Jesus. He lays his life down only if he does so of his own choosing. Listen to me, Alethea my wife, for I'm speaking from knowledge. He has the authority to take his life up again. Yes, he was a man...but he is the Son of God. He and the Father are one." He looked very seriously at Alethea.

"Jason, do you realize what you're saying?" Alethea asked while looking at him very curiously.

"Yeah, I know exactly what I'm saying," Jason said as he put his hands upon Alethea's shoulders and looked straight into her eyes. "There's more. This is the Passover. A sacrificial lamb is offered in the temple for the remission of sins on the Passover. I stood at the cross on which Jesus died. The earthquake had opened a crack upon that escarpment the crosses were in front of. It traveled down right across the base of his cross. The Romans left a deep wound upon the side of Jesus, and there was a large amount of blood and fluid, perhaps water, that ran out of him down into the earth. I believe that Jesus offered himself up to be the ultimate sacrifice for all mankind. He suffered immensely at the hands of the Romans; he did it for us: ALL OF US! The scriptures bear witness to it, although it never made sense to me until now. This is the challenge I spoke of; somehow, I had a sense of what was coming. I passed out at the foot of the cross, when I came around there was a word in my mind: *wait*. Alethea, I've always known who he is. I'm telling you, if he didn't want to die legions of angels would have laid waste to the city. He will rise again; I'm suspecting within three days," Jason said and then stopped while awaiting a response from his wife.

Alethea gazed down while listening to all Jason had told her. She wiped the tears from her eyes, then looked up at her husband with a solemn expression for a long moment. Suddenly, she smiled a huge smile, then embraced Jason.

Morning came, and the warm sunlight was most welcome. Jason and Lukas emerged from their tents almost at the same time. It appeared that Lander and Belen had already left, for their tent was gone.

"They must have left at the crack of dawn. Can't blame them," Lukas commented as he stretched by the remnants of the smoldering fire.

"There's nothing we could have told them to comfort them...yet," Jason said as he threw some wood near where the fire had been. He then knelt to blow upon the embers.

"So today we wait, eh Jason?" Lukas asked. "I'm ready to go back now, but we should have a good morning meal first," he added.

Jason said, "Yes, I'm in agreement with you. I think everyone will wake up hungry this morning, for we've had nothing since that small mid-day meal yesterday."

Orpheus was the next one to emerge and spoke, "I see you two are ready to go back. I'm looking forward to a quiet day; at least I hope it's quiet."

"Are you sure you don't mind staying?" Jason asked his friend.

Orpheus replied, "Well, everyone else has plans, and someone needs to watch over the camp. Cassandra's alright with it. We're going through some of the scriptures today, so that I might point out a few things to her."

Lukas said, "Melina still has her doubts, but she's coming with us."

The morning wore on, and it was probably the quietest morning meal ever. Aegeus and his family left to go into Jerusalem soon after. Jason, Lukas, Alethea, and Melina walked to the garden tomb. They were very surprised to find a handful of Roman soldiers guarding it. The two couples found a fairly comfortable place to hold their vigil at some distance, which was concealed by trees and shrubs. Alethea and Melina were talking between themselves, and soon Melina was seen smiling a bit. By afternoon Jason's curiosity got the better of him, as he and Lukas approached the Roman Guard. They were just sitting around while trying to pass the time in any way they could. Jason sniffed the air as they approached, which caused Lukas to grin a little. The soldiers seemed to welcome a little conversation with a couple of passing strangers.

"Greetings. Are they keeping you busy?" Jason asked in Greek, but prepared to speak in Latin if there was no response.

"Yeah, very busy," one of them replied while sitting against the rock face the tomb had been carved in. The others looked on, as they scrutinized both of them a bit. "Who am I addressing?" he asked.

"I am Jason of Gadara. This is my friend, Lukas," Jason replied.

The guard jumped up, "You're Jason of Gadara?" he asked. "I've heard of you! Show us your arms!" the soldier requested with excitement, and a bit of rudeness.

Jason smiled and pulled back his sleeves revealing his scars.

"You won your freedom in a contest of battle near our eastern camp," the soldier stated, then translated into Latin for the others. They all smiled at Jason and Lukas. "What brings you here?" he asked.

"Curiosity. We came to inquire about this *Jesus* who was crucified yesterday; why are you guarding his tomb?" Jason asked while trying to get information.

The guard replied, "Oh, yeah, we're guarding it because the Jewish Pharisees are concerned someone will try to steal the body. They think his followers will claim he rose from the dead, or some such nonsense."

"Interesting," Jason replied as he attempted to imply that he was indifferent about the whole affair. "What do you think of that?" he asked.

"I think it's an easy assignment," the soldier responded. "Someone may try to steal that body, then we can fill another one or two of these tombs!" he said while smiling, then translated to the others and they all chuckled.

"Do you ever get warm wearing all that metal?" Lukas asked. Jason winced.

"Yeah, a little," the soldier responded with a slight grin. "Cold in the winter too," he added with a curious expression. He was amused.

Jason just looked at Lukas with raised eyebrows. He went on for a few moments engaging in meaningless small talk with the soldier, then he and Lukas went their way. They returned to Alethea and Melina and shared what they had learned. The day proceeded very slowly. They knew their Lord was just beyond the rock barrier they were staring at, but it was incredibly boring. Jason began to envy Orpheus and Cassandra, for he knew they were looking through his scrolls.

Some time went by, then Jason asked Alethea, "Do you remember the man I ministered to a few months ago while we were camping on our way to Gerasa? He left right after you awakened."

Alethea responded, "Yeah, the thief who snuck in to steal from us. You told me his name, but I can't remember."

Jason spoke as he recalled the memory, "Rasmus was his name. We prayed together after I ministered to him. He told me he had prayed that he would meet Jesus before he died."

"What made you remember that now, Jason?" Alethea asked.

Jason looked at her for a moment, then said, "He was hanging on the cross next to Jesus. I approached and he was still alive. He opened his eyes and saw me. With as much agony as he was experiencing...he smiled at me." He then recalled a scripture from the Prophet Isaiah and recited it:

"He had poured out his soul unto death, and he was numbered with the transgressors, and he bare the sin of many, and made intercession for the transgressors."

Alethea teared up and embraced Jason. Lukas and Melina moved in and huddled with them. The day continued to pass slowly. The late afternoon sun began to transform the tomb and surrounding stone with increasing yellow, then amber, and later Auburn tones. The soldiers, at least, provided something other than stone to watch; they walked around, told stories and jokes, played some kind of game with small pieces, and even a couple of mock swordfights. Jason wasn't very impressed. Evening approached. The soldiers started a small fire and had torches. Jason thought to himself that he could watch all night; the others took a dismal view of the idea. Jason agreed to leave, but with the understanding he may return later. He wanted to know what Aegeus had found out.

Orpheus and Cassandra had spent the entire day reading scriptures. Orpheus had read portions of the Prophet Isaiah:

"But he was wounded for our transgressions, he was bruised for our iniquities: the chastisement of our peace was upon him, and with his stripes we are healed. All we like sheep have gone astray; we have turned every one to his own way, and the Lord has laid on him the iniquity of us all. He was oppressed, and he was afflicted, yet he opened not his mouth: he is brought as a lamb to the slaughter, and as a sheep, before her shearers are dumb, so he opened not his mouth."

Orpheus then brought out a small scroll: the same scroll he had given to Jason while he was in prison. "I have pondered this many times; yesterday I realized what it was. This is from the twenty-second Psalm of David, and it was written a thousand years ago:

"My God, my God, why have you forsaken me? Why are you so far from helping me, and from the words of my roaring? O my God, I cry in the daytime, but you hear not; and in the night season, and am not silent. But you are holy, you that inhabit the praises of Israel. Our fathers trusted in you: they trusted, and you delivered them. They cried unto you, and were delivered: they trusted in you, and were not confounded. But I am a worm, and no man; a reproach of men, and despised of the people. All they that see me laugh me to scorn: they shoot out the lip, they shake the head, saying, He trusted on the Lord that he would deliver him, seeing he delighted in him. But you are he that took me out of the womb: you made me hope when I was upon my mother's breasts. I

was cast upon you from the womb: you are my God from my mother's belly. Be not far from me; for trouble is near; for there is none to help. Many bulls have encompassed me: strong bulls of Bashan have beset me round. They gaped upon me with their mouths, as a ravening and a roaring lion. I am poured out like water, and my bones are out of joint: my heart is like wax; it has melted in the midst of my bowels. My strength is dried up like a potsherd; and my tongue cleaves to my jaws; and you have brought me into the dust of death. For dogs have compassed me: the assembly of the wicked have inclosed me: they pierced my hands and my feet. I may tell all my bones: they look and stare upon me. They part my garments among them, and cast lots upon my vesture. But be not far from me, O Lord: O my strength, hasten to help me."

Orpheus couldn't continue as he became a bit emotional. Cassandra embraced him until they heard footsteps approach.

Aegeus and his family returned, then Orpheus shared some of the prophecies with them. It was getting late and they were getting concerned about Jason and the others. The two couples showed up not long after.

Jason greeted everyone, then asked Aegeus what they had found out.

Aegeus explained, "From what I gathered the High Priest Caiaphas had Jesus arrested following some very public demonstrations against them and the temple. The high priest's men seized him, then took him to Pontius Pilate, the Roman governor. The Pharisees incited a large crowd of people to demand his crucifixion despite Pilate wanting to release him. He gave the people a choice of releasing a murderer or Jesus; the people chose the murderer. The strangest thing I heard was that the earthquake struck as the blood of the sacrificial lamb was being offered in the temple. The word is that there was damage within the temple, and the heavy curtain in front of their inner holy chamber was ripped from top to bottom. We heard many conflicting stories, but that is what I believe happened. The disciples of Jesus seem to have scattered, and no one knows of their whereabouts."

Jason shared, "We found out that the tomb Jesus was laid in is being guarded by the Romans. The Sanhedrin fears the body of Jesus will be stolen by his disciples, so they can claim he rose from the dead."

"Is everything going to be alright, Uncle Jason?" Argus asked as he stood in front of him.

Jason grabbed him and embraced the young man. He said, "Yes, young Argus, everything will be alright. The wickedness of this world is fighting back right now, that's all. We will win in the end. Always remember…trust God no matter the circumstance." Jason continued to hold his young friend.

After the meal, Jason asked Lukas privately, "Did you get any sleep last night?"

"No," Lukas replied. "Did you?" he asked.

"No. Alethea and Melina want to stay and sleep," Jason said. "We could return to watch, and take turns sleeping," he added.

"Orpheus and Cassandra coming?" Lukas asked.

"No, they're very tired," Jason informed him. "They want to come tomorrow. Everyone's very tired. We wait until everybody goes into their tents, then we head back, understood?" he asked.

Lukas nodded as he yawned. They stepped back to the fire to join the others. The quiet fellowship with contagious yawning coaxed everyone to their tents a bit early. Jason found himself alone by the fire. He walked over to Lukas and Melina's tent and heard the unmistakable sound of Lukas snoring. Jason just smiled to himself, then went in to kiss a sleeping Alethea and headed back to the tomb.

Upon arriving, Jason saw that the soldiers were mostly sleeping with only two watching. He thought to himself they were doing what He and Lukas were going to do. Jason thought, perhaps, Lukas would sleep awhile, then show up and let him sleep. He chuckled to himself and realized he would likely be alone. Jason was glad he had brought a blanket and wore a heavy outer garment, as the night was chilly. He was wearing only a short Roman tunic underneath. Once he got warm and as comfortable as possible, that was it....

Jason suddenly found himself in a vast cave; a familiar one. He instantly knew he was dreaming; he wasn't sleepy. He decided to stand and wait for he knew a confrontation was imminent. The side table was there as before, so Jason helped himself to a goblet. He was right, this wine wasn't as good as his. Sure enough, the dark figure came up from the depths of the earth. It came close, and Jason was, once again face to face with an empty garment.

"It's been a while," Jason said as he looked into the darkness. "What do you have to say this time?" he asked.

"What do you mean? He's dead...and the whole thing is lost!" The figure said with an aggravated, deep, assertive voice. "What are you going to do now, Gadarene?" it inquired.

"I'm going to wait," Jason said with a voice of confidence that infuriated the spirit. "You think you've won some kind of victory? All you've done is seal your own fate. You no longer hold any real power over us, for you've been defeated," Jason declared.

"He's dead!" the spirit yelled out in it's deep, echoing voice. "His movement is dead! His disciples have scattered!" it shouted.

Jason spoke an acknowledgment, "Yeah, Jesus died, and in doing so he defeated death. He's coming, even now. He's coming to send the likes of you into the abyss!"

Suddenly, a great earthquake hit the cave. The evil spirit was frantic as it ran around screaming. Huge rocks began to fall. Jason leaned against the table while feeling the movement from the earthquake. He smiled as he took another sip of wine....

Jason awoke slowly, as Lukas pushed his shoulder vigorously and shouted at him, "Wake up! Wake up, Jason! Wake up!"

Jason finally managed to open his eyes and saw that it appeared to be mid-morning; he must have been out for some time. He instantly looked out toward the tomb and was immediately and thoroughly shocked. The soldiers were gone, and the huge, round stone covering the tomb entrance was rolled to the side. He looked at Lukas, as he appeared to be as shocked as him.

"I'm sorry, Jason. Melina and Alethea will be here shortly; we were all so tired! Forgive me! We missed it, Jason, we missed it!" Lukas exclaimed. He was sorrowful but very excited.

"Calm down, my friend. Let us go see if we can find out what happened," Jason said as he stood, then the two walked toward the tomb. They were amazed that there was no one around. Jason and Lukas approached the tomb and Jason stepped inside. looking to his right, he saw a stone slab against the back wall that appeared to have been hastily enlarged; Jesus was a tall man. It was empty. Lukas followed Jason in and looked around. Just an empty tomb. They both walked out and looked for anyone who could describe what had happened. They both saw him at the same time; he was sitting a little to the right of the tomb at the base of the stone face. Both men recognized him right away, as he wore his outer garment with his head covered: it was the stranger! Jason and Lukas looked at each other, then slowly approached him.

The stranger spoke, "There are others about, but I thought you both would appreciate someone you know. Do not feel bad, for you needed a rest. Tell me, why are you two seeking the living among the dead? HE HAS RISEN! Go, and tell the others to wait! All will be revealed to those who seek the truth. By the way, Jason, nice going in the cave...."

The stranger vanished right before their eyes. Jason and Lukas looked at each other again, then Lukas began to stagger. Jason immediately put his hands upon his shoulders to steady him, then Lukas got a huge smile upon his face.

"He said to go tell the others, so let us go!" Lukas exclaimed as if his feet weren't fast enough to carry him.

"Are you sure you're alright?" Jason asked with concern.

"Yeah, just got a little shaky from talking to an angel. Let us go!" Lukas shouted as he grabbed Jason's arm and tugged to get him moving.

They met with Alethea and Melina half-way and told them briefly all that had happened. The four rushed back to the camp to tell everyone. They found Aegeus and Calista, as well as Orpheus and Cassandra sitting around the fire. Dimitri and Argus had taken a walk to the city.

Jason excitedly told all that had happened. Orpheus and Cassandra were all smiles, as well as Calista.

Aegeus remained calm and said, "It sounds to me as though that's what they feared would happen. They must have stolen the body as you slept, Jason." Aegeus was unable to accept the resurrection of Jesus.

"What about the angel, Aegeus?" Lukas asked while somewhat indignant that they had been perceived as telling a tale.

"I'm sorry to all of you, but I saw Jesus upon that cross. I can't accept it, until I see with my own eyes...I'm sorry," Aegeus said as he stepped away from everyone.

Jason and Lukas sat by the fire for a bit, as everyone asked questions about the morning. No one seemed as excited about the resurrection of Jesus as them. Alethea sat close beside Jason and put her arm around him. He smiled, but after a while he stood up.

"I need to go somewhere and pray alone," Jason said as he walked away. He didn't have to go far to find a secluded spot within the small forest beside the campsite. He found a stone, then knelt beside it and buried his head in his arms. He felt very tired despite the sleep, and his body ached. He sought God and asked for strength. He cried out to Jesus and asked, "If you've risen, where are you?" He continued to pray for some time. Finally, he got up and started walking back to camp. On the way back he noticed someone in the forest; he assumed it was someone looking for him. All he could see was his outer garment, for his head was covered and his back was facing him. It looked like Aegeus, perhaps, but he carried no staff. Jason approached him.

"Aegeus?" he called out when he drew near. The man turned around. Jason's heart melted within his chest, as he dropped down upon trembling knees. All of the hours he had spent thinking of things to ask and to say suddenly faded into obscurity. There was only one thing that came from his mouth: "MY LORD." Jason bowed his head, and he could see the holes in his feet, though they were healed. Suddenly, there was the sound of shuffling in the forest getting closer. Jason heard a familiar voice calling out his name. A voice pleasing to his heart:

"Jason," Alethea called out, "Ja...son."

Jason peeked behind him and saw Alethea standing there with her mouth open. She immediately dropped to her knees beside her husband....

Aegeus paced back and forth at the camp while nervously tapping the ground with his staff. "They should have been back by now; Alethea went to find him a long time ago. I'm going out to find them myself, for it's my fault Jason had a need to run off like that," he said with remorse.

"Jason can take care of himself, Aegeus," Orpheus said as he walked up to him and placed his hand upon his shoulder. "He'll come back when he's ready. He and Alethea are probably praying together," he speculated.

"Behold, they come," Lukas said as he pointed to the couple emerging from the forest. They had their arms around each other. They were smiling broadly, and everyone saw Jason give Alethea a little kiss upon the cheek as they approached.

"Greetings to you all, and peace be unto you!" Jason shouted with joy as they arrived at the camp.

"Where have you two been?" Aegeus asked. "We were worried about you," he added.

"All of the worries in the world will add nothing to your stature, Aegeus. We've been with Jesus!" Jason said in a very matter of fact way.

There was a collective gasp from everyone assembled. Aegeus was staring at Jason, but unable to speak. Murmuring began to erupt. Aegeus began to speak while holding up his finger, then stopped.

"I see you're still having trouble believing...behold!" Jason exclaimed as he opened his outer garment and threw it upon the ground. Everyone present was intensely and thoroughly shocked. They stared at Jason, for he was wearing a short Roman tunic. Then, one by one, they all began to smile.

Jason spoke with boldness, "We are to return to Jerusalem and wait. We have many friends there. We shall wait, and all of you will see Jesus. We will receive power from on high! We will receive the Holy Ghost! We will be witnesses unto him in Jerusalem, the Galilee, the Decapolis, Perea, Nabataea and throughout the entire earth!" He then asked with a shout, "Are you all with us?"

Aegeus put his arm around Calista and exclaimed boldly, "Yes, we're with you! Dimitri and Argus aren't here, but there's no way they wouldn't be, Uncle Jason!" They were smiling broadly.

"We're with you, Jason!" Cassandra answered for herself and old Orpheus who was weeping a bit.

"Just try to keep us away!" Lukas shouted as he embraced Melina. They were both smiling at Jason.

Alethea stepped around to face Jason and took both of his hands with hers. "By the way...I had come out to tell you something," she said softly as she took his right hand and placed it upon her stomach. She then looked up at Jason with a beautiful smile.

Jason looked upon Alethea with probably the biggest smile he ever had. He then passionately kissed her. She smiled and embraced her husband amid shouting and joyful noise. He stood there a long moment holding his wife, then Jason lifted his hands to the sky and praised God. "PRAISE, HONOR, AND GLORY TO THE ALMIGHTY GOD!" he shouted as he looked up at the beautiful blue sky. It was a truly delightful sight to Jason: the sky framed by his scar-free arms.

The End....

But the adventures continue.

References

King James Bible... (Chapters One and Two) Mark 4:35-41 and 5:1-20, Matthew 8:23-34, Luke 8:22-39, Isaiah 6:3b (Chapter Five) Apocrypha, Enoch Chapter 46:1-4, Isaiah 7:14, 9:6, 11:1, 61:1-2, Luke 4:16-30, Psalm 23 verse one. (Chapter Eight) Mark 7:31- 37, 8:1-9 (Chapter Nine) Psalm 23:1-6, Isaiah 59:19-20, Matthew 8:20 (Chapter Ten) John 11:1-45 (Chapter Eleven) Luke 15:11-32 (Chapter Twelve) Matthew Chapters 21 through 27:1-8, Luke Chapters 19:28 through 22:62 (Epilogue) Isaiah 53:12b, Psalm 22: 1-19

Article: Truth Only Bible, A lesson on evangelism from the Gadarene demoniac, by Dr. Steven Anderson, published September 18, 2015

Article: Gerasa in Gadara DEMON POSSESSED GERASENE, by Bill Heinrich, published January 6, 2016

Article: Quora.com, How was an Inn in 1st century Israel laid out? Have any ruins been discovered that could be described as inns? (caravansary descriptions and images), by William Moran, published July 22, 2016

Article: Jerusalem Perspective, Spoken Languages in the Time of Jesus, Professor Shmuel Safrai, published January 1, 1991

Article: All Bible Is True, Lion Tracks Ministries, Gadara, the Decapolis City by the Galilee, various photographs of ruins and maps, author and date not listed

Article: Biblical Geographic, Jerash, Gerasa, Central Jordan, JORDAN, posted by visitingthebible in JORDAN, author not listed

Video: Flint Steel Fire Starting, YouTube, practicalsurvivor, published August 22, 2010

Article: The Magic of Fire from Steel, Mike Ameling from his website Fire & Steel, date not listed

Article: A History Encyclopedia, A Visual Glossary of Classical Architecture, by Mark Cartwright, published on March 10, 2013

Article: Near east Tourist Agency (NEC), Gadara, Micah Key and Stephen Langfur, date not listed

Video: Lecture at the University of Chicago by Dr. Shelley Wachsmann, Meadows Associate Professor of Biblical Archaeology, Texas A&M University - 'The Sea of Galilee Boat', November 11, 2009, at Oriental Institute, Breasted Hall

Article: I had an Epiphany blogspot, The Jesus Boat, published June 18, 2010, author not listed

Article: A Sense of Belonging, Jesus Baptized Peter, others, published May 30, 2011 by Jayson

Article: Why Did the Disciples Baptize in Jesus Name? by Rev. A.F. Varnell copyright 1956

Article: Bibleinfo.com, Who were the 12 disciples? author and date not listed

Article: AZ 25 Quotes from Epicurus, author and date not listed

Article: (Book Review) by Matt Jackson-McCabe, 'Philodemus and the New Testament World', edited by John T. Fitzgerald, Dirk Obbink, Glen S. Holland, eds. Cleveland State University, Religious Studies Faculty Publications, Published by RBL copyright 2005 by the Society of Biblical Literature

Book: 'The Inside of the Cup: A Devotional Based on Mark's Gospel', by Gerald C. 'Jeb' Monge, Published by AuthorHouse December 5, 2012

Article: Ancient Scripts.com, Article on Nabataean Culture, Date and Author not listed.

Article: 'Religion in the Roman World', An essay by Marianne Bonz describing the myriad of religious options available in the Roman Empire, posted April 1998

Article: Religion Wiki 9 Wikipedia, New Testament Places) Umm Qais, Date and Author not listed.

Article: 'The Demoniacs of Gadara' by Gordon Franz MD, posted March 7, 2011

Article: Bible History Daily, 'Biblical Bread: Baking like the Ancient Israelites', Experimental Archaeology at Tell Halif, Israel, by Cynthia Shafer-Elliott, Published July 21, 2018

Article: Crystalinks - 'Law in Ancient Rome', Author and Date not listed

Article: War History Online, '12 Ranks of Roman Military Officers and What They Did', by Andrew Knighton, Published February 9, 2016

Article: 'The Life of Jesus in the History of LEGIO X FRETENSIS' (Tenth Legion of the Strait), posted by jaysromanhistory.com, Date and Author not listed

Article: Livius.org, Legio X Fretensis, (Tenth Legion of the Strait) by Emil Ritterling, posted July 16, 2017

Book: 'Ancient Rome' by Dr. Simon James, DK Publishing, copyright 2004, 2008

Article: Pilgrim Baptist Church, 'Winemaking in Ancient Israel' by Garrett Peck, posted January 28, 2013

Article: Ancient History Encyclopedia, 'Wine in the ancient Mediterranean' by Mark Cartwright, posted August 26, 2016

Images: (Google searches) First Century Roman Coins, First Century Israel Houses, First Century Clothing, Musical Instruments (Double Aulos), Ancient Greek Cuisine

Video: YouTube, Camel Training 101, How to care for a pet camel, by camelsandfriends, published June 12, 2012

Video: YouTube, Riding Camels Through the Sahara/ Morocco, by Kara and Nate, published December 5, 2016

Video: YouTube, how to ride a camel, by Clair Seaborn, published November 2, 2010

CPSIA information can be obtained
at www.ICGtesting.com
Printed in the USA
BVHW070305260719
554335BV00001B/6/P